The Circle

Also by Bernard Minier

The Frozen Dead

BERNARD MINIER

The Circle

Translated by Alison Anderson

Minotaur Books
New York

THE CIRCLE. Copyright © 2012 by XO Éditions. Translation copyright © 2015 by Alison Anderson. All rights reserved. Printed in the United States of America. For information, address St. Martin's Press, 175 Fifth Avenue, New York, N.Y. 10010.

www.minotaurbooks.com

The Library of Congress Cataloging-in-Publication Data is available upon request.

ISBN 978-1-250-04554-6 (hardcover)
ISBN 978-1-4668-4425-4 (e-book)

Our books may be purchased in bulk for promotional, educational, or business use. Please contact your local bookseller or the Macmillan Corporate and Premium Sales Department at (800) 221-7945, extension 5442, or by e-mail at MacmillanSpecialMarkets@macmillan.com.

First published in France under the title *Le Cercle* by XO Éditions

Previously published in Great Britain under the title *A Song for Drowned Souls* by Mulholland Books, an imprint of Hodder & Stoughton, an Hachette UK company

First U.S. Edition: October 2015

10 9 8 7 6 5 4 3 2 1

The civilized people in the world, the ones who hide behind culture and art and politics . . . and even the law, they're the ones to watch out for. They've got that perfect disguise goin' for them, you know? But they're the most vicious. They're the most dangerous people on earth.

Michael Connelly, *The Last Coyote*

TRANSLATOR'S NOTE

Under French law, when it is believed that a crime has been committed, an officer of the crime unit will inform the district public prosecutor, who in turn appoints an examining magistrate to the case.

Investigations are conducted under the supervision of these magistrates, who answer to the Ministry of Justice. Crimes may be investigated by police commissioners from the crime unit, along with commissioned offficers of the gendarmerie. The gendarmerie, technically, is a branch of the armed forces, but it is in charge of public safety, performing police duties among the civilian population, and thus is often called upon to collaborate with various police units.

Marsac is an imaginary town, but its institutions and inhabitants represent the academic crème de la crème, preparing students for the fiercely competitive entrance exams to the *Grandes Écoles* which, unlike regular universities in France, are selective and groom students to be the future leaders of the country.

Prologue

In the Tomb

In her mind there was a cry, nothing more.

A moan.

A cry of despair, screaming with rage, pain, loneliness. Everything that, for months on end, had deprived her of her humanity.

She was pleading, too.

Please, oh please, have mercy, please . . . let me out of here, I beg you.

In her mind, she was shouting and begging and weeping. But only in her mind: not a sound came from her throat. One fine day she awoke virtually mute. *Mute* . . . And she was someone who had always liked to talk. Words came so easily to her, words and laughter . . .

In the darkness, she shifted her position to ease the tension in her muscles. She was sitting on the dirt floor with her back against the stone wall. Sometimes she would stretch out. Or go over to the flea-ridden mattress in the corner. She spent most of her time sleeping, curled up in a foetal position. When she stood up, she stretched or walked as best she could – four strides this way, four strides back, no more: her cell measured six feet each way. It was pleasantly warm; she had known for a long time that there must be a boiler room on the other side of the door, not only because of the heat but also the sounds: humming, clicking, hissing. She had no clothes on. Naked as a newborn babe. For months, maybe years. She relieved herself in a bucket and had two meals a day, except when he went away: then she might go several days alone without eating or drinking, and hunger, thirst and the fear of death bore into her. There were two holes in the door: one at the very bottom, through which he passed her meals, and another in the middle, which was for watching her. Even when they were closed the holes let in two faint rays of light that pierced the obscurity of the cell. Her eyes had grown accustomed to this half darkness and she could make out details that no one else would have seen.

In the beginning she had explored her cage and listened out for the slightest sound. She had searched for a way to escape, a flaw in his system, the slightest little slackening on his part. Then she had stopped worrying about it. There was no flaw, no hope. She had lost track of how many weeks or months had gone by since her abduction. Since her life *before*. Roughly once a week, maybe more, maybe less, he ordered her to put her arm through the hole and he gave her an injection. It was painful, because he was clumsy and the liquid was thick. She lost consciousness almost at once and when she woke up she would find herself sitting in a dining room in a heavy high-backed armchair, her legs and torso bound to the chair. *Washed, perfumed and dressed.* Even her hair smelled good, of shampoo, and her breath, which must have been pestilential the rest of the time, smelled of toothpaste and peppermint. A fire burned brightly in the hearth, there were lit candles on the dark wooden table which shone like a lake and a delicious aroma rose from the plates. There was always classical music on the stereo. Like a conditioned animal, the moment she heard the music and saw the light from the flames and felt the clean clothes on her skin, her mouth began to water. Before he put her to sleep and removed her from her cell, he always made her go twenty-four hours without food.

From the pain, however, she could tell he had abused her while she slept. In the beginning the thought had filled her with horror and when she awoke back in the cellar she had thrown up her first real meal. Now it no longer affected her. Sometimes he didn't say anything, sometimes he spoke incessantly, but she rarely listened to him: her brain was no longer used to following a conversation. The words *music, symphony, orchestra* constantly cropped up in his speech like a leitmotif, as did one name: Mahler.

How long had she been locked up? There was neither day nor night in her tomb. Because that was what it was: a tomb. Deep down, she knew she would never get out alive. Any hope had abandoned her long ago.

She remembered the simple, wonderful time when she was free. The last time she had laughed, had friends over, seen her parents; the smell of the barbecue in the summer, the evening light in the trees in the garden and her son's eyes. Faces, laughter, games. She saw herself making love to one man in particular. She had thought it was just an ordinary life but in fact it was a miracle. Her regret that she had not appreciated it more fully grew greater by the day. She realised that even the moments of sorrow and pain had been nothing in comparison to the hell she was in now – this non-existence, buried in this non-place. Outside the world. She supposed that only a few feet of stone, cement and earth kept her from the real world, but at the same time, hundreds of doors, miles of corridors and fences could not have separated her further.

One day real life and the real world had been there, so close. For some unknown reason he had been obliged to move her in a hurry. He had dressed her hastily, bound her wrists behind her back and put a canvas bag over her head. Then he made her climb up some steps and she was in the open air. *The open air* . . . She had almost lost her senses with the shock of it.

When she felt the warm sun, and sensed the light through the bag, and breathed the damp smell of the earth and the fields, the perfume of the thickets in flower, and heard the chattering of birds, she had almost fainted. She had wept so profusely that the canvas bag was soaked.

Then he had made her lie down on a metal surface and through the canvas she inhaled exhaust and diesel oil. Even though she couldn't have cried out, he had stuffed her mouth with cotton then covered it with surgical tape as a precaution. He had also bound her wrists and ankles together so that she couldn't kick the side of the van. She felt the vibration of the engine and the van began to bounce over uneven ground before it reached the road. When he suddenly accelerated and she heard the rush of cars overtaking them, she realised they were on the motorway.

The worst of it had been the tollbooth. She could hear voices, music, the sound of engines all around her, *so near* . . . just there, on the other side of the metal. And dozens of human beings. Women, men, children, only a few inches away! *She could hear them.* She was overwhelmed by a flood of emotions. They were laughing, talking, coming and going, alive and free. They had no idea of her presence, her slow death, her life as a slave. She had shaken her head until she was banging it against the metal and her nose bled onto the grimy floor.

It was fine weather the day he moved her, she was almost certain

3

that everything must be in bloom. Springtime. How many more seasons to come until he got tired of her, until she was defeated by madness, until he killed her? The sudden certainty came to her that her friends and family and the police had already given her up for dead: only one person on earth knew that she was still alive, and he was a demon, a snake, an *incubus*. She would never see the daylight again.

Friday

I

Dolls

> *And it was there, in the shady garden,*
> *The killer's shadow in cold ambush,*
> *Shadow against shadow on the grass less green than*
> *Red with evening's blood.*
> *In the trees, a nightingale*
> *Was challenging Marsyras and Apollo.*
> *Deeper down, an aviary of nests and*
> *Mistletoe berries*
> *In rustic setting . . .*

Oliver Winshaw stopped writing. Blinked. At the edge of his vision something had attracted – or rather distracted – his attention. Beyond the window. A flash of light, outside. Like a camera flash.

The storm had broken over Marsac.

That night, as on every other night, he was sitting at his desk. He was writing a poem. His study was on the first floor of the house he had bought with his wife in the southwest of France thirty years earlier; a room with panelled oak walls, almost entirely covered with books. Primarily British and American poetry from the nineteenth and twentieth centuries: Coleridge, Tennyson, Robert Burns, Swinburne, Dylan Thomas, Larkin, e.e. cummings, Pound . . .

He knew he could never hold a candle to his personal idols, but he didn't care.

He had never shown his poetry to anyone. He was approaching the winter of his life, even autumn was behind him now. Very soon he would build a big fire in the garden and into it he would throw 150 black notebooks. All in all, more than 20,000 poems. A poem a day for fifty-seven years. Probably the best kept secret of his life. Even his second wife had not been allowed to read them.

After all these years, he still wondered where he found his inspiration. When he looked back on his life, it was nothing but a long procession of days that always ended with a poem written in the evening in the peace of his study. He never went to bed until he had finished, sometimes at one or two o'clock in the morning, even back in the days when he had been working. He had never needed a great deal of sleep and his job was not physically demanding: English professor at the University of Marsac.

Oliver Winshaw was about to turn ninety.

He was a calm and elegant old man, known by all. When he settled in this picturesque little university town, he was immediately dubbed *l'Anglais*. This was before his compatriots had swooped down like a swarm of locusts onto everything in the region that possessed old stones to be restored, and the nickname became somewhat diluted. Now he was only one among hundreds of other Englishmen in the area. But with the economic crisis the English were heading for destinations that were more financially attractive, such as Croatia or Andalusia, and Oliver wondered whether he would live long enough to find himself once again the only Englishman in Marsac.

> *In the lily pond*
> *The faceless shadow slides*
> *Slender dreary profile*
> *Like the knife's keen sharpened edge.*

He paused once again.

Music . . . He thought he could hear music above the regular patter of rain and the endless echoing of thunder across the sky. Obviously it couldn't be Christine, she had been asleep for a long while. Yes, it was coming from outside: classical music.

Oliver grimaced in disapproval. They must have the volume on full blast for him to hear it in his study despite the storm and the closed window. He tried to concentrate on his poem, but there was nothing for it: bloody music!

Annoyed, he looked again at the window. A lightning glow came through the blinds, and he could see the rain streaming down. The storm seemed to be concentrating its fury on this small town, cutting it off from the rest of the world.

He pushed his chair back and stood up.

He went over to the window and cracked open the blinds. The central drain was spilling over onto the cobblestones. Above the rooftops, the night was streaked with thin bolts of lightning, as if inscribed with the trace of a luminescent seismograph.

In the house across the street all the lights were on. Perhaps they were having a party? The house in question, a townhouse with a garden to one side, was protected from the street and outside observers by a high wall. A single woman lived there; she was a professor at the lycée in Marsac, the most prestigious prep school in the region. A good-looking woman, with brown hair and an elegant figure, in the prime of her thirties. From time to time Oliver spied on her discreetly when she sunbathed in her deck chair, sheltered from all eyes – except his, because her garden was visible from his study window. There was something wrong. All the lights on every floor of the four-storey house were lit. And the front door was wide open, a little lantern clearly guiding the way to the threshold.

But he couldn't see anyone in the windows.

At the side of the house, the French windows were wide open, banging in the wind, and the rain was driving at such an angle that it must be flooding the floor inside. Oliver could see it splashing on the tiles on the terrace and crushing the lawn.

That was probably where the music was coming from. He felt his pulse quicken. He looked slowly over towards the swimming pool.

Thirty feet by twenty. Sand-coloured tiles all around. A diving board.

He felt a sort of dark excitement, the kind that grabs you when something unusual has just interrupted your daily routine. And at his age, routine made up his entire life. His gaze travelled all around the swimming pool. At the end of the garden the forest of Marsac began, 2,700 hectares of woods and paths. There was no barrier on that side, not even a chain-link fence, just a compact wall of vegetation.

Oliver focused his attention on the pool. The surface seemed to be dancing slightly. He narrowed his gaze. First of all, he wondered what he was seeing. Then he realised that several dolls were bobbing on the water. Yes, that's what it was . . . Even though he knew it was only dolls, he felt an inexplicable shiver go through him. They were floating next to each other, their pale dresses rippling on the rain-battered surface. Oliver and his wife had been invited for coffee once by their neighbour from across the street. His wife had been a psychologist before she retired, and she had a theory about the profusion of dolls in the home of a single woman in her thirties. When they got home she explained to her husband that their neighbour was probably a 'woman-child', and Oliver had asked her what she meant. She had gone on to use expressions such as 'immature', 'evading responsibility', 'thinking only of her own pleasure', 'undergone an emotional trauma', and Oliver had beaten a hasty retreat from the conversation: he had always preferred poets to psychologists. But he was damned if he could fathom why there were dolls in the swimming pool.

I ought to ring the gendarmes, he thought. *And tell them what? That there are dolls floating in a swimming pool?* But it wasn't normal. The house all lit up, no one in sight, and those dolls – where was the owner?

He opened the window. A wave of humidity came into the room. The rain beat against his face, he blinked at the strange gathering of plastic faces, with their staring eyes.

He could hear the music perfectly now. It was familiar, although it wasn't Mozart, his favourite composer.

Dammit, what the hell was going on!

A bolt of lightning severed the darkness, immediately followed by a deafening clap of thunder. The noise made the windowpanes vibrate. Like a blinding light from a projector, the lightning showed that someone was there. Someone sitting at the edge of the pool, legs dangling in the water, and Oliver hadn't noticed him because he was swallowed by the shadow of the tall tree in the middle of the garden. *A young man* . . . Bent over the floating tide of dolls, gazing at them. Although he was nearly fifty feet away, Oliver could make out the lost, frantic expression in the young man's eyes, and his gaping mouth.

Oliver Winshaw's chest was an echo chamber, his heart pounding like a demonic percussionist. What was going on here? He rushed over to the telephone and took the receiver from its cradle.

2

World Cup

'Anelka is a loser,' said Pujol.

Vincent Espérandieu looked at his colleague and wondered whether his opinion was based on the striker's poor performance, or on his origins and the fact he came from a housing estate on the outskirts of Paris. Pujol had no fondness for council estates, and even less for their inhabitants.

For once, however, Espérandieu had to admit that Pujol was right: Anelka was useless. Worthless. Hopeless. Like the rest of the team, as it happened. This first match was a heartbreaker. Only Martin seemed not to care. Espérandieu looked over at him and smiled: he was sure his boss didn't even know the name of the manager whom all of France despised and who had been called every name in the book.

'Domenech is one fucking coward,' said Pujol, as if he had been reading Vincent's thoughts. 'If we made it into the final in 2006, it's because Zidane and the rest of the team took over.'

No one disputed the fact, and Pujol wove his way through the crowd to fetch another beer. The bar was packed. 11 June 2010: the opening day and first matches of the World Cup in South Africa, including the match that was on the screen at that very moment, Uruguay-France, 0-0 at half time. Vincent looked again at his boss. He had his eyes glued to the screen, but his gaze was empty. Commandant Martin Servaz was just pretending to watch the match, and his assistant knew it.

Not only was Servaz not watching the match, but he wondered what on earth he was doing there.

He'd wanted to please his team by going along with them. For weeks now there'd been talk of little else but the World Cup at the regional crime squad. What sort of condition the players were in, the catastrophic friendlies they'd played, including a humiliating defeat against China, the selector's choices, the hotel that was expensive beyond belief: Servaz was beginning to wonder if a third world war would have aroused this much attention. Probably not. He hoped that criminals were similarly engrossed and that the crime statistics would go down all on their own without anyone having to lift a finger.

He reached for the cold beer that Pujol had just placed in front of him and raised it to his lips. On the screen, the match had started again. The little men in blue were running around with the same useless energy as before; they hurried from one end of the pitch to the other and Servaz could see absolutely no logic behind their moves. As for the strikers, he was no expert, but they seemed particularly clumsy. He had read somewhere that travel and accommodation for the team would cost the French Football Federation over one million euros, and he would have loved to know where they got their money from, and whether he himself would have to dig into his pocket. But although ordinarily his neighbours in the bar, as taxpayers, were easily riled, this question did not seem to trouble them as much as the ongoing absence of goals. Servaz tried all the same to get interested in what was happening, but there was a constant unpleasant buzzing from the television, as if it were a giant beehive. Someone had explained to him that it was the sound made by the thousands of trumpets the South African spectators had brought to the stadium. He wondered how they could produce and above all how they could stand such a racket: even at this distance, attenuated by microphones and technological filters, the sound was particularly enervating.

Suddenly the lights in the bar flickered and exclamations could be heard all around: the image on the screen shrank and disappeared then suddenly flashed back on. The storm was hovering over Toulouse like a flock of crows. Servaz gave a faint smile at the thought of everyone sitting in the dark, deprived of their football match.

His distracted thoughts veered into a familiar but dangerous zone. *Eighteen months gone by and still no sign of life from Julian Hirtmann.* Eighteen months, but not a day went by that Servaz didn't think about him. The Swiss convict had escaped from the Wargnier Institute during the winter of 2008, only a few days after Servaz had visited him in his cell. At their meeting, he had discovered to his amazement

12

that he and the former prosecutor from Geneva shared the same passion: the music of Gustav Mahler. And then there had been escape for Hirtmann, and for Servaz – the avalanche.

Eighteen months, he thought. Five hundred and forty days, which meant just as many nights having the same nightmare over and over. *The avalanche* . . . He was buried in a coffin of snow and ice, and he was beginning to run out of air, while the cold numbed his limbs . . . Then finally the drill making its way through, and someone furiously clearing the snow above him. A blinding light on his face, gulping fresh air by the lungful, his mouth gaping, until a face filled the open space. Hirtmann's face. He burst out laughing, and said, 'Bye, Martin,' then filled up the hole again . . .

Give or take a few variations, the dream always ended the same way.

He had survived the avalanche. But in his nightmares, he died. And in a way, part of him had died up there that night.

What was Hirtmann doing at that very moment? Where was he? With a shiver Servaz pictured the snowy landscape, its incredible majesty . . . the dizzying summits protecting the lost valley . . . the building with its thick walls . . . locks clanging at the end of a deserted corridor . . . And then that door with the familiar music.

'About time,' said Pujol next to him.

Servaz glanced distractedly at the screen. One player was leaving the pitch, another was replacing him. He gathered it was Anelka again. He looked at the upper left-hand corner of the screen: the seventy-first minute, and the score was still 0-0. Hence the tension that reigned in the bar. Next to him, a big man who must have weighed twenty stone and was sweating abundantly beneath his red beard, tapped him on the shoulder as if they were friends and blew in his face with his booze-heavy breath: 'If I was the coach, I'd give 'em a good kick up the arse to get 'em moving, the wankers. What the fuck, they won't even budge for the World Cup.'

Servaz wondered if his neighbour was much in the habit of moving – apart from when he had to drag himself down here or go and fetch his six-packs at the corner shop.

He wondered why he didn't like watching sports on television. Was it because his ex-wife, Alexandra, unlike him, had never missed a match with her favourite team? They had been the kind of couple who, Servaz had suspected from day one, would not last long. In

13

spite of that, they got married and stuck it out for seven years. He still didn't know how they could have taken so long to realise what was so obvious: they were as mismatched as a member of the Taliban and a supermodel. What did they have left today, other than their eighteen-year-old daughter? But he was proud of his daughter. Oh yes, he was proud. Even if he still hadn't got used to her look, her body piercings and her hairstyle, it was in *his* footsteps Margot was following, not her mother's. Like him, she liked to read and like him, she had qualified for the most prestigious literary prep school in the region. Marsac. The best students went there from miles around, some from as far away as Montpellier or Bordeaux.

If he thought about it, he had to admit that at the age of forty-one he had only two focuses of interest in his life: his job and his daughter. And books . . . but books were something else, they were not merely a focus, they were his *entire* life.

Was it enough? What were the lives of others made up of? He looked at the bottom of his glass, where there was nothing left but a few specks of foam, and he decided he'd had enough to drink for one evening. He felt a sudden urgent desire to pee and he wove his way to the door to the toilets. They were disgusting. A bald man had his back to him, and Servaz could hear his stream striking the urinal.

'That team is nothing but a bunch of no-hopers,' said the man. 'They're a disgrace to watch.'

He went back out without bothering to wash his hands. Servaz soaped and rinsed his own for a long time, dried them, and as he went back out he drew his right hand into his sleeve before taking hold of the door handle.

A quick glance at the screen told him nothing had changed in his absence, even though the match was drawing to a close. The audience was a simmering volcano of frustration. Servaz figured that if things continued like this, there would be riots. He went back to his spot.

His neighbours were shouting, things like, 'Go on!' 'Pass the ball, fuck, pass it!' 'On the right, on the riiight!' which meant that at least something was happening, finally, when he felt a familiar vibration in his pocket. He reached into his trousers and took out his phone. Not a smartphone, but a good old Nokia. The mobile had already transferred the call to his voicemail, and the text read '888'.

Servaz dialled the number to access the message.

And froze.

The voice on the line . . . It took him half a second to recognise it. Half a second of eternity. Time-space contracting, as if the twenty years separating him from the last time he had heard it could be erased in two heartbeats. Even after all this time, he felt something tunnelling deep into his belly.

It was as if the room were beginning to spin. The cries, the shouts of encouragement, the buzzing of the vuvuzelas all receded, lost in a mist. The present contracted, became tiny. The voice was saying, 'Martin? It's me, Marianne. Call me, please. It's very important. I beg you, call me back as soon as you get this message.'

A voice from the past – but also a voice in which he could hear fear.

Samira Cheung tossed the leather jacket onto the bed and looked at the fat man who was leaning against the pillows, smoking.

'You've got to go. I have to go to work.'

The man sitting in her bed was at least thirty years older than she was, had an unmistakeable potbelly and white hair on his chest, but Samira didn't care. He was a good lay, and that, in her opinion, was all that mattered. She herself was no beauty queen. Ever since the lycée she had known that most men found her ugly – or rather that they thought her face was ugly and her body was singularly attractive. Given the strange ambivalence she aroused in them, the scales tipped sometimes one way, sometimes the other. Samira Cheung made up for it by sleeping with as many men as she could; she had known for a long time that the most handsome were not necessarily the best lovers, and she was looking for men who were good in bed, not Prince Charming.

The big bed creaked as her round-bellied lover lifted his legs out from under the sheets and leaned over to retrieve his neatly folded clothes. Samira pulled on a pair of knickers and a T-shirt then disappeared through the trap door in the floor.

'Booze or coffee?' she shouted from below.

She made her way through the little red kitchen that was so narrow it looked like a ship's galley, and switched on the capsule coffee maker. With the exception of the bare bulb over her head, the big house was plunged into darkness. And for a reason: Samira

15

had bought the ruin twenty kilometres from Toulouse the year before. She was gradually restoring it, choosing her occasional lovers from various trades – electricians, plumbers, masons, painters, roofers – and for the time being she lived in only one-fifth of the inhabitable space. The rooms on the ground floor were completely empty of furniture, draped in plastic tarpaulins, the walls covered with scaffolding, pots of dripping paint and tools, as was half of the first floor, and she had made the attic into a bedroom for the time being.

The man went heavily down the ladder. She handed him a steaming espresso and took a bite from an apple that had already been started and was going brown on the countertop. Then she vanished into the bathroom. Five minutes later she went into the 'dressing room'. All her clothes were hanging temporarily from long metal rods encased in thin plastic covers, while her underwear and T-shirts were stored in small dressers with plastic drawers, and dozens of pairs of boots stood in a row against the wall.

She pulled on a pair of jeans with holes in, flat-heeled ankle boots, a clean T-shirt and a leather belt with studs. Then the holster for her service weapon. And a military parka for the rain.

'You still here?' she said, re-entering the kitchen.

The fat fifty-year-old wiped the jam from his lips. He pulled her closer and kissed her. She submitted for a moment, then pulled away.

'When are you going to fix my shower?'

'Not this weekend. My wife is coming back from her sister's place.'

'Find a day. This week.'

'My schedule is full,' he protested.

'No plumbing, no fucking.'

The man frowned.

'Maybe Wednesday afternoon. I'll have to see.'

'The keys will be in the usual place.'

She was going to say something else when a mixture of electric-guitar riffs and horror-film screams could be heard somewhere. The first bars of a song by Agoraphobic Nosebleed, an American grindcore group. By the time she found her mobile, the screaming had stopped. She looked at the number on the screen: Vincent. The phone vibrated. A text message:

Call me back.

Which she did at once.

'What's up?'

'Where are you?' he asked without answering.

'I'm at home, I was about to leave. I'm on duty tonight.'

On a night like this, every man in the squad who had managed to call in sick had done so.

'What about you, you're not watching the match?' she asked.

'We've had a call.'

An emergency. Probably the deputy on call at the public prosecutor's office. Hard luck for any football fans. At the law courts, as well, the televisions must be overheating. She'd even had trouble finding a lover for the evening: it was obvious that football was winning over fucking that night.

'Did the prosecutor's office call?' she asked. 'What's going on?'

'No, it wasn't the prosecutor's office.'

'It wasn't?'

She could hear unusual tension in Espérandieu's voice.

'I'll explain. No point going to the crime division. Take your car and get over here. Have you got something to write with?'

Paying no attention to her guest, who stood next to her growing impatient, Samira opened a kitchen drawer and took out a pen and a Post-it.

'Hang on . . . okay, right.'

'I'll give you the address, meet us there.'

'Go ahead.'

She raised an eyebrow as she wrote it down, even though he couldn't see her.

'Marsac? That's way out in the country. Who called you, Vincent?'

'I'll explain. We're already on our way. Meet us there as soon as you can.'

'Us? Who's us?'

'Martin and me.'

'Fine. I'll come as quick as I can.'

She hung up. Something was wrong.

3

Marsac

The rain hammered relentlessly on the roof of the car. It danced in the headlights, flooded the windscreen and the road, banished animals to their burrows and isolated the rare passing vehicles from one another. It had come from the west, like an army invading new territory. This was no simple downpour; it was a deluge. From time to time, flashes of lightning scored the sky but the rest of the time they could see nothing beyond the headlights. It was as if a cataclysm had drowned all inhabited land and they were making their way along the bottom of the ocean.

Servaz peered out at the road. The pulsing of the windscreen wipers echoed that of his heart, which was contracting and dilating far too quickly. They had left the motorway a while ago and were driving now through hills plunged in rural darkness. Vincent had slipped a CD by Queens of the Stone Age into the player and for once Martin had not objected.

He was far too absorbed by his own thoughts.

For a split second Espérandieu took his eyes from the road. He saw the glow from the headlights and the to and fro of the wipers reflected in his boss's black pupils. Servaz was staring at the tarmac the way he had been staring at the television screen not long before: without seeing it. His deputy thought of the telephone call again. From the moment he'd got it, Martin had been transformed. Vincent gathered that something had happened in Marsac, and that the person at the other end of the line was an old friend. Servaz wouldn't say anything more. He had told Pujol to stay and watch the match and asked Espérandieu to go with him.

The rain eased up a bit just as the Renault headed into the tunnel of plane trees that marked the entrance to the town, and they wound their way through the little streets in the centre, jiggling along the cobblestones.

'To the left,' said Servaz when they reached a square with a church.

Espérandieu could not help but notice the number of pubs, cafés and restaurants. Marsac was a university town. 18,503 inhabitants. And almost as many students. Faculties of letters, science, law, economy, and management, and the renowned prep school. Newspapers, always eager for a pithy epithet, had dubbed it 'the Cambridge of the Southwest'. From a strictly police point of view, the influx of so many students meant recurring problems with drink and drug driving, dealing, and damage caused during student protests. But there was nothing that fell within the remit of the crime squad.

'It looks as if the power is out.'

The streets were engulfed in darkness. They could just make out moving flickers of light behind the windows: torches. *The storm,* thought Vincent.

'Go around the square and take the second street on the right.'

They drove around the little circular piazza and left by a narrow cobblestone street that wound its way up past tall facades. Through the downpour, twenty metres further along, they could make out the swirl of revolving lights. The gendarmerie. Someone had called them.

'What's going on here?' said Espérandieu. 'Did you know that the gendarmerie was in on this?'

They pulled over behind a Renault Trafic and a Citroën C4, both of which were painted in the colours of the gendarmerie. Since his boss didn't answer, Vincent turned and looked at him. Martin looked more tense than usual. He gave his assistant a puzzled, reticent look and climbed out of the car.

In less than five seconds Servaz's hair and shirt were drenched. Several members of the gendarmerie were stoically sheltering beneath waterproof windbreakers. One came over to them and Servaz pulled out his warrant card. The gendarme raised his eyebrows to convey his astonishment that the crime squad was on the scene before the prosecutor had even referred the case to them.

'Who's in charge?' asked Servaz.

'Captain Bécker.'

'Is he inside?'

'Yes, but I don't know whether—'

Servaz walked past the gendarme without waiting to hear the rest.

'*Martin!*'

He turned his head to the left. A Peugeot 307 had pulled in a bit further down the narrow street. There was someone standing on the driver's side, behind the open door, someone he had thought he would never see again.

The streaming rain, the dazzling, spinning lights from the vehicles, the faces beneath the windbreakers, everything was a blur. But he would still have recognised her among thousands. She was wearing a raincoat, the collar turned up. *It really was her.* She was standing straight with her hand on the door, her chin up, the way he remembered. Her face was ravaged by fear and sorrow, but she had not abandoned her pride.

That was what he had loved, back then, that pride. Until it became a wall between them.

'Hello, Marianne,' he said.

She hurried over to him. A moment later she was embracing him. He felt a sort of seismic shock go through him, along with the sobs that were shaking her. He put his arms around her, without holding her tighter. A gesture that spoke more of protocol than intimacy. How many years had it been? Nineteen? Twenty? She had cast him out of her life, had gone off with someone else, and found a way to leave him with the blame. He had loved her, yes. Perhaps more than any other woman before or since. But it had all happened in another century, so long ago . . .

She took a step back and looked at him, and her long hair, now drenched, caressed his cheek as she did so. Once again he felt a slight tremor go through him, magnitude 4 on the Servaz scale. Her eyes, so close, like two green and shining pools. He read a multitude of contradictory emotions in them, including pain, sorrow, doubt and fear. But also gratitude and hope. A tiny, timid hope. That she placed in him. He looked elsewhere to calm the pounding of his heart. Nineteen years and she had hardly changed at all, beyond the fine wrinkles at the corners of her eyes and her mouth.

He brought to mind her words on the telephone: '*Something terrible has happened.'* At the time, he thought she was talking about herself, something she had done, until he realised it was about her son: *'Hugo . . . he found a woman in her house, dead. Everything makes him look guilty, Martin . . . They'll say he did it . . .'* As she spoke her voice was so broken by sobs, her throat so tight, that he hadn't understood half of what she was saying.

'What happened?'

'He just called me. He was drugged . . . He woke up in this woman's house and she was . . . dead . . .'

It was absurd, what she was telling him, it made no sense. He wondered if she had been drinking, or had taken something.

'Marianne, I don't understand. What are you talking about? Who is this woman?'

'A teacher. In Marsac. One of his teachers.'

Marsac . . . That's where Margot was studying. Even on the telephone he had found it difficult to hide his distress. Then he said to himself that between the university, the lycée and the secondary school, there must be at least a hundred teachers in Marsac. What were the odds that Margot had been one of her students?

'They're going to accuse him, Martin . . . He's innocent. Hugo could never do such a thing. I beg you, you have to help us . . .'

'Thank you for coming,' she said now. 'I—'

'Not now . . . go on home. I'll be in touch.'

She gave him a desperate look. Without waiting for her answer, he turned on his heels and headed towards the house.

'Captain Bécker?'

'Yes.'

He flashed his card for the second time, even though it was difficult to see anything inside the house.

'Commandant Servaz, Toulouse crime squad. This is Lieutenant Espérandieu.'

'Who called you?' asked Bécker right away.

A stocky man in his early fifties, he looked like the sort who slept badly, judging from the bags under his eyes. He also looked as if he had been very shaken up by what he had seen. And he was in a foul temper. *Yet another man who'd been dragged away from his football.*

'A witness,' said Servaz evasively. 'Who called you?'

Bécker sniffed, reluctant to share his information with strangers.

21

'A neighbour. Oliver Winshaw. An Englishman who lives there, across the street.'

He pointed over the wall.

'What did he see?'

'The window of his study overlooks the garden. He saw a young man sitting beside the pool and a load of dolls floating in the water. He thought it was peculiar, so he called us.'

'*Dolls?*'

'Yes. You can see for yourself.'

They were standing in the living room: the house was in complete darkness, like all the houses in Marsac. The door to the street was open and the only light in the room came from the headlights of the vehicles parked outside, stretching the men's shadows across the walls. In the obscurity Servaz could make out an open-plan kitchen, a round glass table sparkling with reflected light, four wrought-iron chairs, a dresser and, behind a column, a stairway leading to the floor above. The humid air wafted in through the French windows, and Servaz noted that someone had blocked them so they wouldn't bang.

A gendarme walked past them; the beam from his torch lit up their silhouettes for a moment.

'We're in the process of setting up a generator,' said Bécker.

'Where's the kid?' asked Servaz.

'In the van. In safe custody. We're going to take him back to the gendarmerie.'

'And the victim?'

The gendarme pointed to the ceiling.

'Up there. In the attic. In the bathroom.'

From his voice, Servaz could tell he was still in shock.

'Did she live alone?'

'Yes.'

Judging from what he had seen from the street, it was a big house: four floors, if you included the attic and the ground floor – even though each level was no more than fifty square metres.

'She was a teacher, right?'

'Claire Diemar. Thirty-two years old. She taught I don't know what in Marsac.'

Servaz's gaze met the captain's in the darkness.

'The kid was one of her students,' said Bécker.

'What?'

The thunder had drowned out the gendarme's words.

'I said, the kid was in one of her classes.'

'Yes, I know.'

Servaz stared at Bécker in the dark, both of them lost in thought.

'I suppose you're more used to this sort of thing than I am,' said the gendarme at last. 'But let me warn you: it is not a pretty sight. I've never seen anything so . . . revolting.'

'Excuse me,' said a voice. They turned towards it. 'May I know who you are?'

Someone was coming down the stairs.

'Commandant Servaz, Toulouse crime squad.'

The man held out a leather-gloved hand. He must have been almost seven feet tall. At the top of his body Servaz could just make out a long neck, a strange square head with protruding ears and hair cut very short. The giant crushed his still-damp hand in the soft leather.

'Roland Castaing, public prosecutor for Auch. I've just had Catherine on the telephone. She told me you were on your way. May I ask who filled you in?'

He was referring to Cathy d'Humières, chief prosecutor for the Toulouse region, whom Servaz had worked with several times before, in particular on the case that had taken him to the Wargnier Institute a year and a half earlier. Now Servaz hesitated.

'Marianne Bokhanowsky, the young man's mother,' he replied.

A silence fell.

'Do you know her?'

The prosecutor's tone was slightly astonished and suspicious. He had a deep, solemn voice that rolled over his consonants like the wheels of a cart over pebbles.

'Yes. A bit. But I hadn't seen her for years.'

'So why, in that case, did she call you?' asked Castaing.

Once again Servaz hesitated.

'Undoubtedly because my name has been in the news.'

For a moment the man remained silent. Servaz could tell that he was examining him, looking down on him from his great height. Even in the dark he could tell the prosecutor's gaze was on him, and he shivered: the newcomer made him think of a statue from Easter Island.

'Ah yes, of course . . . The killings at Saint-Martin-de-Comminges. Of course, that was you . . . an incredible business. I imagine it must leave a mark, a case like that, Commandant?'

There was something about the magistrate's tone that Servaz found extremely unpleasant.

'That still doesn't explain what you are doing here.'

'I told you: Hugo's mother asked me to come and take a look.'

'The case has not yet been assigned to you,' said the magistrate sharply.

'No, it hasn't.'

'It falls within the jurisdiction of the public prosecutor's office at Auch. Not Toulouse.'

Servaz almost replied that the office in Auch had only a very small investigation squad, and that not a single major criminal investigation had been assigned to it in recent years, but he refrained.

'You've come a long way to get here, Commandant,' said Castaing. 'And I suppose, like all of us, you had to sacrifice the evening's television. So go on up and have a look, but I warn you: it's not a pretty sight. Although it's true that, unlike most of us, you've seen worse.'

Servaz merely nodded. Suddenly he knew that he had to be on this case, no matter what.

The dolls were looking at the night sky. Servaz thought to himself that a corpse floating in the swimming pool would have more or less the same expression. They were rocking, their pale dresses undulating to the same rhythm, and sometimes they bumped together lightly. He was standing at the edge of the pool with Espérandieu. His assistant had opened an umbrella the size of a parasol over their heads. The rain was ricocheting off it, and off the flagstones and the toes of their shoes.

'Fuck,' said Espérandieu, simply.

This was his favourite way of summing up a situation that, in his opinion, was incomprehensible.

'She collected them,' he said. 'I don't think whoever killed her brought them with him. He must have found them in the house.'

Servaz nodded. He counted. *Nineteen* . . . Another flash of lightning lit up their streaming faces. The most striking thing was all those staring expressions. He knew that a similar expression

24

would be waiting for them upstairs, and he prepared himself mentally.

'Let's go.'

Once they were indoors, they put on gloves, caps over their hair, and nylon overshoes. Darkness enveloped them; the generator wasn't working yet, apparently there was a technical problem. They prepared themselves in silence; neither Vincent nor Servaz felt like talking. Servaz took out his torch and switched it on. Espérandieu did the same. They began to climb the stairs.

4

Illumination

The lightning flashing through the skylights illuminated the steps as they creaked beneath their feet. The glow from the torches sculpted their faces from below, and Espérandieu could see his boss's eyes shining like two black pebbles while he looked, head lowered, for traces of footprints on the stairway. As he climbed he placed his feet as close as possible to the skirting board on either side, spreading his legs like an All Blacks rugby player during the haka.

'Let's just hope that our friend the prosecutor went up and down the same way,' he said.

Someone had left a storm lamp on the top landing. It cast an uncertain brilliance on the door.

Servaz paused on the threshold. He looked at his watch. 23.10. A particularly bright flash of lightning lit up the bathroom window as they went in. An ear-splitting clap of thunder immediately followed. They took another step and swept their torch beams over the space under the roof. They had to hurry. The crime scene officers would be here soon, but for the moment they were on their own. The attic room was completely dark, with the exception of the fireworks beyond the window . . . and the bath, which formed a sort of light blue rectangle in the darkness at the far end of the room.

Like a swimming pool . . . *lit up from inside* . . .

Servaz could feel his pulse pounding in his throat. He moved the beam of his torch over the floor. Then he forced himself to go closer to the bath, hugging the walls. It wasn't easy: there were bottles and candles everywhere, small pieces of furniture and a basin, a towel rack, a mirror. A double curtain framed the bath. It had been pulled open and Servaz could now see water gleaming against the porcelain. And a shadow.

There was something in the bath . . . Something, or rather, someone.

The bath was an old-fashioned clawfoot model in white cast iron. It was nearly two metres long, and it was deep – so deep that Servaz had to walk the last metre from where he stood to be able to see into the bottom.

He took another step. Wanted to recoil, repressed the urge.

She was in there, looking at him with her blue eyes wide open, as if she were waiting for him. She also had her mouth open, which made it seem as if she were about to say something. But of course that was impossible, because her expression was dead. There was nothing living left in it.

Bécker and Castaing had been right: even Servaz had rarely seen anything so horrifying. Except perhaps the decapitated horse on the mountainside . . . But unlike them, he knew how to control his emotions. Claire Diemar had been tied with an absolutely unbelievable length of rope, wound many times over around her torso, her legs, her ankles, her neck and her arms, passing under her armpits, between her thighs, and crushing her chest, the rough rope biting deep into the victim's skin in every place. Espérandieu stepped forward in turn and looked over his boss's shoulder. One word immediately sprang to mind: *bondage*. There were so many knots and loops in some places, so complicated and tight, that Servaz figured it would take the pathologist hours to cut through them, then examine them once he got back to the lab. He had never seen such a tangled skein. Trussing her up like that would not have taken that long, however; whoever had done this could have acted in brutal haste before laying her in the bath and opening the tap.

He hadn't turned it off properly, because it was still dripping.

A deafening noise in the silent room every time a drop fell on the surface of the water.

Perhaps he had beaten her first. Servaz would have liked to put one hand into the bath, lift her head out of the water and hold up her skull to feel the occipital and the parietal – two of the eight flat bones that make up the cranium – through her long brown hair. But that was the pathologist's job.

The light from his torch rebounded on the water. He switched it off and there was only one source of light now. *It was as if the water had sequins in it . . .*

Servaz closed his eyes, counted to three, then opened them again: the light was not in the bath, but in the victim's mouth. A tiny little torch, no more than two centimetres in diameter. It had been rammed down her throat. Only the end emerged, and it lit up the dead woman's palate, tongue, gums and teeth, while its beam was diffracted through the surrounding water.

Like a lamp with a human lampshade . . .

Puzzled, Servaz wondered what the meaning of this final gesture might be. A signature? Its pointlessness and its undeniable importance left him thoughtful. The symbol remained to be found. He thought about what he could see there before him, as well as the dolls in the swimming pool, and tried to determine how significant each element might be.

Water . . .

Water was the main thing. And he could also make out organic substances at the bottom of the bath, a faint whiff of urine. She must have died in that cold water.

Water here and water outside. *It was raining.* Had the murderer waited for this stormy night to act?

He considered how he had not seen any traces on the stairs on his way up. If the body had been tied up somewhere else, then dragged up here, in all likelihood there would have been scrapes on the skirting boards, or twists and tears in the carpet. He would ask the technicians to examine the stairway and take samples, but he already knew the answer.

He looked at the young woman again. He felt dizzy. She had had a future. Who deserved to die so young? Her expression in the water told him what else had happened: that before she died she had been afraid, terribly afraid. She had understood that it was all over, that she had used up all her credit before she'd even had a chance to find out what getting older was about. What had she been thinking about? About the past, or the future? About all the missed opportunities, the second chances she would not have, the plans that would never come to be, about lovers or the love of her life? Or was she just thinking about surviving? Judging by the wounds the rope had left, she must have struggled with the wild desperation of an animal caught in a trap. But she was already confined in her narrow prison of cords by then, and she would have felt the level of the water rising slowly, inexorably, around her. While panic was howling like a hurricane in her brain and she would have liked to cry out for real, the little torch in her mouth had prevented her from doing so, more efficiently than any gag, and she could only breathe through her nose while her throat was hurting, swollen around a foreign object, and her brain was beginning to lack oxygen. She must have choked when the water came into her mouth, then panic would have changed to pure terror when the water entered her nostrils, covered her face, and lapped against her wide-open eyes . . .

Suddenly the light came back on and they both jumped.

'Bloody fucking hell!' exclaimed Espérandieu.

'Can you tell me why I should let you handle this case, Commandant?'

Servaz raised his head and looked at Castaing. The magistrate took out a cigarette and wedged it between his lips. The cigarette crackled in the rain when he lit it. He looked like a totem pole, standing in the glow from the headlights.

'*Why?* Because everyone expects you to. Because it's the most reasonable choice. Because if you don't and the investigation turns into a monstrous cock-up, everyone will ask you why you didn't.'

Castaing's beady little eyes were sparkling, and Servaz could not decide whether it was in anger or amusement, or a mixture of the two. The huge man's body language was astonishingly difficult to read.

'Cathy d'Humières is unstinting in her praise of you.'

His tone betrayed his scepticism.

'She said your investigation team is the best one she's ever worked with. That's no small compliment, is it?'

Servaz remained silent.

'I want to be kept informed of all your movements and every breakthrough in the investigation, is that clear?'

Servaz merely nodded.

'I will refer the case to the regional police and call your director at once. Rule number one: no hiding things and no mucking about with procedure. In other words, you're to take no initiatives without my prior consent.'

From beneath his prominent brows, Castaing sought a sign of assent. Servaz nodded again.

'Rule number two: everything regarding the press goes through me. No speaking to the journalists. I'll take care of that.'

Well, well, he wanted his fifteen minutes, too. With his little formula Andy Warhol had sown the seed of discord, and now everyone wanted to be in the limelight at least once before vanishing: the refs on the pitch, overacting; union leaders taking managers hostage – to defend their jobs, yes, but also to be on the telly; and provincial prosecutors, the minute the camera got switched on.

'No doubt you would have preferred to work with Cathy d'Humières, but you'll just have to make do with me. I will refer matters to you for the duration, and I'll start a preliminary investigation as soon as the suspect is brought in. If I'm not satisfied with your work, if it isn't producing results, or if I am of the opinion that you are not doing enough, I will have the judge take you off the case and put the gendarmerie investigation squad on it. But in the meantime you have carte blanche.'

He turned on his heels and walked over to his Skoda parked further along.

'Great,' said Espérandieu. 'Nice to know he trusts us, isn't it?'

'At least we know what to expect,' added Samira, who had just arrived. 'What level of law court do they have in Auch?'

She had shown up as they were coming back downstairs, and had not failed to attract the attention of the gendarmes with her *Zombies versus Vampires* parka.

'It's a county court . . .'

'Hmm.'

He guessed what she was driving at: he was willing to bet that this was the first case of such importance that the prosecutor had had to handle. To make up for his lack of experience, he was asserting his authority. There were times when the law and the police were in step, but sometimes it was as if they were pulling at opposite ends of the same rope.

They went back inside. The CSI team had arrived; they had put up police tape, switched on their projectors, unwound metres of electric cable, laid down tabs of yellow plastic to indicate possible clues, and they were sweeping the walls with the beam of their special lamps to look for traces of blood, sperm, or God knows what. They came and went between the ground floor, the stairs and the garden, silently, in their white overalls, each one knowing exactly what to do.

Servaz went into the garden. The rain had slackened off somewhat. But he still felt as if his head were being pounded by it. Marianne's voice on the telephone was still resonating in his ears. She had told him that Hugo had called to explain he had just woken up in his teacher's house. His voice was unrecognisable. He had no idea what he was doing there or how he had got there. Sobbing, he told her how he had searched the garden because the French windows were open, and had been astonished to find a collection of dolls floating in the swimming pool. Then he had set about searching the house, one room at a time, one floor after the other. He thought he would pass out when he discovered Claire Diemar's body in the bath on the top floor. Marianne had explained to Servaz that for at least five minutes her son could do nothing but cry and speak incoherently. Then Hugo had pulled himself together and gone on with his explanations. He had grabbed Claire in the water, shaking her to wake her up while he tried to undo the knots, but they were too tight. And in any case, he could see that she was already dead. Horribly upset, he dragged himself out of the house and to the swimming pool, in the rain. He had no idea how long he'd been out there by the swimming pool, his mind drained of thoughts, before calling his mother. He told her that he felt weird – as if his head were full of fog. That was the expression he had used. As if he'd been drugged . . . then, while he was still groggy, the gendarmes had shown up and handcuffed him.

Servaz went over to the swimming pool. A technician was fishing the dolls out with a net. He would catch one, then let it slide into one of the big transparent bags a colleague was holding out. There was something surreal about the scene: the projectors had been switched on, and the dolls' white, ghostly faces glowed in the harsh light, as did their blue, staring eyes. Except, thought Servaz with a shiver, Claire Diemar's gaze looked as dead as could be, while the dolls' gazes seemed strangely alive. Or, to be more exact, their hostility seemed alive . . . What rubbish. Servaz berated himself for having such thoughts.

He walked slowly around the pool, careful not to slip on the wet tiles. He sensed something in the victim's behaviour must have attracted the predator. As in nature, where an animal can picture its prey, and does not hunt by chance.

Everything about the way the crime had been staged told him that in this case, too, the victim had not been chosen by chance.

He stopped by the wall that separated the garden from the street and looked up. Above the wall he could see the upper floor of the house across the street. One window looked directly over the swimming pool. That must be where the English neighbour had seen Hugo and the dolls. If Hugo had sat on the other side of the pool, at the foot of the high wall, no one would have seen him. But he had been sitting on the side where Servaz was now standing. Perhaps he hadn't even thought about it, perhaps he was too stoned, too lost, too distraught after what had just happened to care about anything else. Servaz frowned. There was something not right about the whole business.

5

The Hunting of the Snark

Oliver Winshaw was an old man with eyes as bright as those of a fish straight out of the water. And although it was late, he didn't seem the least bit tired. Servaz observed that his wife had not said a word, but she never took her eyes off them, and she didn't miss a thing. Just like her husband, she was anything but sleepy. Two alert old people, who had surely led interesting lives and intended to keep their neurons working as long as possible.

'One more time, just to get this straight, you haven't noticed anything unusual lately?'

'No. Nothing. I'm sorry.'

'Even something like a man lurking about the house, or someone ringing at your neighbour's door, a detail you might not have noticed at the time but which, in light of what has just happened, might seem fishy now. Please concentrate, it's important.'

'I think we are quite aware of how important it is,' said the woman firmly, speaking for the first time. 'My husband is trying to help you, Commissioner, you can see that.'

Servaz looked at Oliver. The old man's left eyelid was twitching almost imperceptibly. He didn't bother to correct her use of 'commissioner'.

'Mrs Winshaw, would you mind leaving me alone with your husband for a moment?'

The woman's expression hardened and she parted her lips.

'Look, Commissioner, I—'

'Christine, please,' said Winshaw.

Servaz saw that his wife was startled. Apparently she was not used to seeing her husband take charge. There was a touch of alertness in Oliver Winshaw's voice: he had enjoyed hearing his wife being put in her place, and he liked the idea of finding himself alone among men. Servaz looked at his two assistants and motioned to them to leave the room as well.

'I don't know if you are allowed to drink while on duty, but I would be glad of a Scotch,' said the old man when they were alone.

'You won't tell anyone?' said Servaz with a smile. 'Without ice, thank you.'

Winshaw flashed him a smile yellowed with tannin. He had a gentle, mischievous gaze, and an old man's thinning hair. Servaz got up and went over to the bookshelf. *Paradise Lost, The Rime of the Ancient Mariner, Hyperion, The Hunting of the Snark, The Waste Land*: row upon row of English poetry.

'Are you interested in poetry, Commandant?'

Servaz took the glass the old man was holding out to him. The first sip went down like fire. It was good, with a very pronounced taste of smoke.

'Only Latin poetry.'

'Did you study it?'

'I studied literature, a long time ago.'

Winshaw nodded vigorously in approval.

'Only poetry can tell of man's inability to understand the meaning of our passage on earth,' he said. 'And yet, when given the choice, humankind always prefers football to Victor Hugo.'

'What, you don't like sport?' said Servaz teasingly.

'Bread and circuses. Nothing very new about that. At least the gladiators put their lives at risk, and that gave them an altogether different allure than these kids in shorts running after a ball. The stadium is only an exaggerated version of the schoolyard.'

'Plutarch said, "Nor is it good to scorn physical exercise",' said Servaz.

'Then let's drink to Plutarch's health.'

'Claire Diemar was a beautiful woman, wasn't she?'

Oliver Winshaw paused with his glass a few inches from his lips. His pale, gentle gaze seemed to retreat somewhere far from the room.

'Very.'

'As much as that?'

'You saw her, didn't you? Unless . . . Don't tell me that she . . . that she . . .'

'Let's just say that she wasn't looking her best.'

The old man's gaze clouded over.

'Oh, Lord . . . Here we are joking and drinking, with what just happened right over the road . . .'

'Did you watch her?'

'What?'

'Over the wall, when she was in her garden, did you watch her?'

'What are you getting at, for goodness' sake?'

'She sunbathed: that was obvious from her tan lines. She must have walked around her garden. Stretched out on the deckchair. Gone swimming, I would imagine. A beautiful woman . . . There must have been times when you noticed her without meaning to, as you walked by your window.'

'Rubbish! Don't beat about the bush, Commandant. You want to know if I was a bit of a voyeur?'

Oliver Winshaw was not at a loss for words. He shrugged.

'Then let me tell you: Yes, I did occasionally watch her. And so what? She had one hell of an arse, if that's what you want to hear. And she knew it.'

'In what way?'

'That girl wasn't born yesterday, Commandant, believe me.'

'Did she have visitors?'

'Yes. A few.'

'People you knew?'

'No.'

'None of them?'

'No. She didn't associate with the locals. But I had already seen that boy.'

The old man looked Servaz straight in the eyes, clearly enjoying the interest he aroused in the policeman.

'You mean that he had already come to see her?'

'Yes.'

'When?'

'A week ago. I saw them together in the garden. They were talking.'

'Are you sure?'

'I'm not senile, Commandant.'

'And any other times? Were there other occasions?'

'Yes, I had already seen him before.'

'How many times?'

'I would say at least a dozen. Not to mention the times I must have missed him. I'm not always at my window.'

Servaz was convinced that wasn't true.

'Were they always out in the garden?'

'I don't know . . . I don't think so, no . . . Once or twice, he must have rung the bell and they stayed inside. But don't go thinking I'm insinuating anything.'

'How did they behave towards each other? Did they seem to be . . . intimate?'

'Like lovers, you mean? No . . . maybe . . . Honestly, I really don't know. If you're looking for juicy details, you'll have to ask someone else.'

'Had it been going on for long?'

The old man shrugged.

'Did you know that he was one of her students?'

This time there was a spark in the old man's eye.

'No, I didn't know that.'

He took a swallow of his whisky.

'And doesn't that seem odd, a student who visits his teacher when she is at home alone? A teacher who is that beautiful?'

'It's not for me to judge.'

'Do you talk with your neighbours, Mr Winshaw? Were there any rumours about her?'

'*Rumours*? In a town like Marsac? What do you think? I hardly speak with the neighbours: that's Christine's job. She's much more sociable than I am, if you see what I mean. You'll have to ask her that.'

'Had you ever been inside her house, you and your wife?'

'Yes. When she moved in, we invited her for coffee. She returned the invitation, but only once, probably out of politeness.'

'Do you recall whether she collected dolls?'

'Yes. My wife used to be a psychologist. I remember very well that when we came home, she voiced a theory about the dolls.'

'What sort of theory?'

Winshaw told him.

At least the riddle about the origin of the dolls had been solved. Servaz had no more questions. He looked at a small table where three books lay open: a Torah, a Koran and the Bible.

'Are you interested in religion?' he asked.

Winshaw smiled. He took a sip of his whisky, his eyes twinkling mischievously above his glass.

'It's fascinating, don't you think? Religion, I mean. How these lies can blind so many people. You know what I call this table?'

Servaz raised an eyebrow.

'"The stupid bastards' corner".'

6

Amicus Plato sed major amicus veritas

Servaz dropped a coin into the coffee machine and pressed the button for an Americano with sugar. He had read somewhere that, contrary to popular belief, there was more caffeine in 'long' coffees than in espressos. The cup fell sideways from the dispenser, half the liquid spilled to one side and he waited in vain for the sugar and the stir stick.

He drank it down all the same, to the last drop.

Then he crumpled the cup and tossed it in the bin.

Finally, he went through the door.

The gendarmerie in Marsac did not have an interview room, so they had set aside a little meeting room on the first floor. Servaz immediately noticed the location of the window and frowned. The prime danger in this sort of situation was not so much that the suspect might attempt to escape, but rather commit suicide, if he felt driven to it. Even if it seemed highly unlikely that he would throw himself from the first-floor window, Servaz didn't want to take any chances.

'Close the shutters,' he said to Vincent.

Samira had opened her laptop and was preparing the statement, noting the time they had begun. Then she swivelled it so she'd be able to film the suspect. Once again, Servaz felt behind the times. Every day his young assistants reminded him how quickly the world was changing and how maladjusted he was. He reflected that some day soon the Koreans or the Chinese would invent robot-investigators and he would be put out to pasture. The robots would be equipped with lie detectors and lasers that could detect the slightest inflection in the voice or movement of the eye. They would be infallible and emotionless. But lawyers would probably find a way to ban them.

'What the fuck are they doing?' he asked, annoyed.

Just then the door opened and Bécker came in with Hugo. The boy wasn't wearing handcuffs. Servaz observed him. He seemed absent. And tired. He wondered whether the gendarmes had already tried to interrogate him.

'Have a seat,' said the captain.

'Has he seen a lawyer?'

Bécker shook his head.

'He hasn't said a word since we took him in.'

'But you did remind him that he had the right to see one?'

The gendarme shot him a nasty look and handed him a typed sheet of paper without bothering to reply. Servaz read, 'Has not requested a lawyer.' He sat down at the table opposite the boy. Bécker went to stand near the door. Servaz told himself that since Hugo's mother already knew he was here, there was no one else he needed to inform.

'Your name is Hugo Bokhanowsky,' he began, 'and you were born on 20 July 1992, in Marsac.'

No reaction. Servaz read the next line. And gave a start.

'You are in the second year of literary preparatory classes at the lycée in Marsac . . .'

Hugo would be eighteen in one month. And he was already taking the advanced preparatory classes. A very intelligent boy . . . He wasn't in the same class as Margot – who was in the first year – but he was nevertheless at the same school. Which meant there was a good chance that Margot had also had Claire Diemar as a teacher. He made a note to ask her.

'Would you like a coffee?'

No reaction. Servaz turned to Vincent.

'Go and get him a coffee and a glass of water.'

Espérandieu stood up. Servaz looked closely at the young man. He was keeping his eyes down and his hands wedged tightly and defensively between his knees.

He's scared shitless.

He was slim, with the sort of good looks that girls go for, his hair cut so short that it formed a light, silky down on his round skull, which shone in the neon light. A three-day beard. He was wearing a T-shirt advertising an American university.

'Do you realise that everything seems to point to your guilt? You were found at Claire Diemar's house the same evening she was assaulted in a particularly barbaric fashion. According to the report I have here, you were clearly under the influence of alcohol and drugs at that time.'

He looked closely at Hugo. The boy didn't move. Perhaps he was still under the influence of the narcotics.

'Your footprints were found all over the house.'

Hugo said nothing.

'With traces of mud and grass from your shoes after you had been in the garden.'

Still no response.

Servaz looked questioningly at Bécker, who answered with a shrug.

'Identical traces were discovered on the stairs and in the bathroom where Claire Diemar was found murdered.'

The boy still said nothing.

'Your mobile phone indicates that you called the victim no fewer than eighteen times in the last two weeks alone.'

Silence.

'What did you talk about? We know she was your teacher. Did you like her?'

No answer.

Shit, we're not going to get anything out of him.

He had a fleeting thought for Marianne: her son was behaving in every way as if he were guilty. For a moment he thought of asking her to get him to cooperate.

'What were you doing at Claire Diemar's house?'

No answer.

'Fuck, are you deaf or what? Don't you know you're in deep shit?'

Samira's voice. She had burst in, as sharp and shrill as a saw. Hugo jumped. He deigned to look up and for a split second he seemed slightly disconcerted on seeing the large mouth, protruding eyes and little nose of the French-Chinese-Moroccan woman. But his reaction lasted only a fraction of a second before his gaze returned to his knees.

A storm outside, and silence within. No one seemed prepared to break it.

Servaz and Samira exchanged glances.

'I'm not here to torment you,' he said at last. 'We just want to get at the truth. *Amicus Plato sed major amicus veritas.*'

I love Plato, but I love the truth even more.

Was that the Latin formula?

This time, there was a reaction.

Hugo was looking at him.

His eyes were extremely blue. *His mother's eyes*, thought Servaz, although her eyes were green. He could see Marianne in the shape of her son's face. Their physical resemblance was disturbing.

'I have spoken with your mother,' he said suddenly, without thinking. 'We used to be friends, years ago. Very good friends.'

Hugo said nothing.

'It was before she met your father—'

'She never mentioned you.'

The first words out of Hugo Bokhanowsky's mouth fell like a blade. Servaz felt as if he'd had a fist in his stomach.

He knew that Hugo was telling the truth.

He cleared his throat.

'I studied in Marsac, too,' he said. 'Like you. And now my daughter is studying there. Margot Servaz. She's in the first year.'

Now he had the young man's attention.

'Margot is your daughter?'

'Do you know her?'

The young man shrugged.

'Everyone knows Margot. She doesn't exactly go unnoticed at Marsac . . . She's a great girl. She didn't tell us her father was a cop.'

Hugo's blue gaze was on him now and didn't let go. Servaz realised he'd been mistaken: the boy wasn't afraid, he had simply decided not to speak. And even if he was only seventeen, he seemed much more mature. Servaz continued, gently.

'Why won't you speak? You know you'll only make your case worse if you behave like this. Would you like us to call a lawyer? You can speak with the lawyer and then we'll talk.'

'What's the use? I was on the premises when she died, or not long afterwards . . . I have no alibi . . . Everything points to me . . . So I'm guilty, aren't I?'

'Are you?'

Those blue eyes, staring right at him. Servaz could read neither guilt nor innocence in them. There was nothing to be deciphered from such a gaze, only patience.

'In any case, that's what you think . . . so what the fuck difference does it make whether it's true or not?'

'It makes a huge difference,' said Servaz.

But that was a lie, and he knew it. French prisons were full of innocent people, and the streets were full of guilty ones. Judges and lawyers pretended to cloak themselves in their robes and their virtue as they doled out their speeches about morality and the law, but for all that they tolerated a system they knew was producing judicial errors by the shovelful.

'You called your mother to tell her you woke up in the house and that there was a dead woman there, is that correct?'

'Yes.'

'Where were you when you woke up?'

'Downstairs in the living room.'

'Whereabouts?'

'On the sofa. Sitting.'

Hugo looked at Bécker.

'I already told them.'

'And then what did you do?'

'I called out for Mademoiselle Diemar.'

'Did you go on sitting there?'

'No. The French windows were open, and the rain was coming in. I went out that way.'

'Didn't you wonder where you were?'

'I recognised the house.'

'You had already been there?'

'Yes.'

'So you recognised the place. Did you go there often?'

'Often enough.'

'What do you mean by "enough"? How many times?'

'I don't remember.'

'Try to remember.'

'I don't know . . . maybe ten . . . or twenty . . .'

'Why did you go to see her so often? And why did you call her all the time? Did Mademoiselle Diemar receive all the students from Marsac in this way?'

'No, I don't think so.'

'So, why you? What did you talk about?'

'About my writing.'

'What?'

'I'm writing a novel. I had mentioned it to Clai— to Mademoiselle

Diemar. She was very interested in it; she asked if she could read what I had written. We spoke about it regularly. On the phone, too.'

Servaz looked at Hugo. A tremor. He too had started writing a novel when he was a student at Marsac. The great modern novel . . . The glorious dream of every apprentice writer . . . The one that would make publishers and readers say, 'A masterpiece!' The story of a quadriplegic man who lived for his thoughts alone, whose inner life was as luxuriant and intense as a tropical jungle, and far richer than that of the majority of people. He had stopped the day after his father committed suicide.

'You called her Claire?' he asked.

A hesitation.

'Yes.'

'What was the nature of your relationship?'

'I just told you. She was interested in my writing.'

'Did she give you advice?'

'Yes.'

'She thought it was good?'

Hugo's gaze. A gleam of pride in his pupils.

'She said . . . she said she hadn't read anything like it for a long time.'

'Will you tell me the title?'

He saw Hugo hesitate. Servaz put himself in his shoes. No doubt the young author did not feel like sharing this sort of thing with a stranger.

'It's called *The Circle*.'

Servaz would have liked to ask what it was about, but he didn't. He felt the stirrings of a deep bewilderment, and at the same time a surge of empathy for the young man. He was no fool: he knew it was because Hugo reminded him of himself, twenty-three years earlier. And perhaps, too, because he was Marianne's son. But for all that Servaz still wondered if it was possible that Hugo could have killed someone who understood and appreciated his work.

'Let's go back to what you did after that, after the garden.'

'I went back into the house. I called out to her. I searched every-where.'

'You didn't think of calling the police?'

'No.'

'And then?'

43

'I went upstairs, I searched all the rooms, one by one . . . until I reached the bathroom . . . and then . . . *I saw her.*'

His Adam's apple bobbed up and down.

'I panicked. I didn't know what to do. I tried to get her head out of the water, I slapped her to wake her up, I shouted, I tried to untie the knots. But there were too many, and they were too tight, and I couldn't do it: the water had made them swell up. And before long I realised it was too late.'

'You say you tried to revive her?'

'Yes, that's what I did.'

'And the torch?'

Servaz saw Hugo's eyelids flutter almost imperceptibly.

'You did see the torch in her mouth, didn't you?'

'Yes, obviously . . .'

'So why didn't you try to pull it out?'

Hugo hesitated.

'I don't know. Probably because . . .'

He paused, and Servaz prompted him with his gaze.

'Because I couldn't put my fingers in her mouth . . .'

'You mean, in a dead woman's mouth?'

Servaz saw Hugo's shoulders slump.

'Yes. No. Not just that. In Claire's mouth . . .'

'And before that? What happened? You said you woke up in Claire Diemar's house – what did you mean by that?'

'Just that. I regained consciousness in the living room.'

'You mean you had lost consciousness?'

'Yes . . . well, I suppose . . . I already explained all this to your colleagues.'

'Explain it to me: what were you doing when you lost consciousness, do you remember?'

'No . . . not really . . . I'm not sure. It's like, as if there were a blank . . .'

'A blank in time, in the chain of events?'

Servaz saw that Bécker was staring at him and not Hugo. The gendarme's gaze was eloquent. He also saw that the blow had struck home. Hugo was intelligent enough to understand that this blank was not good news.

'Yes,' he admitted reluctantly.

'What's the last thing you remember?'

'I was with friends at the Dubliners, earlier that evening.'

Servaz was taking notes, in shorthand. He didn't trust the webcam any more than he trusted gadgets in general.

'The Dubliners?'

He knew the place. The pub had been there in his day. Servaz and his friends had made it their headquarters back then.

'Yes.'

'What were you doing there? What time was it?'

'We were watching the World Cup, the opening match, and we were waiting for the one with France.'

'"Waiting"? You mean you don't remember seeing Uruguay-France?'

'No . . . maybe . . . I don't know any more about what I did during the evening. It may seem strange, but I don't know how long it lasted . . . or exactly when I passed out.'

'Do you think someone knocked you out, is that it? Did someone hit you?'

'No, I don't think so, I checked. I don't have a bump. And I don't have a headache, either. But when I came round I was all fuzzy, as if my head were full of fog . . .'

He slumped further into his chair, as if realising that the more he talked, the more everything pointed to him.

'Do you think someone drugged you?'

'It's possible.'

'We'll check that. Where were you sitting in the pub?'

'I don't remember.'

Servaz exchanged looks with Bécker. The gendarme's gaze said, unequivocally: *guilty.*

'I see. Maybe it will come back to you. If it does, let me know, it's important.'

Hugo shook his head bitterly.

'I'm not stupid.'

'I have one last question: do you like football?'

A glow of surprise in his blue eyes.

'Yes, why?'

'Your coffee's going to get cold,' said Servaz. 'Drink it. It could be a long night.'

★

'A woman alone in an unlocked house,' said Samira.

'And no sign that it was broken into,' said Espérandieu.

'She must have let him in. He's her student, after all; she had no reason to be wary. And he said so himself: he had already been there. And he called her eighteen times over the last two weeks . . . to talk about books? A likely story!'

'He did it,' decreed Vincent.

Servaz turned to Samira, and she nodded her head in agreement.

'I think so too. He was arrested at the victim's. And there are no traces of any other individuals. Nothing. Anywhere. Not the slightest proof that a third person was there. But his traces are everywhere. The breath test came up with 0.85 grams of alcohol in his blood; the analysis will tell us whether he had also taken drugs – which is probable, given the state we found him in – and the amount. The gendarmes said that when they caught him his pupils were dilated and he was completely out of it.'

'He said someone drugged him,' said Servaz.

'Oh, come on . . . Who? We found his car parked nearby. So someone else drove it? And even if we suppose it was someone else, he said he woke up in the house: that means the actual murderer would have had to have run the risk of taking Hugo out of the car and dragging him all the way to Claire's house. And no one saw a thing? It doesn't add up. Several houses overlook the street, and there are three terraced houses right across from the victim's—'

'Everyone was watching the football,' protested Servaz. 'Even we were.'

'Not everyone: the old man across the street saw him all right.'

'But he didn't see him arrive, that's just it. No one saw him go in. Why would he sit there waiting for someone to come and get him if he did it?'

'You know the statistics as well as I do,' answered Samira. 'In fifteen per cent of cases, the perpetrator of a crime hands himself in to the police, in five per cent he informs a third party who tells the police, and in thirty-eight per cent of cases he waits calmly at the crime scene for the police to arrive, fully aware that a witness must have contacted them. That's what this kid did. In fact, nearly two-thirds of cases are solved within the first few hours because of the perp's attitude.'

Servaz did indeed know the figures.

'Yes, but they don't go on to claim they are innocent.'

'He was stoned. Once he started to come back down, he realised what he had done and what he was in for,' said Espérandieu. 'He's simply trying to save his skin.'

'The only question worth asking right now,' said Samira, 'is whether the assault was premeditated.'

His two assistants were staring at him, waiting for him to react.

'The crime was staged and it's a pretty unusual way to kill someone, isn't it?' he replied. 'The ropes, the torch, the dolls . . . none of it is anything like an ordinary crime. We should be careful not to jump to conclusions.'

'The kid was high,' said Samira with a shrug. 'He probably had some sort of spell of delirium. It wouldn't be the first time a junkie does something completely crazy. I don't trust this kid. And anyway, everything points to him, doesn't it? Shit, boss . . . In any other circumstances, you would come to the same conclusion.'

He started. 'What's that supposed to mean?'

'You said it yourself: you were well acquainted with his mother. And she's the one who called for help, if I'm not mistaken.'

Servaz arched his back, stung by her insinuation. There were still a number of details that didn't fit. *The way it was staged, the torch, the dolls . . .* he thought. *And the timing as well . . .* There was something about the timing that was bugging him. If the kid had lost it, why was it on that very night, when everyone was glued to the television?

Was it chance, coincidence? In sixteen years on the job, Servaz had learned to scratch such words from his vocabulary. Hugo liked football. Would someone who liked watching the World Cup choose that evening to kill someone? *Only if he wanted to be sure no one would notice . . .* But Hugo had stayed on the spot and let himself be caught; he hadn't tried to hide.

'This investigation is over before it's even begun,' concluded Samira, cracking her knuckles.

He stopped her with a wave of his hand.

'Not quite. Go back there and check whether the technicians had a good look at Hugo's car, and ask them to go over it with cyanoacrylate.'

He wished he had a shed available to go over the interior and exterior of the car with a fine-toothed comb. A painting shed like the ones that body shops used, equipped so that cyanoacrylate – a sort of superglue – could evaporate by being heated. Upon contact with the oily traces that fingers left, cyanoacrylate vapours made the fingerprints appear in white. Unfortunately there were no sheds like that available within a radius of over 500 kilometres: consequently, the technicians had to make do with 'cyano shots' – portable diffusers. In any event, the violent downpour had probably washed the body-work clean.

'And then question the neighbours. Do all the houses on the street, one by one.'

'A house-to-house – at this hour? It's two o'clock in the morning!'

'Well then, get them out of bed. I want answers before we go back to Toulouse. I want to know whether anyone saw anything, heard anything, noticed anything, tonight or on any day leading up to today, anything unusual, anything at all – even if it has no connection with what happened this evening.'

He met their incredulous gazes.

'Get to work!'

7

Margot

They'd been driving through the hills. It was September, and it was still warm; summer was all around them, and since the air-conditioning wasn't working, Servaz had rolled down the windows. He had slotted a Mahler CD in the player and he was in an excellent mood. Not only was the weather fine and he had his daughter for company, but he was taking her to a place he knew well, even though he hadn't been back there in a long time.

As he drove, he thought about how Margot had been an average pupil in primary school. Then there had been the adolescent crisis. Even now, with her piercings, her strange hair colour and her leather jackets, his daughter didn't look at all like she'd be at the top of her class. But despite her punky look she had earned very good marks. And Marsac was the most demanding prep school in the region. You had to prove you were good to be admitted. As he drove through the summer land-scape that morning, he felt himself swelling with pride like a soap bubble.

'It's so beautiful here,' said Margot, removing her headphones from her ears.

Servaz glanced quickly around him. The road wound its way through green hills, sunny forests and silky blond fields of wheat. As he slowed down to go around a bend, they could hear the birds singing and the chirring of insects.

'It's a bit dead, no?' said Servaz.

'Hmm. What is Marsac like?'

'A small town. Quiet. I suppose they still have the same student pubs. Why did you choose Marsac rather than Toulouse?'

'Because of Van Acker. The lit prof.'

Even after all this time, Van Acker's name elicited a reaction, like an electrical impulse stimulating a long inactive zone in his heart. He tried nevertheless to keep his voice neutral.

'He's that good?'

'He's the best in 500 kilometres.'

Margot knew what she wanted. No doubt about that. He recalled the words of his daughter's married lover, the only time he had met him, on the place du Capitole, a few days before Christmas: 'Beneath her rebellious exterior, Margot is a wonderful girl, brilliant and independent. And a lot more mature than you give her credit for.' A difficult conversation; bitter, full of reproach, but which in the end had made him conclude that he did not know her very well at all.

'You could have made more of an effort with your clothes.'

'Why? It's my brains they're interested in, not my clothes.'

That was Margot all over . . . Still, he wasn't sure her argument would carry much weight with the staff. They had driven through the vast Marsac forest, which went on for miles, with its bridle trails, footpaths and car parks, then they had entered the town by way of the long straight avenue lined with plane trees which Servaz had gone up hundreds of times in his youth.

'You don't mind being a boarder from Monday to Saturday?' he asked.

'I don't know.' She was looking out of the open window. 'I haven't given it much thought. I suppose I'll meet interesting people here; it'll be a nice change from those idiots at the other lycée. What was it like when you were here?'

The question had caught him unawares. He didn't feel like talking about it.

'It was good,' he said.

There were a lot of bicycles on the streets, mostly with students perched on the saddle, but also a few professors with leather panniers stuffed with books over their rear wheels or in front of the handlebars. Marsac had several faculties: law, science, humanities . . . The town seemed to have yielded to its preference for youth. Except during the holidays, half the population was under twenty-five.

They drove north out of town. A green meadow, with a dense line of trees in the distance.

'Here,' he announced.

There was a long, tall building on the right, a short way from the road, at the end of a broad meadow. It looked very old-fashioned, with its roofs clustered with chimneys, its facade with mullioned windows. Around it there were several low, modern concrete buildings, set down upon the lawn like incongruous dominoes. Memories assailed him. He saw once again the pensive statues, the pools with green water, the copses colonised by mistletoe, the tennis courts overrun by dead leaves in November, the running track, the little woods where he liked to go for walks, which led to a high, gently sloping hill and the view it offered over the undulating hills as far as the Pyrenees, white from autumn to spring.

It was as if a cold fist had squeezed his heart, causing a rush of nostalgia.

He hadn't realised it, but his fingers were gripping the steering wheel. He had dreamt for so long of a second chance, and had eventually understood that there wouldn't be one. He had missed his chance. He would finish his adult life the way he had begun it: as a cop. In the end, his dreams had turned out to be as transient as clouds.

Fortunately the sensation only lasted a second, and the next instant it was gone.

They left the road to head up the paved driveway. It led between a white gate, which separated them from the broad meadow and the main building on their left, and a row of old oaks beyond a ditch to their right. Horses were frolicking in the meadow. He couldn't help but think of his investigation during the winter of 2008.

'Follow your dreams,' he said suddenly.

His voice was stifled.

Margot turned to look at him, surprised. He wished he could have hidden the fact that his eyes had misted up.

'This preparatory class is very demanding. It is meant for students who are very motivated and who are not afraid to work hard. The two years you are going to spend with us will be an opportunity for you to bloom and make the most of your education, not to mention the unprecedented experiences you will have. The knowledge we pass on to you does not neglect the human side. Unlike other establishments, we are not obsessed with statistics,' explained the headmaster with a smile.

Servaz was certain the opposite was true. Behind the headmaster, the window was open. He could see ivy and hear the sound of a lawnmower, and someone hammering. He knew that the headmaster's office was at the top floor of a circular tower, and that his window overlooked the rear of the building: Servaz knew the place like the back of his hand.

'No pupils are kept down the first year, except in the event of an accident or serious illness. However, the difficulty of the entrance examinations to the institutes of higher education often necessitates repeating the second year. This possibility is open to all students who have shown the required qualities during their two years here.'

A beam of sunlight fell upon the folder with Margot's name on it when the headmaster opened it and pulled out a sheet of paper.

'Let's take a look now at the choice of options. This is a very serious matter. You must not choose lightly, young lady, because even if your choice for the exam is only finalised at the beginning of the second year, it will depend on what you choose in the first year. And I advise against increasing the options simply to, shall we say, cover all eventualities . . . The workload is considerable, and such a decision would inevitably be detrimental to the quality of your work.'

He counted on his fingertips.

'In first year, you already have five hours of French, four hours of philosophy, five of history, four of living languages 1, three of classical languages and culture, two of geography, two of living languages 2 and two of physical education, and—'

'I've already chosen my options,' interrupted Margot. 'Speciality units Latin and Greek, level confirmed. And drama. As my living language number 1, I'll be taking English. Living language number 2, German.'

The head's pen scratched across the paper.

'Very good. You are bound by your choices for the entire year, you realise that?'

'Yes.'

He turned to Servaz with a delighted smile.

'Here is a young person who knows what she wants.'

8

Music

Servaz went back into the interrogation room. It was half past two in the morning. Hugo's features were drawn, and Servaz sensed that the atmosphere had changed. So much pressure, so much fear. The time had come for confessions. Spontaneous confessions, fake confessions, truthful confessions, fantastical confessions, extorted confessions . . . I confess, because it relieves me of the burden of my guilt; I confess because I've had enough, because I'm exhausted and helpless, because I have an irresistible desire to go for a wee; I confess because that stupid bastard won't stop blowing his stinking breath in my face; I confess because he's driving me crazy, screaming at me, and because he frightens me; I confess because that's what they all want, basically, and because I'll end up having a heart attack, coronary thrombosis, hypoglycemia, kidney failure, epilepsy . . . He lit a cigarette and handed it to Hugo, in spite of the pictogram on the wall. The young man took it. He inhaled his first puff with the gratitude of a shipwreck survivor who has been handed a flask of fresh water, and he allowed the poison to flow slowly down his throat and into his lungs. Servaz noticed that he didn't inhale, but he definitely seemed to feel better afterwards. Hugo observed him in silence. Outside, the rain drummed noisily on a row of dustbins.

They were alone – as was always the case, once it became clear that one member of a team of investigators had a better rapport with the detainee than the others did. It didn't matter whether it was the leader of the team or a subordinate: the main thing was to get the detainee talking.

'Would you like another coffee?'

'No, thank you.'

'Something to drink? Another cigarette?'

The young man shook his head.

53

'I had stopped smoking,' he said.

'How long ago?'

'Eight months ago.'

'You don't mind if we go on?'

He gave Servaz a worried look.

'I thought we had finished.'

'Not quite. There are a few things to clear up,' said Servaz, opening his notepad. 'Would you like to postpone it until later?'

Once again, Hugo shook his head.

'No, no. It's fine.'

'Good. Another hour or two and you'll be able to get some sleep.'

'Where?' Hugo asked, his eyes widening. 'In prison?'

'In a custody cell for the moment. But we're going to have to take you back to Toulouse. From now on the investigation will be under the jurisdiction of the regional police force.'

He saw the boy's expression wilt.

'I'd like to call my mother—'

'We're not obliged to let you. But you'll be able to call her as soon as we've finished, all right?'

The young man leaned back in his chair, his hands behind his neck. He stretched his long legs under the table.

'Try to remember if anything seemed strange to you that evening.'

'Such as?'

'I don't know, anything . . . a detail . . . Something that might have made you feel uneasy, for example. Something that wasn't where it belonged. Just tell me everything that goes through your head.'

Hugo shrugged. 'I really can't think of anything.'

'Make an effort, it's your hide that's at stake.'

Servaz had raised his voice. Hugo looked at him, surprised. Outside, the thunder rumbled once again.

'The music . . .'

Servaz looked at him closely.

'What music?'

'I know it seems ridiculous, but you asked me to—'

'I know what I asked you. Well? What music?'

'When I regained consciousness, there was music coming from the stereo.'

'That's it? What was so unusual about that?'

'Well . . .' Hugo was thinking. 'Claire did use to put music on when I was there, but . . . never that kind of music.'

'What kind of music was it?'

'Classical.'

Servaz looked at him. Classical . . . He felt a tremor go down his spine.

'She didn't generally listen to classical music?'

Hugo shook his head.

'Are you sure?'

'Not to my knowledge . . . She put on jazz, or else rock. Even hip-hop. But I don't remember ever hearing classical music at her house until that evening. I remember that at the time, when I woke up, it immediately seemed . . . *weird*. This sinister music coming from downstairs, the house wide open and no one answering my calls. It really wasn't the sort of thing she'd do.'

Servaz began to feel a gnawing anxiety welling up inside. Something vague, diffuse.

'Nothing else?'

'No.'

Classical music . . . He had an idea but he banished it; it seemed too far-fetched.

When he went back to Claire Diemar's house, he found everything still in upheaval. Now the street was cluttered with vehicles, and the media had joined in the fray as well, despite the late hour – or early, depending on your point of view – with their microphones, cameras and professional agitation. Judging by the presence of a van fitted with a satellite dish, football commentary was not the only subject about to occupy the day's news. But Servaz felt sure that the murder of the classics professor would be relegated to a spot long after the pitiful showing of the national team.

He pulled up the collar of his jacket, which had more or less been reduced to a dishrag, and crossed the slippery cobblestones, masking his face with his hands when the cameras flashed.

Inside the house only a narrow passage, marked off by the forensic team's tape, had been preserved between the front door and the French windows leading to the garden. Servaz spotted the stereo, but some men were already working on it. He decided to go over the garden in the meantime. The dolls had vanished. Technicians were planting numbered signs in the grass, among the trees, wherever there were hypothetical clues. The pool house was open and brilliantly lit. Servaz went up to it. Two technicians in white boiler suits were crouched down inside. He saw a sink, folded deck chairs, shrimping nets, games, and big bottles of products for treating the swimming pool.

'Have you found anything?'

One of them looked at him, his gaze enlarged by the lenses of his thick orange glasses, and shook his head.

Servaz walked around the swimming pool. Slowly. Then he crossed the waterlogged lawn towards the forest. It formed a compact wall of greenery where the lawn came to an end. There was no fence, but the vegetation was thick enough to serve as a natural barrier. He did notice two small gaps, however, and went closer. It was dark in there, and the rain splashed noisily on the foliage overhead without reaching him. The first gap led to a dead end within a few metres. He made his way back, then tried the second gap. This one seemed to lead further. It was no more than an almost indiscernible breach between the trunks and the hedges, and he had to lean this way and that to make his way through, but the breach led stubbornly on into the darkness like a seam of silver in rock. The trees almost completely blocked the rain and Servaz's torch grazed the branches, which seemed to want to hold him back. He stumbled over a bed of leaves and dead wood, and he went for a dozen metres or so without the passage ever getting any wider. Eventually he turned round and promised himself he would come back in daylight. He had nearly reached the way out when in almost total darkness he saw something white on the ground, and he aimed the beam of his torch in that direction.

A little pile of light cylinders, on the leaves and the dark ground. Cigarettes.

He leaned closer. Cigarette butts. At least half a dozen.

Someone had stayed here smoking for quite a while. Servaz raised his head. From where he was standing, he could clearly see the side of the house that gave on to the garden – the French windows and even inside the living room, lit by the projectors. Through one upstairs window he could see furniture. An ideal lookout post . . .

The fine hairs on his neck rose. Whoever had waited here was familiar with the place. He tried to convince himself that it must be a gardener. Or even Claire Diemar herself. But that didn't make sense; he could see no valid reason to lurk in the undergrowth smoking one cigarette after another, if it were not to spy on what the young woman was doing.

Hugo had entered through the front door and left his car on the street. Why would he have spied on Claire from the woods? He had admitted coming here several times: would he have felt the need to play the voyeur on other occasions?

Servaz suddenly got the unpleasant impression that he was watching a magic trick, where the entertainer draws your attention one way while what is actually significant is happening elsewhere. One hand in the light for the spectators, the other hand acting in the shadow. *Someone wanted to make them look in the wrong place . . .* That person had set the scene, chosen the décor, the actors, and perhaps even the spectators . . . Servaz thought he could see a hidden shadow moving behind the drama and his anxiety returned, stronger than ever.

Frowning, he went back into the house. He wiped his soaking feet on the doormat. In the little living room, the technicians had finished with the stereo.

'Do you want to take a look?' one of them asked, handing him some latex gloves, shoe covers, and one of those ridiculous caps which made all the cops in the crime squad look as if they were customers at a ladies' hairdresser's.

Servaz took them and slipped them on before lifting the tape.

'There's something weird,' said the technician.

Servaz looked at him.

'We found the kid's mobile in his pocket. But there is no trace of the victim's. And yet we searched everywhere.'

Servaz pulled out his notepad and wrote this down. He underlined the word telephone twice. He remembered they had found eighteen calls to the victim on Hugo's mobile. Why would he have got rid of Claire Diemar's and not his own?

'And did you find anything on this?' he asked, gesturing towards the stereo with his chin.

The technician shrugged.

'Nothing special. Fingerprints on the player and on the CDs, but they're the victim's.'

'No CD in the player?'

The technician looked at him, not understanding. He was clearly wondering why that should matter. On a piece of furniture there was a small pile of transparent sealable plastic bags, waiting to be taken to the lab. The man picked up one of them and handed it to Servaz wordlessly. Servaz grabbed it.

He looked at the case inside the bag.

And recognised it.

Gustav Mahler . . .

The *Kindertotenlieder*, '*Songs on the Death of Children*'. The 1963 version conducted by Karl Böhm, with Dietrich Fischer-Dieskau. He had exactly the same one.

9

Whiteness

Hugo had mentioned music. But he hadn't said exactly which music. Music that sent Servaz back to the investigation in 2008. Snow, wind, whiteness. Above all whiteness, outside and in. In the East, the colour of death and of mourning. The colour, too, of rites of passage. And it had been such a rite on that December day in 2008 – when they had gone up the valley buried in snow, among the fir trees, beneath the indifferent gaze of a sky as grey as a blade.

And the place. Isolated. The Wargnier Institute. Stone walls typical of that early twentieth-century mountain architecture, used in that era for hotels and hydroelectric power plants alike. An era where things were built to last, and where people believed in the future. Deserted corridors, armoured doors and biometric security locks, cameras, guards. Although there were not so many guards after all, considering the dangerous nature and number of inmates. And the mountain all around: enormous, hostile, disturbing. Like a second prison.

And then there was the man himself.

Julian Alois Hirtmann. Born forty-five years earlier in Hermance, in the French part of Switzerland. He and Servaz had only one thing in common: a love of Mahler's music. Both of them knew everything there was to know about the Austrian composer's oeuvre. Beyond that, they shared nothing: one was a cop from the crime squad, and the other a serial killer. Hirtmann was a former prosecutor from Geneva, who organised orgies at his villa on the shore of Lake Geneva, and who had been arrested for the double murder of his wife and her lover on the night of 21 June 2004. Subsequently, documents had been discovered at his home suggesting that Hirtmann was the author of forty or more murders spread over a period of twenty-five years. Which made him one of the most feared serial killers of modern times. He had been sent to several psychiatric establishments before ending up at the Wargnier Institute, a facility unique in all of Europe, where murderers who had been declared insane by the courts in their respective countries were locked up. Servaz had been involved in the investigation which had preceded – and in a way led to – Hirtmann's escape; he had met the man in his cell shortly before.

Then Hirtmann went over the wall and vanished into thin air, disappeared in a cloud of smoke like the genie in the lamp. Servaz had always been convinced that he would eventually resurface. Sooner or later, without the appropriate treatment, his impulses and hunting instincts would reawaken.

Which did not mean that it would be easy to catch him.

As Simon Propp, the forensic psychologist who had taken part in the investigation, had emphasised, Hirtmann was not only a manipulator and an intelligent sociopath: he was in a class of his own. He belonged to that rare category of serial killers who are capable of having an intense and gratifying social life alongside their criminal activity. It was usual for the personality disorders from which compulsive murderers suffered to affect their intellectual faculties and social life in some way or other. But for twenty years or more the Swiss murderer had managed to occupy a position of great responsibility in the Geneva law courts, while continuing to kidnap, torture and murder over forty women. Tracking Hirtmann down had become a priority: several cops were devoting most of their time to it, both in Paris and Geneva. Servaz had no idea where they stood with their investigation – but he had their telephone numbers somewhere.

Again he pictured Hirtmann in his cell, his dark brown hair and very pale, almost translucent skin. He was thin and unshaven, wearing a boiler suit and T-shirt, of a whitish colour that had gone grey from frequent washing. Yet he was urbane, smiling, extremely polite. Servaz was sure that even if he were homeless Hirtmann would preserve that veneer of education and *savoir-vivre*. He had never met someone who looked so little like a serial killer. But there was something in his expression as electrifying as a Taser, and he never blinked. Something both severe and punitive about his face, yet the lower half, his mouth in particular, belonged to a sensualist. He could have been a hypocritical resident of Salem, Massachusetts in 1692, sending so-called witches to the stake; or a member of the Holy Inquisition; or an accuser at a Stalinist trial . . . or what he had been: a prosecutor who had a reputation for being intransigent, but who organised sado-masochistic soirées at his villa, where his own wife was subjected to the whims of powerful, corrupt men. Insatiable men who, like him, were in search of emotions and pleasures that went far beyond convention or public morality. Businessmen, judges, politicians, artists. Men with power and money. Men whose appetites knew no bounds.

Servaz wondered what Hirtmann looked like nowadays. Had he resorted to cosmetic surgery? Or had he merely let his hair and beard grow, or dyed them and started wearing contact lenses? Had he put on weight, changed the way he walked or spoke, found a job? So many questions . . . If he wore make-up and dressed in a totally different manner, would Servaz recognise him if he passed him in a crowd? A shudder went through him.

He handed the bag with the CD back to the technician.

There was a knot in his stomach.

It was that same piece of music, the *Kindertotenlieder*, that Julian Hirtmann had selected the night he had murdered his wife and her lover. Servaz knew that once they had finished with the initial search and the house-to-house, he would have to get hold of a few people. He did not understand how one crime scene could involve both the son of a woman he had been in love with for a long time, and this music that evoked the most horrific murderer ever to cross his path, but he did know one thing: not only had the public prosecutor's office allowed him to lead the investigation, he was also personally involved.

They drove back to Toulouse at around four o'clock in the morning. They locked Hugo up in one of the detention cells. At the police station the cells were in a row on the opposite side of the corridor from the offices: that way, detainees did not have to go far to be interrogated. Servaz checked his watch.

'Right. Let's let him get some rest,' he said.

'And then what do we do?' asked Espérandieu, stifling a yawn.

'We still have some work ahead. Keep track of the hours he spends resting, and make sure he initials them – and ask him if he's hungry.'

Servaz turned around. Samira was unloading her weapon in the bullet bin, a sort of metallic padded and armoured Kevlar dustbin. To avoid any accidents, when agents came back from a mission they emptied their guns into the bin. Unlike most of her colleagues, Samira wore her holster on her hips. Servaz thought it made her look rather like a cowboy. As far as he knew, she had never yet had to use her gun, but she had excellent results at the shooting range – unlike Servaz, who could have missed an elephant in a corridor. He was the despair of his trainer, who had baptised him 'Daredevil'. Since Servaz didn't understand, the instructor explained that 'Daredevil' was a superhero in a comic strip who was very intuitive but blind. Servaz himself had never used the bullet bin. First of all because he generally forgot to take his weapon, and secondly because he simply locked it up when he came back from a mission and most of the time the magazine was empty anyway.

He walked across the hall and into his office.

The night was not yet over, and he still had a pile of paperwork to get through. The very idea of it depressed him. He went over to the window and looked out at the canal in the rain. The night sky was fading, but the day had not yet risen, so what he saw in the windowpane was his own reflection. His forehead, mouth and eyes were blurry, but before he had time to arrange his features, he surprised an expression that displeased him. That of a man who was anxious and tense. A man who was on his guard.

'Someone wants to speak to you,' said a voice behind him.

He turned around. One of the officers on duty.

'Who?'

'The family lawyer. He's asked to see the kid.'

Servaz frowned.

'The boy didn't ask for a lawyer, and visiting hours are over,' he said. 'He ought to know that.'

'He does. But he's asking for a favour: to speak with you for five minutes. That's what he said. And he says it's the kid's mother who sent him.'

Servaz paused. Should he comply with the lawyer's request? He could understand Marianne's anxiety. What had she told the lawyer about Servaz and herself?

'Where is he?'

'Downstairs. In the lobby.'

'Okay. I'll be down.'

★

When he came out of the lift, Servaz ran into two officers setting up a little television behind the counter. He saw something green on the screen and tiny figures in blue running in every direction. Given the time, it must be a repeat. He gave a sigh, and mused that entire countries were on the verge of collapse, that the names of the Four Horsemen of the Apocalypse were finance, politics, religion and the depletion of resources, and they were whipping their horses as hard as they could, but the ant farm continued to dance on a volcano and be fascinated by things as insignificant as football. Servaz thought that the day the world came to an end – in a blaze of climate catastrophes, stock market collapses, massacres and riots – there would still be men stupid enough to score goals and others who were even more inane going to the stadiums to cheer them on.

The lawyer was sitting in the gloomy, deserted lobby. During the day, the chairs were besieged by anyone who had a reason to be there. No one came to the police station for the pleasure of it, and the officers on duty had to deal with crowds of desperate, furious or frightened people. But at this time of day, the little man was all alone, his briefcase on his lap, his knees close together, and in the dim light he was cleaning his glasses.

The lawyer heard the lift doors open. He put his glasses back on his nose and looked up in Servaz's direction. Servaz motioned to him to follow him and the man walked round the reception with his hand extended. A cool, limp handshake. After that, he smoothed his tie as if he were wiping his hand.

Servaz got straight to the point. 'Sir, you know you have no business here. The boy did not request your presence.'

The little man evaluated him carefully, and Servaz was immediately on his guard.

'I know, I know, Commandant. But Hugo wasn't really thinking straight when you asked him. He was under the influence of the drugs he'd been given, as the tests will show. So I'm asking you to put the question to him again, now that he may have regained his faculties.'

'Nothing obliges us to do so.'

A brief flash behind his glasses.

'I am aware of that. So I am calling upon your . . . humanity, and your sense of justice – not merely the code.'

'My . . . humanity?'

63

'Yes. Those were the very words used by the person who sent me. You know, I think, who I am talking about.'

The lawyer kept his gaze on him, waiting for an answer.

He knew about Marianne and him . . .

Servaz felt a burst of anger. 'I advise you not to—'

'As you can imagine,' the lawyer broke in, 'she is very upset by what is going on. And "upset" is a weak word . . . desperate, shattered, terrified, would be more appropriate. It's just a little gesture, Commandant. I am not trying to put a spanner in the works. I am not here to make things more difficult for you; I simply want to see him. She is begging you to agree to my request: that is also the word she used. Put yourself in her position. Imagine how you would feel if it were your daughter who was in Hugo's place. Ten minutes. Not a minute more.'

Servaz stared at him. The lawyer held his gaze. The cop tried to read scorn, affliction or embarrassment in his eyes, but there was nothing. Other than his own reflection in the lenses of the man's glasses.

'Ten minutes.'

Saturday

IO

Memories

It was as if the sky were pouring out bile rather than tears, as if someone up there were squeezing a dirty sponge over their heads: the rain fell relentlessly on the roads and the woods from a sky the yellow-grey colour of a decomposing corpse. The air was sultry, sticky and humid. It was Saturday, 12 June, and not yet eight o'clock in the morning. Servaz was already on the road for Marsac, on his own this time.

He'd slept for barely two hours in one of the cells, had rinsed his armpits and his face in the washroom, dried himself with paper towels from the distributor, and now he was having trouble keeping his eyes open.

With one hand on the steering wheel, the other clutching a thermos of lukewarm coffee, he blinked to the same sleepy rhythm as the windscreen wipers. He was also holding a cigarette in the thermos hand, and he inhaled the smoke with a rage. Everything was coming back to him now, and he was acutely aware, stunningly lucid, as if his memory were on fire. The years of his youth. They had the flavour of the countryside he was going through. In autumn, the dead leaves scattered to the side of the road as he drove by, music on full blast; the long, silent, gloomy corridors bathed in a grey light as the rain fell relentlessly all through the endless November weeks; and then, the white illumination of the first snow in December, rock music resonating joyfully through the dormitories from behind people's doors as Christmas approached; the buds in spring and flowers bursting forth everywhere, like a siren's call, a lost paradise, inviting them to leave this place, just as the work rhythm was intensifying and the written exams of April and May were fast approaching. And finally, the stifling heat of June, the pale blue sky baking with heat, the dazzling light and the buzzing of insects . . .

Faces, too.

Dozens of faces . . . youthful, honest, clever, spiritual, fervent, concentrated, friendly, all filled with hopes, dreams and impatience. And then, Marsac itself: its pubs, its art-house cinema showing Bergman, Tarkovsky and Godard; its streets, its squares. He had loved those years. Oh, God, how he had loved them. Even if, at the time, he had lived through them with a sort of unconsciousness punctuated by moments of astonishing happiness, or despair as violent as coming down from an acid trip.

The worst one was called Marianne . . .

Twenty years on, the wound, which he had thought would never heal, had closed, and he could look back on that time with the detached curiosity of an archaeologist. Or at least so he had thought, until yesterday.

The Cherokee bumped over the old cobblestones when he reached the town. It didn't look at all like it had the night before. The smooth faces of the students in their shining rain gear, the rows of bicycles, the shop windows, the pubs, the dark awnings dripping over the outdoor cafés: he was stunned to see it all, as if nothing had changed in twenty years, as if the past had been looking out for him, waiting for him, hoping, all these years, to grab him by the neck and immerse him headfirst in his memories.

I I

Friends and Enemies

Servaz climbed out of the car and looked at a group of lycée students trotting past him, their blank-faced gym teacher in the lead, and he remembered a similar instructor who liked to humiliate and harden his students. He went into the building.

'I am Commandant Servaz,' he said to the secretary sitting in the office beyond the lobby, 'I'm here to see the director.'

She gave his wet clothes a suspicious look.

'Do you have an appointment?'

'I'm in charge of the investigation into the death of Professor Diemar.'

He saw her gaze cloud over behind her glasses. She picked up the telephone and spoke in a low voice. Then she stood up.

'There is no need. I know the way,' he said.

He saw her hesitate for a second, then sit back down, looking as if something were troubling her.

'Madame Diemar . . .' she said. '*Claire* . . . She was such a good person. I hope you're going to punish whoever did this.'

She had not said *find*, she had said *punish*. He was sure that everyone in Marsac knew that Hugo had been arrested. Servaz moved away. Silence reigned in this part of the lycée; courses were held elsewhere, in the concrete cubes out on the lawn and in the ultra-modern amphitheatre which hadn't been there in his day. Out of breath, he reached the top of the spiral stairs inside the circular tower. The door opened almost at once. The headmaster had put on an appropriately grave expression, but his surprise destroyed the effect.

'I know you. You are—'

'Margot's father, yes. I'm also in charge of the investigation.'

The headmaster's face fell.

'What an awful business. Not to mention the reputation it will give our establishment: a professor killed by one of her students!'

Obviously . . .

'I didn't know that the investigation was already over,' said Servaz as he walked into the room. 'Or that the specifics had been made public.'

'Hugo was arrested at Mademoiselle Diemar's place, was he not? Well then: everything points to him.'

Servaz shot him a gaze that had the temperature of liquid nitrogen.

'I understand that you would like the investigation to be wound up as quickly as possible,' he said. 'In the interests of the establishment . . .'

'Precisely.'

'But let us do our work. You must understand that I cannot tell you more.'

The headmaster nodded vigorously, blushing.

'Yes, of course. Of course, naturally . . . it goes without saying . . . of course, of course.'

'Tell me about her,' said Servaz.

The big man looked panicked.

'What . . . what do you want to know?'

'Was she a good teacher?'

'Yes, well, we did not always agree when it came to her . . . *pedagogical* . . . methods, but her students, the students . . . uh . . . they liked her.'

'What sort of relationships did she have with them?'

'What do you mean?'

'Was she close to them? Distant? Strict? Friendly? Maybe she was too close for your liking? You just said that they liked her.'

'A normal rapport.'

'Were there any students or professors who might have had a grudge against her?'

'I don't understand the question.'

'She was a good-looking woman. Colleagues, or even students, might have made a pass at her. Did she ever report anything of the sort?'

'No.'

'She had no inappropriate relationships with her students?'

He grunted in the negative. 'Not to my knowledge.'

70

The difference between his two answers did not go unnoticed; Servaz told himself he would delve further into this question later on.

'May I see her office?'

The headmaster took a key from the drawer and went to the door, swaying heavily.

'Follow me.'

They went down to the floor below, then along a corridor. Servaz remembered where the teachers' offices were. Nothing had changed. The same smell of beeswax, the same white walls, the same creaking floorboards.

'Oh!' said the headmaster suddenly.

Servaz followed his gaze and saw a mass of colour at the foot of one of the doors: bouquets of flowers, little handwritten or printed letters, and a few candles on the waxed floor. They looked at each other and for a moment a certain solemnity came over them. That didn't take long, thought Servaz, and he guessed that the news had already spread through the dormitories. He bent down, picked up one of the little notes and unfolded it. A few words written in purple ink: *'A light has gone out. But it will never stop shining in us. Thank you.'* Nothing else. He was strangely moved. He decided not to read the other ones; he would delegate the task to someone else.

'What do you think? What should I do with this?'

The headmaster's tone was more annoyed than moved.

'Don't touch anything,' answered Servaz.

'But for how long? I don't think the other teachers will be too pleased.'

It's mainly you who isn't pleased, you heartless git, thought Servaz.

'For the duration of the investigation. It's a crime scene,' he replied, with a wink. 'They are alive, she is dead – that should suffice for them.'

The man shook his shoulders and opened the door.

'Here we are.'

He did not seem to want to go in. Servaz went ahead, climbing over the bouquets and candles.

'Thank you.'

'Do you still need me?'

'Not for the time being. I think I can find my way out.'

The headmaster grunted again. 'Don't forget to bring back the key when you've finished.'

Servaz pulled on some gloves and closed the door. A white room. In a huge mess. The desk in the middle was buried beneath a lamp, a telephone, a mountain of papers, elastic-bound folders, colourful Post-it pads, and pots full of pencils and pens. Through the window behind him Servaz saw the two tree-lined playgrounds, one for the regular lycée students and the other for those who were in the prep classes; beyond them were the playing fields and the woods, swept by rain. Three white shelves covered with books and binders ran all along the wall on the right. To the left of the window, in the corner, was a massive and outdated computer. Finally, the entire left-hand wall was covered with dozens of drawings and reproductions of works of art, tacked on the wall at random, occasionally overlapping, creating something like a scaly, many-coloured skin. He recognised most of them.

Slowly he scanned the room. He went around the desk and sat in the armchair.

What was he looking for? First of all, to understand the woman who had lived and worked here. Even an office is a mirror of the occupant's personality. *What did he see?* A woman who liked to surround herself with beauty.

'Beauty will be convulsive or will not be at all.'

The sentence was written in big letters on the wall, in the middle of the pictures. Servaz knew its author: André Breton. What had this sentence meant to Claire? He stood up and went over to the books on the opposite wall. Classical Greek and Latin literature (familiar terrain), contemporary authors, drama, poetry, dictionaries – and a great many books about art history: Vasari, Vitruve, Gombrich, Panofsky, Winckelmann.

Suddenly he recalled his father's books. *So similar to Claire's . . .*

A jagged metal edge lodged in his heart. Not deep enough to kill but enough to hurt . . . How long must a son carry the shadow of a dead father? His gaze settled on the rows of books, but he was looking far beyond. In his youth he thought he had got rid of it; he had believed that this type of memory would fade over time and eventually become perfectly innocuous. Like all the others. But gradually he had come to realise that the shadow was still there. Waiting for him to turn his head. It had eternity on its side, while Servaz did not. It said clearly: *I will never let you go.*

He had come to realise you could rid yourself of the memory of a woman you had loved, or a friend who had betrayed you, but not of a father who had committed suicide and chosen you to find his corpse.

For the thousandth time Servaz saw the bright evening light angling in through the study window, caressing the book bindings, like in a Bergman film, dust floating in the ambient air. He heard the music: Mahler. Saw his father sitting in his armchair, dead, his mouth open, a white froth dripping down his chin. Poison . . . Like Seneca, like Socrates. It was his father who had given him a liking for that music and those authors, back in the days when he was still a sober professor much liked by his students. His wife had died, or more precisely, had been raped and murdered *before his eyes,* and he had survived. Survived for ten more years, a slow descent into hell, ten years of punishing himself for not having been able to do anything because he was tied to a chair and was begging them to stop, the two famished wolves who had shown up at their house one July evening. And then one fine day his father had decided to put an end to it. Once and for all. No slow drunkard's suicide, this time: it would be final, he'd do it the old way, with poison. And the father had arranged it so that the son would find him. Why? Servaz had never found a satisfactory answer to the question. But a few weeks after he had found the body, he quit his studies and took the exams to enter the police.

He shook himself. *Concentrate! What are you looking for here? Concentrate, dammit!* He was beginning to get an idea of Claire Diemar's personality. She was someone who lived alone, but was not a lonely person, someone who cared for beauty, was elitist, original and somewhat bohemian. A frustrated artist, who had fallen back on teaching.

Suddenly he saw a notebook open before him on the desk. He leaned over and read:

'Sometimes the word friend is drained of meaning, but enemy, never.' on the first page.

He turned the pages. They were blank. He raised the notebook to his nose. It was new. Apparently, Claire Diemar had just bought it. Puzzled, he read that sentence again. What had she meant by these words? And for whom were they intended? For herself, or someone else? He wrote it down in his own notebook.

His thoughts focused on the victim's phone.

If Hugo was guilty, he had no reason to make it disappear when everything already pointed to him: his presence in her house, the state he was in, and also his own mobile phone, with the proof of how often he had called her. It was absurd. And if the murderer was not Hugo, and that person had got rid of the victim's mobile, then they were complete idiots. With or without a phone, in a few hours, the telecom companies would have provided the police with a list of incoming and outgoing calls. And so? Weren't most criminals imbeciles, fortunately? Except, if one were to suppose that Hugo had been drugged and left there to serve as a scapegoat, and if one were to suppose that a clever magician was hiding in the shadow, that magician would not have made such a mistake.

There was a third possibility. Hugo was indeed guilty and the telephone had disappeared for reasons that had nothing to do with the crime. Often in an investigation, a stubborn little detail resembled a thorn in the investigator's side, until the day they realised it had absolutely nothing to do with all the rest.

The atmosphere in the room was stifling and he flung open the central window. A wave of moisture caressed his face. He sat down at the computer. The ancient machine moaned and creaked for a moment before the screen appeared. There was no password. Servaz identified the icon for her inbox and clicked on it. This time, a password was required. He looked at his notes, tried a few combinations with her date of birth and the initials, backwards and forwards. Nothing happened. He typed the word *Dolls*. That didn't work either. Claire taught classics, so he spent the next half hour testing the names of Greek and Latin poets and philosophers, the titles of works, the names of gods and mythological characters, and even terms such as 'oracle' or 'Pythia', the name given to the oracle at Delphi. Every time, he got the message 'incorrect login or password'.

He was about to give up when once again he glanced at the wall covered with pictures, and the sentence displayed there. He typed *André Breton* and the mailbox opened at last.

Empty. A white screen. Not a single message.

Servaz clicked on 'Sent' and 'Trash'. Same thing. He flopped back into the armchair.

Someone had emptied Claire Diemar's mailbox.

Servaz knew he was right to think this business was not as simple as it seemed. There was a blind spot. There were too many elements that did not fit. He took out his mobile and dialled the technological tracking service. A voice answered on the second ring.

'Was there a computer at Claire Diemar's?' he asked.

'Yes. A laptop.'

It was now routine to go through every victim's communications and hard drives.

'Have you examined it?'

'Not yet,' said the voice.

'Can you take a look at the e-mail program?'

'Okay, I'll finish what I'm on and look right away.'

He leaned over the old PC and disconnected all the plugs one by one. He did the same with the landline telephone, after lifting a mountain of papers to follow the trajectory of the cable, then he took a plastic evidence bag from his jacket and slipped the open notebook into it.

He went to the office door, opened it, went back to pile the landline telephone and notebook on top of the computer, and lifted the entire pile. The computer was heavy. He had to pause twice.

Out on the steps, he put his load down once again, removed the electronic key from his pocket, unlocked the Cherokee from a distance, and then hurried over, watching as raindrops fell onto the waterproof bag where the notebook was sealed. He would take the computer and telephone the technological tracking service and have the notebook examined by the criminal records office. Once he had put everything on the back seat, he stood up straight and lit a cigarette.

The storm was soaking him but he didn't feel it. He was far too deep in thought. He puffed on his cigarette, and the stimulating caress of the tobacco made its way into his lungs and his brain. *The music* . . . He could hear it again. The *Kindertotenlieder* . . . Was it possible?

He looked all around him – as if Hirtmann might be there – and suddenly something caught his eye.

There was someone there.

A silhouette. Wrapped up in rain gear, his head shadowed by a hood. Servaz could make out the youthful lower half of the face.

A student.

He was watching Servaz from a little hillock a dozen or so metres away, beneath a grove of trees, his hands in the pockets of his plastic cape. A faint smile hovered over his lips. As if they knew one another, thought the cop.

'Hey, you!' he called.

The young man turned away and began walking unhurriedly towards the classrooms. Servaz had to run after him.

'Hey, wait!'

The student turned round. He was slightly taller than Servaz, his blond hair and beard glistening in the outline of the hood. Large, clear, questioning eyes. A wide mouth. Instantly, Servaz wondered if Margot knew him.

'Excuse me? Are you talking to me?'

'Yes. Morning. Do you know where I can find Professor Van Acker? Does he teach on Saturday morning?'

'Room 4, the cube over there . . . but if I were you, I would wait for him to finish. He doesn't like to be disturbed.'

'Oh . . .'

The boy's smile spread wider. 'You're Margot's father, aren't you?'

Servaz was briefly surprised. In his pocket his mobile vibrated but he ignored it.

'And who are you?'

The young man took his hand out of his cape and extended it.

'David. I'm taking the prep classes. Glad to meet you.'

Servaz reasoned that he must be in the same class as Hugo. He squeezed his hand. A frank, strong handshake.

'So, you know Margot?'

'Everybody knows everyone, here. And Margot doesn't exactly go unnoticed.'

The same words Hugo had used.

'But you know that I'm her father.'

The young man trained his golden gaze on Servaz's.

'I was there the day you came with her for the first time.'

'Oh, I see.'

'If you're looking for her, she must be in class.'

'Did you have Claire Diemar as a teacher?'

The young man paused. 'Yes, why?'

Servaz showed him his warrant card. 'I'm in charge of the investigation into her death.'

'Bloody hell, you're a cop?'

He said it without animosity. It was more that he was stunned. Servaz could not help but smile.

'Indeed.'

'We're all devastated. She was a really wonderful teacher, we all liked her. But . . .'

The young man lowered his head and looked at the toes of his trainers. When he looked up again, Servaz could read a familiar glow in his eyes. The one he often saw in the gaze of people who were close to the accused: a mixture of nervousness, incomprehension and disbelief. A refusal to admit the unthinkable.

'I can't believe Hugo did it. It's impossible. It's not him.'

'Do you know him well?'

'He's one of my best friends.'

The young man's eyes had misted over. He was on the verge of tears.

'Were you with him at the pub last night?'

David's gaze was unwavering.

'Yes.'

'And do you remember what time he left?'

David looked at him more cautiously this time. He took the trouble to think before replying.

'No, but I remember he didn't feel well. He felt . . . weird.'

'Is that what he said to you? Weird?'

'Yes. He didn't feel right.'

Servaz held his breath.

'Did he say anything else?'

'No. Just that he really wasn't well and he . . . he wanted to go home. We were all . . . surprised. Because the match . . . the match was about to start.'

The young man had hesitated over his final words, realising that what he said could make things worse for his friend. But Servaz saw it quite differently. Had Hugo used this as a pretext to get away and go to Claire Diemar's – or was he really sick?

'And then?'

'Then what?'

'He left and you didn't see him again?'

Once again, the young man hesitated.

'Yes, that's right.'

'Thank you.'

He saw that David looked concerned, worried about how his words might be interpreted.

'He didn't do it,' he said suddenly. 'I'm sure he didn't. If you knew him as well as I do, you would know that too.'

Servaz nodded.

'He's really brilliant,' the boy insisted, as if it could help Hugo. 'He's enthusiastic, full of life. He's a leader, someone who truly believes in his destiny and who knows how to share his passions. He really has everything. He's a loyal friend. This isn't like him at all!'

As he spoke his voice trembled. He wiped away the raindrops dripping from the end of his nose. Then he turned around and walked away.

For a moment Servaz watched him go.

He knew what David meant. There was always someone like Hugo at Marsac: an individual who was even more talented, more brilliant, more outstanding and more sure of himself than anyone else, someone who caught everyone's eye and had a flock of admirers. In Servaz's day, that person had been Francis Van Acker.

He looked to see who had called him. The tracking service. He called them back.

'Her password is on file,' said the voice. 'Anyone could get at her mailbox. And someone emptied it.'

12

Van Acker

He stopped by the concrete cube and leaned against a tree as he took another cigarette from the pack. The voice reached him through the open windows. It hadn't changed in the last fifteen years. As soon as you heard it you knew that you were dealing with someone who was smart, formidable and arrogant.

'What I have here is nothing more than the excretions of a group of adolescents who are incapable of seeing beyond their tiny little emotional world. Priggish pedantry, sentimentalism, masturbation and acne. For God's sake! You all think you're so brilliant – wake up! There isn't a single original idea in any of this.'

Servaz clicked the lighter and lit a cigarette – the time it would take for Francis Van Acker's declamatory prose to come to an end.

'Next week we are going to study three books side by side: *Madame Bovary*, *Anna Karenina* and *Effi Briest*. Three novels published between 1857 and 1894, which established the form of the novel. Might there, miraculously, be one of you who has already read all three of them? Does that rare bird exist? No? Does anyone at least have an idea what these three books have in common?'

Silence, then a girl's voice said, 'They're all stories about adulterous women.'

Servaz shuddered. Margot's voice.

'Exactly, Mademoiselle Servaz. Well, I see there is at least one person in this class whose reading is not limited to *Spider-Man*. Three stories about adulterous women, another common thing being that they were written by men. Three masterly ways to deal with the same subject. Three absolutely major works. Which goes to show that Hemingway's sentence, according to which one must write what one knows, is hogwash. As are a good number of other sayings by dear old Ernest. Good. I know that some of you have plans for the weekend and that the school year is more or less over, but I want you to have read these three books before the end of next week. Don't forget that your essays are due on Monday.'

A scraping of chairs. Servaz hid round a corner of the building. He did not want to run into Margot now; he would go and see her later. He watched her walk away amongst the other students. He emerged from his hiding place just as Van Acker was coming down the steps, opening his umbrella.

'Hello, Francis.'

Van Acker was briefly startled. The umbrella pivoted.

'Martin . . . I suppose I should have been expecting your visit, given what's happened.'

His blue eyes were still just as piercing. His nose was fleshy, his lips were thin but sensual and his beard was carefully groomed. Francis Van Acker was just as Servaz remembered him. He literally *radiated* charm. Only a few grey hairs were visible in his beard and in the lock of chestnut hair that swept over his brow.

'What are we supposed to say to each other in this kind of situation?' he asked ironically. '"It's been ages"?'

'*Fugit irreparabile tempus,*' replied Servaz.

Van Acker gave him a dazzling smile.

'You always were best in Latin. You cannot imagine how that exasperated me.'

'That's your weakness, Francis. You always wanted to be first in everything.'

Van Acker didn't answer. But before long his provocative smile reappeared.

'You've never come back to see us. Why not?'

'You tell me.'

Van Acker's gaze did not leave him. In spite of the moisture in the air, he was wearing the same kind of dark blue velvet jacket that Servaz had always seen him in. When they were students, it even became the subject of a joke: Francis Van Acker had a wardrobe full of identical blue jackets and white shirts.

'Well, we both know, Edmond Dantès,' said Van Acker.

Servaz felt his throat go dry.

'Like the Count of Morcerf, I stole your Mercedes. Only I didn't marry her.'

For a fraction of a second, Servaz felt a twist of anger in his gut, like an ember flaring. Then the ash of years covered it over again.

'I have heard that Claire died in the most awful way.'

'What are people saying?'

'You know Marsac, everyone knows everything in the end. The gendarmes turned out to be rather talkative. The grapevine did the rest. Tied up and drowned in her bath, that's what people are saying. Is it true?'

'No comment.'

'Dear Lord! Yet she was a good sort. Brilliant. Independent. Stubborn. Passionate. Not everyone agreed with her teaching methods, but I thought they were rather, shall we say, interesting.'

Servaz nodded. They were walking alongside the concrete cubes; the windows were dirty.

'What an atrocious way to die. You'd have to be mad to kill someone that way.'

'Or very angry,' corrected Servaz.

'*Ira furor brevis est.* "Anger is a brief madness".'

Now they were walking past the deserted tennis courts, where the nets were drooping like the ropes of a ring beneath the weight of an invisible boxer.

'How is Margot doing?' asked Servaz.

Van Acker smiled.

'The apple never falls far from the tree. Margot has true potential, she's getting on quite well. But she will be even better when she understands that systematic anti-conformist behaviour is another form of conformity.'

It was Servaz's turn to smile.

'So you're in charge of the investigation,' said Van Acker. 'I could never understand why you joined the police.' He raised his hands to forestall any objection. 'I know it had something to do with your father's death and, if you go back further, with what happened to your mother, but for Christ's sake, you could have done something else. You could have been a writer, Martin. Not one of those hacks, but a real writer. You had the gift. Do you remember that text of Salinger's we used to quote all the time, about writing and brotherhood?'

'*Seymour, an Introduction*,' answered Servaz, trying not to yield to emotion.

He realised that although he had not read the book for years, every sentence was intact, branded in blazing letters upon his memory. In those days, it had been their sacred formula, their mantra, their password.

Van Acker stopped walking.

'You were my big brother,' he said suddenly, his voice surprisingly emotional, 'you were my Seymour – and for me, in a way, that big brother committed suicide the day you joined the police force.'

Servaz felt his anger return. Really? *Then why did you take her from me?* he would have liked to ask. *Of all the women you could have had and whom you did have, you had to go and take her . . . And why did you abandon her?*

They had reached the edge of the pine woods, where the view, when the weather was fine, revealed a panorama for miles around, as far as the Pyrenees, forty kilometres away. But clouds and rain had cloaked the hills in wisps of mist. This was where they used to come twenty years earlier, Van Acker, Servaz himself and . . . Marianne – before Marianne became a barrier between them, before jealousy, anger and hatred tore them apart; and perhaps, who knows, Van Acker still came here, although Servaz doubted it would be in memory of the good old days.

'Tell me about Claire.'

'What do you want to know?'

'Did you know her?'

'Do you mean personally, or as a colleague?'

'Personally.'

'No. Not really. Marsac is a little university town. It's like the court at Elsinore. Everyone knows everyone else, they all spy on each other, stab each other in the back, spread vile gossip . . . Everybody makes sure they have something to say about their neighbours, preferably something snide and juicy. All these academics have raised backstabbing and gossip to an art form. Claire and I used to run into each other at parties, we only made small talk.'

'Were there any rumours about her?'

'Do you really believe that in the name of our erstwhile friendship I'm going to fill you in on all the gossip going around?'

'Oh really, there was that much?'

There was the whoosh of a car on the little road winding past the foot of the hill.

'Rumours, speculation, gossip . . . Is that what they call a house-to-house investigation? Not only was Claire an independent and attractive woman, she also had very set ideas on an entire host of subjects. She had a tendency to be a bit too . . . *militant* at times, at work dinners.'

'And besides that? Were there any rumours about her private life? Do you know anything about that?'

Van Acker bent down to pick up a pine cone. He threw it into the distance, down the slope.

'What do you think? A beautiful woman, single, intelligent . . . Naturally she was surrounded by men. And she hadn't been raised in a convent.'

'Did you sleep with her?'

Van Acker gave him an indecipherable look.

'I say, Maigret, is that the way you work in the police? You throw yourself on the first evidence you can find? Might you have forgotten the difference between exegesis and hermeneutics? May I remind you that Hermes, the messenger, is a deceitful god. The accumulation of proof, the search for hidden meaning, the descent into the unfathomable structure of intentionality: Kafka's parabolas, Celan's poetry, the question of interpretation and subjectivity in Ricoeur – you turned all that to your advantage, once upon a time.'

'Had she received any threats? Did she confide in you? As a colleague or as a friend, did she ever talk to you about a complicated relationship, or a break-up, or was anyone harassing her?'

'She didn't confide in me. We weren't that close.'

'She never mentioned any strange calls or e-mails?'

'No.'

'No suspicious graffiti concerning her, in or around the lycée?'

'Not to my knowledge.'

'And Hugo, what sort of student is he?'

The trace of a smile passed over Van Acker's face.

'Seventeen years old, and already in the preparatory classes – and top of his class. Do you get the picture? And a good-looking kid too, with all the girls, or nearly all of them, at his feet. Hugo is the boy that all the others dream of being.'

He broke off and stared at Servaz.

'You should go and see Marianne.'

There was something like a faint shift in the air – or perhaps it was the effect of the wind in the pine trees.

'I intend to, for the investigation,' said Servaz coldly.

'I'm not just referring to that.'

Servaz listened to the murmur of the rain on the bed of pine needles. Like Van Acker, he was staring at the horizon of hills immersed in gloom.

'You've always been anything but level-headed, Martin. Your acute sense of injustice, your anger, your fucking idealism . . . Go and see her. But don't reopen the old wounds.' Then, after a moment of silence: 'You still hate me, don't you?'

Servaz suddenly wondered if it was true, if he hated this man who had been his best friend. Was it possible to hate someone for years and never forgive him? Oh yes, it was possible. He realised that deep in his pockets his nails were digging into his palms. He turned and walked away heavily, crushing the pine cones beneath the soles of his shoes. Francis Van Acker did not move.

Margot was coming in his direction, straight through the mass of students in the corridors. She looked exhausted. He could tell how tired she was from her hunched shoulders and the way she was carrying her books. And yet she smiled when she saw him.

'So I hear they've given you the investigation?'

He closed Hugo's locker – where he had found nothing but sports things and books – and tried to smile in turn. He gave her a hug there in the middle of the dense crowd, jostled as the young people swirled round them, calling out and bumping into each other. They were kids, just kids, he thought. They came from a planet known as *Youth*, a planet every bit as far away and peculiar as Mars. A planet he did not like to think about on evenings when he was alone and feeling nostalgic, because it reminded him that being an adult is a curse.

'Are you going to question me as a witness, too?'

'Not right away. Unless you have some confession to make, of course.'

He winked and saw her relax. She checked her watch.

'I don't have a lot of time. History class in five minutes. Are you leaving or are you here for the day?'

'I don't know yet. If I'm still here this evening, maybe we could have dinner, what do you think?'

She made a face.

'Okay. But a quick one. I have an essay to finish for Monday and I'm behind.'

'Yes, so I heard. You did well, speaking up this morning.'

'Speaking up when?'

'In Van Acker's class.'

'What are you talking about?'

'I was there. I heard everything. Through the window.'

She looked down at her feet.

'Did he . . . did he say anything about me?'

'Francis? Oh yes. He's full of praise where you're concerned. And coming from him, that's rather rare. He said, I quote, "the apple never falls far from the tree".'

He saw her blush with pleasure and for a moment he thought that she was just like he had been at that age: desperately in need of recognition and approval. And unlike the young man he had been, she hid this insecurity behind a rebellious attitude and a facade of independence.

'I'm off,' she said. 'Happy sleuthing, Sherlock!'

'Wait! Do you know Hugo?'

His daughter turned around, her face inscrutable.

'Yes. Why?'

He waved his hand.

'Just wondered. He spoke about you, too.'

She came back up to him.

'Do you think he's guilty, Dad?'

'What do you think?'

'Hugo is a good person, that's all I know.'

'He said the same thing about you.'

He saw her resist the temptation to ask more.

'And did you have Claire Diemar as a teacher?'

She nodded.

'What was she like?'

'She knew how to make her classes interesting. The students liked her. Couldn't we talk about it some other time? I really am going to be late.'

'But what was she like?'

85

'Joyful, exuberant, enthusiastic, very pretty. A bit crazy, but super cool.'

He nodded and she turned to go, but he saw that her shoulders and her back had slumped forward again.

He walked along the corridor to the entrance hall, making his way through the crowd, glancing at the noticeboards covered with announcements, rules, offers, opportunities for swaps – that hadn't changed, either, since his day – and went back out. His mobile vibrated in his pocket. He looked at the number: Samira.

'Yes?' he replied.

'We may be on to something.'

'What?'

'You did tell us not to focus on the kid, right?'

He felt his pulse beat faster.

'Out with it.'

'Pujol remembered a case he worked on a few years ago. Assault and rape of a young woman in her own home. He tracked down the man who did it. And he dug up the files from the archives. This guy had several convictions for sexual assault. In Tarbes, Montauban and Albi. Elvis Konstandin Elmaz is his name. He has a fairly unsavoury record: at the age of twenty-five he'd already been convicted a dozen times or more for drug trafficking, serious assault, and theft . . . He's twenty-seven now. A predator. His method is enough to send shivers down your spine: the guy was in the habit of going onto dating sites to find his victims.' Servaz thought of Claire's empty mailbox. 'In 2007 he met one of his victims in a public place in Albi, took her back to her own house at knifepoint, tied her to the radiator and gagged her, then took her bank card once he'd got the code off her. Then he raped her and threatened her with reprisals if she filed a complaint. Another time, he assaulted a woman in a park in Tarbes, after nightfall, then he tied her up and put her in the boot of his car, until he changed his mind and abandoned her in a bush. It's just a miracle he hasn't killed anyone yet—' She broke off. 'Well, if we exclude . . . In short, he got out of prison this year.'

'Mmm.'

'There is a snag, though . . .'

Through the receiver he heard a spoon clinking against a cup.

'It would seem that our resident Elvis has a solid alibi for last night. He got in a fight in a bar.'

'That's a solid alibi?'

'No, he was also taken to Rangueil by ambulance. He was admitted to the casualty ward at around ten p.m. He's still in hospital as we speak.'

Ten o'clock . . . By then, Claire was already dead and Hugo was sitting by the side of the pool. Would Elvis Elmaz have had time to go back to Toulouse and start a fight to ensure an alibi? If that were the case, when would he have found the time and the opportunity to drug Hugo?

'Is his name really Elvis?'

He heard her laugh on the other end of the line.

'It is indeed. I looked into it: apparently it's a fairly common name in Albania. In any case, with this bastard, we're a lot closer to "Jailhouse Rock" than to "Don't Be Cruel".'

'Uh-huh,' said Servaz, who wasn't sure he grasped what she meant.

'So what do we do, boss? Shall I interview him?'

'Don't move, I'm on my way. Just make sure the hospital doesn't let him vanish into thin air in the meantime.'

'No danger of that: I'll stick to the bastard like a leech.'

Interlude 1

Hope

Hope is a drug.

Hope is psychotropic.

Hope is a far more powerful stimulant than caffeine, khat, maté, cocaine, speedball or amphetamines.

Hope was accelerating her heartbeat and her breathing, raising her blood pressure, dilating her pupils. Hope was amplifying her auditory and olfactory perception. Hope was contracting her viscera. Her brain was doped up on hope, recording everything with a sharpness she had never known before.

A bedroom.

It wasn't hers. For a tiny moment she thought she had woken up at home, that the endless months spent down in the cellar were only a nightmare. That morning had come, placing her back in her life before, her marvellous, ordinary life – but the bedroom wasn't hers.

This was the first time she had ever seen it. An unfamiliar room.

Morning. She turned her head slightly and saw the ever-brighter stream of light coming through the netting between the curtains. The red figures on the alarm clock on the night table said 6.30. There was a refrigerator on the far side of the room. She raised her head and in the mirror she could see her feet, her legs, and between them, her own face in the semi-darkness, looking like an anxious little animal's, terrified.

There was someone next to her, asleep.

Hope returned. He had fallen asleep and had forgotten to take her back down to the cellar before the drug he'd administered stopped working! She could not believe her eyes. A mistake, a single mistake at last after all these months of captivity. This was her chance! She felt as if her heart were coming loose.

Hope – delirious hope – spread through her brain. She turned her head cautiously towards him, aware of the deafening pounding of her blood in her ears.

He was sleeping with his fists closed tight. With absolute neutrality she looked at his long naked body next to her. She felt neither hatred nor fascination. Even his close-cropped blond hair, his dark little beard and his arms black with tattoos like a scaly second skin no longer drew her attention. She saw a few filaments of dried sperm in the hairs on his thighs and shuddered. But it was nothing like the nausea and revulsion that had gripped her in the beginning. She was well beyond that stage.

Hope increased her strength. Suddenly she was burning with the hope that she might be able to leave this hell behind and be free. So many contradictory emotions . . . This was the first time since the beginning of her captivity that she had seen daylight. Even through a window and curtains. And the first time that she had woken up in a bed and not on the hard dirt floor in her cellar, in darkness. The first bedroom in months, perhaps years . . .

It can't be possible. Something has happened.

But she mustn't get distracted. The light in the room was getting progressively brighter. He would wake up. Such an opportunity would never come again. She instantly felt afraid.

There was one solution. To kill him. Now, right away. To split his skull with the bedside lamp. But she knew that if she got it wrong, he would have the advantage, he was much too strong for her. There were two other options: find a weapon – a knife, a screwdriver, a sharp object.

Or run away . . .

She preferred this second solution. She was so weak, she had so little strength left to confront him. But where would she go? What would she find outside? The only time he had moved her from one place to another, she had heard birds singing, and a cock crowing, and the smells were those of the countryside. An isolated house . . .

With her heart in her throat, convinced he was going to wake up any second, she pushed back the sheet, slipped out of the bed, and took a step towards the window.

Her heart stopped beating.

It wasn't possible . . .

She could see a sunny clearing and the woods beyond. Like in a fairytale from her childhood, the house was all alone in the middle of a forest. She could see tall grass, poppies, yellow butterflies fluttering everywhere. Even through the window she could hear the twittering of birds welcoming the new day. All these months of hell below ground when the simplest, most beautiful life was just there, so near.

She looked at the bedroom door beckoning irresistibly. Freedom was just beyond that door. She glanced at the bed. He was still sleeping. She took a step, and then another one, then a third, and she went around the bed and her torturer. The doorknob turned soundlessly. She couldn't believe it. The door opened. A corridor. Narrow. Silent. Several doors to the right and to the left, but she went straight ahead, and came out in the big dining room. She instantly recognised the big wooden table, dark as a lake, and the dresser, the stereo, the big fireplace, the chandeliers, and before her eyes there were the platters of food, and the flickering candles, and in her ears there was the music, in her nostrils the smell of the food. The nausea returned. *Never again . . .* The shutters were closed, but the sun outside carved long slices of light through the slits.

The vestibule, the front door – just there, to her right, in the shadow. She took two more steps. She could tell that the drug he had given her had not quite stopped working. It was as if she were moving through water, as if the dense air were resisting her. Her gestures were heavy and clumsy. Then she stopped. She couldn't go out like this. Naked. She looked behind her and her belly contracted. *Anything rather than go back into that room.* There was a throw on the sofa. She grabbed it and draped it around her shoulders. Then she went to the front door. Like the rest of the house, it was old, made of rough wood. She lifted the latch and slid back the bolt.

The sunlight blinded her, the birdsong burst into her areas like a clanging of cymbals, flies assailed her with their buzzing, the smell of grass and woodland hurt her nostrils, the heat caressed her skin. For a fraction of a second her head was spinning, she blinked, dazzled, breathless. She felt dizzy with the onslaught of the heat, the light, the life. But fear returned at once. She had very little time.

There was an outbuilding on the right, a sort of former barn that was open and half collapsed, with exposed beams. Inside was a pile of old household devices, tools, a woodpile, and a car . . .

She hurried towards the car, barefoot over the ground already warm with the sun. The door on the driver's side opened with a creak and for a moment she was afraid the noise would wake him. Inside it smelled of dust, leather and motor oil. She groped about, her hand trembling, but there was no key. She searched in the glove box, beneath the seat, everywhere. In vain. She went back out. *Run away*. Don't wait . . . She looked around her. A track suitable for motor vehicles: no, not that way. Then she saw the beginning of a vague footpath in the dappled light of the forest. Yes. She ran in that direction, and realised how weak she was and how poorly her legs responded. But hope was filling her with a new energy.

The undergrowth was cooler but just as noisy. She ran along the path, and several times she scraped the soles of her feet on sharp pebbles or thorns, but she didn't care. She crossed a little wooden bridge above a stream that flowed through the shade with a clear ripple. The loosely fitted planks vibrated as she ran over them.

Then she began to suspect that something was wrong.

On the ground, in the middle of the path, a bit further along . . .

A dark object. She slowed her pace and went closer. An old cassette player playing music. She recognised it immediately, and started with horror. She had heard it hundreds of times. She sobbed. It was unfair. Infinitely cruel. Anything, but not this . . .

She froze, her legs shaking. She couldn't go on that way, nor could she go back the way she had come. On her right, there was a gully, wide and deep, with a stream flowing by at the bottom.

She rushed to her left, climbed over an embankment and hurried along a faint path through the ferns.

She followed the path, running breathlessly, glancing over her shoulder, but she saw no one. The undergrowth was still bursting with birdsong, and the sinister music was audible behind her, carried by the echo, like an omnipresent threat.

She thought she had left that threat behind her when suddenly she came right up against a sign nailed to a tree trunk, where the path she was following split in two, creating a fork among the ferns. Painted on the sign was a double arrow indicating the two options available to her. Above the arrows were two words: FREEDOM on one side, DEATH on the other.

She sobbed again. Bent down to vomit in the ferns by the edge of the path.

She stood up straight and wiped her mouth with a corner of the throw, which, she now realised, stank of stale air and dust and death and madness. She felt like crying, like collapsing to the ground and not moving any more, but she had to do something.

She knew it must be a trap. One of his perverse games. Death or freedom . . . If she chose 'freedom', what would happen? What sort of freedom was he offering her? Certainly not that of returning to her former life. Would he deliver her from her prison by killing her? And what if she chose 'death'? Was it a metaphor? For what? The death of her suffering, the end of her ordeal? She rushed off in that direction: the way that sick man's mind worked, the offer that seemed more attractive on the surface would certainly be the worst one.

She ran another hundred metres before she saw it: a long dark shape hanging above the path.

She slowed down again, running less quickly, then walking – and finally she stopped altogether when she realised what it was. A cat was hanging from a branch, and the string used to strangle him was so tight that it was only a matter of time before he was decapitated. A sliver of pink tongue emerged from his white mouth, and his body was as stiff as a plank.

She had nothing left in her stomach, but she felt the urge to vomit regardless, the taste of bile in her mouth. At the same time, an icy fear went all down her spine.

She moaned. She felt hope fading like the guttering of a dying candle. Deep down she knew that these woods and that cellar were the last places she would ever see. There was no way out. No more today than on any other day. But she still wanted to believe, just that tiny little bit.

Was no one else out walking in this wretched forest? She suddenly wondered where she was: was she in France, or somewhere else? She knew there were countries where you could walk for hours or even days without meeting a single soul.

She hesitated, trying to decide which way to go. Certainly not the way that madman had chosen for her, in any case.

She rushed into the thicket and the trees, far from any trace of a path, tripping over roots and the uneven ground, which caused her bare feet to bleed. Soon she reached another stream, full of the trunks of trees felled by a recent storm. She had great difficulty making her way between them; branches as sharp as daggers tore the flesh on her calves and her toes twisted on sharp stones and pieces of dead wood.

There was a new path on the other side. Breathless, she decided to take it. She still hoped she might run into someone, and trying to make her way through the undergrowth was too exhausting.

I don't want to die.

She ran, stumbled, continued on her way.

She was running to save her skin, her lungs were on fire and her heart about to burst, her legs grew heavier and heavier. The woods around her were getting thicker and thicker, and the air was getting hotter. The scents of the forest mingled with the smell of her own acrid sweat, which stung her eyes. She could hear the gurgling of a nearby stream. No other sound. Silence behind her.

I don't want to die . . .

This thought filled all the free space in her mind. Abject, inhuman fear.

I don't want . . . I don't want . . . I don't want . . .

To die . . .

She could feel bitter tears streaming down her cheeks. She would have killed her father and mother to get out of this nightmare.

And suddenly her heart leapt. *There was someone, there . . .*

She screamed.

'Hey! Wait! Wait! Help! Help me!'

The person didn't move, but through the blur of her tears she could see them clearly. A woman. Wearing a buttoned sundress. Oddly, she was completely bald. She used every ounce of strength to reach her, but the woman still did not move. As she got closer, her blood went thick as syrup, as she began to understand.

It wasn't a woman.

A plastic dummy. Leaning against a tree trunk. Frozen in an artificial pose, like in a shop window. And she recognised the dress the dummy was wearing: it was her own, the one she had been wearing the night when . . . except now it was splattered with red paint.

She felt as if all her strength were abandoning her, as if someone were sucking it out of her body. She was sure he had filled this cursed forest with a host of other traps, all equally sinister. She was the rat in the labyrinth, his toy – and he was there, right nearby . . . She felt her legs give way beneath her as she lost consciousness.

13

Elvis

Servaz parked on the lower level of the car park and headed towards the lifts. The University Hospital Centre at Rangueil rose like a fortress on top of a hill to the south of Toulouse. To reach it from the car park, which was halfway up, you had to take a lift then walk over a long footbridge hanging several metres above the trees, with an impressive view over the university buildings further down and the outskirts of the city. As was often the case, the external aesthetics had been given priority over the internal infrastructure. The hospital might employ 2,800 doctors and 10,000 staff members, and treat over 180,000 patients a year, the population of a medium-size city, but Servaz had already noticed that many services were cruelly lacking, and not only medical ones.

He went quickly from the sole cafeteria where staff, visitors and patients in hospital gowns mingled, and down the long corridor to the inner lifts. Contemporary artwork from charitable donations tried in vain to brighten the walls: art has its limits. Servaz noticed the door to the chapel, with the chaplain's visiting hours posted on it. He wondered how God could find his place in this world where human beings were reduced to plumbing, taken apart and put back together like an engine, and sometimes sent to the scrap heap, but not before a few spare parts had been salvaged in order to repair other engines.

Samira was waiting for him in front of the lifts. He was tempted to light a cigarette, but his gaze landed on the no smoking sign on the wall.

'*Crash*,' he said, in the lift.

'Huh?' asked Samira; her gun, strapped to her waist, was attracting considerable attention.

'A novel by J.G. Ballard. The marriage of surgery, mechanics, mass consumerism and desire.'

94

She stared at him blankly and he shrugged. The doors opened on the next floor and they heard a voice shouting, 'Bloody wankers, you got no right to keep me here against my will! Call that fucking doctor, I want to see him right away!'

'Is that our Elvis?' asked Servaz.

'Could well be.'

They turned right, then left. A nurse headed them off. Samira waved her warrant card.

'We're here for Elvis Konstandin Elmaz.'

The woman's face hardened. She pointed to a frosted glass door at the end of the corridor, just past a bed on wheels where an old man waited with a tube in his nose.

'He needs to rest,' she said sternly.

'So it seems,' said Samira ironically.

The woman gave them a look full of scorn then walked away.

'Fuckin' hell! The pigs, all we needed!' exclaimed Elvis when they entered the room.

The air was warm and damp despite a fan struggling in the corner. Elvis Konstandin Elmaz was sitting bare-chested at the head of the bed. He was watching television with the sound off.

'*One for the money, two for the show,*' hummed Samira, swaying her hips and taking a few dance steps. 'Hiya, Elvis.'

Elvis took his time to inspect the female cop, and he frowned at what he saw: that day, Samira was wearing half a dozen necklaces over a T-shirt which proclaimed LEFT 4 DEAD.

'Who the fuck's this, then?' he said to Servaz. 'You call this a cop these days? Fuckin' hell, what's the world coming to!'

'Elvis Elmaz?'

'No, Al Pacino. What d'you want? You're not here about my complaint.'

'No, we're not.'

'Course not. Doesn't take long to see you're from the KFC.'

Yobs had adopted the name of the famous fast-food chain as a nickname for the parent company – in other words the Criminal Division. Elvis Konstandin Elmaz was small and very sturdy, with a skull that was perfectly smooth, a strip of beard over his thick jaw, and a tiny cubic zirconia stud in his ear. Unless it was actually a diamond. A bandage was wrapped several times around his muscular torso, from his lower belly to his diaphragm. Another one circled his right biceps.

'What happened to you?' asked Servaz.

'As if you didn't know. I got stabbed, mate. Three times in my belly and once in my arm. It's a miracle those fuckers didn't kill me. "No vital organs were touched, it's a miracle, Mr Elmaz," so that pompous doctor said. He doesn't want to let me out before tomorrow; he says if I move around too much it could open again. I'm no doctor, he's the one who knows. But I've got pins and needles in my legs and the food here is worse than in the slammer.'

'*Those* fuckers?' asked Samira.

'There were three of them. Serbs. In case you didn't know, those fucking Serbs and us Albanians, not a good mix. Serbs are all scum.'

Samira nodded. She had heard the same refrain from the other side. And she didn't say it, but she also had a little bit of Bosnian blood in her veins, and probably Italian blood as well: her family had been around . . .

'What happened?'

'We started arguing inside the caff, and then we went out on the pavement. I'd had a few, I have to admit.'

He looked at each of them in turn.

'Except that that midget had two mates and I didn't know. Before I could do a thing they laid into me and then cleared off. And I was lying on the pavement pissing blood. I really thought that this time I was done for. I suppose there must be a god for bad guys, too. Babe, you wouldn't have a cigarette, would you? I'd kill my own mother for a fag.'

Samira resisted the temptation to lean over and prod his ribs through the bandage with her index finger.

'Can't you see the sign?' she said nastily. 'No smoking. What was the reason for the altercation?'

'Altercation . . . Fuck, listen to the way you talk, love! I told you: I'm Albanian, they were Serbian.'

'That's it?'

They saw him hesitate.

'No.'

'What else?'

'A woman, for fuck's sake. This bird had been sniffing around me.'

'Ah, she was with them?'

'Yup.'

'Pretty?'

Elvis Konstandin Elmaz's face lit up like a Christmas tree.

'Better than that! A real stunner. And classy, too. You had to wonder what she was doing with those three losers. I couldn't help looking at her, shit. Eventually she noticed, and she came over for a chat. Maybe she wanted to annoy them, who knows? Maybe she was afraid of them, or she'd had an altercation, as you say . . . That's when things got out of control.'

'So you ended up in casualty last night, you were operated on during the night and you've been stuck here ever since?'

A little gleam lit up his brown eyes.

'What's the big deal? You don't give a damn about my story, do you? It's what happened afterwards that you're interested in. Something's happened.'

'Monsieur Elmaz, you got out of prison four months ago, is that correct?'

'Yes.'

'You have been convicted of theft, along with violence, abduction, sexual assault and rape . . .'

'So what's all this about? I served my time.'

'Every time, it was young, pretty, brown-haired women you went after.'

Elvis's gaze clouded over.

'What are you getting at? That was a long time ago.' His eyes were darting back and forth. 'What happened last night? Some woman got attacked, is that it?'

Servaz saw a newspaper lying on the rolling table next to the bed. It took him half a second to grasp what he was seeing. And less time than that for the blood to drain from his face:

YOUNG PROFESSOR MURDERED IN MARSAC

Policeman who solved St-Martin case placed in charge of investigation

Shit! He paid no further attention to Samira's questions or Elmaz's answers as he grabbed the paper. He turned the pages, looking for the article.

There were only a few lines, on page 3. It explained that '*Commandant Servaz, from the Toulouse Criminal Affairs Division, the officer who led the investigation into the Saint-Martin murders during the winter of 2008, the most significant crime in recent years in the Midi-Pyrenees region, has been entrusted with the investigation into the murder of a Marsac professor from an elite lycée in the region.*' A bit further on, the author of the article specified that the young woman had been found at home, '*tied up and drowned in her bath*'. At least the press department had not mentioned the detail of the torch – no doubt to be able to trip up all the crazies who would be calling in the hours to come. But they had handed the journalists his name on a platter. Brilliant. Servaz felt his anger welling up. He would like to get hold of the moron who had passed on the information. An involuntary leak – or had it been orchestrated? Could it have been Castaing himself?

'What time did the argument take place?' Samira was asking.

'Half past nine, ten o'clock . . .'

'Were there any witnesses?'

A hoarse guffaw, followed by a cough.

'Dozens!'

'And before that, what were you doing?'

'Are you deaf? I was drinking, and eyeing up that girl. Dozens of people saw me, I tell you. I know I made mistakes in the past. But shit, those girls I assaulted, what were they doing out at night, huh? In Albania, women don't go out at night. They're respectable.'

Samira Cheung chose a spot at random and jabbed her index finger into the Albanian's side. Hard. Servaz saw Elvis wince with pain. He was going to intervene when Samira removed her finger.

'Your alibi had better be solid,' she said in an ugly, cold voice. 'You really have a problem, Elvis. I don't suppose you're impotent, are you? Or maybe you're a repressed fag . . . Yes, that's it. Of course that's it. Did you enjoy taking showers in the nick?'

Servaz watched as the man's face was transformed, his gaze turning as black as a pool of oil, no light in his eyes. In spite of the heat in the room, it was as if icy water were trickling down his spine. His pulse began beating faster. He swallowed. He'd seen that sort of look before, a long time ago. *He had been ten years old . . .* The little boy in him could not forget. Once again he thought about the men who had shown up in the garden of his family home one July evening. Two men like this one, wolves, lost creatures with empty gazes. He remembered his mother, crying and begging, and his father, tied to a chair. And little Martin, locked in the cupboard beneath the stairs, hearing everything, guessing everything – and how many times had he come across people like them since he had joined the police? Suddenly he was desperately in need of air, he had to get out of that room, that hospital. He began running towards the toilets before the nausea had time to overwhelm him.

'It's not him.'

Servaz nodded. They were heading back up the corridor towards the lobby. He had a terrible desire to smoke, but there were no smoking signs everywhere, constantly calling him to order.

'I know,' he said. 'His alibi is solid and, in any case, I don't see how he could have emptied Claire Diemar's mailbox at the lycée, or why he would have followed Hugo and drugged him.'

'That guy should not be out of jail,' said Samira as they walked past the cafeteria.

'There are no laws about putting people in prison just because they're dangerous,' he said.

'He'll do it again, sooner or later.'

'He served his sentence.'

Samira shook her head as they crossed the lobby.

'The only valid therapy for his sort is chopping off their balls,' she decreed.

Servaz looked at his assistant. Apparently she wasn't joking. With relief he saw the glass doors coming closer and dug his hand in his pocket, but there was one last no smoking sign on the other side – he felt as if he were an adolescent again, on the running track, his lungs on fire, sure he would never manage to run the last twenty metres.

The doors opened at last. Heat and damp engulfed them. He stiffened. His lungs were clamouring for nicotine, demanding their poison, but there was something else . . . What was it? Ever since they had gone past the first no smoking sign earlier that afternoon, his unconscious had been at work – but he couldn't put his finger on what it was seeking.

'If it's not Elmaz, then we're back to square one,' said Samira.

'Meaning?'

'Hugo . . .'

Servaz managed to check his watch as he took out his cigarette.

99

'Let's go back to the office. You put pressure on the tracking service. I want results by the end of the day. If it is Hugo, can you tell me why he would have emptied out Clare's computer but not cleared his own mobile?'

She raised her hands in a gesture of ignorance. An ambulance arrived, siren wailing, and stopped in front of the barrier, waiting for it to lift.

Suddenly it dawned on him. He knew why he had been so obsessed by the no smoking signs.

As he walked across the long footbridge above the trees, he took out his mobile, found Margot's phone number and hit dial. Horrible music replied, and he made a face. He was pleased to know that Margot switched her mobile off during class, but it was bad timing. With one finger he typed a text message:

Does Hugo smoke? Call me back. Urgent.

He had just finished when his telephone began to vibrate.

'Margot?' he said, as he reached the lifts.

'No, this is Nadia,' said a woman's voice.

Nadia Berrada was in charge of the tracking service. He pressed the button to call the lift.

'The computers have spoken,' she said.

His hand was suspended in mid-air.

'And?'

'The mailboxes had indeed been emptied, but we were able to recover the messages, both sent and received. The last one is from the day she died. It's the usual stuff: e-mails to colleagues, personal messages, announcements for staff meetings and seminars, and junk mail.'

'Were there any messages sent or received from Hugo Bokhanowsky?'

'No. Not a one. However, there was one correspondent who showed up on a regular basis. "Thomas999". And his messages seem . . . how shall I put it? *Intimate.*'

'Intimate in what way?'

'Intimate enough for him to write—' She broke off before reading: '"Life in the future will be so much more exciting because we are in love", "Amazing. Incredible. Miss you absolutely", "I am the lock and you are the key, I am yours forever, your darling, for now and all eternity" . . .'

'Who wrote that, him or her?'

'Both of them. Well, she wrote seventy-five per cent of them . . . He seemed slightly less expressive, but completely hooked all the same. Shit, that woman was really passionate!'

From the tone of her voice, he supposed that the e-mails had made Nadia wistful. He remembered what he and Marianne had been like . . . In those days there were neither e-mails nor text messages, but they had exchanged hundreds of letters in a similar vein. Glorious, lyrical, naïve, ardent, funny letters. Even though they saw each other almost every day. They had known that intensity, that fire. He was on to something – he could tell. *That woman was really passionate* . . . Nadia had got it spot-on. He looked at the treetops swaying in the rain beneath the footbridge.

'Ask Vincent to get a warrant,' he said. 'We need the identity of this Thomas999 as quickly as possible.'

'It's already done. We're waiting for the answer.'

'Perfect. Let me know as soon as you have it. And Nadia, please, could you take a quick look at the list of exhibits?'

'What do you want to know?'

'Whether there was a pack of cigarettes among the items found in the kid's pockets.'

He waited. The doors to the lift opened, but he did not go in, for fear that the metal walls would prevent the signal from getting through. Nadia came back on the line after four minutes.

'No packet, no cigarette, no joints,' she said. 'Nothing of the kind. Does that help?'

'It may do. Thank you.'

While picturing Nadia rummaging through the exhibits, he'd had a thought concerning the notebook he had found on Claire's desk and the sentence written there:

Sometimes the word friend is drained of meaning, but enemy, never.

He felt a tingling at the base of his spine. Claire Diemar had written this in a brand-new notebook not long before she died, and she had left it open on her desk. Was she aware of any imminent threat? Had she made an enemy? Could this sentence have anything at all to do with the investigation? His thoughts were getting clearer. He took out his phone again.

'Are you at your desk?' he asked when Espérandieu picked up.

'Yes, why?' said his assistant.

'Could you run a sentence through Google?'

'Through Google?'

'That's what I said.'

'Like some sort of quote?'

'Uh-huh.'

'Hang on . . . Okay, go ahead, I'm listening.'

Servaz repeated the sentence.

'What is it? For some quiz show?' joked his assistant. 'Wait . . . aren't you the one who studied literature?'

'Out with it.'

'Victor Hugo.'

'What?'

'It's a quotation. From Victor Hugo. Would you care to explain?'

'Later.'

He hung up. Victor *Hugo*. Could it be just a coincidence? Claire Diemar had not written anything else in the notebook and she had left it in plain sight. She was referring to an *enemy* . . . Hugo? Servaz was aware that they were dealing with Marsac, a university town, a place, as Francis had pointed out, where people had a sense of discretion as well as of malicious gossip, where daggers were drawn but with elegance and refinement – and where any direct accusation would be seen as an unforgivable breach of taste. He must not forget that he was dealing with scholars, with people who liked puzzles, allusions, hidden meaning; people who liked to show how subtle they could be, even in dramatic circumstances. The sentence had not been written in the notebook by chance.

Could it be that Claire, in an allusive, indirect way, had indicated the name of her enemy – even that of her future killer?

14

Hirtmann

Back at the Criminal Division, Servaz went straight to Espérandieu's office.

'How is the kid doing?'

His assistant removed his headphones, where the lead vocalist from Queens of the Stone Age was singing 'Make It Wit Chu', and shrugged.

'He's calm. He asked me if I had something to read. I gave him one of my comics. He didn't want it. I should remind you that his detention ends in six hours.'

'I know. Call the prosecutor. Ask for an extension.'

'On what grounds?'

It was Servaz's turn to shrug his shoulders.

'I don't know. Pull something out of your bag of tricks.'

Once he was in his office, he hunted in his drawers for a moment before he found what he was looking for. A telephone number. In Paris. He looked at it, thoughtfully. He had not called this number in a long time. He had hoped he would never have to; he had hoped the whole business was behind him.

Servaz looked at the time, and dialled. When a man's weary voice answered, he introduced himself.

'It's been a long time,' said the voice on the other end of the line ironically. 'To what do I owe the honour, Commandant?'

He explained what had happened the night before and finished with the discovery of the Mahler CD. He was expecting the man to say, 'You called me for *that*?' but he did no such thing.

'Why didn't you call me at once?' he asked instead.

'For a CD found at a crime scene? It probably has nothing to do with it.'

'A crime scene where, as if by chance, the son of one of your former acquaintances has been found, where the Toulouse crime squad has, quite logically, been put on the case, and the victim happens to be a young woman in her thirties who has the same profile as his other victims? And where, to top it all off, the music that Julian was playing the night he killed his wife was playing? You must be joking!'

Servaz noticed the use of 'Julian'. As if after all this hunting for the man, his pursuers had ended up fraternising with him. He held his breath. The cop was right. He had had exactly the same hunch when he first saw the CD, and then he'd moved on to something else. But seen from this angle, the elements fitted together in a disturbing way. He told himself that to grasp all this so quickly the guy at the other end of the line must really know his stuff.

'It's always the same old story,' sighed the voice on the line. 'People get in touch when they have the time, when they've put aside their ego, or when all the other trails have gone cold.'

'And do you have anything new at your end?'

'You'd like me to say that I do, wouldn't you? I'm sorry to disappoint you, Commandant, but we have so much information that we're drowning in it. As if it were pouring down on us. Most of it is so far-fetched that we don't even check it any more, other leads have to be checked all the same, and it all takes a great deal of time. He's been spotted all over the place: Paris, Hong Kong, Timbuktu . . . One witness was certain he was a broker at the casino in Mar del Plata where he plays every evening, another saw him at the airport in Barcelona, or in Düsseldorf, there's a woman who suspects her lover is Hirtmann . . .'

Servaz could hear the discouragement and extreme weariness in the speaker's voice. Then all of a sudden his voice changed, as if he had just thought of something.

'It's Toulouse, right?'

'Yes, why?'

The man didn't answer. Instead, Servaz heard him speaking to someone else. His hand over the receiver made his words inaudible, but a few seconds later he came back on the line.

'Something happened quite recently,' he said, and Servaz noticed the change of tone. 'We put his portrait online. We Photoshopped his image and made a dozen different versions: beards, moustaches, long hair, short hair, dark, fair, a different nose and so on. You get the picture. In short, we had hundreds of replies. We looked at every single one: a long, painstaking job . . .'

The weariness in his voice once again.

'Among the sightings there was one more interesting than the others: a guy who runs a service station on a motorway, who swears that Hirtmann stopped there for petrol and to buy the papers. According to this fellow, he was on a motorbike, had dyed his hair, let his beard grow, and was wearing sunglasses, but the guy was categorical: he looked just like one of the portraits online, the height and shape matched, and the biker spoke with a slight accent that could have been Swiss, according to the witness. For once, we lucked out: we were able to check the shop's video surveillance tapes. And the manager was right: it could be him – I repeat, *it could be* . . .'

'And where is this service station? When was it?'

'Two weeks ago. You'll like this, Commandant: it's called Bois de Dourre, on the A20, north of Montauban.'

'Was the motorcycle filmed? Do you have the number plate?'

'Whether by chance or deliberately, he parked it out of sight of the cameras. But he showed up at a tollbooth further south, in the Paris–Toulouse direction. The picture isn't very sharp, but we have the beginning of the registration. We're working on it . . . Do you see now why your story is so important? If it really was Hirtmann on that bike, there's a very good chance he's in your sector as we speak.'

Dumbfounded, Servaz stared at the results of his search. He had typed the words 'Julian Hirtmann' into Google and obtained no less than 1,130,000 hits.

He flung himself back in his chair and thought.

He spent a long time looking for any report containing the slightest bit of information concerning Hirtmann after his escape; he had been through newspapers, dispatches and newsletters, had made dozens of phone calls, had harassed the unit in charge of tracking him, but the months had gone by, then the seasons – spring, summer, autumn, winter, spring again . . . and he had given up. Time to move on. It was no longer his business. Enough. *The End. Finito.* He had tried to banish him from his thoughts.

He scanned the page of hits on the screen. He knew that freedom of expression was of key concern to Internet users, and it was up to each individual to filter, sort and use their discrimination, but he was gobsmacked by what he discovered on the web. Julian Hirtmann had thousands of fans, and there were dozens of sites that glorified him. Some articles were relatively neutral: photographs of Hirtmann during his trial and others where he was shown before the trial in the company of his ravishing spouse – the one he had electrocuted in his basement along with her lover. Hirtmann was compared to other European serial killers like José Antonio Rodriguez Vega in Spain, who raped and killed no fewer than sixteen women aged from sixty-one to ninety-three between August 1987 and April 1988, or Joachim Kroll, the 'cannibal of the Ruhr'. In the photographs Hirtmann had a firm, clearly outlined face, somewhat stern, regular features and an intense gaze; far from the pale, tired man Servaz had met at the Institute.

Servaz could associate that face with a voice – deep, pleasant, steady. The voice of an actor, or an orator. The voice of a man who was used to being in charge and expressing himself in court.

He could also associate it with the more or less blurry faces of about forty women who had disappeared over the last twenty-five years. Women of whom there was not the slightest trace but whose names had been written, with a quantity of other details, in the former prosecutor's notebooks. Somewhere, there was a group of victims' parents who were clamouring for Hirtmann to be forced to talk. How? With some truth serum? Hypnosis? Torture? Every solution had been envisaged by the usual zealots on the web. Including sending him to Guantánamo or burying him in the desert, his head covered in honey, next to a colony of red ants.

Servaz knew that Hirtmann would never talk. Locked up or at liberty, he had more power over those families than any evil god would ever possess. He would always be their tormentor. Their nightmare. And that was the role he wanted. He was characterised by a total absence of remorse or guilt – like all major psychopathic perverts. He might crack if he was subjected to waterboarding or to electric shock but it was unlikely that he would crack during detention or a psychiatric interview – if they were even able to get their hands on him, which Servaz doubted.

ARE YOU READY?

Servaz jumped.

The words had just appeared on the screen.

For a moment he thought that Hirtmann had somehow managed to get into his computer.

Then he understood that without realising it he had just clicked on one of the numerous sites on the list. Immediately afterwards, the words disappeared and on the screen he saw a picture of a dense crowd and a stage. A singer walked up to the microphone, his eyes hidden behind dark glasses, even though it was night time, and the crowd began chanting the killer's name. Servaz could not believe his ears. He hurriedly left the website, his heart pounding.

The next three links simply referenced encyclopaedia sites. Two more were general websites about serial killers. Fourteen in a row were forums where the name Julian Hirtmann was invoked for one reason or another, and Servaz didn't bother to consult them. The next link immediately drew his attention:

The Valley of the Hanged *is being filmed in the Pyrenees.*

He saw that his hand was trembling when he double-clicked. When he had finished reading, he pushed his chair far away from the screen and closed his eyes. Breathed deeply, for a long time.

A film was going to be made the following winter. It would be based on his investigation in the Pyrenees and above all on Hirtmann's escape from the Wargnier Institute. The names had been changed, of course, but the premise of the film was transparent. Two very well-known actors had been approached to play the serial killer and the *commissar* (sic). Servaz felt sick to his stomach. This was what their society had become, he thought: exhibitionism, voyeurism, commodification.

He felt angry, but also frightened. All this agitation . . . In the meantime, where was Hirtmann? What was he plotting? He told himself that Julian Alois Hirtmann could just as easily be in Canberra, in Kamchatka or in Punta Arenas as in an Internet café at the end of the street. Servaz thought about the time Yvan Colonna had been on the run. The media, the police, the anti-terrorist services had all thought he was in South America, in Australia, anywhere – but in fact the Corsican criminal was hiding in a sheepfold not thirty kilometres from where he had committed the crime he was wanted for.

Could Hirtmann really be in Toulouse?

Over one million inhabitants, if you included the greater urban area. A diverse population. A tangle of streets, squares, roads, bypasses, flyovers, slip roads. Dozens of nationalities – French, English, German, Spanish, Italian, Algerian, Lebanese, Turkish,

Kurdish, Chinese, Brazilian, Afghan, Malian, Kenyan, Tunisian, Rwandan, Armenian . . .

Where do you hide a tree? In a forest . . .

She wasn't unlisted, he found her number in the directory, but she hadn't included her first name: *M. Bokhanowsky.* He hesitated for a good while before he dialled. She picked up on the second ring.

'Hello?'

'It's Martin,' he said. For a split second he faltered. 'Can we meet? I have a few questions for you . . . about Hugo.'

Silence.

'I want you to tell me the truth,' she said, 'right now: do you think he did it? Do you think my son is guilty?'

Her voice quivered, as taut and fragile as a spider's silk thread.

'Not on the telephone,' he replied. 'But if you must know, I have increasing doubts about it. I know how difficult it is for you, but we have to talk. I can be in Marsac in an hour and a half, roughly. Is that all right, or would you prefer to wait until tomorrow?'

'Marianne?' he said at last, as she did not answer.

'Forgive me, I was thinking . . . In that case, why don't you stay for dinner? I'll do some shopping.'

'Marianne, I'll be perfectly frank with you. I don't know, given that I'm the investigator, whether I should—'

'That's fine, Martin. You don't need to shout it from the rooftops. And you can ask me your questions at the same time. After two glasses of wine, I'm a good deal more talkative.'

'I know,' he said.

It was an attempt to ease the tension, but he instantly regretted his words: he did not want to refer to the past, still less to let her think that he might have any motivations other than professional ones, particularly at the moment.

He thanked her and hung up, then looked up the address in the directory: *5, Domaine du Lac.* He still remembered the geography. Marianne lived in west Marsac. That was where the most luxurious villas were, on the north shore of a little lake. They had names like Belvedere, The Cask, or Villa Antigone, and most of them were set back from huge lawns that sloped gently down to a jetty where small dinghies or motorboats were moored. In the summer, the children of the rich lakeside inhabitants learned to sail and water ski. Their parents worked in Toulouse, as academics or in eminent positions in the aeronautics or electronics industries. Coincidentally, given what was on his mind, the other inhabitants of Marsac had baptised this district 'Little Switzerland'.

His mobile buzzed. He quickly pulled it out of his pocket and opened it. Margot.

'What's going on?' she said. 'Why do you need to know that?'

'No time to explain. Does he smoke or not?'

'No. I've never seen him smoke.'

'Thanks. I'll call you back later.'

15

North Shore

It was already three minutes past eight when he reached the east shore of the lake, where the café-concert restaurant Le Zik sat on stilts above the green water. Servaz drove around it and headed north. The Marsac lake was shaped like a bone or a dog biscuit, running east–west, seven kilometres in length. Most of it was bordered by thick woodland. Only the eastern area was urbanised, and 'urbanised' might be pushing it: every villa was huge, and generally situated on a property 3 to 5,000 square metres in size.

The address corresponded to the last house on the north shore, just before the woods and the part where the lake narrowed before widening again further along. The building must have been at least a hundred years old with its gables, balconies, chimneys and Virginia creeper. A house that was much too big for a mother and her son, he thought. The gate was open and Servaz drove beneath tall fir trees over the gravel, as far as the porch. He went up the steps and heard Marianne calling to him through the open door. A suite of rooms led to the terrace.

The rain was still sweeping over the lake. Kingfishers circled above the choppy surface before dive-bombing then reappearing in a shower of drops with their dinner in their beaks. To the left, beyond the other properties, he could see the roofs of Marsac and its steeple, veiled in mist. On the opposite shore there were dark woods and what local people pompously referred to as 'the Mountain': a rocky massif which rose a few dozen metres above the surface of the lake.

Marianne was setting the table. He stopped for a moment to look at her. She was wearing a khaki tunic dress that buttoned in front with two pockets on the chest and a fine woven belt, which gave her an almost military look. She had undone the top button, presumably because of the heat. Servaz noticed her bare suntanned legs and the absence of any jewellery around her neck. She was wearing only a faint touch of lipstick.

'What awful weather,' she said. 'But we won't let that get us down, will we?'

She was speaking without conviction, her voice as hollow as a metal box. When she kissed him on the cheek, he caught a whiff of her perfume.

'I brought this.'

She took the bottle, looked briefly at the label and set it down on the table. Then she went back to what she had been doing.

'The corkscrew is over there,' she added after a moment, as he stood there, arms hanging limply by his side.

She disappeared inside and he wondered if he had made a mistake by agreeing to come to dinner. He knew he shouldn't be there, that the little lawyer with the intense gaze would use this against him if Hugo was found guilty. He also sensed that the investigation was taking up all his thoughts, and it would be hard for him to talk about anything else. He should have questioned Marianne according to procedure, but he hadn't been able to resist the invitation. After all these years . . . He wondered whether Marianne had known what she was getting into, inviting him like that. Suddenly, without knowing why, he was on his guard.

'Why?'

'Why what?'

'Why did you never come back?'

'I don't know.'

'No letters, no e-mails, not a single text or call – nothing, in twenty years.'

'Twenty years ago there were no text messages.'

'That's not much of an answer, Commandant.'

'I'm sorry.'

'That's not an answer either.'

'There is no answer.'

'Of course there is.'

'I don't know . . . it was a long time ago.'

'A white lie, but a lie all the same.'

Silence.

'Don't ask me why,' he said.

'Why not? I wrote to you. Several letters. You never answered.'

She was probing him, her green gaze sparkling in the shadow of her face. Just the way it used to.

'Was it because of Francis and me?'

Again he said nothing.

'Answer me.'

He stared at her wordlessly.

'So that was it . . . Oh, for Christ's sake, Martin! All those years of silence, because of Francis and me?'

'Perhaps.'

'You're not sure?'

'Yes. Yes, I am sure. For God's sake, what difference does it make now anyway?'

'You wanted to punish us.'

'No, I wanted to move on. To forget. And I did.'

'Oh really? And that student you met after me? What was her name again?'

'Alexandra. I married her. And then we got divorced.'

It was strange how you could sum up a life in so few words. Strange and depressing.

'And now, are you seeing anyone?'

'No.'

Silence.

'So that explains your appearance,' she said. 'You look like a confirmed old bachelor, Martin Servaz.'

She was trying to sound light-hearted, and he was grateful to her for the attempt to ease the tension. The darkness of evening was stealing over them, along with the faint distortion of the senses that the wine induced.

'I'm afraid, Martin,' she said suddenly. 'I'm terrified, scared out of my wits . . . Tell me about my son. Are you going to charge him?'

Her voice almost broke on the last words. Servaz saw her pained expression, the fear in her eyes. He understood that from the start this had been the only question that really mattered to her. He took the time to choose his words carefully.

'As things stand at the moment, if he were up in court, there is a good chance he would be charged.'

'But you told me on the telephone that you had your doubts?'

Her tone was that of a desperate plea.

'Listen. It's too soon. I can't talk about it. But I need some information,' he said. 'And some time . . . There are one or two things . . . I don't want to give you any false hope.'

'I'm listening.'

'Does Hugo smoke?'

'He quit a few months ago. Why do you ask?'

He swept his question away with a wave of his hand.

'You knew Claire Diemar.'

This time it wasn't a question.

'We were friends. But not close friends. Acquaintances. She lived on her own in Marsac, and so did I. That sort of friends.'

'Did she talk to you about her private life?'

'No.'

'But did you know anything?'

'Yes, of course. Unlike you, I didn't leave Marsac. I know everyone and everyone knows me.'

'What sort of things?'

He saw her hesitate.

'Rumours . . . about her private life.'

'What sort of rumours?'

Again she hesitated. In the old days, Marianne had hated gossip. But her son's freedom was at stake.

'People said that Claire collected men. That she used them and tossed them out like tissues. That she played with them and that she had broken a few hearts in Marsac.'

He looked at her. Thought about the messages on the computer. They expressed a sincere, violent, absolute love. They did not match this portrait.

'But she was discreet about it, at any rate. And if you want me to name names, I don't have any.'

What about you, he wanted to ask, *where do you stand, in that respect?*

'The name Thomas, does that mean anything to you?'

She stared at him as she inhaled her cigarette, then shook her head.

'No. Nothing at all.'

'Are you sure?'

She blew away the smoke.

'That's what I said.'

'Did Claire Diemar listen to classical music?'

'What?'

He repeated the question.

'I have no idea. Does it matter?'

Suddenly another question came to him.

'Have you noticed anything peculiar lately? A guy hanging around the house? Anyone following you in the street? Something, anything, that made you feel uneasy?'

The look she gave him said she failed to understand.

'Are we talking about Claire, now, or me?'

'About you.'

'No. Should I have?'

'I don't know . . . if anything comes to mind, let me know.'

She stared at him intensely, but did not say anything more.

'And you,' he said suddenly. 'Tell me about yourself, about your life over all these years.'

'Is this still the cop talking?'

He looked down, then up again.

'No.'

'What do you want to know?'

'Everything . . . These past twenty years, Hugo, your life since . . .'

Her gaze clouded over in the fading light. She took the time to gather her memories. And to sort through them. Then she told him. A few carefully weighed sentences, nothing melodramatic. And yet there was plenty of drama; hidden, deep. She had married Mathieu Bokhanowsky, one of the members of their gang. Bokha, thought Servaz. Bokha the boor, the oaf. Bokha the good guy, occasionally the third wheel – there was always one like that – and openly scornful of girls and any form of romance. Bokha with someone like Marianne: back then, it would have seemed unimaginable. Bokha, against all expectations, had turned out to be a good, tender and affectionate guy, even funny. 'A fundamentally decent man, Martin,' she insisted. 'He wasn't pretending.' Servaz lit a cigarette and waited for her to go on. She had been happy with Bokha. Truly happy. With his kindness, simplicity and incredible energy, Mathieu had turned out to be someone who could move mountains, and he had almost managed to make her forget the scars left by Servaz and Van Acker. 'I loved you. Both of you. God knows I loved you. But you were both inaccessible, Martin: you had the burden of your mother's memory, your hatred of your father, that anger; and Francis had his ego.' Mathieu was calming, Mathieu didn't ask for anything in exchange for what he gave. He was simply there, whenever she needed him. Servaz listened to her as she unravelled the skein of years, no doubt leaving many things out, touching up some things and embellishing others, but isn't that what we all do? Back in the days when they were friends, no one, starting with Marianne herself, would have bet a centime on Bokha's future, and yet he had turned out to be not only extremely gifted at human relations but also endowed with a practical intelligence, something he had not really needed in the days when Francis and Martin spent their time talking about books, music, cinema and critical theory. Bokha had studied economics, created a chain of computer stores, and made a fortune that was as unexpected as it was sudden.

In the meantime, Hugo was born. Bokha the mediocre oaf, the underling of the gang, now had everything a man could want: money, recognition, the prettiest girl in the neighbourhood, a home, and a son.

Too much happiness, no doubt – at least that was Marianne's opinion, and Servaz thought, without saying it, of hubris, that lack of moderation which to the ancient Greeks was a capital sin: the man who committed it was guilty of wanting more than his share, and so he drew down the wrath of the gods. Mathieu Bokhanowsky was killed in a car crash one night on his way home from the opening of an umpteenth store. There were rumours: according to some, his alcohol level was over the limit. Others said that they had also found traces of cocaine in the car. Or that he hadn't been alone: his pretty secretary was with him, who escaped with only a few bruises.

'Slander, lies, jealousy,' hissed Marianne.

She had lifted her knees up against her chest and her bare feet clung to the edge of the wooden chair like claws. For a moment he observed them, those pretty tanned feet.

'There were also rumours implying that Mathieu was ruined. They were untrue. He had invested his money in life insurance and shares, but I found a job so I wouldn't have to sell the house. I'm an interior decorator for people who have no taste; I design websites for various organisations . . . It's a long way from our dreams of being artists, but still, it's not as far as—' She broke off, but he knew she had almost said, 'as being a cop.' 'I've been bringing Hugo up alone since he was eleven years old,' she concluded, crushing her cigarette in the ashtray. 'I've managed fairly well, I think. Hugo is innocent, Martin. If you charge him, it's not just my son you'll be sending to prison, but also an innocent boy.'

He got the message. She would never forgive him.

'It doesn't depend just on me,' he answered. 'It's up to the judge.'

'But it depends on what you say to him.'

'Let's get back to Claire. There must be some people in Marsac who disapproved of her way of life?'

She nodded.

'Of course there were. There was constant gossip. I was the target of similar gossip after Mathieu died, whenever married men came to visit.'

'Married men came to visit you?'

'Completely above board. I have a few friends here, perhaps Francis told you. They helped me get over it. This is a new thing, this judgmental attitude . . .'

'It's the job, I can't help it,' he said.

She stood up.

'You should forget your job from time to time.'

Her tone was as harsh as a whip, but she softened it by placing her hand on his shoulder as she walked by. She turned on the light on the terrace. The sky was getting dark. Servaz could hear frogs. Insects gathered around the lamp, and wisps of mist began to appear on the surface of the lake.

She came back with another bottle. He felt good, relaxed – but he wondered where this was heading. He noticed that he was following every move she made, that he was hypnotised by the way she filled the space. She uncorked the bottle and poured him another glass. Neither one of them felt the need to speak now, but she looked at him often. He suddenly understood that something else was happening, in his guts: he desired her. Violently. It had nothing to do with their history together. It was a desire for *this* woman, the Marianne she was today.

It was one in the morning by the time he reached his flat. He took a burning-hot shower to rid himself of the fatigue that was knotting his muscles and he put Mahler's Fourth Symphony on low in the living room. He thought about everything he had learned in the last twenty-four hours, and tried to organise his thoughts.

Servaz sometimes wondered why he liked these symphonies so much. Probably because they were complete worlds where he could lose himself, because in each one he found the same intensity – cries, pain, chaos, storms and mournful omens, the same ones as out in the real world. Listening to Mahler meant taking a path from darkness to light and back to darkness, from boundless joy to the tempest assailing the fragile craft of human existence and eventually capsizing it. The greatest conductors had taken on this Everest of symphonic art, and Servaz collected the various interpretations the way others collected rare stamps or seashells: Bernstein, Fischer-Dieskau, Reiner, Kondrashin, Klemperer, Inbal . . .

Music, however, did not prevent him from thinking. On the contrary. He absolutely had to get some sleep; five or six hours, no more – just enough to charge his batteries – but his mind would not rest until he had sorted and classified his mass of bare facts and impressions and come up with a strategy for the following day.

It was Sunday, but he had no choice: he would have to call in his team, because Hugo's remand was due to end in a few hours. Judging from the elements they had in the file, Servaz knew that the magistrate would not hesitate to request pre-trial detention. Marianne would be devastated and the kid would lose all his innocence; a few days in the rat-trap and his vision of the world would change. Urgency was boiling Servaz's blood. He took his notepad and began summing up the evidence:

1. *Hugo found sitting by the side of the pool at Claire Diemar's; she is dead in her bath.*
2. *Claims he was drugged and regained consciousness in the victim's living room.*
3. *No trace of any other person.*
4. *His friend David said he left the Dubliners pub before the Uruguay-France match: had plenty of time to go to Claire's and kill her. Also said that Hugo was not feeling well: pretext or reality?*
5. *Was clearly under the influence of drugs when the gendarmes found him. Two hypotheses: was drugged by someone else/got himself high.*
6. *Cigarette butts. Someone was spying on Claire. Hugo or someone else? According to Margot and Marianne, Hugo doesn't smoke.*

7. *Hirtmann's favourite music in the CD player.*
8. *Who deleted Claire's e-mail? Why would Hugo bother when he didn't touch his own mobile? Who got rid of the victim's phone?*
9. *The sentence: 'Sometimes the word friend is drained of meaning, but enemy, never.' – Is it referring to Hugo? Is it important?*
10. *Who is Thomas999?*

Servaz underlined the last two questions. He lifted his pencil from the page, sucked on it, and reread what he had written. Soon, the tracking service would give him an answer to question number 10. This would mean some headway with the investigation. He went over the facts again slowly, one by one, and worked out a chronology: Hugo left the pub shortly before the Uruguay-France match; an hour and a half later, roughly, he was seen by a neighbour sitting by the side of Claire Diemar's pool, and the gendarmerie found him shortly afterwards, distraught and clearly under the influence of alcohol and drugs, while the young professor lay at the bottom of her bath. The kid asserted he had lost consciousness and only came to in the victim's living room.

Servaz flopped back in his chair and mulled this over. There was a contradiction between the apparently spontaneous nature of the crime and its very elaborate staging. Once again, the image of Claire Diemar tied up in her bath, with a torch down her throat, sprang into his mind. He was suddenly convinced that this was not the killer's first crime: the modus operandi pointed to someone experienced, not a beginner. At the same time it was proof of a highly unbalanced personality. There was something ritualistic about the whole thing. And the presence of a rite almost always implied the threat of a series of deaths . . . a series to come or already underway? he wondered. The idea had occurred to him when he found the corpse, but he had rejected it because serial killers are rare, except in films and novels, and no cop on the crime squad ever thinks of them spontaneously: most of them have never even met one. *Hirtmann?* No, it couldn't be. And yet, question number seven worried him more than anything. He found it very difficult to believe that the Swiss criminal could have anything to do with this case; it was just too fantastic – and it would have meant that Hirtmann was very well acquainted with Claire's life. But then he recalled his phone call with the man in Paris, the business with the biker at the motorway service station. . . He found that hard to believe as well. Could it be that the members of the unit in charge of finding Hirtmann had gone after so many ghosts that they had ended up mistaking their dreams for reality?

Servaz walked around the open-plan kitchen, took a beer from the fridge and slid open the glass door to the balcony.

He went over to the edge and looked down at the street below him, as if Hirtmann might be there, somewhere in the rain, spying on his every move. A shiver went through him. The street was deserted, but cities never truly sleep at night, he knew that. As if to prove him right, a police car went by his building before disappearing, its siren fading progressively into the permanent hum of a city on standby.

He went back inside and switched on his computer to check his e-mail, the way he did every night before going to bed. Adverts offered him low-cost train journeys anywhere in Europe, hotels by the sea at rock-bottom prices, villas for rent in Spain, online dating . . . Suddenly his gaze was caught by an e-mail entitled 'Greetings'.

The blood went cold in his veins. The message was sent by a certain Theodor Adorno.

He moved the mouse and clicked on it:

From: theodor.adorno@hotmail.com
To: martin.servaz@infomail.fr
Date: 12 June
Subject: Greetings

Do you remember the first movement of the Fourth, Commandant? Bedächtig . . . Nicht eilen . . . Recht gemächlich . . . The piece that was playing when you came into my 'room' that famous day in December? I've been thinking about writing to you for quite some time. Are you surprised? I'm sure you'll believe me if I tell you I've been very busy lately. You can only truly appreciate your freedom, like your health, when you've been deprived of it for a long time.

But I won't bother you any more, Martin. (Do you mind if I call you Martin?) Personally I hate being bothered. You'll have news of me soon. I doubt you will like it very much – but I am sure you will find it interesting.

Regards, JH.

16

Night

The moon made a brief appearance then disappeared again, engulfed by clouds. The sound of rain hammering on the tiles came in through the open window, and the moisture clung to her skin like a wet towel while the drops fell to the floor at her feet, but Margot stayed motionless by the window, inhaling her cigarette. It was stifling in the little garret room beneath the eaves.

Smoking wasn't allowed, but she didn't care. Her tank top clung to her burning skin, the sweat was trickling between her shoulder blades and under her arms. She looked at her watch. Ten minutes past midnight. Her roommate was sound asleep, and snoring. As usual.

Margot wondered which was noisier, the summer rain or her roommate. She liked the girl – shy, on the chubby side – but her snoring was driving her crazy. Fortunately, she had her iPod to fill her ears with 'Welcome to the Black Parade' by My Chemical Romance. A headache was drilling into her temples. Fifteen minutes earlier they had still been working on their philosophy essay.

She leaned outside and glanced up at the old ivy-draped round tower in the corner, crowned with a pointed roof. At the top of the tower there was a light on in the headmaster's office. As there often was at this time. Disgusting Old Pig must be downloading porn while his wife was sound asleep.

She smiled at the thought.

More than once she had caught him sneaking glances at girls' legs, and she was sure his mind was a gallery of smut.

Suddenly a flash of light at the edge of her vision drew her attention and she looked over towards the garden. Another flash of light. Once. Twice . . . Then nothing more.

Shit, Elias, she thought. *You're out of your mind!*

Before closing the window she tossed her cigarette butt out and it made an incandescent arc in the night. She also closed her laptop, which had been open on the bed, its screen glowing in the dark. She pulled on her khaki shorts, fastened the big silver buckle of her studded belt, and slipped her bare feet into some fluorescent trainers.

On the wall above her bed were three posters from horror films: the main character from *Halloween*; Pinhead, the Cenobite with his head prickling with needles from *Hellraiser*, and Freddy Krueger, the bogeyman with the burned face who haunted the nightmares of teenagers on Elm Street. She loved horror films. Just as she loved heavy metal and novels by Anne Rice, Poppy Z. Brite and Clive Barker. She knew that her reading and her taste in music and movies stuck out like a sore thumb in Marsac, and that none of these authors stood the slightest chance of ever finding their way onto the modern literature syllabus. Even Lucie, who went to a lot of trouble to please her roommate, had ventured to question the choice of posters she saw nightly as she dropped off to sleep. Just as she had objected to Margot's habit of smoking in their room, even with the window open.

Margot leaned over the little sink, splashed her face with cold water and rinsed under her arms.

Then she stood up and inspected herself in the mirror. Her two ruby studs, one in her eyebrow, the other below her lower lip, shone like little red stars in the neon light. She was slender, with muscular legs and medium-length brown hair, and she didn't look anything like the other girls in Marsac, which was a source of pride to her.

The cupboard door creaked when she opened it to grab her anorak from a hanger. Lucie protested feebly in her sleep.

The corridor was deserted. Light shone at the end of the corridor from under the doors of the students who were in scientific prep classes. In some of their rooms the light would stay on until three o'clock in the morning. There was no movement at all in the corridor and she went along to the staircase, feeling as if the very soul of this place was weighing on her shoulders. The building was almost three centuries old.

She went down the stairs and out into the storm, and felt a child-like joy. The warm rain crackled on the hood of her jacket while she hugged the wall of the former stables. Then she went through the soaking grass to the first hedge, moving from shadow to shadow, choosing a path that made her invisible. She stopped between the hedge, the trunk of a cherry tree and a tall statue on a pedestal. She looked up. The statue was peering down at her with empty eyes.

'Hey,' said Margot. 'Stinking weather, even for you, right?'

The entrance to the maze was a bit further along. More than once the administrative body of the lycée had discussed closing the maze, or even tearing it down, because there had been several issues with hazing as well as 'inappropriate behaviour' in the hedges between students of both sexes – but the maze was on the register of historical monuments, like the main building, so they weren't allowed to touch it. All they could do was hang a sign on a chain that said: 'PRIVATE. ENTRANCE FORBIDDEN TO STUDENTS', which obviously only dissuaded the most obedient. Margot was not one of them. She bent down and slipped under the chain.

At this time of night, the interior of the maze was not the most cheerful place in the world. She shivered and cursed Elias.

'Where are you?' she shouted, to make herself heard above the rain.

'Over here!'

The voice came from directly opposite, but on the other side of the tall hedge that blocked the way. The first lane of the maze led to two corners, to the right and to the left.

'Right. Either you tell me which way to go, or I'm going home.'

'Go left,' he answered.

She started walking. A laugh.

'No: go right.'

'Elias!'

'Go right, go right . . .'

She turned around. She felt as if she were inside a bubble. She went around the corner at the end of the lane. There was another right angle turn to the left two metres farther along, then another to the right immediately after that . . . Then there was a crossroads with three possibilities: straight ahead, to the left, or to the right.

'Which way?'

'To the left!'

She obeyed, went around two more bends and saw him at last, sitting on a moss-covered stone bench, his endless legs stretched out in front of him. His brown hair clung to his head, streaming with water and covering nearly his entire face.

'Elias, you are completely sick!'

'I know.'

She wiped the end of her nose.

'Fuck, if anyone sees us, they'll think we're completely crazy.'

'Calm down, no one will see us.'

'Yeah, right!'

Elias and Margot were in the same class. In the beginning she hadn't paid much attention to this beanpole who seemed encumbered by his body and hid behind his hair as if it were a curtain. During breaks between classes he spent most of his time well away from the others, smoking and reading, sitting in a corner of the courtyard. He wouldn't speak to anyone except when it couldn't be helped, and before long his misanthropy was attracting a fair number of sidelong looks and harsh commentary. 'Antisocial', 'nutter' and 'weirdo' were the adjectives most often applied to him. As well as 'virgin', when it was the girls talking. Except Elias didn't seem to give a toss about what anyone thought of him. This was probably what had eventually drawn Margot to him. She was perfectly aware of the looks she had inspired when she had undertaken her initial efforts at friendship but, like Elias himself, she didn't care what others thought. But unlike him, she had managed to create a sufficiently solid network of friends within the lycée.

'Watch out,' he had said right at the start, 'you might catch my disease if you get too close.'

'What disease?'

'Solitude.'

'Your misanthropy doesn't faze me.'

'So what are you doing here?'

'I'm trying to figure something out.'

'Figure what out?'

'Whether you're a genius, a slob, or just a guy who likes to show off.'

'You're barking up the wrong tree, babe. Don't waste my time with your psychobabble.'

That was how it had begun. She was not attracted to Elias. But she liked the way he was different, and didn't care.

Margot looked up. The moon greeted her briefly through a tear in the clouds, then disappeared again. Elias handed her his pack of cigarettes and she took one.

'Have you heard about Hugo?'

'Obviously. That's all anyone is talking about.'

'So you know they found him completely stoned next to Mademoiselle Diemar's swimming pool,' he said.

'So?'

'I heard your dad was in charge of the investigation.'

She stopped fiddling with her lighter.

'Who told you that? I thought you didn't speak to anyone except me.'

'Some girls next to me this morning were talking about it . . . News travels fast. All you have to do is tune your antennae,' he said, fanning his hands on either side of his head.

'Right. So what's your point?'

'I was at the Dubliners, last night, before it happened . . . Hugo and David were there, too.'

'So? I heard the pub was packed, because of the match . . .'

'Hugo left the pub before the match started. Roughly an hour before Mademoiselle Diemar was killed.'

'That's the rumour that's going around.'

'It's not just a rumour. I was there. Nobody paid any attention to him at the time, everybody was waiting for the fucking match. Everyone except me.'

A smile played on Margot's lips as she thought of her father.

'Sports really aren't your thing, huh, Elias? And so what were you doing all that time? Playing the fucking voyeur? Were you asleep? Were you reading *Brothers Karamazov*?'

'Why don't we focus on what's really important,' he said, putting her in her place.

'So what's important, according to you?'

'David left the pub, too.'

This time he had her attention. The clouds parted like a zip, showing the white breast of the moon, then closed again.

'What?'

'Exactly. A few seconds later.'

'You mean—'

'That David didn't stay and watch the match, either. No one noticed because no one gave a fuck about anything except that stupid football . . . Except maybe Sarah.'

'Was Sarah with them?'

'Yes, at their table. She's the only one of the three who didn't move. Later, David came back. But Hugo didn't, as you know.'

Margot's senses were suddenly all on the alert.

'How much later?'

'I don't know. I didn't keep track. As you can imagine, I had no way of knowing what was going on. I just noticed that David had come back at one point. That's all.'

Sarah was in the prep classes with David and Hugo. Easily the prettiest girl in the lycée, she liked wearing little hats set jauntily on her short blonde hair. Sarah, David, Hugo and another girl called Virginie – a little dark-haired girl with glasses and an assertive character – went everywhere together.

'Why are you telling me all this? So that I'll tell my father to question Sarah?'

He smiled. 'Don't you want to find out more?'

'What do you mean?'

'Like father, like daughter, no? I mean, who better than us to conduct a little investigation inside the lycée?'

'You're not serious?'

He stood up. He was a good head taller than her.

'Oh, I certainly am.'

'Shit, Elias!'

'If we sum it up: we've got Hugo, who's been accused of murder and was found at the scene of the crime; we've got David, who left the pub a few seconds after him; we have Sarah, who saw everything, but who's keeping her mouth shut; and we have the top four second-year students – in other words the four most brilliant young minds for miles around – who make up an inseparable quartet. You have to admit that, put that way, things look far more interesting, right? There's a hitch somewhere.'

'And you want us to go sticking our noses in? Why?'

'Think about it. Outside of those four, who are the smartest kids in the lycée?'

She shook her head, incredulous.

'And just supposing I go along with this, how do we do it?'

A smile spread across Elias's face.

'If one of them has anything to do with what happened, he – or she – will be wary of your father, of the cops, of the teachers – of everyone except the other students. That's our chance. We'll share the job of watching them and we'll wait and see what happens. Whoever did it is bound to slip up at some point or other.'

'I'd never realised, but you are truly out of your mind.'

'Think about it, Margot Servaz. Don't you think it's strange that a guy like Hugo got caught so easily?'

'So why should I help you?'

'Because I know that you like him,' he answered, lowering his voice and looking at his feet. 'And because no one who's innocent deserves to rot in prison,' he added with a gravity that was unusual for him.

Touché . . . Uneasy, she looked at the maze around them. A flash of lightning broke the darkness above the hedges, and a thought flared in her mind, just as blinding.

'Do you realise what this means?' she said.

He looked at her questioningly.

'If it isn't Hugo, then there's someone really sick running around out there.'

Sunday

17

Ubik Café

'Caffeine,' said Servaz.

'Caffeine,' said Pujol.

'Caffeine,' said Espérandieu.

'I'll have tea,' announced Samira Cheung, going back out of the meeting room to help herself at the hot drinks dispenser next to the lift, while Vincent got up to start the coffee machine.

It was nine o'clock in the morning on Sunday, 13 June. Servaz glanced at his colleagues. That morning, Espérandieu was wearing a close-fitting Kaporal T-shirt, which emphasised the fact that he kept in moderately good shape, and a pair of jeans full of pockets, with patches on the knees. Servaz had found it hard to get used to his deputy's style in the beginning (and he wasn't sure he ever really had). And then Samira Cheung had joined the force and Vincent had begun to seem almost . . . tame. Although on this June morning she was relatively sober: a sequined waistcoat over a T-shirt that proclaimed DO NOT DISTURB, I'M PLAYING VIDEO GAMES, a denim miniskirt with a large buckle, and a pair of brown cowboy boots. But Servaz was less interested in his investigators' look than in what they had in their heads, and since Vincent and Samira had arrived, his investigation team had the highest rate for solving crimes in the entire regional crime squad – despite the official boasts about the city's quality of life, cultural heritage and dynamic environment, the crime rate in Toulouse was well above the national average.

Servaz liked to say that if you let a little old lady with a handbag loose on the streets of Toulouse at midnight, you would see half the scooters in town show up to snatch it off her. They would probably even kill each other for the privilege. The officers in the crime squad had to deal with a growing whirlwind of offences.

To curb delinquency, the city had come up with a bright idea that only showed how much they were in denial where crime was concerned: the creation of an 'Office of Tranquillity'. Why not an office of sexual freedom to combat rape, while they were at it? Or an office of healthy living to combat drug trafficking? They could have opened it on a square where the cops and customs officials regularly conducted raids that simply scattered the dealers and pushers of contraband cigarettes for a few hours. Then they drifted back, to exactly the same place – like ants momentarily deterred by the kick of a boot.

It's natural law, thought Servaz as he stood up. Survival of the fittest. He went down the corridor. In the men's toilets, he went over to the row of sinks. He had shadows beneath his eyes, his eyelids were red, and he looked like death warmed up. He splashed his face with cold water. He had got very little sleep after the e-mail, and all the caffeine already speeding through his veins was making him nauseous. The sun was beaming in the skylights above the urinals, causing the dust to dance around him; the stuffy air smelled of industrial cleaner. The space behind him made him feel uncomfortable. The fear was there. He could recognise its electric caress on the back of his neck.

When he got back to the meeting room he saw that Samira and Vincent had already opened their laptops, although Samira still had her headphones around her neck. Servaz wondered silently when she would start having hearing problems. He saw that even Pujol had bought a smartphone, and he sighed as he took out his notepad and a finely sharpened pencil.

At forty-nine, Pujol was the oldest in the group. He was an old-school cop, hard-boiled, an advocate of 'muscular' methods. Physically, he was a sturdy bloke, intimidating, with a thick mane of greying hair in which he plunged his fingers when he was thinking – which he didn't do often enough, in Servaz's opinion. Given his experience, he was a useful tool, but there were certain aspects of his personality that Martin found hard to take: his racist jokes, his borderline behaviour with female recruits fresh out of the academy, his scarcely concealed homophobia. These attitudes had become only too apparent when Espérandieu and Samira Cheung arrived in the division. With a few other colleagues, Pujol had piled on the petty harassment – until the day Servaz decided to put a stop to it. He'd had to resort to methods he generally frowned upon, and he had made a few enemies as a result. But he had also earned his two young assistants' eternal gratitude.

The coffee finished brewing with a gurgle and Espérandieu filled the cups. The other two were absorbed in reading the e-mail.

'Theodor Adorno,' said Samira. 'Does that name mean anything to you, boss?'

'Theodor Adorno was a German philosopher and musicologist, a great specialist in Mahler's work,' he confirmed.

'Julian Hirtmann's favourite composer, but yours too,' said Espérandieu.

Servaz frowned. 'There are millions of people who appreciate Mahler's music.'

'What's to say it isn't a hoax?' asked Samira, looking up with her teacup in her hand. 'We've had dozens of bogus calls since Hirtmann escaped, and a heap of e-mails every bit as fantastical.'

'This one came to his personal e-mail address,' Espérandieu pointed out.

'At what time?'

'Roughly six o'clock,' said Servaz.

'The time it was sent is written there,' said Espérandieu, pointing to the top of the sheet with one hand and holding his coffee in the other.

'So what does that prove?' asked Samira. 'Hirtmann had this address? Did you give it to him, boss?'

'Of course I didn't.'

'So it proves nothing.'

'Have they traced it?' asked Pujol, sitting back in his chair to stretch and crack his knuckles.

'The cyber unit is working on it,' said Espérandieu.

'How long is it going to take?' asked Servaz.

'Dunno. For a start, it's Sunday – though they have brought a technician back in. Secondly, he made a bit of a fuss and pointed out that they'd already told him to work on Claire Diemar's hard disk. He wanted to know which he should do first. Thirdly, there's another case that takes precedence. The gendarmerie are working on a paedophile network. Hundreds of e-mail addresses to check.'

'And here I was thinking a serial killer who's about to strike again might be a priority.'

The comment cast a pall over the room. Samira took a long swallow of her tea and seemed to find it bitter.

'It is,' she said quietly. 'But when it's kids, you know, boss—'

Servaz felt his cheeks flush.

'Okay, okay,' he said.

'If it even is Hirtmann,' said Pujol.

Servaz felt his hackles rise.

'What do you mean?'

'I agree with Samira,' said Pujol, to everyone's surprise. 'The e-mail proves absolutely nothing. There are bound to be people out there who know how to get hold of your e-mail address. Privacy on the Internet – everyone knows that's a load of rubbish. My kid is thirteen years old and he knows ten times more than I do about it. I've heard there are quite a few little jokers among the hackers and computer whizzes.'

'How many people would know what piece of music was playing in Hirtmann's cell the day I went there, in your opinion?'

'Are you one hundred per cent certain that no journalists got wind of it? That the information wasn't published somewhere? They did a fair amount of digging at the time. Every single protagonist in that case was contacted by the press. Maybe someone talked. Have you really been through all the articles?'

Of course not, he thought, furious. He had carefully avoided reading them. And Pujol knew it.

'Pujol is right,' said Samira approvingly. 'It's bound to be some arsehole. Ever since he escaped, Hirtmann has never given a single sign of life. It's been eighteen months. Why would he do it now?'

'Good question,' said Vincent. 'And I have another one: what has he been up to in the meantime?'

His question made them shiver.

'What does someone like him do once they're free again, do you think?' asked Servaz. 'Okay, so how many of us think it's him?'

He raised his hand to set the example, saw Espérandieu hesitate but eventually keep his hand down.

'And how many think the opposite?'

Pujol and Samira, somewhat embarrassed, raised their hands.

'No opinion,' said Espérandieu when the others looked at him questioningly.

Servaz felt anger welling up in him. They thought he was being paranoid. And what if he was?

'There was a CD in Claire Diemar's stereo. A Mahler CD,' he began. 'Naturally that information must not leave this room and above all must not find its way into the media.'

He saw the other three stare at him, surprised.

'And I've called the unit in Paris.'

He related his conversation with Paris. Everyone was silent.

'But the CD could very well be a coincidence,' said Samira, not about to back down. 'And this business about a biker filmed on the motorway, that just seems bogus. Those people in Paris have to justify the existence of their unit, after all.'

He felt like exploding. They were behaving just like those researchers who analyse the results of their experiments depending on what they want to find. They didn't want Hirtmann involved in this investigation. So before they even got started they were convinced that any information about him could only be fantastical or unreliable. It had to be said in their defence that they'd been flooded with messages and phone calls from people claiming to have seen him here or there, all of which had turned out to be false or unverifiable. Hirtmann seemed to have been wiped off the surface of the planet. The possibility of suicide had even been evoked, but Servaz didn't believe it: the killer could easily have put an end to his days at the Wargnier Institute if he'd wanted to. In Servaz's opinion, Hirtmann wanted only two things: to regain his freedom, and resume his activities.

'I'm going to call Paris all the same and send them the e-mail,' he said.

He was about to add something when they heard a shout from the next room.

'That's it! We've got him!'

Servaz looked up from his notebook. They had all recognised the voice of one of the computer specialists. A tall, thin young man, who looked like a cross between Bill Gates and Steve Jobs, made a triumphant entry into the room, a paper in his hand.

'Have I got news!' he shouted, waving the paper. 'I found out where the e-mail came from.'

Servaz looked around him. All gazes were now focused on the newcomer. The nervousness and excitement were palpable.

'Well?'

'It was sent from here. From a cybercafé. In Toulouse.'

The Ubik Café, on the rue Saint-Rome, was squeezed in between a sandwich shop and a women's clothing boutique. Servaz recalled there used to be a bookstore there when he was a student. An Aladdin's cave that smelled of paper and ink and dust, and the inexhaustible mysteries of the written word. The only vestige of that era were the two semi-circular arcades in which the window of the cybercafé was set.

The interior was divided by an invisible frontier: a café to the left, with a bar counter and tables, and the multimedia space to the right, not unlike a hairdresser's with its row of armchairs. Two customers were sitting at computer monitors, talking into micro-phone-headsets. Servaz scrutinised them, as if Julian Hirtmann might be among them. The woman who stood behind the counter – her name was Fanny, according to the badge on her chest – had a faint smile and an ample bosom. Espérandieu showed her his card and asked her if she had been there the previous day at around six o'clock in the evening. She turned and called out to someone called Patrick. They heard Patrick grumbling from the back room. He took his time coming out. He was a big fellow in his thirties, wearing a white shirt with the sleeves rolled up and black trousers. He gave them a wary look from behind his glasses and Servaz immediately filed him in the 'not very cooperative' category. He had pale little eyes, cold and stubborn.

'What do you want?' he asked.

Espérandieu stepped forward and showed his card once again. Servaz preferred to stand back. His assistant was a geek, far better acquainted with the whole world of computers than he was: the invasive influx of mobile phones, social networks and tablet computers was already enough to cause him to break out in a rash. Espérandieu also didn't look like a cop.

'Are you the boss here?'

'I'm the manager,' corrected the big man cautiously.

'An e-mail was sent from here yesterday evening at around six o'clock. We'd like to know if you remember the man who sent it.'

The manager raised his eyebrows above his glasses and shot them a look which implied, *What do you think, mate?*

'There are roughly fifty people or more who come through here every evening. You think I stand over their shoulders to see what they're doing?'

Espérandieu and Servaz had a photo of Hirtmann on them, but they had decided not to show it: if the guy recognised the serial killer who had been on the front page of all the papers the previous year, he might go telling everyone what had happened, and the news that Hirtmann was in Toulouse sending e-mails to the police would make its way into the papers in less time than it took Usain Bolt to run 100 metres.

'A very tall, thin guy,' said Espérandieu. 'In his forties. He might have been wearing a wig. He might have attracted attention because of his rather . . . strange behaviour. And he might have had a slight accent.'

The manager's gaze went back and forth between the two of them, like a spectator at the French Open; he seemed to think that they were perfect morons. He shrugged.

'Is this some sort of joke? That's a lot of "might have"s, don't you think? Really doesn't ring a bell with me, no.'

Then he seemed to remember something.

'Wait a minute . . .'

He saw them looking at him and broke off. His faded blue eyes sparkled behind his glasses and Servaz understood that the man was enjoying their interest and their impatience.

'Someone did come in, yes, now that you mention it . . .'

He smiled. Acted as if he were thinking. Waited for their reaction. Servaz was beginning to feel exasperated.

'This is a nice place you have here,' said Espérandieu, as if he couldn't care less what came next. 'Is your local network on WiFi?'

The man seemed disconcerted by the visitor's sudden loss of interest in him, but he was flattered by his interest in the café.

'Uh . . . no, I've still got cable. With thirty computers, even if I had a top-end WiFi router, it couldn't cope. Because of all the games on the network.'

Espérandieu nodded his approval.

'Hmm . . . Yes, of course. So, someone did come?'

This time the manager of the Internet café felt a need to kindle the flames somewhat.

'Yes, but not the guy you described. It was a woman.'

The two cops' interest was fading to zero.

'So what's that got to do with the man we're looking for?'

A smile returned to the manager's face.

'Because she told me you would come. She told me that some guys would come and see me and ask me questions about a message she had sent. But she didn't tell me they'd be from the police.'

Gotcha. They were riveted.

'And that's not all . . .'

Stupid bastard, thought Servaz. One more minute like this and he would grab him by the collar.

'She left this . . .'

They watched as he bent down to open a drawer and take something out.

An envelope.

Servaz felt a chill down his spine.

Patrick handed the brown envelope to Espérandieu, who had already pulled on a pair of gloves.

'Who's touched it, besides you?'

'No one.'

'Are you sure?'

'Yes. I'm the one who took it and put it in the drawer.'

'Do you have a letter opener, or a pair of scissors?'

The man rummaged in a drawer and handed him a bread knife. Espérandieu delicately tore open the envelope and placed two fingers inside. Servaz looked at his gloved hand as he pulled out a shining metallic disc. Espérandieu examined it on both sides. Over his shoulder, Servaz did the same. The disc was blank: there was nothing written on it, nor any fingerprints that he could see.

'Can we have a look?' he asked the manager.

The man waved to the row of computers in the multimedia space.

'No, not there. Somewhere more private.'

Patrick went back to the other side of the bar and drew open a red curtain, revealing a tiny windowless room filled with computer packaging material, crates, a defunct percolator and, in one corner, a desk with a lamp and a computer.

'This woman who handed you the envelope,' said Servaz, 'was she alone?'

'Yes.'

'What sort of impression did she make?'

Patrick thought for a moment.

'She was cute, I remember. Other than that, rather on the serious side. Come to think of it, I get the impression she actually was wearing a wig.'

'And she asked you to give this to us? Why didn't you call the police?'

'Because there was no mention of the police or any hint that it was anything illegal. She just told me that some people would come and ask me about her and that I had to give them this envelope.'

'Why did you agree? Didn't you find it a bit dodgy?'

The man broke into a smile.

'There were two fifty-euro notes along with it.'

'That's even dodgier, don't you think?'

The man didn't answer.

'So you didn't notice anything else, besides the wig?'

'No.'

'Do you have CCTV?'

'Yes. But it only turns on at night, once the place is closed. It's activated by a motion detector.'

He could read the disappointment in Servaz's eyes and seemed delighted. Patrick didn't seem particularly concerned about the fate of his fellow citizens, but on the other hand he was clearly very eager not to make things too easy for the police. No doubt he read George Orwell and was convinced that his country was a police state.

'The notes, do you still have them?'

Another smile.

'No. Money comes and goes, here.'

'Thank you,' said Espérandieu to dismiss him.

Servaz watched as his assistant leaned over the computer. The man didn't budge.

'Who's this guy you're looking for?'

'You can go now,' said Servaz with a broad smile. 'We'll call you if we need you.'

The manager gave them a look. Then he shrugged and walked off. Once he was on the other side of the curtain, Espérandieu slipped the disc into the drive. A window opened on the computer screen and the media software program started up automatically.

Instinctively, Servaz felt tense. What should they expect? A message from Hirtmann? A video? And who was this woman the manager was talking about? An accomplice? The tension was affecting them physically. Servaz could see a triangle of sweat darkening his assistant's T-shirt, and it wasn't just because it was hot in the tiny room.

The silence seemed to last forever, broken only by the crackling of static in the loudspeakers. Espérandieu turned the volume up.

All of a sudden there was a blast of music that made them both jump as if a gun had gone off.

'Bloody hell!' exclaimed Espérandieu, hurrying to turn down the volume.

'What is that?' said Servaz, his heart pounding fit to burst, while the music continued, more quietly.

'Marilyn Manson,' answered Espérandieu.

'There are people who listen to this?'

In spite of the tension, Espérandieu could not help but smile. The song played to the end. They waited for a moment, then the CD stopped.

'That's it,' said Espérandieu, looking at the cursor on the screen.

'There's nothing else?'

'No, that's it.'

On Servaz's face, fear had given way to bewilderment and disappointment.

'What do you think it means?'

'I don't know. It looks like a hoax. One thing is for sure: it wasn't Hirtmann.'

'No.'

'So it wasn't Hirtmann who sent you the e-mail, either.'

Servaz got the message and felt his anger return.

'You all think I'm paranoid, don't you?'

'Listen, the lunatic is out there somewhere. Every police force in Europe is looking for him, but they haven't got the slightest clue. He could be anywhere. And before he disappeared he confided in you.'

Servaz looked at his assistant. 'There is one thing I do know,' he replied, aware that his words could be yet another piece of evidence for the file on his paranoia: 'Sooner or later, that lunatic is going to show up again.'

18

Santorini

Irène Ziegler looked down at the cruise ship anchored in the volcanic crater 100 metres below her. From this vantage point, the huge ship looked like a pretty toy, all white. The sea and the sky were almost artificially blue, contrasting with the blinding white terraces, the red ochre cliffs, and the black of the little volcanic islands at the centre of the bay.

She took a sip of very sweet Greek coffee then a long draw of her cigarette. Eleven o'clock in the morning. It was already hot. On the neighbouring terrace, an English couple wearing straw hats were writing postcards. On yet another, a man in his thirties gave her a friendly little wave while talking on the phone. At €225 a night in low season, the hotel catered to a rather wealthy clientele. Fortunately she wasn't the one, on her gendarme's salary, who was paying for the room.

She waved back, and stood up. A little sea breeze struggled against the rising heat, but she felt, all the same, a trickle of sweat run down her back. She went through the French windows.

'Don't move,' said a voice in her ear.

Ziegler jumped. The voice was full of menace.

'If you make a single move, you'll regret it.'

She felt a rope go round her wrists behind her back and her forearms prickled with goosebumps, despite the heat. Then everything went dark as a blindfold covered her eyes.

'Go over to the bed. Don't try anything.'

She obeyed. A hand pushed her roughly onto the bed on her stomach. Her skirt and bathing suit were immediately yanked off.

'Isn't it a bit early for this?' she asked, her face in the sheets.

'Shut up!' said the voice behind her, followed immediately by a stifled laugh. 'It's never too early,' added the voice, with a slight Slavic accent to her French.

She was turned over onto her back and her tank top was removed. A body as naked and hot as her own lay on top of her. Moist lips kissed her eyelids, nose and mouth, then a wet tongue ran over her body. Irène freed her wrists, removed the blindfold and looked at Zuzka's brown head moving down towards her belly. A wave of desire broke in the hollow of her back. With her fingers in her companion's silky black hair she arched, rubbed against her and moaned. Then Zuzka's face came back up, and they kissed.

'What's that weird taste?' she asked suddenly between kisses.

'*Yaourti me meli*,' answered the voice. 'Yoghurt with honey. Quiet.'

Irène Ziegler gazed at Zuzka's body stretched out next to her. She was naked except for a Panama straw hat over her face and strappy little leather sandals on her feet. She was asleep.

For three weeks they had been hopping from one island and one ferry to another: Andros, Mykonos, Paros, Naxos, Amorgos, Serifos, Sifnos, Milos, Folegandros, Ios and finally Santorini, where they had spent their time swimming, diving, and sunbathing on the black sand beaches, and shutting themselves away in their hotel room to make love. Especially to make love . . . From time to time, they would go and sip a Marvin Gaye at the Tropical Bar, just before the rush of hysterical revellers drove them away. Then they would enjoy a moment wandering hand in hand through the calm streets, kissing under awnings and in dark corners, or jumping onto the scooter to head for a moonlit beach – but even there it was difficult to get away from the drunks and the bores and the thumping echo of techno.

Ziegler stood up soundlessly, so as not to wake her girlfriend, and opened the fridge to take out some bottled fruit juice. She drank a tall glass, then went into the bathroom for a shower. It was their last day. The next day they would fly back to France and each of them would resume her usual life: Zuzka in the nightclub where Irène had met her two years earlier, where she was both manager and head stripper, and Ziegler to her new assignment: the investigation squad in Auch.

Not really a promotion when you came from the investigation squad in Pau, a much bigger place . . .

The winter 2008 investigation had left its mark. Paradoxically, Commandant Servaz and the Toulouse crime squad had stood up for her, and it was her own superiors who had punished her. For a moment she closed her eyes against the memory: that sinister session where her superiors, all lined up in their dress uniforms, had listed the charges against her. Against all the rules, she had wanted to play the lone warrior, and she had hidden information from the members of her team; she had also hidden certain aspects of her past with regard to the investigation, and she had concealed an important piece of evidence where her name appeared. The only reason she had not been punished more severely was thanks to Martin's intervention and that of the prosecutor, Cathy d'Humières, who had insisted that she had saved the policeman's life and also risked her own to capture the murderer.

So when she got back she would be taking up her position in the investigation squad of the county town of a region of 23,000 inhabitants. A new life and a new departure. In theory. She already knew that the cases she would deal with there would have little in common with the cases she had previously worked on. Her only consolation was that she would be the head of the department, as her predecessor had retired three months earlier. Auch did not have a court of appeal the way Pau did; there was a county court, and she had already noticed that the trickier cases were sent to the regional section of the Criminal Affairs Division, to the departmental public security police, or to the regional gendarmerie in Toulouse. She let out a sigh, came out of the shower, wrapped herself in a towel and emerged again on the terrace, where she picked up her sunglasses before leaning over the little wall of stones.

She lost herself in the contemplation of the ships criss-crossing the caldera. This was the last chance to stock up on memories.

She wondered where Martin was, what he was doing at that moment. She was fond of him, and although he didn't know it, she was watching over him. In her own way. Then her thoughts drifted again. *Where was Hirtmann? What was he doing at that very moment?* Deep inside, her restlessness and her hunter's instinct were stirring. A little voice told her that the Swiss killer was at it again, that he would never stop. She suddenly realised she was eager for the holidays to be over. She was in a hurry to get back to France, to continue the hunt . . .

Servaz spent the rest of his Sunday doing a bit of housework and thinking. At around five o'clock the telephone rang. It was

Espérandieu. Sartet, the examining magistrate, together with the magistrate for custody and release, had decided to charge Hugo and place him in provisional detention. Servaz's mood clouded over. He wasn't sure the young man would emerge unscathed from such an experience. He would go through the looking glass, and see what was hidden behind the veneer of their society; Servaz could only hope that Hugo was still young enough to forget what he was about to see.

He thought again about the sentence in Claire's notebook. There was something odd about it. It was both too obvious and too subtle. For whom was it intended?

'Are you still there?' he asked.

'Yes,' replied Espérandieu.

'Do what you can to find a sample of Claire's handwriting. And ask for a graphological comparison with the sentence in the notebook.'

'The Victor Hugo quotation?'

'Yes.'

He went out onto the balcony. The air was still heavy, and a threatening sky hung over the city. The thunder was only a distant muffled echo, and it was as if time had stood still. There was electricity in the air. He thought about an anonymous predator moving around in the crowd, about Hirtmann's victims who had never been found, about his mother's murderers, about war and revolution, and about the world that was using up all its resources, including those of salvation and redemption.

'To last night in Santorini,' said Zuzka, raising her glass of margarita.

Just beyond their table the white terraces, tinged blue with night, plummeted dizzyingly towards the edge of the cliff, a Legoland of balconies and lights piled up above the void. All the way down at the bottom, the caldera sank slowly into the night. Still anchored in the bay, the cruise ship glittered like a Christmas tree.

A salty offshore breeze ruffled Zuzka's hair and she turned to look at Ziegler. In the candlelight her irises were a very pale blue with a darker edge bordering on violet. Irène could not get enough of looking at her.

'Cheers to the world,' she said, raising her glass again.

Then she leaned across the table and kissed Irène, beneath the curious gazes of their neighbours. She tasted of tequila, orange and lime. Eight seconds, no less. There was some applause.

'I love you,' declared Zuzka, out loud, oblivious of their surroundings.

'Same here,' answered Irène, her cheeks on fire.

She had never been the demonstrative sort. She had a Suzuki GSR600 motorcycle, a helicopter pilot's licence and a firearm, and she liked speed, deep-sea diving and motorsports, but next to Zuzka, she felt shy and awkward.

'Don't let those macho bastards mess your head, all right?' (Zuzka occasionally had difficulty with idiomatic expressions.)

'You can count on it.'

'And I want you to call me every night.'

'Zuzik . . .'

'Promise.'

'I promise.'

'At the slightest sign of . . . *depresia*, I'll be right over,' said Zuzka threateningly.

'Zuzik, I've got a company flat, in a building full of gendarmes . . .'

'So?'

'They're really not used to this sort of thing.'

'I'll put on a fake moustache, if that's what worries you. We can't spend life hiding. You should change jobs, you know?'

'We've already discussed this. I like my job.'

'Maybe. But your job doesn't like you. Why don't we go for little walk to beach, so we enjoy last Greek night?'

Ziegler nodded, lost in thought. The holidays were over. Back to the norm, to life in the Southwest. She liked her job. *Really?* So many things had changed since that notorious winter. Suddenly, she saw herself as she had been eighteen months earlier, when she'd been carried away by the avalanche, casting a desperate look at Martin before he disappeared from sight, up there in the mountains. She thought for the hundredth time of that psychiatric hospital lost in the snow, with its long corridors and its electronic locks, and the enigmatic man, pale and smiling, who had been locked up in there – and Mahler's music . . .

★

143

A full moon was shining over the Aegean, inscribing a silver triangle on the surface of the water. They held hands, and walked barefoot at the edge of the waves. The sea breeze blew harder here, caressing their faces. Now and again strains of music came to them from one of the tavernas along the immense beach at Perissa, then the wind shifted and the roar of the sea grew louder.

'Why didn't you say anything, earlier, when I said you should change job?' asked Zuzka.

'Say anything about what?'

'That I too should change my job.'

'You are free to choose, Zuzka.'

'You don't like what I do.'

'It's thanks to your job that we met.'

'And that's exactly what frightens you.'

'What do you mean?'

'You know very well what I mean. Do you remember? When I was stripping and you showed up in the room, you and that other gendarme . . . Do you think I have forgotten your look? You tried to hide it, but you couldn't take your eyes off my body. And you know I have same effect on other clients.'

'Why don't we change the subject?'

'Ever since we've been together, you haven't been back to *Pink Banana,* or just that once, that night when I left letter to say I was leaving you,' continued Zuzka.

'Zuzka, please . . .'

'I haven't finished. And you know why? You are afraid to see other clients gazing at me the way you did. You are afraid I'll find someone like I found you. Well, you're wrong. I found you, Irène. We found each other. And no one can come between us, you have nothing to fear. There is only you. The only thing that can come between you and me is your job.'

Ziegler didn't answer.

'You are too sensitive for that job,' said Zuzka, walking on. 'All those months where I saw it interfere in your private life, where I put up with your dark moods, your silences, your fears. I don't want to live through that again. Because if you cannot separate private life from your fucking job, if you cannot disconnect when we're together, it's not some dyke who comes to stare at me you have to be afraid of; no, it's you: you are the only person who can separate us, Irène.'

'Then you don't need to worry. Where I am now, all I have to deal with is a few stolen handbags and some drunken brawls.'

She said this wearily. Zuzka grabbed her by the hand and stopped her.

'I'm going to be honest with you. For me, this is excellent news.'

Ziegler said nothing. Zuzka pulled her close. She kissed her and took her in her arms. Irène could smell her skin and her hair, her light perfume. She felt her desire return. She had never felt this before meeting Zuzka, never with such intensity.

'Hey, girls, you're not on Lesbos here!'

A drunken voice, heavy with laughter. They pulled apart, swung round in the direction of a little group that had just come out of the shadow. Young Brits, full of alcohol. The scourge of Mediterranean beaches . . . There were three of them.

'Look at those fucking dykes!'

'Hi, girls,' said the smallest one, stepping away from the other two.

Ziegler looked around her quickly. There was no one else on the beach.

'A nice moonlit night, huh, girls? Super romantic and all that. Aren't you bored all alone?' he said, turning to look at his friends.

The other two burst out laughing.

'Fuck off, arsehole,' said Zuzka coldly in perfect English.

Ziegler started. She placed a hand on her girlfriend's arm.

'You hear that, lads? They're not the kind to give in easily, eh? Hey, want something to drink?'

'No thank you,' Ziegler replied.

'Suit yourself.'

His tone was too conciliatory. The gendarme felt every muscle of her body tense and harden. Out of the corner of her eye, she kept watch on the other two.

'What about you, bleedin' cow – want some?'

Irène's hand squeezed Zuzka's arm. Zuzka said nothing this time. She had grasped the danger.

'Cat got yer tongue? Or you only use it to insult people and go down on her?'

A strain of music drifted over from one of the tavernas. It occurred to Ziegler that even if they screamed no one would hear them.

'You're pretty stacked for a dyke,' said the redhead, looking Zuzka up and down.

Ziegler watched the other two. They weren't moving. They were waiting to see what would happen. They were followers . . . Or maybe they were already too drunk to react. How many hours had they been drinking? It did matter, after all. She turned her attention to the leader. He was a bit too chubby, with an ugly face, a strand of hair falling in his eyes, thick glasses and a long pointed nose that made him look like a fucking rat. He was wearing white shorts and a ridiculous Manchester United sweatshirt.

'Maybe you could change the menu, for once. Have you ever sucked off a man, love?'

Zuzka didn't budge.

'Hey, I'm talking to you!'

Irène had already grasped that things wouldn't stop there. Not with this dickhead. She evaluated the situation in silence. The other two were definitely taller and sturdier, but they did look heavy and slow. In the short term, the ginger wanker was the most dangerous. She wondered if he had anything in his pocket, a knife. She was sorry she had left her can of mace at the hotel.

'Leave her alone,' she said, to distract his attention from Zuzka.

The Englishman swung around to face her. She saw his little eyes sparkling with fury in the moonlight. Yet his gaze was blurred with alcohol. So much the better.

'What d'you say?'

'Leave us alone,' said Ziegler again, her English shaky but adequate.

She had to get him to come closer.

'Shut up, bitch! Stay out of this.'

'Fuck you, bastard,' she replied.

The Englishman's face was distorted; he opened his mouth. Under different circumstances his expression might have looked hilarious.

'Whaaa d'you say?'

His voice hissed like a snake. She was trembling with rage.

'Fuck you,' she repeated, very loudly.

She saw the other two move and an alarm bell went off in her mind. Watch out: maybe they weren't as drunk as they seemed; they had managed to grasp, after all, that the situation was evolving.

The chubby little guy moved too; he took a step in her direction. Without knowing it, he had just entered her zone. Make a move, she thought, so intently she wondered if she hadn't said it out loud. *Make a move . . .*

He raised his hand to hit her. In spite of the booze and his excess weight, he was quick. And he was reckoning on the effect of surprise. With anyone else it would have worked – but not Irène. She stepped easily to one side and aimed a kick in the direction of the most vulnerable part of any male. Bingo, bull's eye. The redhead let out a shout and fell to his knees in the black sand. Irène saw one of the other two rush towards her and she was about to deal with him when she saw Zuzka empty her can of mace in his face as he went by. The second Englishman screamed, lifting his hands to his face and bending double. Weighing up the situation, the third man hesitated to get involved. Ziegler turned her attention back to the first. He was already back on his feet; she didn't wait for him to be fully upright but grabbed his wrist and rotated it in a movement she had learned at the academy, twisting his arm behind his back. She didn't stop, now that she had the advantage. If she let them get their wits about them, she and Zuzka would be fucked. Maintaining her momentum, she twisted his arm until a bone cracked somewhere. The redhead let out a roar like an injured animal. She let him go.

'She broke my arm! Fuck! She broke my arm, that dyke,' he whined, holding his shattered limb.

Ziegler sensed a movement to her right. She turned her head just in time to see a fist come in her direction. The shock made her head fly back and for a split second she felt as if she were being plunged underwater. It was the third yob – he'd eventually made a move. She fell stunned into the sand, and immediately afterwards felt a kick to her ribs. She rolled over to cushion the blow.

She waited for more blows. But to her great surprise, there weren't any. She raised her head and saw that Zuzka had jumped on the back of the third one and was clinging to him. With a quick glance Irène saw the second one was beginning to recover. She got to her feet and rushed to her girlfriend's aid, directing a kick straight into the guy's chest. He collapsed, his breath taken away. Zuzka pushed him over in the sand to get away from him.

The redhead hadn't completely given up. He rushed at Ziegler. This time, he held a blade in his good hand: she saw it gleam in the moonlight for a second. She stood easily to one side, grabbed the Englishman by his broken arm and pulled.

'Ahhhhhh!' he screamed, falling for the second time.

She let him go. She grabbed Zuzka by the hand.

'Come on, let's get out of here.'

The next instant they were fleeing, running flat out towards the lights, the music and their scooter.

'You're going to have nice black eye,' said Zuzka, caressing her swollen eyebrow.

Ziegler looked at herself in the bathroom mirror. A bump was starting to show, mustard yellow to violet. And around her eye, all the colours of the rainbow.

'Just what I needed to go back to work.'

'Lift your left arm,' said Zuzka.

She obeyed. And winced.

'Does it hurt there?'

'Ow!'

'You maybe have broken rib,' said Zuzka.

'I can't have.'

'Anyway, as soon as we get home, you go and see a doctor.'

Ziegler nodded, pulling on her tank top with some difficulty. Zuzka opened the minibar and took out two miniatures of Absolut and two bottles of fruit juice.

'And since we can't go out in this fucking rathole without getting attacked, we'll drink here. It will calm the pain. Whoever is less drunk puts the other one to bed.'

'It's a deal.'

The phone woke him up. He had dropped off on the sofa. He sat up, reached out towards the coffee table where his mobile phone was buzzing and vibrating like an evil insect.

'Servaz.'

'Martin? It's me. Did I wake you?'

Marianne's voice . . . The voice of someone at breaking point – and who had been drinking, also.

'Hugo's been remanded in custody. Did you know?'

'Yes.'

'Then for fuck's sake why didn't you call me?'

There was more than mere anger in her words. There was rage.

'I was going to, Marianne, I promise you . . . and then I . . . I forgot.'

148

'*Forgot?* Fuck, Martin, my son gets sent to jail and you forget to tell me?'

That wasn't entirely true. He had wanted to call, but he had hesitated for a long time. And he'd eventually fallen asleep, exhausted.

'Listen, Marianne, I . . . I don't think he's guilty. I . . . you have to trust me, I'll find the culprit.'

'Trust you? I don't know where I am any more . . . My thoughts are all over the place, I'm losing my mind, I picture Hugo all alone at night in that prison and I want to go mad. And you . . . you forget to call me, you don't say a thing, you act as if nothing had happened – and you let the judge send my son to jail even though you told me you believed he was innocent! And you want me to trust you?'

He would have liked to say something, to stick up for himself. But he knew it would be a mistake. The time wasn't right. There was a time for discussion and a time for silence. He had already made this mistake in the past: wanting to justify himself, whatever the cost, wanting to impose his point of view no matter what, to have the final word. It didn't work. It never worked. He had learned . . . He said nothing.

'Are you listening?'

'I've been doing nothing else.'

'Goodnight, Martin.'

She hung up.

Monday

19

Vertigo

On Monday morning Servaz had an appointment at the morgue for the autopsy results. Translucent windows. Long echoing corridors. Some laughter came from behind a closed door, then silence, and he was alone as he went down to the basement.

In his memory a little boy was dancing and running around his mother. Dancing and laughing in beams of sunlight. His mother, too, was laughing.

He banished the image and went through the swing doors.

'Good morning, Commandant,' said Delmas.

Servaz glanced over at the big table where Claire Diemar lay. From where he stood he could see her pretty profile. Except that her skull had been meticulously sawn open and he could see the grey mass of her brain gleaming in the neon light. The same went for her torso, split into a Y, her pink viscera showing on the surface of her abdomen. There were samples on a work surface, sealed in hermetically closed tubes. The rest had been put in a bin for anatomical waste.

Servaz thought of his mother. She had suffered the same fate. He looked away.

'Right,' said the little man, 'do you want to know whether she died in her bath? I may as well inform you straight away, deaths by drowning are a right nuisance. And when the drowning occurred in a bath, it's even worse.'

Servaz looked at him questioningly.

'Diatoms,' explained Delmas. 'Rivers, lakes and oceans are full of them. When water is inhaled, they spread throughout the organism. At present they are still the best sign of drowning we have. Except that urban water is very low in diatoms, so do you see my problem?'

The pathologist removed his gloves, tossed them into a pedal bin and went up to the tap.

'What's more, any traces of blows to the body are difficult to interpret because of the immersion. Fortunately she wasn't in the water for very long.'

'Are there traces of blows?' asked Servaz.

Delmas gestured towards the back of his own neck, his chubby pink hands covered in antiseptic soap.

'A haematoma on the parietal and a cerebral oedema. A very violent blow with a heavy object. I'd say her fate was sealed at that moment, but I suspect she actually died from drowning.'

'You *suspect?*'

The pathologist shrugged.

'I told you, the diagnosis is rarely straightforward in cases of drowning. Perhaps the analyses will tell us a bit more. The blood strontium, for example – if the concentration in the blood is very different from the usual, and very close to that of the water where she was found, we can be almost certain that she died at the time she was immersed in that bloody bath.'

'Hmm.'

'Same thing for the postmortem lividity: the water delayed it. And then the histological exam didn't come up with much, either . . .'

He seemed quite put out.

'And the torch?' asked Servaz.

'What about the torch?'

'What do you think of it?'

'Nothing. Interpretation is your job. I limit myself to facts. In any case, she panicked, and struggled so hard that the ropes left very deep wounds in her flesh. The question is to determine *when* she struggled. Which would in all likelihood exclude the hypothesis of a mortal blow to her skull.'

Servaz was beginning to have enough of the pathologist's cautiousness. Delmas was a competent guy, he knew. And it was precisely because he was competent that he was also extremely cautious.

'I'd prefer a conclusion that would be slightly more . . .'

'Precise? You'll get one, when they've done the tests. In the meantime I'd say there's a ninety-five per cent chance that she was put in that bath while still alive, and that she died from drowning. Not a bad likelihood, eh?'

Servaz thought about how the young woman must have panicked, fear exploding in her chest as the water rose, the dreadful sensation of suffocation. He thought about the pitilessness of the perpetrator, watching her die like that. The pathologist was right: interpretation was Servaz's job. And his interpretation told him that he was not dealing with an average killer.

'By the way, have you read the paper?' asked Delmas.

Servaz threw him a cautious glance. He hadn't forgotten the article he'd seen in Elvis's room. The pathologist turned round, reached for *La Dépêche* on a work surface and handed it to him.

'You should like this – page 5.'

Servaz turned the pages. He didn't have to go far. Huge headline: 'HIRTMANN WRITES TO POLICE.' For God's sake! The article was only a few lines, and reported an e-mail sent to *'Commandant Servaz of the regional crime squad'* by someone calling himself Julian Hirtmann. *'According to police sources, it has not been possible at this stage to determine whether it was from the Swiss killer or a hoaxer . . .'* Servaz couldn't believe it. He began to boil with rage.

'Great, isn't it?' said the pathologist. 'I'd love to know which wanker passed on the information. In any case, it must be someone from your squad.'

'I've got to go,' said Servaz.

Espérandieu was listening to 'Knocked Up' by the Kings of Leon when Servaz burst into the office.

'Have you seen your face?'

'Come with me.'

Espérandieu looked at his boss and understood that this was not a time for questions. He removed his headset and stood up. Servaz had already gone back out. He was striding towards the double doors and the corridor leading to the director's office. They went through the bulletproof door one after the other, past the little waiting room with its leather sofas, and past the reception desk.

'He's in a meeting!' shouted the secretary as she saw them go by.

Servaz did not stop. He knocked on the door and went in.

' . . . lawyers, notaries, auctioneers . . . We've been using kid gloves, but we haven't lost a thing,' Stehlin was saying to several members of the Financial Affairs Division. 'Martin, I'm in a meeting.'

Servaz went over to the big table and tossed the newspaper, open to page 5, in front of the director of the crime squad. Stehlin leaned over to look at it, examined the headline. And raised his head, jaws clenched.

'Gentlemen, we will conclude this meeting at another time.'

The four men got up and went out, their expressions full of surprise.

'The leak must be internal,' said Servaz at once.

Divisional Commissioner Stehlin was in his shirtsleeves. He had opened all the windows to let in the still relatively temperate morning air, and the noise from the boulevard filled the room. The air-conditioning had been out of order for several days. He nodded his head towards the chairs opposite his desk.

'Do you have any idea who it could be?' he enquired.

In one corner, a scanner was spitting out messages; the commissioner kept it turned on all the time. Servaz said nothing. He had noted Stehlin's tone and knew what this meant: beware of any unfounded accusations . . . He could not help but compare his new boss to his predecessor, Divisional Commissioner Wilmer, with his carefully groomed goatee and the smile plastered to his lips like a cold sore. For Servaz, the fact that Wilmer had filled this position was proof that an imbecile can go far if he has other imbeciles above him. At his farewell party, the atmosphere had been chilly and formal, and when Wilmer had embarked on his little thank you speech, the applause was reticent. Stehlin had kept his distance, not wearing a tie, in his shirtsleeves like he was today, looking like just another cop. And he had carefully observed his future colleagues. Servaz had observed him, too. He had concluded that his new boss must have grasped how much work lay ahead to repair the damage done by his predecessor. Servaz liked Stehlin. He was a good cop, had been in the field and knew his stuff – he was not some technocrat who opened his umbrella the minute there was a drop of rain.

'I am sure of one thing,' said Servaz. 'It isn't Vincent or Samira; I trust them one hundred per cent.'

'Then that doesn't leave too many possibilities,' said Stehlin.

'No.'

Stehlin looked unhappy. He crossed his fingers over the desk.

'What do you suggest?'

Servaz reflected.

'Let's leak some item only *he* could know. Some erroneous item . . . If it shows up tomorrow in the newspaper, we'll have killed two birds with one stone: we'll know for sure that it is *him,* and we'll be able to make a formal rebuttal, thus discrediting both the journalist and his source . . .'

He hadn't suggested any names, but he knew that the divisional commissioner and he were thinking of the same person. Stehlin nodded.

'An interesting idea . . . and what sort of information did you have in mind?'

'It has to be sufficiently credible for him to take the bait . . . and sufficiently important for the press to want to talk about it.'

'You've just come from the pathologist,' suggested Espérandieu. 'We could imply that Delmas found some vital clue. A clue that would prove the kid's innocence beyond a shadow of a doubt.'

'No,' said Servaz. 'We can't do that. But we can say we found a Mahler CD at Claire Diemar's . . .'

'But that's the truth,' said Stehlin, puzzled.

'Precisely. That's the trick. We'll give them the wrong title. When the time comes, we can say with complete sincerity that it was totally wrong, that we never found the Fourth Symphony at her place – without going on, obviously, to specify that we found another CD . . .' Servaz gave a twisted smile. 'Consequently, the Hirtmann connection to the Diemar case will be made to look ridiculous and the journalist who published the scoop will be discredited. I'm calling a meeting in five minutes with my team.'

He was already heading towards the door when Stehlin's voice stopped him.

'Did you say "Hirtmann connection"? Are you suggesting there is a Hirtmann connection?'

Servaz looked at his boss, shrugged as if to feign ignorance, and went out.

Distant rumbling, heat, motionless air and grey sky. The very countryside seemed expectant, frozen like an insect trapped in resin. Barns and fields looked deserted. At around three o'clock, he stopped for lunch at a roadside café where the men were chatting noisily about the performance of the French team and the incompetence of the coach. He gathered that the next match was against Mexico. Servaz almost asked them whether Mexico had a good team but caught himself in time. His sudden interest in the tournament caught him by surprise, and he realised that he was nourishing a secret hope: that the French team would be eliminated, and soon, so that they could get on with other things.

Lost in thought, he entered the paved streets of the little town almost without realising. He was thinking back to the lorry drivers' conversation in the restaurant, and he was suddenly struck by the fact that everything had happened on a Friday evening in the space of a few hours, during a football match that had the entire country glued to the television. That short period of time was where they had to look. They had to concentrate on what happened just before, and painstakingly reconstitute the unfolding of events. He took his thoughts one step further. He had to start at the beginning: the pub Hugo left a short while before the crime was committed. He was convinced that whoever they were looking for had not chosen the place or the time by chance. He parked his car on the little square beneath the plane trees, switched off the engine and looked at the terrace of the pub. It was packed with youthful faces. Students, boys and girls. As in his day, ninety per cent of the clientele was under twenty-five.

Margot Servaz poured herself an insipid coffee at the drinks dispenser in the hall, added an additional dose of sugar she had taken from the canteen, and rammed her earphones into her ears – a sign which meant 'don't bug me' – and glanced discreetly at David, Sarah and Virginie at the far end of the crowded, noisy hall. They had met up during the break. She bit her lower lip as she spied on them, pretending to be interested in the noticeboard. In the jumble of posters there was one advertising an 'END OF YEAR BALL 17 MAY ORGANISED BY THE MARSAC STUDENTS' ASSOCIATION' as well as 'FRANCE-MEXICO, GIANT SCREEN, THURSDAY, 17 JUNE, 20.30, HALL F IN THE SCIENCE FACULTY. COME ONE COME ALL! BEER AND TISSUES PROVIDED!' At the top someone had scribbled with a felt tip, in big red letters, 'SEND DOMENECH TO THE BASTILLE!'
  She was sorry she hadn't learned how to lip read. She averted her gaze when Sarah looked in her direction, pretended to be grumbling to herself as she rummaged in the change slot of the dispenser. When she looked up again, they were walking towards the courtyard. Margot followed, taking out her cigarette papers and her tobacco.
  She looked for them in the crowd. Spotted them. They'd split up.

Sarah and Virginie were smoking in silence; David had joined another group. She focused her attention on him. He had dropped out of sight for the entire weekend, but Margot knew that, like Elias and herself, he hadn't gone home. Where had he been? Ever since he'd shown up again he had seemed agitated and tense. David was Hugo's best friend. It was rare to see one of them without the other. She'd talked to him on several occasions and had found herself exasperated by his habit of never taking anything seriously, but she sensed that behind his joker-ish facade there was something serious, a hurt that sometimes troubled his gaze. It was as if the smile that constantly played on his lips was nothing but a shield. But what was he protecting himself from?

Margot knew that she had to focus her attention on him.

'Have . . . noticed . . . Davi . . . nerv . . . ?'

The words had difficulty penetrating the wall of sound in her ears, just as Marilyn Manson was screaming, 'Fuck! Eat! Kill! Now do it again!'

'Elias,' she said, noticing him.

She removed one of her earphones.

'I've been following you ever since we got out of class,' he said.

She raised an eyebrow. Elias was observing her from under his hair.

'Well?'

'I can see what you're up to – you're watching them. I thought you thought my idea was stupid?'

She shrugged, put her earphone back in place. He pulled it out.

'In any case, you should be a bit more discreet,' he shouted, too loudly, in her ear. 'Besides, I made enquiries: no one knows where David was this weekend.'

The Dubliners was run by an Irishman from Dublin who asserted, naturally, that Joyce was the greatest writer of all time. He had been there in Servaz's student days. Servaz and Francis had never known more than his first name: Aodhágán. He was always behind the bar. Like Servaz, Aodhágán was twenty years older now – except that in the old days he had been the age the cop was now.

Aodhágán's pub was the only one in Marsac where in addition to the wood and copper and the porcelain beer handles, you could find shelves full of books in English. The majority of the customers were students and representatives of the local Anglophone community. Servaz himself went there as a student several times a week, alone or with Van Acker and a few others, and from time to time he would take a book from the shelves while he drank a beer or a coffee. He spent glorious days lost in the pages of *Catcher in the Rye*, *Dubliners* or *On the Road* in the original, a voluminous Anglo-French dictionary at his side.

'Dear Lord, is that young Martin before me or am I seeing things?'

'Not so young any more, you old fogey.'

The Irishman's hair and beard were more grey than brown now, but he still looked like a cross between a commando and a DJ from a 1960s pirate radio station. He walked around the bar and gave Servaz a hug, patting him on the back.

'What have you been up to?'

Servaz told him. Aodhágán frowned.

'And here I thought you'd be the next Keats.'

Servaz could hear the disappointment in his voice, and for a fraction of a second he was overwhelmed with shame. Aodhágán gave him another pat on the back.

'This one's on me. What will you have?'

'Do you still have your famous stout?'

Aodhágán replied with a wink, his entire face creased with joy. When he came back with the beer, Servaz pointed to the seat next to him.

'Sit down.'

The Irishman gave him a look of surprise. And wariness. Even after all these years, he knew the tone – and he had no more affection for the French police than for the British.

'You've changed,' he said, pulling over a chair.

'Yes. I became a cop.'

Aodhágán looked down.

'If there's one job I could never have seen you in . . .' he said quietly.

'People change,' said Servaz.

'Not everyone . . .'

There was a note of pain in the Irishman's voice. As if it hurt him to call to the surface all the betrayals, denials and renunciations in his life. His own, or others'? wondered Servaz.

'I have a few questions for you.'

He looked at Aodhágán.

Who looked right back. Servaz felt that the mood was changing. They were no longer the Martin and Aodhágán of the old days. They were a cop and a bloke who didn't like dealing with cops.

'The name Hugo Bokhanowsky – does that mean anything to you?'

'Hugo? Of course it does. Everyone knows Hugo. He's a brilliant lad . . . a bit like you were, back in the day. No, more like Francis . . . You were more discreet, more withdrawn – even if you were every bit as brilliant.'

'Did you hear that he's been arrested?'

Aodhágán nodded his head in silence.

'He was in your pub on the evening Claire Diemar was killed. And according to witnesses he left the pub not long before the murder. Did you notice anything?'

The Irishman thought. Then he looked at Servaz the way the apostles must have looked at Judas.

'I was at the bar, serving, nowhere near the door . . . the pub was filled to bursting that night. And like everyone else, I was watching what was happening on the telly. No, I didn't notice anything.'

'Do you remember where Hugo and his friends were sitting?'

Aodhágán pointed to a table just below the television screen on the wall.

'There. They came early to get the best spot.'

'Who was at the table?'

Again, the Irishman thought.

'I can't be sure. But I think there were Sarah and David. Sarah, she's a beauty, the prettiest young woman to grace my pub. But she doesn't act the princess. A lovely girl. Bit of an introvert. Sarah, Virginie, David, Hugo: they're practically inseparable. They remind me of Francis, Marianne and you at that age . . .'

Servaz felt a serpent unwind in his belly and close round his insides.

'Do you remember? When you came here to transform the world, to talk politics . . . You talked about rebellion, revolution, changing the system . . . Ha! Ha! Dear Lord, youth is the same the world over! Marianne . . . she was something, do you remember? Even pretty Sarah can't touch her. Marianne drove you all mad, it was plain to see . . . and I've seen my share of pretty students. But Marianne was unique.'

Servaz gave him a sharp glance. He hadn't realised it at the time, but Aodhágán would only have been about forty in those days. Even he must not have been totally impervious to Marianne's charms. To that aura of mystery and superiority she gave off.

'David is Hugo's best friend.'

'I know who David is. And Virginie?'

'A little brown-haired girl, on the chubby side, with glasses. Very lively, very intelligent. A lot of authority. That girl is cut out to be a leader, believe me. And the others, as well. That's what you were all programmed for, wasn't it? To end up in charge, human resources directors, ministers, God knows what.'

Suddenly Servaz remembered something.

'There was a power outage when we arrived in Marsac on Friday night . . .'

'Yes, fortunately I have an emergency generator. It happened ten minutes before the end of the match . . . Dear Lord, I can't get over it,' mumbled Aodhágán.

'Get over what?'

'That you became a cop.' He let out a long sigh. 'You know, in the 1970s, I was a prisoner at Long Kesh, the most filthy prison in Northern Ireland. Have you heard about the H-blocks? Maximum-security quarters. They got the name because seen from the sky they formed a big letter H. Dilapidated facilities, filth, humidity, broken windows, lack of hygiene . . . And those bloody screws were right Nazis. In the winter it was so cold we couldn't sleep. I took part in the famous hunger strike in 1981, when Bobby Sands died after sixty-six days. I took part in the blanket strike in 1978, too, when we refused to wear the prison uniform, and we wandered around naked with nothing but flea-ridden blankets in spite of the freezing cold. The food they gave us was off, they beat us, tortured us and humiliated us. I never gave in, I didn't yield an inch. I hate uniforms, young Martin, even when they're invisible.'

'So it was true . . .'

'What was true?'

'That you belonged to the IRA.'

Aodhágán didn't answer.

'I heard that in those days the IRA behaved like a police force themselves in the ghettos,' suggested Servaz.

Anger flared in the Irishman's eyes. 'Hugo is a good kid,' he said, changing the subject. 'Do you think he's guilty?'

Servaz hesitated.

'I don't know. That's why you have to help me, whether I'm a cop or not.'

'I'm sorry, but I didn't see anything.'

'Maybe there's another way . . .'

Aodhágán gave him a questioning look.

'Talk about it to others around you, ask questions, try to find out if anyone saw or heard anything.'

The Irishman stared at him incredulously.

'You want me to play informant for the police?'

Servaz brushed aside his objection.

'I want you to help me get an innocent kid out of prison,' he retorted. 'A kid who, as of yesterday, is in provisional detention. A kid you care for. Is that enough to convince you?'

Once again, Aodhágán glared at him. Servaz saw him thinking.

'Here's the deal,' he said at last. 'I will share any information for the defence that happens to come my way, and keep anything incriminating to myself, whether it involves Hugo or anyone else.'

'For fuck's sake!' protested Servaz, raising his voice. 'A woman was killed – tortured and drowned in her bath! And there might be some sick fuck walking round scot-free, ready to do it again!'

'You're the cop,' said the Irishman, getting to his feet. 'Take it or leave it.'

At 17.31, he walked back out onto the little square. He looked at the sky; it was full of clouds as black as ink. The anxiety was still there. Servaz recognised the sensation in the pit of his stomach.

Friday evening, he thought. Hugo says he's not feeling well. It's not yet half eight, the match hasn't started. He starts walking towards his car. Someone comes out right behind him. Someone who blended into the crowd in the pub and who's been waiting for this moment.

An hour and a half later, Hugo will be found by the gendarmes at Claire Diemar's. So what happens in the seconds that follow his departure from the pub? Is he alone or is there someone with him? At what point does he lose consciousness?

Servaz swept his gaze over the car park. On the far side of the square was the tallest building in Marsac – ten floors of concrete

– an ugly wart in the middle of the little nineteenth-century buildings. On the ground floor there was a canine grooming salon, an employment agency and a bank. *The bank's surveillance cameras . . .* Servaz spotted them right away. There were two of them. The first one filmed the entrance, the second one the rest of the square. And the car park along with it. He swallowed. This would be really good luck, wouldn't it? Too good to be true. But he had to double-check all the same.

He locked the Jeep again and walked up the row of cars towards the camera.

And saw that it was pointed in the right direction. He turned back towards the entrance to the pub. It was at least twenty-five metres . . .It would all depend now on the quality of the image. The camera was probably too far away to identify anyone leaving the pub – unless, maybe, you already knew who you were looking at. And maybe, also, it wouldn't be too far away to see if someone did go out after Hugo . . .

He rang the doorbell to the bank and the mechanism buzzed to let him in. Inside, he walked across the big lobby past the clients who were waiting by the counter, and took out his warrant card.

He asked to see the director of the establishment immediately, and the employee picked up the telephone. Two minutes later a man in his fifties walked up to him, his hand held out but his expression impenetrable.

'Come with me,' he said.

In a glassed-in office at the end of the corridor, the director asked him to sit down. Servaz answered that it wouldn't be necessary. He explained quickly what his visit was about. The director placed a finger on his lower lip.

'I don't think that should be a problem,' he said finally, clearly relieved. 'Come with me.'

They left the office and crossed the hall. The man opened the door into a space the size of a box room, lit by a tiny window with frosted glass. On the table there was something that looked like an extra-flat DVD player and recorder, with a remote control. Next to it was a nineteen-inch screen. The director switched it on.

'There are four cameras in all,' he said, 'two inside and two outside. The insurance company didn't require even that much. They just wanted the cashpoint to be under video surveillance. Here we are.'

The director picked up the remote. A mosaic of four images appeared on the screen.

'It's this camera which interests me,' said Servaz, placing his finger on the rectangle showing the car park, on the upper left-hand side.

The director pressed the number four on the remote and the image filled the monitor. Servaz noticed that it was slightly blurry at the back, by the entrance to the pub.

'Does it record continuously or only when movement is detected?'

'Continuously for the indoor cameras, except the one by the cashpoint, which is on a sensor and records when there's movement. The recordings are on a loop.'

Servaz was disappointed.

'So does this mean that the recording from last Friday was taped over during the days that followed?' he said.

'I don't think so, no,' smiled the director. 'The camera you're talking about also works on a sensor, like the cashpoint one. It only comes on when there is something going on in the car park, which happens fairly regularly during the day but not much at night. Also, the camera records a limited number of images per second to save space. And if my memory serves me well, it has a hard disk of one teraoctet. That ought to be plenty. We keep the recordings as long as is legally required.'

Servaz felt his pulse increase slightly.

'Don't ask me how it works,' said the director, handing him the remote. 'Would you like me to call the guy who installed it? He could be here in half an hour.'

Servaz looked at the clock in the corner of the screen. Then at a sheet of paper in a plastic sleeve taped to the table. At the top was written 'Surveillance System – Operating Instructions'.

'No need, I should be able to manage on my own.'

The director looked at his watch.

'We're closing in less than ten minutes. Maybe you could come back tomorrow . . .'

Servaz thought about this. He was overwhelmed by curiosity and a sense of urgency. He didn't want to waste a single minute.

'No, I'll stay here. Tell me how to lock up behind me.'

The director seemed annoyed.

'I can't leave the bank open like that after closing time,' he protested. 'Even if you are inside.' He hesitated for a second. 'I'll lock you in.

But I'll switch off the alarm: I don't want you setting it off without realising then have the gendarmerie show up.' He showed Servaz the screen of his BlackBerry. 'When you're finished, call me on this number, and I'll come and lock up behind you and turn on the alarm. I live right nearby.'

Servaz entered the banker's number into his phone. The director went back out, but he left the door to the box room ajar. Servaz heard the last clients leaving, then the employees gathered their belongings, said goodbye, and left the establishment in turn.

'Will you be okay?' asked the director five minutes later, sticking his head through the door, a briefcase in his hand.

Servaz nodded, even though he was beginning to wonder. The operating instructions seemed bloody complicated – at least for someone like him who had a serious technology handicap. He began by manipulating the buttons on the remote; the image disappeared then came back; then he got a full-screen image, but it was the wrong one. He swore to himself. Nowhere in the bloody instructions could he find how to replay the recordings. Obviously . . . had he ever found a single instruction manual that was useful from first page to last?

At 18.45, he realised he was in a sweat. It had to be 35 degrees in the room. He opened the little window, which was protected by two thick bars embedded in the wall. It had started raining again, and the sound of the rain entered the tiny space at the same time as the welcome cool air.

At 19.07 he finally understood what he had to do. When he managed to get the camera recordings that had filmed the car park, he realised there was only one way to get to the scene he was looking for – if it existed – that had occurred slightly before 20.30 the previous Friday: fast-forward the recording.

He made a first attempt but, mysteriously, the fast-forward jammed after a few minutes and the recording went back to the beginning.

'Shit, shit, shit!'

His voice echoed down the empty corridor and lobby. He took a deep breath. Calm down. You'll get there. He decided to fast-forward the recording up to a certain point, then watch it normally, then fast-forward it again a bit further along.

At 19.23 his heart began to beat more quickly. 20.12 said the screen. He pressed play, at normal speed. Something had set off the camera at that moment. A car was leaving the car park. A succession of fixed images. Servaz watched the car drive by the camera. A flash of lightning lit up the screen. The storm broke over Marsac, the vehicle's windscreen wipers came and went and it was virtually impossible to see anything inside. Until he was able to make out for a fleeting moment a couple in their fifties . . . Once again, he was disappointed. The recording stopped, then switched back on at 20.26. Another car went by, behind the curtain of rain and the car park. The light was fading, but the system made up for it. In the background, however, the entrance to the pub was getting more and more blurry. He wondered if he would be able to make out anything at all if someone were to leave at that moment . . . He rubbed his eyelids. His eyes were burning from staring at the screen. The sound of the rain was deafening. It was as if it were coming from the recording. Suddenly he stiffened. *Hugo* . . . He had just come through the door of the pub. In spite of the storm and the blurry image, there could be no doubt. The clothes were the same ones he had been wearing the night of the murder. The haircut and shape of the face matched. Servaz swallowed, aware that the seconds that followed would be decisive.

Go on, go ahead . . .

His eyes riveted to the screen, he saw the young man walk across the square between the cars. The speed of a dozen images per second made his progress seem somewhat choppy. The young man stopped suddenly in the middle of the street, raised his eyes to the sky, and stood there for a few seconds.

What the fuck are you doing, for Christ's sake?

Hugo was so motionless that Servaz wondered if the image weren't stuck again. At the same time, he watched the entrance to the pub. But nothing was happening there . . . His sweating fingertips left a damp trace on the remote. *Come on . . .* Servaz tried to make out the car, the one that Hugo had left outside Claire Diemar's place, but he couldn't see it. It must be there, though, somewhere, in that row . . . Suddenly, Hugo pivoted to the right and disappeared. *Shit!* There was some sort of equipment shed right in the middle of the car park, and Hugo had parked behind it! Servaz swore once again and was about to bang his fist on the table when, in the background, the door to the pub opened . . .

Jesus Christ!

He'd been right. He opened his mouth, eyes glued to the screen. There was just a chance. A very slight one. Tiny even. *Come closer* . . . The figure turned into the car park, walking towards the camera, also with that slightly jerky gait, heading towards the spot where Hugo had parked. Servaz's throat went dry. The newcomer was tall and thin. He was wearing a sweatshirt with the hood pulled up. Shit! Suddenly, Servaz was certain he would not see his face and he was filled with rage. But at least there was one positive thing: this recording would lend greater credibility to Hugo's statements. Even if it did not constitute definitive proof. The silhouette in the hoodie disappeared in turn behind the equipment shed.

And now?

There was still a slight chance . . . The car had to back up, and come into the camera's visual field at some point. Maybe he'd be able to see who was driving. Servaz waited, his throat tight, his nerves on edge. Too long. It was taking too long . . . Something was going on.

A sound.

He sat up straight as if someone had kicked him. He'd heard something – not from outside, but in the bank.

'Is there anyone there?'

No answer. Maybe he'd imagined it. There was so much noise from the rain through the window that he couldn't be sure. He wanted to turn his attention back to the screen. *No, he had heard something* . . . He pressed the pause button and stood up. Went out into the corridor.

'Hey! Who's there!'

His voice echoed down the corridor. On the far side was a metal emergency exit door with a horizontal bar. It was locked.

He hesitated, then finally began walking towards the lobby. No one. The counter, the rows of coloured armchairs, the white line . . . The lobby was deserted. He turned around.

Except . . . He could feel it now . . .

A draught, ever so slight.

A draught, between the window of the box room and . . . another window open somewhere. He swung around in the middle of the lobby and looked through the glass doors at the deserted square. The doors were locked. Inside, darkness was creeping into every corner of the lobby. Darkness and silence. It was as if someone were rubbing a grater over his nerves. He felt for the gun on his hip, and opened the holster. A gesture he had not made in many months, not since that winter of 2008, to be exact.

Not since Hirtmann . . .

Servaz walked past the counter. There was a second corridor on the other side. Now he was taking measured steps, his weapon firmly in his hand. He hoped no one would pass the glass doors of the bank just then and notice him. He wasn't altogether sure this wasn't simply a fit of paranoia. Nevertheless, he kept his weapon in the prescribed position, hoping he wouldn't have to use it. Sweat trickled from his eyebrows into his eyes, and he blinked.

The other corridor was not as long as the first one. There was only one door, leading to the toilets.

He bent his knees, held his hand down to the ground, to the gap of two centimetres beneath the door.

The draught was coming from there.

He opened the door very slowly, encountering a slight resistance from the door closer. A smell of industrial cleaner. All of a sudden the draught of air increased and more than ever he was on his guard. The door to the men's toilets.

It was open.

Someone had forgotten to close that window, and as the director had not connected the alarm system, no one had noticed. He was trying to think of a simple explanation. The idea that someone might have come into the bank to go after him, when they could easily have gone after him anywhere and at any time, seemed terribly far-fetched.

He stood with both feet on the toilet bowl and pulled himself up to the little window. It had the same bars as in the box room. There was nothing to see here. He was climbing back down when he heard a new sound, outside the toilets but inside the bank. This time, the blood surged into his veins like water from a dam into a turbine. Now he was afraid. He turned to the door, heart pounding, legs like jelly. *There was someone out there* . . . He tightened his hold on his gun, but his hand slipped on the moist grip.

Call for back-up. But what if he was mistaken? He could just see the headlines: *Cop Loses It in Empty Bank.* He could also call the director and tell him that he couldn't play the recordings. And then?

Would he stay locked inside here waiting for someone to show up? He had got as far as this in his deliberations when he heard the sound of the emergency exit door closing with a bang.

Bloody hell!

He rushed out of the toilets and past the counter, skidded at the corner and ran as fast as he could to the end of the corridor. He went through the same metal door. A stairway. He heard footsteps above him. *Shit!* He took off after them. Two flights of concrete stairs and a door between each floor. The stairs vibrated beneath his feet. He listened out to try and hear whether the fugitive had left the staircase, but he felt certain that he was still climbing. After three flights, Servaz was out of breath, his chest burning. He clung to the metal railing. On the sixth floor, he stopped to catch his breath, bent double, his hands on his knees. His lungs were making a wheezing sound. His target was continuing to climb: he could feel the vibrations beneath his feet. He resumed his climb. He had reached the seventh floor when a metal door squealed, then banged noisily, closing above him. He opened the door to the seventh floor. It didn't squeal and didn't close, either. So he hadn't gone through there . . . His heart was pounding fit to burst. For a split second he wondered if he might die of a heart attack, climbing up some stairs in pursuit of a murderer.

He continued on up past the eighth floor.

His muscles were like cement when he finally made it up the last two flights of stairs. *The roof* . . . The metal sound had come from here. This was where they were hiding. Servaz's apprehension returned, full blast. He recalled the investigation in the Pyrenees. The vertigo. His fear of the void. He hesitated.

He was soaked in sweat. As he passed his weapon from one hand to the other, he wiped his palms on his trousers, then sponged his face with the back of his sleeve. He waited for his heart to ease a little, and he stared at the closed metal door.

What was behind it? What if this were a trap?

He knew that his fear would make him weak. But he had a weapon . . .

And what if the fugitive was armed, too?

He hesitated, unsure how to proceed. At the same time, impatience and urgency were snapping at his heels. He placed a trembling hand on the metal bar. The door squealed when he pushed it. He was immediately overwhelmed by the storm: lightning, wind and rain. The wind was much stronger up here, out in the open. The soles of his shoes crunched on gravel. The terrace was a vast flat space with a concrete edge not more than twenty centimetres high. His stomach went into a knot. He could see the roofs of Marsac below. He let the door close behind him. Where had they gone? The wind mussed his hair. He looked to the left and the right: a row of masonry pillars one metre high, with openings for ventilation, rose up out of the roof. There were also huge pipes running along the ground, and three satellite dishes – and that was all.

Where had they gone?

It was raining harder than ever, pounding on his skull, streaming down his face. Black clouds hovered above the town. The hills were pale in the lightning. He felt as if he were suspended in mid-air.

The wind in his ears.

A sound, over to the left . . .

He turned his head, his gun pointed. At the same time his brain analysed the situation, and in flash he knew it was a trap. A pebble, an object . . . Something had been tossed that way to lure him in the wrong direction.

Too late he heard the footsteps running towards him, and he felt a brutal blow against his spine as he was rammed full on, seized by the waist and thrust forward. His legs arched. He let go of his gun, his hands flapping at the air.

He was hustled along, dragged. His aggressor had the advantage of the initial impulse and surprise. And before he even had time to react, he was being propelled at full speed towards the edge of the roof.

The void.

'NOOOO!'

He heard himself scream, watched as the edge of the roof and the entire countryside leapt up to meet him, altogether too quickly, despite the soles of his feet desperately clinging to the gravel.

Ten storeys.

His vision grew larger and blurred, distorted by fear, rain, vertigo . . . He screamed again. He saw the entire square in the darkness, the row of balconies below him, the vertical, convergent lines of the rain, the toes of his shoes striking the concrete edge. His body plunging forward, hovering perilously.

For a split second he swung out over the edge of the abyss, and was only kept from falling by a hand at his back.

Then he felt a violent blow to his head. He fell into a black hole.

Irène Ziegler and Zuzka Smatanova landed at Toulouse-Blagnac airport from Santorini at 20.30 that night. They claimed their luggage and headed towards Hall D. From there a free shuttle would take them to the 'budget' car park where their car had been waiting for a month. Altogether, 108 euros in parking fees. Ziegler had spent the entire trip calculating the amount in her head. Her girlfriend had paid for almost all of their holiday; Irène had paid only for her return ticket and two restaurants. No doubt about it, a stripper and nightclub manager earned more money than a gendarme. Irène had already wondered what her superiors would say if they ever found out that her partner was the manager of a strip joint, but she had decided once and for all that if she ever had to choose between her job and Zuzka, she would not hesitate for a second.

They were dragging their wheeled suitcases behind them, looking out of the window at the downpour, already nostalgic for the Greek sunshine, when they went past a newspaper stand. Irène stopped short.

'What is it?' asked Zuzka.

'Wait.'

Zuzka gave her a questioning look. Irène had put down her suitcase. She went up to the display: the photo was poor quality but the face was familiar. Martin Servaz was looking at her from the front page of the newspaper, his face white from the flashbulbs. The headline declared, HIRTMANN WRITES TO POLICE.

20

Clouds

Grey, bruised clouds, bulbous as mushrooms. Piled high in the sky like monuments. As he looked up at them, he felt a drop of rain hit his cornea. Hard as a marble. Then a second, and a third. He blinked. Rain was hitting him in the face. With his mouth open, he felt it on his tongue.

There was a terrible pain at the back of his skull, where his head was resting on the gravel. He raised his head; the pain grew worse, spread like tentacles around his neck and shoulders. Wincing, he rolled over to one side, to the left. He found himself staring out into the abyss, and a wave of nausea came over him. He was lying on the edge of the roof! Only a few centimetres from a fatal fall. Terrified, he rolled the other way, then crawled out of harm's way before getting up on his shaky legs.

He raised one hand to his skull and touched it cautiously. The pain immediately radiated throughout his head and he took his hand away. But he had had time to feel the enormous bump beneath his scalp. He looked at his fingers, and rain washed away the blood. It didn't necessarily mean anything: the scalp always bled abundantly.

He saw his gun a bit further away. He took two steps and bent down to pick it up. He dragged himself over to the metal door, which, on this side, was equipped with a handle. He tried to figure out what had happened.

And he knew at once. *The recording . . .*

He hurried unsteadily down the stairway from the roof, opened the door to the tenth floor and rushed over to the lifts. Once he was on the ground floor, he looked for the door to the staircase. He went through it and located the bank's emergency exit. The automatic door closer had shut it. He went back out of the building and over to the glass doors of the bank. They were locked, and he could not get back in. He took out his telephone and called the manager.

'Have you finished?'

'No. But something happened.'

Five minutes later, a Japanese 4x4 pulled onto the square. The manager got out and came over, looking worried. He typed in a code and Servaz heard the buzzing of the electronic lock. He pushed open the door and hurried to the box room.

The little recorder had vanished. All that was left were the cables on the table.

This was what his attacker had wanted. To get hold of the recording. *He had taken a considerable risk. Without a doubt, that's who it was . . . the person in the hoodie.* He was the one who had killed Claire Diemar, who had drugged Hugo. Servaz no longer had any doubts. He had been there all that time, spying on him, following him. He had seen him go up to the surveillance camera and into the bank. He had realised what Servaz was about to do. He had no way of knowing whether someone would recognise him, so he had taken a crazy risk. He must have got into the bank with the other clients, then gone to the toilets and stayed there until closing time. Then he had lured Servaz away from the box room and he had stolen the hard drive and disappeared. Or something to that effect.

Servaz let out an oath.

'Do you think he was on that recording . . . that he came into *my* bank . . . the man who killed that young woman?'

The manager's voice was almost trembling: he was beginning to realise what had happened. He had gone pale. Servaz was in such pain that it was as if someone were ramming a metal bar into his skull. He had to see a doctor. He called the CSI people and asked them to send a team over.

'You can go home,' he said to the manager.

Then he left the room and went into the lobby. With every step his shoes squelched with water. From a big cardboard display, a pretty employee gave him a radiant smile. Around her neck she was wearing a scarf with the bank's colours. Servaz suddenly found himself cursing all those ad men who, with their psychological manipulation, polluted everyone's daily lives, everyone's minds, and practically every aspect of existence from birth to death. That evening he was angry with the entire world. He let the doors shut again behind him, and in the shelter of an overhanging balcony he lit a cigarette. No matter how he analysed what had just happened, he always came to the same conclusion: *he had let the murderer slip through his fingers.*

It was getting darker and darker. The shadows were lengthening beneath the trees on the square. He looked at his watch. Half past ten. The forensic team wouldn't get here for a good hour at least.

His stomach was churning with fear. He was aware that some-where, not far away, lurked a murderer who did not hesitate to go after the police, acting with terrifying determination and sang-froid. Servaz felt the hair on his neck rise at the thought.

His mobile buzzed in his pocket. He looked at the number: Samira.

'They've identified Thomas999,' she said. 'His name isn't Thomas at all.'

Suddenly he was miles away from the bank.

'You're not going to believe it,' she told him.

Someone knocked on the door. Margot looked over at her sleeping roommate, then at her laptop on the bed, and checked the time in the corner of the screen. 23.45. She got up and opened the door. It was Elias. His pale, moonlike face – or at least the half that wasn't hidden by his hair – stood out against the darkness of the corridor.

'What the fuck are you doing in the girls' dormitory? Don't you know how to text?'

'Come with me,' he said.

'What?'

'Get a move on.'

She was on the verge of slamming the door in his face, but his tone dissuaded her. She went back to her bed, grabbed a pair of shorts and a T-shirt and pulled them on. It was almost midnight, she had been in her bra and knickers, and Elias hadn't paid the slightest attention to her body, although she knew that in general boys liked it. There were two possibilities: either he really was a virgin, the way some girls said he was, or he was gay, which was what some of the boys said.

They headed towards the stairs. At the bottom of the steps, in the lobby, two marble busts watched as they opened the door leading out to the garden. Outside, there was a lull in the storm. Between the clouds the moon clawed at the night like a pale fingernail.

'Where are we going?'

'They've gone out.'

'Who?'

He rolled his eyes.

'Sarah, David and Virginie. I saw them go into the maze, one after the other. They must have agreed to meet there. We have to hurry.'

'And what if we run into them? What will we say?'

'We'll ask them what they're doing there.'

'Great.'

They hurried into the shadow. They went past the statue beneath the tall cherry tree and entered the maze, slipping under the rusty chain. Elias stopped to listen. Margot did likewise. Silence. Everywhere the vegetation was shaking in the wind, dripping, anticipating the next shower. This made it difficult to identify any other sounds, but it also hid any that they might make.

She saw Elias hesitate then turn left. At every turn, she was afraid they would run into the threesome. The hedges had not been trimmed in a long time and now and again a branch scratched against her face in the dark. The cloud cover had returned. She couldn't hear anything but the sound of the wind, and she was beginning to wonder whether Elias was mistaken.

Until suddenly they heard their voices. Right nearby.

Ahead of her Elias stopped and raised his hand, like in war films where commandos lurk in enemy territory. She almost laughed. But deep down she was beginning to feel very uneasy. She held her breath. They were right there, around the next bend. They took two more steps and this time they heard David's voice, loud and clear.

'It's scary, bloody horrible,' he was saying.

'What else can we do?'

Margot immediately recognised Sarah's soft, veiled voice. 'All we can do is wait . . .'

'We can't just leave him,' protested David.

Margot felt an electric current go through the down on her arms. She had only one desire: to go back to her bedroom. David's voice was a toneless moan. His speech was approximate, tripping haltingly over certain syllables. As if he were drunk, or high.

'I have a bad feeling about it. There's . . . surely there's something we can do . . . Shit, we can't just . . . We can't just abandon him.'

'Shut up.'

Virginie's voice. Sharp as a whip.

'You're not going to crack now, do you hear?'

But David didn't seem to hear. Through the hedge Margot detected a sobbing sound. Like a dull, prolonged moan. Or teeth grinding.

'Oh, shit, shit, shit,' he groaned. 'Fuck, fuck . . .'

'You're strong, David. And we're here. We're your only family, don't forget that. Sarah, Hugo, me and the others . . . We're not going to abandon Hugo.'

A silence. Margot wondered what Virginie was talking about. David came from a well-known family: his father was the CEO of the Jimbot group. By greasing palms at every level, by making a fuss over the deputies and financing their electoral campaigns, he had landed the vast majority of contracts for motorways, public works and regional development in recent decades. David's older brother had studied in Paris and at Harvard and had gone on to run the family business with their father. David hated them, Hugo had told her one day.

'We have to call an urgent meeting of the Circle,' said David suddenly.

Another silence.

'We can't. The meeting will be held on the seventeenth, as planned. Not before.'

Virginie's voice again. Full of authority.

'But Hugo is in prison!' moaned David.

'We won't abandon Hugo. Ever. That cop will eventually get the picture and, if we have to, we'll help him . . .'

Margot felt the blood draining slowly from her face. The way Virginie had spoken about her father sent a chill down her spine; there was something shockingly brutal about the girl's voice.

'That cop is Margot's father.'

'Exactly.'

'Exactly what?'

Silence. Virginie did not answer.

'Don't worry, we'll keep an eye on him,' she said finally. 'And his daughter, too.'

'What you talking about?'

'I'm simply saying that we have to make that cop understand that Hugo is innocent . . . one way or the other . . . and as for everything else, we have to be careful . . .'

'Haven't you noticed lately that every time you turn your head she's there?' said Sarah. 'Always hanging about wherever we happen to be . . .'

'Who is?'

'Margot.'

'Are you implying that Margot is spying on us? That's absurd!'

That was David. Elias gave Margot a questioning look in the darkness. She blinked nervously.

'What I mean is, we have to be careful. That's all.'

Sarah's voice, fluid as an icy stream. Margot suddenly felt it was time to get out of there.

Suddenly her smartphone rang out from her pocket, quietly but clearly, the sound of a harp. Elias cast her a furious glance, his eyes as round as saucers. Margot's heart flipped over.

'I'll talk to her if you want—' David began.

'Shh! What was that noise? Didn't you hear?'

'What noise?'

'It sounded like . . . a harp, something like that . . . there . . . just nearby.'

'I didn't hear anything,' said David.

'I heard it too,' said Sarah. 'There's someone here!'

'*Run,*' murmured Elias in Margot's ear. He grabbed her hand and they began to sprint towards the way out, not even trying to hide their presence.

'Fuck!' screamed David. 'There was someone there!'

They heard him take off after them, followed by the other two. Elias and Margot were running as fast as their legs could carry them, taking the corners as quickly as possible, brushing against the hedge as they went by. Behind them, the others were running too, and Margot could hear the pounding of their footsteps. She felt as if her blood were trying to burst through her temples. As if the corners and lanes of the maze would never end. When they scrambled underneath the chain at the entrance, the rusty sign scratched her back and she winced with pain. She wanted to go the way they had come, but Elias yanked her back.

'Not that way!' he muttered in rebuke. 'They'll see us.'

He pulled her in the opposite direction, dodging into a narrow space between two hedges she hadn't been aware of, and they found themselves in complete darkness under the trees. They zigzagged between the tree trunks and emerged in front of the large windows of the semi-circular amphitheatre. They went around the side to a little door she had never noticed. She saw Elias rummage in his pockets, then, to her great surprise, insert a key in the lock. A second later they were inside, their running footsteps echoing down the deserted corridors.

'Where did you get that key?' she asked as she ran behind him.

'Later!'

A staircase. It wasn't the one they had taken. This one was older and narrower and it smelled of dust. They climbed up to the floor where the dormitories were. Elias opened the door. Margot couldn't believe it: they were just outside the girls' dormitory. The door to her room was only a few metres away.

'Hurry!' he murmured. 'Don't get undressed! Get in bed and pretend you're asleep!'

'What about you?' she asked.

'Don't worry about me, run!'

She obeyed and hurried to her door, opened it, and looked behind her: Elias had disappeared. She closed the door and was beginning to unbuckle the belt of her shorts when she remembered his words. She lifted the sheet and slipped underneath.

A few seconds later her pulse went wild when she heard rapid footsteps coming down the corridor; and when someone turned the door handle she froze with fear. She closed her eyes and left her mouth slightly open like someone who's sleeping, trying to breathe deeply and calmly. Through her closed lids she could sense the light from a torch playing over her face. She was sure that from where they were standing they must be able to hear her heart pounding wildly, and see the sweat on her forehead and the blush on her skin.

Then the door closed, the footsteps faded away and she heard Sarah and Virginie go into their room.

She opened her eyes in the dark. White spots were dancing before them.

She sat up in bed. She was trembling from head to toe.

21

Roman Holiday

The radio was switched on. The voice in the speakers was deep and steady. 'What does an MP's job consist of? Spending one's time on charitable committees, at neighbourhood meetings and departmental assemblies, applauding speeches, inaugurating supermarkets, being an expert on local boxing, shaking hands and knowing when to say yes. Above all when to say yes. Most of my colleagues do not believe that the evils of society can be resolved by any particular legislation, nor do they believe that promoting social progress is part of their job description. They believe in the religion of privilege, the creed of greed and the dogma of perks – for themselves, naturally.'

Servaz leaned closer and turned up the volume, not taking his eyes from the road. The voice filled the car. This was not the first time he had heard it. With his insolence, youth, and gift for sound-bites, the speaker had become the darling of the media. The one who got invited to all the talk shows and morning radio programmes, the one who gave his listeners a hard-on.

'Are you referring to your political opponents or those who are on your side?' asked the presenter.

'Weren't you listening? I said "most of". Have you heard me talking in a partisan manner?'

'Well, I just hope you realise you won't be making friends by saying things like that.'

Another pause. Servaz could still feel the sharp pain throbbing like a vein at the back of his skull. He checked the screen of his GPS. The forest whizzed by in the beam of his headlights. There were white fences, lampposts every fifty metres, and the sides of the road were carefully maintained. Behind the trees he could make out spacious modern houses.

'Voters elected me so I would tell them the truth. Do you know why people vote? For the illusion that they are in control. Control is as important to humans as it is to rats. In the 1970s researchers showed that by giving electrical shocks to two groups of rats, the ones that had the means to control the shocks had more antibodies and fewer ulcers.'

'Perhaps that's because they received fewer shocks,' joked the presenter lamely.

'Well, this is what I do and what I want to go on doing,' continued the voice, unruffled. 'To give control back to my constituents. And not just the illusion of control. That is why they elected me.'

Servaz slowed down. Hollywood. That's what all these illuminated houses among the trees made him think of. Not a single one smaller than 300 square metres. Straight out of the pages of a home decoration magazine, with vintage wines in the cellar and jazz turned on low.

'We have one representative for every 100 inhabitants in this country, and one doctor for every 300. Don't you think it ought to be the other way around? A certain sum is allocated, up there at the top, at the very top, to be used for this or that purpose, and then – how should I put it? – the money . . . *trickles down* . . . and at every level in between a part of the total evaporates. By the time it gets to the bottom, and reaches the people or purpose for which it was intended, most of it will have vanished in operating costs, salaries, contract awards, and so on.'

'You're just saying this because the left won almost every region last March,' said the presenter dryly.

'Of course. Still, you pay taxes, don't you? I am willing to bet that—'

Servaz turned the sound off. He was almost there. The programme may have been recorded, but there was no guarantee he would find his prey at home. However, this was where he wanted to meet him. Not back at the precinct. He hadn't informed anyone of his plans, other than Samira and Espérandieu. Vincent had simply said, 'Are you sure you haven't got things the wrong way round?'

What had the honourable member just said? *Control is as important to humans as it is to rats* . . . Well, it is indeed, he'd buy that, and that's why he wanted to keep control over his own investigation.

Servaz left the road. The drive led straight ahead for a dozen metres or so, ending in front of a building that gave onto the woods and which was just the opposite of Marianne's house: it was modern, one storey, all concrete and glass. But it was certainly no bigger than Marianne's house. After the north shore of the lake, this neighbourhood nestled among the trees was the most elegant in Marsac. Besides, Marsac was one of those towns that broke all the laws regarding low-cost housing quotas. And for good reason: there was hardly anyone who could afford to live there. Sixty per cent of the population was made up of university professors, executives, bankers, airline pilots, surgeons, and engineers from the aerospace industry in Toulouse. Which explained the two golf courses, the tennis club and the two-star Michelin restaurant. Marsac was a sort of chic suburb for the region's elite, a place where people kept to themselves, far from the turbulence of the big city.

Servaz switched off the ignition. He stared at the illuminated building and at the night falling with stifling slowness. Horizontal lines, a flat roof, large glass surfaces intersecting at right angles along an elevated terrace. The rooms – an ultramodern open-plan kitchen, lounge areas, corridors – were all completely visible, in spite of the Venetian blinds. It looked like something Mies Van der Rohe might have designed. Servaz told himself that Paul Lacaze, the rising star of the right, believed in his celebrity status to the point where he followed their taste in architecture. He opened the car door and got out. Someone was watching him through one of the picture windows. A woman . . . He saw her turn her head and speak to someone behind her.

Suddenly his telephone buzzed.

'Martin, are you all right? What's going on?'

Marianne . . . He looked for the woman in the picture window. She had vanished. A man's silhouette had replaced her.

'I'm all right. Who told you?'

'The director of the bank is a friend . . .' (*Of course*, he thought. Marianne herself had told him she knew everyone here.) 'Listen . . .' he heard her sigh on the other end of the line. 'I'm sorry about last night . . . I know you're doing what you can. I – I would like to apologise.'

'I have to go,' he said. 'I'll call you back.'

He turned his attention to the house. One of the glass doors had slid open and the silhouette was now standing on the terrace.

'Who are you?'

'Commandant Servaz from the crime squad,' he said, taking out his warrant card and starting up the stairs. 'Paul Lacaze?'

Lacaze smiled.

'Who do you think? Don't you ever watch television, Commandant?'

'Not really, no. But I just heard you on the radio . . . very interesting.'

'What brings you here?'

Servaz looked at him more closely. Forty years old. Medium height, solid build, Lacaze seemed to be in good physical shape. He was wearing a tracksuit with a hood which made him look like a boxer who'd just finished a workout. Which was what he was. A fighter. The type who would rather hit than dodge. The tracksuit wasn't the same as the one on the surveillance tape, but that didn't mean anything.

'Don't you know?'

His expression became less friendly.

'Claire Diemar,' said Servaz.

For a moment the MP stood stock still.

'Darling, what is it?' called a woman's voice behind him.

'Nothing. The monsieur is from the police. He's investigating that murder. And since I am deputy mayor of the town . . .'

Lacaze gave him a penetrating look. Servaz saw Lacaze's wife come forward through the glass door. She was wearing a scarf tied around her head with a curly wig underneath. Her eyebrows had been replaced by thick lines of black pencil and even in this dark grey half-light, she did not look well. In spite of that, she was still pretty. She held out her hand, and Servaz took it. Her hand in his weighed no more than a feather; it had neither strength nor energy.

In her eyes he read that the cancer was winning, and suddenly he felt like apologising and getting out of there.

'What a terrible business,' she said. 'That poor woman . . .'

'I won't take much of your time,' he said apologetically. 'It's a simple formality.'

He looked at her husband.

'Why don't we go to my study, Commandant?'

Servaz nodded. Lacaze pointed to the ground. Servaz looked down and saw a doormat. Obediently, he wiped his feet. Then they went into the house. Crossed a lounge where a large flatscreen television was showing a subtitled black-and-white film with the sound turned off. Servaz noticed two glasses half filled with Scotch on the coffee table, and a bottle on the bar counter. A corridor lit by spotlights. Lacaze opened a door at the end of it. The study was spacious, modern and comfortable, and the ebony walls were covered almost entirely with framed photographs.

'Have a seat.'

Lacaze went behind his desk and collapsed into an armchair. He switched on an anglepoise lamp. Servaz's chair was made of chrome tubes and supple leather.

'No one told me you were coming,' said Lacaze.

All his suave politeness had vanished.

'I took it upon myself.'

'Right. What do you want?'

'You know very well.'

'Get down to the facts, Commandant.'

'Claire Diemar was your mistress.'

Lacaze did not hide his surprise. Servaz was not so much asking him a question as asserting a statement.

'Who told you?'

'Her computer. However, someone went to the trouble to empty both her mailboxes, the one at work and the one at home. A rather stupid manoeuvre, if you want my opinion.'

Lacaze stared at him, clearly failing to understand. Or else he was a good actor.

'"Thomas999", that's you, isn't it? You were exchanging passionate e-mails.'

'I loved her.'

His answer, laconic and direct, took Servaz by surprise. Apparently Lacaze cultivated frankness in every domain. A sincere politician? Servaz was not so naïve as to believe that even one specimen of the species might exist.

'And your wife?'

'Suzanne is ill. I love her, Commandant. Just as I loved Claire. I know that must be hard for you to understand.'

More of this apparent frankness. Servaz was wary of people who made a show of honesty

'Are you the one who deleted Claire Diemar's e-mails?'

'What?'

'You heard me.'

184

'I don't know what you're talking about.'

'You know the usual question of an alibi,' he said.

'You're not being serious?'

'I am.'

'I don't have to answer.'

'That's true, but I would like you to all the same.'

'Shouldn't you have consulted the judge before coming to bother my wife and me at such a late hour? I suppose you've heard of parliamentary immunity?'

'The term is not unfamiliar.'

'So, you're talking to me as a witness, is that it?'

'Precisely. Just a little conversation between friends.'

'A conversation I can put an end to at any time.'

Servaz nodded.

The MP stared at him, then threw himself back into his armchair with a sigh.

'What time?'

'Friday. Between 19.30 and 21.30.'

'I was here.'

'Alone?'

'With Suzanne. We were watching a DVD. She likes American comedies from the fifties, you see. Lately, I've been doing everything I can to make her life more pleasant. Friday, let's see – it was *Roman Holiday*, I think, but you'll have to ask her. I'm not sure. She can testify to that if it comes to it . . . But it won't come to that, will it?'

'For the time being, this conversation does not exist,' confirmed Servaz.

'That's what I thought.'

Two boxers weighing in. Lacaze was gauging him. He liked his adversaries to be worthy.

'Tell me about *her*.'

Servaz used the pronoun intentionally. He knew what a strange chemistry the word could trigger in the brain of a man in love. He knew from experience.

And indeed, he saw Lacaze's gaze falter. Touché. The boxer took the blow.

'Oh . . . dear God . . . is it true what they say?'

Lacaze was struggling with the words.

'That she died . . . *tied up* . . . *drowned* . . . Oh, shit . . . I think I'm going to be sick.'

Servaz saw him leap out of his chair and rush to the door. But before he reached it, he'd already turned round. He swayed for a few seconds in the middle of the room, as if he were lying against the ropes, groggy, before he returned to his chair and collapsed into it – and the analogy continued in Servaz's mind: all that was missing now was a bucket and a second in the corner of the ring. A faint film of sweat was pearling on the man's forehead, and all the colour had drained from his face.

'Yes,' said Servaz gently, answering the question. 'It's true.'

Servaz saw Lacaze lower his head until he was almost touching the blotter with his forehead. His elbows on the desk, he put his hands behind his skull, interlacing his fingers.

'Claire . . . oh, fuck, Claire . . . Claire . . . Claire . . .'

Lacaze's voice was a long lament rising from the back of his throat. Servaz couldn't get over it. Either the man was madly in love with that woman, or he was the best actor on the planet. It was as if he didn't give a damn whether anyone saw him in this state.

Then he sat up. His red eyes looked daggers at Servaz. Servaz had rarely seen someone this upset.

'Did that kid do it?'

'Sorry. I can't answer that question.'

'But you must have a lead, at least?'

He asked this almost imploringly. Servaz nodded. Did he have one? He was beginning to wonder.

'I'll do everything I can to help you,' said Lacaze, gathering his wits. 'I want you to catch the scum who did it.'

'In that case, answer my questions.'

'Go ahead.'

'Tell me about her.'

Lacaze took a deep breath and, like the exhausted boxer back in the ring, he thrust himself forward.

'She was a very intelligent girl. Magnificent. Gifted. Claire had everything going for her, she was blessed by the gods.'

Blessed by the gods until Friday evening, thought Servaz.

'How did you meet?'

Lacaze told him. In detail. With, noted Servaz, a certain complacency. Every year since he had become the deputy mayor of Marsac,

186

he had been invited to visit the lycée. He knew all the teachers, and every member of staff: the lycée was window dressing for the town, attracting the best students in the region. He had been introduced to the new classics teacher. Something had happened the moment they met, he explained. They had chatted, with their drinks in their hands. She had explained to him that she used to teach French and Latin in a secondary school, and that she had obtained her accreditation and taught in another lycée before she was offered this prestigious post. He had immediately sensed that she was on her own and that she needed someone by her side. It had been clear in his mind that they would not leave things as they stood. And that was exactly what had happened, not even two days later, when they ran into each other at a car wash. They went straight from the car wash to the hotel. That was how it had begun.

'Was your wife already ill at that point?'

Lacaze jumped as if he'd been slapped.

'No!'

'And then?'

'The usual thing. We fell in love. I was a public figure. We had to be discreet. The situation was weighing on us. We would have liked to declare our love to the whole world.'

'She asked you to leave your wife and you didn't want to?'

'No. You've got it all wrong, Commandant. I wanted to leave Suzanne. And it was Claire who was against the idea. She said she wasn't ready, that it would ruin my career, she refused to take that responsibility, since she didn't know whether she wanted to share my life.'

There was a hint of regret in his voice.

'And then Suzanne fell ill and everything changed . . .' He gave Servaz a wounded look, his eyes infinitely sad. 'My wife made it clear to me that I had a destiny, that Claire was too self-centred, too focused on herself to help me attain it. That she was the type of woman who never brings anything to others but drains them of their substance in order to nourish her own. She made me promise, if she were to die, not to give up my future for . . . for *her* . . .'

'How did she find out about your affair?'

He saw the man's eyes cloud over.

'She had found clues, and conducted her own little investigation. My wife used to be a journalist. She has a good nose.'

'Do you smoke?'

Lacaze raised an eyebrow.

'Yes.'

'What brand?'

Lacaze gave him an intrigued look, but answered all the same.

'So you had been to Claire's house?'

'Yes. Of course.'

'You weren't afraid that someone would see you?'

He saw Lacaze hesitate.

'There is a passage . . . through the woods, which leads straight to her garden.' Servaz did not show any reaction. 'On the far side, there is a little picnic area, in the forest, by the side of the road. I would park there and go the rest of the way on foot. The path is virtually impossible to find if you don't know it's there. The only people who could have seen me were the neighbours across the street: their windows overlook Claire's garden. But it was a risk I was willing to take. And I always wore a hood.' He smiled. 'It was hard on us, but it was exciting too, to be honest. We felt like conspirators. Teenagers who have run away. You know, the "us against the world" syndrome.'

At the end his voice cracked: the best memories became crosses that were hard to bear under certain circumstances, thought Servaz. What about the passage through the woods: would Lacaze have mentioned it to him if he were the man who was spying on Claire, smoking in the hedge? Had he spied on her and discovered that she was seeing someone else? Hugo? . . . He always wore a hood – was it Lacaze he had seen on the video? The figure had seemed taller and thinner, but he could be wrong. Why had Lacaze felt he ought to mention it? Was the politician unconsciously challenging him to prove his guilt?

'Well, do you have any other questions?'

'Not for the time being.'

'Good. As I told you, I will do everything in my power to help you; on the other hand, you must be aware of my position.'

Clearly Lacaze had his wits about him again. Servaz gave him a look that was deliberately confused.

'My position as a public figure,' explained the politician, annoyed. 'The political class in this country is dying. Moribund. We have no more faith in ourselves, we've been sharing power for so long that we no longer have the slightest new idea, or the slightest hope of changing anything. Commandant, I'm not ashamed to say it: I am one of the party's rising stars. I believe in my destiny. Two years from now, when our president loses the election – because he will lose it – I will be in charge of the party, and I'll be the frontrunner in 2017. And the Left, too, will have to confront its poor showing. Europe, along with the rest of the world, will be nothing but an arena of rebellion. Men like me are the future. Do you understand what's at stake? It goes far beyond your investigation, the death of Mademoiselle Diemar, or the salvation of my marriage.'

Servaz could not believe what he was hearing: this man was consumed by ambition.

'Which means?'

'Which means I cannot allow the slightest shadow, the least suspicion, do you understand? Because this is what the public want: brand-new, immaculate people. Unsullied by corruption, strangers to the old ways of doing things, not implicated in affairs of any kind. You must conduct your investigation with absolute discretion. You know that even if I am innocent, if my name appears anywhere there will always be someone prepared to say that there is no smoke without fire, to feed the rumour, to tarnish my reputation . . . But why don't we speak about your career, instead of mine. I can help you, Commandant. I have powerful allies. At the national as well as the regional level. People in high places listen to me.' Lacaze took a deep breath. 'I am counting on your diplomacy. And your loyalty. Don't get me wrong: I want the bastard who did this to be found as badly as you do – but I also want the investigation to be discreet.'

Well, well, what a surprise . . . Servaz felt a surge of rage. The 'I'll do everything to help you' had already been forgotten. Lacaze was suggesting an exchange of services: you scratch my back and I'll scratch yours. Servaz got to his feet.

'Don't bother yourself with that. I haven't voted in nearly twenty years. That doesn't make me very receptive to those kinds of arguments. I have one last question.'

Lacaze waited.

'Other than the fact that you visit the lycée once a year, were you already familiar with the prep classes in Marsac?'

'Of course; I was a student there myself. It's . . . how to explain it. A very special place. Very different from—'

'No need to explain. I know it, too.'

Lacaze gave him a surprised look. Servaz left the room and went down the corridor.

When he turned into the lounge, he almost bumped into Lacaze's wife. She was standing ramrod straight in front of him and the look she gave Servaz was as cold as ice. She was looking at him, defying him, her lips white and pursed. He understood the implicit message: *she knew* – and she also hoped that he would be discreet. But for other reasons.

'You have blood on your collar, at the back,' she said.

'Forgive me,' he muttered, blushing. 'I'm sorry to have disturbed you at this late hour.'

'People who don't believe there is anything after life are wrong,' she said, looking at the bottom of her glass. 'There's an eternity of silence. It isn't an easy thing to face.' She raised her eyes to his. 'Get the fuck out of here.'

He left the corridor and crossed the lounge towards the picture window. She followed him with her gaze, saying nothing, as he went out onto the terrace. He felt crushed. Crushed by the weight of the darkness that reigned here. Crushed by his own past. Crushed by the aftermath of what he had been through on the roof of the bank. He stopped for a moment and looked at the black, hostile country-side. The pain was still throbbing at the back of his skull, as if to remind him of something – *but what?*

He lifted his collar and went sadly into the night.

22

Nostalgia

She leaned over the toilet bowl to vomit. Rinsed out her mouth. Brushed her teeth. Rinsed again. Then she stood up straight and looked at the ghost staring at her from the mirror. She gave it a defiant glance as she had been doing for months. But she felt that the ghost was no longer afraid of her, and that it was getting stronger by the day.

Officially, the ghost had begun to grow ten months earlier, in her neck, but she knew that it had been there longer. In the form of a single little cell to start with, as solitary as it was lethal, biding its time until the moment it began to divide into thousands, millions, then billions of immortal cells. The irony of fate: the greater the number of immortal cells, the closer she would be to her own death. Another irony: the enemy was not outside her but within. She had given birth to it. Molecular mechanism, cellular division, mutagenic agents, secondary hosts . . . she had become a specialist. It was as if she could feel, physically, the proliferation of the cancer in her body, the armies of cancer moving about on the motorways of her circulatory system, spilling onto the slip roads, interchanges, secondary roads of her capillaries and her lymph glands, besieging her lungs, her spleen and her liver, sending metastases all the way to her groin and her brain. She opened the medicine cabinet, looking for the anti-emetic. She had nothing in her stomach besides alcohol, but she had no more appetite. She had started chemo again at the beginning of the week. She began humming 'Feeling Good'. Muse's version or Nina Simone's. The more she died, the more she felt like singing. On leaving the bathroom, she heard the voice from the study. He had left the door ajar. Barefoot, she went closer. He was worried. He was speaking feverishly into the phone.

'We've got a problem, I tell you. That cop won't just leave it. He's a tough one.'

She placed a hand on her scarf and her wig to check their position and felt another wave of nausea. Suddenly she propelled herself far away from there. Planets born and dying, stars far out in space that stopped shining, a baby about to emerge from a womb while another person passed away, a wave forming far out to sea which she rode on a surfboard aged fifteen, a Schubert sonata she played on the piano at nineteen, a hundred people applauding, monitor lizards in the jungle, a lagoon, a volcano, a backpack, a trip around the world when she was twenty-eight with a much older, married man whom she loved, then. She would have liked to rewind the film. To start from square one, start everything all over again . . .

Again the panicked voice coming through the door.

'I know what time it is! Call him and ask him what's going on. No, not tomorrow, tonight, shit! He can get the prosecutor out of bed, for fuck's sake!'

Where were you on Friday evening and what were you doing?

She smiled. The media darling was afraid. Scared shitless. She had loved him, oh yes. More than anyone else. Before she began to despise him – more than anyone else as well. Her scorn was in proportion to the amount of love she'd once felt. Was it one of the side effects of the disease? It should have made her more understanding, shouldn't it? More . . . *empathetic*, as those people said. Her *friends* – journalists, politicians, doctors, company directors, petty bourgeois. She realised now the degree to which she was surrounded by priggish, pretentious pedants and posers, their lips spouting fine words, witty phrases and hollow platitudes, which they passed back and forth. How she missed the uncomplicated people of her childhood. Her father, her mother: simple craftsmen . . .

'Right. Get back to me.'

She heard him hang up and she moved away quietly. She had heard him tell the cop that they had spent the evening together watching a DVD. That she loved American comedies from the fifties – the only bit of truth in a web of lies. *Roman Holiday*! She almost burst out laughing. She could picture him as Gregory Peck and herself as Audrey Hepburn on their Vespa, dashing through the streets of Rome. Ten years earlier, they had looked like that, it was true. The perfect couple. The one everyone admired, envied . . . At all the parties, everyone looked at them: she was the brilliant, attractive journalist, he was the young politician with a bright future ahead of him. Their gazes had been full of wonder and envy. He was still a politician with a bright future ahead of him . . .

They hadn't watched a film together for a long time.

She'd heard him moaning like a wounded animal about the death of that slut. He didn't even give a damn that there was a cop sitting across from him. Had he loved her that much?

Where were you on Friday?

One thing was for sure: he hadn't been at home that night. Any more than on all the other nights.

She didn't want to know. There was enough darkness around her. He could roast in hell or languish in prison – once she was dead. Sadness, solitude and the fear of death tasted like chalk dust in her mouth. Or maybe it was the ghost, playing another trick. She wanted to die in peace.

Ziegler opened the wardrobe and took out several uniforms, one after the other, and lay them on the bed.

One jacket in navy and royal blue waterproof cloth, with two stripes marked GENDARMERIE on the back and the chest. A blue jacket with reinforcements at the elbows and shoulders. Several long-sleeved polo shirts, two pairs of trousers, three straight skirts, shirts, a black tie and a tie clip, several pairs of court shoes and two pairs of walking boots, gloves, a cap, and a hat that she found every bit as ridiculous as the last time she had worn it, just before the holidays.

Except that now she wasn't wearing these outfits just at certain ceremonies but on a daily basis. The uniform that most of her colleagues wore with pride was, in her eyes, a symbol of her loss of rank and her disgrace.

She had spent two years as an investigator with the gendarmerie's crime investigation division, wearing civvies. And now here she was back to square one.

She had dreamt of being promoted to a major city. A city full of lights, of sound and fury. Instead, she was back out in the country. The countryside might seem idyllic, and crime might be less visible, but it was everywhere all the same. New technologies had enabled crime to spread to the most remote of backwaters. There were the hardened urban criminals who no longer hesitated to move into places with less police presence; and even in a village with a few hundred inhabitants you could find one or two brainless cretins whose dreams of grandeur consisted in committing acts as evil as those of their urban counterparts. It was plain to see that here, as elsewhere, there were two professions with no danger of obsolescence: the law, and the police.

But she also knew that the moment an important case came along, it would be immediately taken out of her hands and entrusted to a more competitive investigation squad than her modest one could ever hope to be.

She made sure all her outfits were clean and ironed, then hung them back up in the wardrobe and tried to forget them. Her holiday wasn't over until tomorrow morning. In the meantime she refused to succumb to negative thoughts.

Ziegler went out of the room, crossed the tiny lounge of her company flat and picked up the newspaper from the coffee table. Then she headed towards the little desk by the window, switched on her computer and sat down.

She found the article. There was no information on the newspaper's website other than what was already in the paper version. However, one link referred back to an older article that had appeared while she was in Greece. It was entitled: 'YOUNG PROFESSOR MURDERED IN MARSAC. *Policeman who solved St-Martin case placed in charge of investigation.*' She felt a tingling.

'Good God, do you have any idea of the time?'

The minister spluttered into the receiver, reaching with one hand for the bedside lamp. He glanced at his wife, sound asleep in the middle of the big bed: the ringing telephone had not even woken her up. The man at the other end of the line did not turn a hair. He was, after all, the president of the assembly parliamentary group and he was not in the habit of waking people up over trifles.

'You must realise that if I'm calling you it's a matter of extreme importance.'

The minister sat straight up in bed.

'What's going on? Has there been a terrorist attack? Did someone die?'

'No, no,' said the voice. 'Nothing like that. Still, in my opinion it could not wait until tomorrow.'

The minister felt like telling him that opinions were roughly as numerous and varied as what they both had between their legs, but he refrained.

'So what is the matter?'

The head of the parliamentary group explained. The minister frowned and, swinging his legs out of bed, he shoved his feet into a pair of slippers. He left the room and went into the study.

'You say he was the woman's lover? Is that rumour or fact?

'He confessed to the policeman,' the other man replied.

'Fuck! He's even stupider than I thought! And he didn't tell you, by any chance, whether he'd killed her?' said the minister, his voice dripping with sarcasm.

'In my opinion, he didn't,' replied the man soberly. 'I don't think Paul is capable of such a thing. To my mind, he's a weak man who wants to pass himself off as a strong one.'

The president of the parliamentary group was quite pleased with this witticism, which excused his rival while at the same time debasing him. He was well aware of Paul Lacaze's ambition. He knew that the young MP was after his post, and he despised the man. He was a mad dog posing as the white knight of politics. The problem with white, he mused, is that it gets dirty. He was not at all displeased by what had happened. But on the other end of the telephone line the minister sighed.

'I advise you to erase the words "opinion" and "to my mind" from your vocabulary,' he said curtly. 'Voters don't care for opinions, they want deeds and facts.'

The head of the parliamentary group felt like answering back, but he was savvy enough to know when to keep his mouth shut.

'What do we know about the cop?'

'He's the one who brought down Eric Lombard a year and a half ago,' he replied.

Silence on the other end of the line. The minister was thinking. He checked his watch. Twelve minutes past midnight.

'I'll call the Minister of Justice,' he decided. 'We must keep a lid on this story before it explodes in our face. You call Lacaze back. Tell him we want to see him. First thing tomorrow. I don't care what he's got on his agenda. He'll just have to figure it out.'

He hung up without waiting for an answer and looked for the number of the woman in charge of the Ministry of Justice. She would have to find out what she could, and very quickly, about the magistrates assigned to the case. For a moment, he felt nostalgic for the days when judges were subservient to those in power, where any affair in the country could be hushed up, where the life of France's chief cop consisted of illegal phone-tapping, writing compromising reports on one's rivals and other dirty tricks. He would have loved to be around during that era, but it was no longer possible. Nowadays, the little judges went nosing into everything, and you had to be careful not to make the slightest faux pas.

Servaz looked at the clock on the dashboard. Twenty minutes past midnight. Maybe it wasn't too late. Did he have the right to show up like this, without warning? He decided he did. Instead of going back to Marsac, he left the residential neighbourhood behind him and continued on through the woods, then turned left at the next crossroads, amidst the fields. The road led directly to the lake. When he reached it, the first house along the north shore would be Marianne's. There was a light shining on the ground floor. She wasn't in bed yet. He drove up to the gate and got out.

'It's me,' he said simply, after he'd pressed the button and heard the electric crackling in the intercom – and he realised that his heart was beating a bit too fast.

She didn't answer, but there was a click and the gate slowly opened as he got back behind the wheel. He drove over the gravel, his headlights carving out the low-hanging branches of the fir trees. At the top of the steps the front door was open.

He closed it behind him and let the sound of the television guide him. He found her sitting among the cushions on her sand-coloured sofa, her legs tucked beneath her, a glass of wine in her hand. She held it up.

'Cannoneau de Sardegna,' she said. 'Would you like some?'

She did not seem surprised by his late visit. He had never heard of the wine. She was wearing short satin pyjamas and the electric blue cloth emphasised her blonde hair, her light eyes and her suntanned legs, and he could not help but admire them.

'I'd love some,' he said.

She rose from the sofa in a single supple movement and went to fetch a large stem glass from the bar, set it down on the coffee table and filled it one-third full. It was certainly a good wine, but slightly too full-bodied for his tastes. However, he had to admit he was no expert. She muted the TV, but left the picture on. The reflex of a person who lives alone, he thought. Even without the sound, television was a presence. She looked exhausted and sad, with shadows under her eyes; she wore no make-up, but he found her even more attractive. Aodhágán was right. No one could touch her then and no one could touch her now. Even without make-up, her hair uncombed, wearing nothing but those pyjamas, she could have shown up at a party and she would have eclipsed all others, regardless of their jewellery, their designer gowns and their last-minute trips to the hairdresser's.

She sat back down. He collapsed on the sofa next to her.

'What brings you here?' she asked.

Before he had time to answer, she gave a start.

'Christ, Martin, you've got blood all over your collar. And in your hair!'

She leaned closer and he could feel her fingers delicately parting his hair.

'You've got a very nasty wound . . . You have to see a doctor . . . How did you do that?'

He told her as he took another swallow of wine. He knew that one or two more gulps like that and his head would begin to spin. He glanced at the label on the bottle. Fourteen per cent, no less . . . He told her about the surveillance videos at the bank, the second figure, the sound, and the chase up to the roof.

'Does this mean that . . . does this mean that the person caught on tape is the actual culprit, in your opinion?'

He could hear that her throat had tightened with hope. Immense, immoderate hope.

'Maybe,' he said cautiously.

She didn't add anything, but he guessed that her mind was racing, while she went on mechanically parting his hair with her fingertips.

'You can't stay like this . . . You need stitches.'

'Marianne . . .'

She got up again and left the room, returning five minutes later with cotton, alcohol and a box of Steri-Strips.

'It won't work,' he said. 'You'll have to shave my head.'

'It's worth a try.'

He realised it was doing her good to do something, to think about someone else besides Hugo for a while. He could feel the alcohol burning as she disinfected his scalp, and he trembled from the pain when she pressed a bit too hard. She took a Steri-Strip out of the box, removed the protective strip and tried to apply the butterfly stitch. But she had to give up almost immediately.

'You're right, I would have to shave you.'

'No way.'

'Wait. Let me have another look.'

She leaned over him again. Her fingers were still rummaging in his hair. She was close. Too close . . . He could see how thin the satin pyjamas were. He became aware of the warm, brown skin beneath. Her lips, like his, too big. It used to make them laugh, back in the old days. They used to say that *their mouths had found each other.* Marianne's fingers were caressing the back of his neck . . . He turned his head.

He saw her eyes, how they were shining.

He knew this was not the right time, that it was the last thing he should do. The past was the past. It would not return. Not like before. Not a past like theirs. All they would accomplish would be to lay waste to their most beautiful memories, and destroy a large part of the magic they had preserved up to this day. There was still time to press 'pause': there were a million good reasons why he should.

But it was a wave he could not stop. Marianne's fingers seemed to flow through his hair like water and for a few seconds all he saw was her face and her wide-open eyes, shining like a lake in moonlight. She kissed him on the corner of his mouth and he felt her arms slipping around him. Suddenly the silence seemed to grow denser. They kissed, looked at each other, kissed again. As if they needed reassurance that it was all real, and that it was truly what they wanted. They found the familiar gestures again, instinctively, their own particular way of offering themselves to each other: deep kisses, complete abandonment as they let themselves go, totally – whereas Alexandra had always remained on the threshold, with a reserve that betrayed her need to control, even during lovemaking. If he had been blind Servaz would have recognised Marianne's tongue, her mouth, her kisses. It was true what they had said: *their mouths had found each other.* He had known other women – after Marianne and even after Alexandra – but never again had he found such complicity, such a complementary nature. Only she could kiss him that way.

He undressed her quickly. How familiar, too, her long neck, broad shoulders, her birthmark, the tips of her breasts, the hair between her thighs. Her narrow waist and thin arms, and her hips, fuller: their ample curve, spreading wider, and her legs as solid as an athlete's, with the same astonishingly muscular belly. He knew, too, the movement of her hips as they arched and came to meet him, the abundant wetness beneath his fingers. It was all so familiar that he realised that the memory of these sensations had been embedded, inscribed somewhere in the convolutions of his reptilian brain, simply waiting to be reborn. And he felt as if he were home at last.

Ziegler wasn't sleepy. She had gone back to her regular routine, which kept her awake every night. Her passion, her manhunt. Revising her notes on her MacBook Air after one month's holiday, during which Zuzka had obliged her to disconnect.

The photographs and press cuttings pinned to the walls of her study testified to her obsession. If the members of the unit in Paris that Servaz had contacted had been able to get into Irène Ziegler's computer, they would have been astonished by the quantity of information she had managed to amass in just a few months regarding Julian Alois Hirtmann. And maybe they would have thought she'd make an excellent colleague. Clearly Ziegler had read a great deal on the topic. In fact, she had read everything.

In the archives of the Swiss press the gendarme had found an almost inexhaustible mine of information about Hirtmann's childhood, his law studies at the University of Geneva, his career as a prosecutor, and his three-year stint at the International Criminal Court in The Hague. A Swiss reporter had questioned both close and distant relatives at length, as well as the neighbours and inhabitants of Hermance, the little town on Lake Geneva where Hirtmann had grown up. The childhood of a serial killer always contains warning signs, all the experts know this: shyness, solitude, a liking for morbid things, animals disappearing in the neighbourhood, all of it fairly typical . . . The journalist had discovered one element of particular interest to the investigators. When he was ten years old, Hirtmann had lost his younger brother Abel, who was eight, in circumstances that had never been clear. It happened in the middle of the summer, when he and his little brother were on holiday with their grandparents; their parents had just divorced. The grandparents had a farm, a large, typical Swiss building with a vast panorama, blue above and below, overlooking the lake of Thun in the Bernese

Oberland: behind the house was an entire alignment of glaciers, 'like plates on a rack', in the words of Charles Ferdinand Ramuz. A veritable postcard. According to the journalist, various witnesses referred to a solitary child, who avoided others and played only with his little brother. At their grandparents', Julian and Abel were in the habit of going on long bike rides around the lake, which could last all afternoon. They would sit in the tall grass and from the top of the gentle, graceful slope of the hill, they would look at the boats criss-crossing the lake, and listen to the bells in the valley slowly chiming the hours, their joyful sound rising like kites on atmospheric currents.

One evening, however, Julian came home alone. He declared, in tears, that he and his brother had made the acquaintance of a stranger named Sebald. They had met him at the beginning of the holidays and went every day to meet him in secret. This Sebald – an adult in his forties – taught them 'lots of stuff'. That day he had been acting strangely and irritably. When Julian told him that Abel was hiding two Basler Läckerlis in his pocket, Sebald wanted to try one. But the little brother had obstinately refused to share his biscuits. 'What shall we do?' asked Sebald in a syrupy voice, and this had caused both of them to tremble. And when Abel, who was beginning to be afraid, had expressed his desire to go home, Sebald had ordered Julian to tie him to a tree. The young boy wanted to please the grown-up, even though he was afraid of him, so he had obeyed, in spite of his little brother's pleading. Then the man had told him to put some earth and leaves in Abel's mouth to punish him while they ate the biscuits in front of him. That was when Julian ran away, abandoning his little brother.

Immediately after they heard the story, the grandparents and their neighbours rushed to the place, but there was no trace of Abel or Sebald anywhere. In the end, Abel's body had washed up by the lake one week later. The autopsy revealed that his head had been held under water. As for the mysterious Sebald, despite an exhaustive search by the Swiss police, no trace of the man was ever found, or even any proof of his existence.

Another journalist had matched his various trips to countries bordering Switzerland with the disappearance of a certain number of young women. Several articles mentioned the three years Hirtmann had spent at the International Criminal Court in The Hague, where he had had to rule, among other crimes, on cases of rape, torture and murder committed by the armed forces – including the UN peacekeeping force.

Ziegler had compiled a list, by no means exhaustive, of the former prosecutor's 'possible' victims in Switzerland, but also in the Dolomites, the French Alps, Bavaria and Austria, and she had noted a number of suspicious disappearances in Holland during the period Hirtmann had been living there – including that of a man in his thirties, a ferreting little journalist who, it would seem, had been onto him before anyone else had. He was undoubtedly Hirtmann's only male victim, apart from his wife's lover. The disappearance of an American tourist in the Bermudas when he was on holiday a few miles from there was also taken into account, even though the authorities had put her death down to a shark attack. At the time of his arrest, the press and the police had attributed to him forty or more cases spread over twenty-five years. Ziegler's calculations brought the figure closer to 100. Not a single one of the victims had ever been found . . . If there was one domain where Hirtmann was a master, it was in knowing how to make bodies disappear.

Ziegler leaned back in her chair. For a moment she listened to the silence of the sleeping building. Eighteen months had gone by since the Swiss criminal had escaped from the Wargnier Institute. Had he killed anyone in all that time? She was willing to bet he had. How many victims should she add to the list? Would they ever know?

The dark side of Julian Alois Hirtmann had been revealed after the double murder of his wife and her lover, the judge Adalbert Berger, a colleague from the Geneva public prosecutor's office, in his house on Lake Geneva on the night of 21 June 2004. The investigation that followed led to the discovery of several binders filled with press cuttings regarding the disappearance of dozens of young women in five neighbouring countries. Hirtmann declared that he was interested in these cases for professional reasons. When this line of defence proved to be untenable, he began to manipulate the psychiatrists. Like most individuals of his ilk, he knew exactly the type of response the psychiatrists and psychologists expected from someone like him; a good number of hardened criminals are experts in the art of turning the system to their advantage. Hirtmann confessed to his jealousy on discovering that his parents loved his little brother more than they loved him, to his mother's scorn, and his father's violence and alcoholism, and even to sexually inappropriate gestures on the part of his mother.

Julian Hirtmann had stayed in several different psychiatric hospitals in Switzerland before ending up at the Wargnier Institute. That was where Servaz and Irène had met him. That was where he had escaped from, two winters earlier.

Ziegler went back to the two recent articles in the press, the one entitled 'HIRTMANN WRITES TO POLICE' and the one that mentioned Martin's investigation in Marsac. Who was behind the leak? She thought about Martin, the state of mind he must be in. She was worried about him. They had spoken at length after the investigation in the winter of 2008, and he had eventually told her about the trauma that had been haunting him since childhood. She had seen it as a great sign of trust, because she was sure he hadn't spoken to anyone about it in years. That day she had decided she would watch over him, in any way she could, even behind his back – like a sister, like a friend.

She sighed. Over these past months she had refused to allow herself to go digging into Martin's computer. The last time she had hacked into it was when the Council of Inquiry – the disciplinary board of the gendarmerie – had been handed her case by head office. In those days, she had shown an aptitude for computer hacking, which the Ministry of Defence would no doubt have found *interesting*, if they had known about it. So she had read the report Martin sent to the disciplinary board about her. It was very favourable, and emphasised her contribution to the investigation and the risks she had taken. The report recommended that the council act with clemency. As she was not meant to have read it, she had not been able to thank him.

On more than one occasion she had been tempted to obtain news of Martin this way – she knew how to hack into both his computers, the one at the Criminal Division and the one he had at home – but every time, she had decided not to. Not only out of loyalty, but also because she didn't want to stumble upon things that she might regret knowing later on.

Everyone has their secrets, everyone has something to hide, and no one is exactly what they seem.

Which held true for her as well. She wanted to preserve the image she had of Martin, the one that he had left her with: that of a man she might have found attractive if she'd been into men, a man who was caught up in his contradictions, haunted by his past, full of anger and tenderness at the same time, whose slightest gesture or word suggested that he knew that the weight of humanity is made up of all the combined acts of every man and woman on the planet. She had never known a more melancholy man. Or a fairer one. Sometimes Ziegler found herself hoping that Martin would find someone to bring peace and a little lightness to his life. But somehow, too, she knew this would never happen.

Haunted – that was the word that sprang to mind whenever she thought about him.

She typed something quickly on the keyboard, and this time she did not back out. *It's in your interest that I'm doing this.* Once she was in, she found her way with the dexterity of a burglar in a dark flat. She scrolled through his inbox and there it was: the e-mail that the newspaper was referring to, the e-mail he had received recently. He had transferred it to Paris, to the unit in charge of the manhunt for the Swiss killer:

From: theodor.adorno@hotmail.com
To: martin.servaz@infomail.fr
Date: 12 June
Subject: Greetings

Do you remember the first movement of the Fourth, Commandant? Bedächtig . . . Nicht eilen . . . Recht gemächlich . . . The piece that was playing when you came into my 'room' that famous day in December? I've been thinking about writing to you for quite some time. Are you surprised? I'm sure you'll believe me if I tell you I've been very busy lately. You can only truly appreciate your freedom, like your health, when you've been deprived of it for a long time.

But I won't bother you any more, Martin. (Do you mind if I call you Martin?) Personally I hate being bothered. You'll have news of me soon. I doubt you will like it very much – but I am sure you will find it interesting.

Regards, JH.

She read it, and then read it again. Until she had absorbed the words. She closed her eyes, squeezed her eyelids, concentrated. Opened them again. Then she went through the e-mails Martin had exchanged with the unit in Paris, and she gave a start: Hirtmann may have been seen on the motorway between Paris and Toulouse, on a motorbike. There was an attachment, and she hurried to open it. The picture was slightly blurred, filmed by a surveillance camera at a tollbooth: a tall man with a helmet on a Suzuki motorbike. He was leaning over to pay, his gloved hand reaching out, his face invisible beneath the helmet. Another picture followed. A tall, blond man with a little beard and sunglasses at a supermarket till. The jacket was identical; there was an eagle on the back and a little American flag on the right sleeve. Ziegler felt goosebumps rising all along her skin. Was that Hirtmann or not? There was something familiar about the way he was walking, the shape of the face . . . But she was wary of her eagerness to identify him; she didn't want to jump to any conclusions.

Hirtmann in Toulouse . . .

She saw herself again, with Martin, in that cell in unit A, the high-security unit where the most dangerous inmates of the Wargnier Institute were locked up. She had sat in on the interview, at least at the beginning, until Hirtmann asked to speak to Martin alone. Something happened that day. She had felt it. It happened without warning, but they had all felt it: between the serial killer and the cop, there had been some sort of connection; they were like two chess champions, sizing each other up, acknowledging each other. What had they said to each other, once they were alone? Martin had not been very talkative on the subject. What Irène remembered above all was that as soon as they went into the cell, the two men immediately struck up a conversation about the music on the CD player that day: it was Mahler – or at least according to Martin it was, because Ziegler couldn't tell Mozart from Beethoven. It was like watching a heavyweight boxing match between two adversaries who respect each other.

'*You'll have news of me soon. I doubt you will like it very much – but I am sure you will find it interesting.*'

She shivered. Something was going on. Something extremely unpleasant. Ziegler switched off the computer and stood up. She went into her room and got undressed, but the wheels in her mind went on turning.

Interlude 2

Resolution

She'd had a childhood.

She had had an eventful life, full of joy and sadness, a full life. A life like millions of others.

Her memory was like all memories: an album full of yellowing photographs, or a series of jerky little Super 8 film clips, stored away in round plastic boxes.

An adorable little blonde girl who made sandcastles on the beach. A preteen who was more beautiful than her peers, whose curls and soft gaze and precocious curves troubled some of her parents' adult male friends, who had to struggle to ignore her. A mischievous, intelligent kid who was her father's pride and joy. A student who had met the love of her life, a brilliant, melancholy young man with a big mouth and an irresistible smile, who would talk to her about the book he was writing – until she realised that he was carrying a burden that could not be prised from his grip, and even she could do nothing against the ghosts.

Then she betrayed him.

There was no other word. It made her want to weep. *Betrayal.* There was nothing more painful, more sinister, more despicable than that word. For the victim and the traitor. Or, in this case, the traitress . . . She curled up in a foetal position on the hard bare earth of her tomb. Was that what she was expiating? Was God punishing her through the pervert upstairs? These months of hell: was that what she was paying for, her betrayal? Did she deserve what was happening to her? Did anyone on earth deserve what she was going through? She would not have inflicted such a punishment on her worst enemy . . .

She thought about the man who lived there, just over her head – who was living, unlike her; who came and went in the world of the living while keeping her in the antechamber of death. She suddenly went cold all over. What if he didn't tire of this game? What if he *never* got tired of it? How long could it last? Months? Years? Decades? Until *he* died? And how much longer before she went completely insane? She could already see the beginnings of her madness. Sometimes, for no apparent reason, she began laughing uncontrollably. Or she would recite, hundreds of times, 'Blue eyes go to the skies, grey eyes go to paradise, green eyes go to hell, and black in Purgatory dwell.' There were times when her mind went completely astray, she had to admit. Where reality vanished behind a screen of fantasy. Welcome to Saturday's special screening. Tears and emotion guaranteed. Get out your handkerchiefs. Next to me, Fellini and Spielberg are desperately lacking in imagination.

She would end up crazy.

It was so obvious it terrified her. That, and the thought that it would never end. And that she would get old in this tomb, while at the same time he was getting old up there. They were almost the same age . . . No! Anything but that. She felt as if she were going to pieces, as if she were going to fall into a dead faint. *No no no no anything but that.* And suddenly, she felt even colder. Because she had just caught a glimpse of the way out. She had no choice. She would never get out of there alive.

So she would have to find a way to die.

She picked at her thought, looked at it every which way. The way she might have examined a butterfly, or an insect.

To die . . .

Yes. She had no choice. Up to now she had refused to look at what was staring her in the face.

She could have done it already: that time when she thought she'd escaped, when he'd just been pretending to be asleep, the better to play with her in the forest afterwards. No doubt she could have found a way to put an end to it if she'd been determined enough at the time. But back then all she could think of was running away, getting out of there alive.

Had there been others before her? She had often wondered and she was sure that there had. She was only the latest in a long series: his system was too perfect, not a single detail was left to chance. It was a masterly piece of work.

Suddenly, with icy clarity, she saw the solution.

She had no way to commit suicide. So she had to drive him to kill her.

It was as simple as that. She felt a sudden rush of enthusiasm, as incongruous as it was fleeting, like a mathematician who has found the solution to a particularly complicated equation. Then the difficulties became apparent, and her enthusiasm vanished.

But she did have one advantage over him: she had time.

Time to brood, to think, to go crazy, but also time to devote to her strategy.

Slowly, she began to come up with what is conventionally known as a plan.

Tuesday

23

Insomnia

The moonlight filtered through the open French windows, spreading throughout the room. If he looked to his left, he would see it sparkling on the surface of the lake. He could hear the water lapping against the shore, a rustling as quiet as that of cloth crushed between fingers.

He felt Marianne's warm, soft body beside him. Yes, a body beside him, something that had not happened to him for months. Her thigh on his, her bare breasts against his torso, and her arm around him, trusting. A strand of fine blonde hair was tickling his chin. She was breathing regularly and he did not dare move for fear of waking her. The strangest thing of all was her breathing: there is nothing more intimate than someone sleeping and breathing so close to you.

Through the window, he could see the dark mass of the Mountain. It had stopped raining. The forest beneath the starry sky was motionless.

'You're not asleep?'

He turned his head. Marianne's face in the moonlight, her big, light eyes, curious and gleaming.

'What about you?'

'Mmm. I think I was dreaming. A strange dream, neither pleasant nor unpleasant.'

He looked at her. She did not seem to want to say any more about it. A thought occurred to him and vanished the moment he began to wonder whom she had been dreaming about: Hugo, Bokha, Francis – or himself?

'Mathieu was in my dream,' she said at last.

Bokha . . . Before he could say anything, she stood up and went to the bathroom. Through the half-open door he could hear her urinating, then she opened a cabinet. He wondered if she was looking for another condom. What was he to make of the fact that she had a supply of them? It was the first time they had ever used one. The fact that he had shown up without one had, however, seemed to cheer her. He looked at the clock radio: 2.13.

Back in the room she took a cigarette from the night table and lit it before lying down next to him. She inhaled twice then placed the cigarette between his lips.

'Do you have any idea what we're doing here?' she asked.

'It seems pretty obvious to me,' he tried to joke.

'I wasn't talking about fucking.'

'I know.'

She caressed between his thighs.

'What I mean is . . . that I don't have the slightest idea,' she added. 'I don't want to . . . to make you suffer all over again, Martin.'

Servaz's cock, in all honesty, was thinking neither of suffering nor of all the years it had taken him to forget her, to get her out of his life. It didn't care about any of that and immediately went hard. She pulled back the sheet and lay on top of him. She rubbed his belly, from top to bottom, exerting a delicious pressure. She kissed him again, then resumed her intimate strokes, scrutinising him intensely; her pupils were dilated, there was a smile on her dry lips, and he wondered if she had taken something in the bathroom.

She leaned closer and suddenly bit his lower lip until it bled; the pain made him shudder, and the coppery taste of blood filled his mouth. She squeezed his head, hard, crushing his ears between her palms, while he kneaded her lower back and sucked at her nipple, erect like a bud. He could feel the soft, wet back-and-forth against him. Finally she raised herself up, her fingers closed around him and she gave a strange guttural moan as she straddled him and brought him inside her. He remembered then that it had been her favourite position, in the old days, and for a fraction of a second, which almost spoiled everything, he felt a pang of sadness, devastating sadness.

Was it the night, the moonlight, the time? They let themselves go in a way that left him both drained and distraught. When she headed once again to the bathroom, he raised his fingers to his wounded lip. He had scratches on his back, and she had also bitten him on the shoulder. He could still feel the fire in his skin, the burn of her caresses – and he gave a smile that was both solemn and victorious, solemn because he knew his victory was only provisional. Was it even a victory? Or more of a relapse? What should he think? He wondered again whether Marianne had taken something before making love. He was feeling increasingly uneasy. Who was this woman? Not the one he used to know . . .

She came back and flopped onto the bed. Then she kissed him with a tenderness she had not shown since they'd started making love that night. Her voice was hoarser and deeper than usual when she rolled over onto her side.

'You should watch out: everyone I grow attached to comes to a bad end.'

He looked at her. 'What do you mean?'

'You heard me.'

'What are you talking about?'

'Everyone I love comes to a bad end,' she said again. 'You, with what happened back then . . . Mathieu . . . Hugo . . .'

He felt a column of ants nibbling at his belly.

'That's wrong. You've forgotten Francis. He's not doing too badly, by the looks of it.'

'What do you know about Francis's life?'

'Nothing, other than that he ditched you, not long after you left me for him.'

She stared at him.

'That's what you think. That's what everyone thinks. Actually, I'm the one who called it quits. After that, he went shouting from the rooftops that he had ended our relationship, and that it was his decision.'

He gave her an astonished look.

'And it wasn't true?'

'I left him a note, one day, after we'd argued for the umpteenth time, where I said that it was over.'

'So why didn't you set the record straight?'

'What difference would it have made? You know Francis – everything always has to revolve around him.'

One point to her. She looked at him, and in her eyes he saw the gaze of the Marianne from the old days, full of attentiveness, insight and tenderness.

'You know . . . when your father committed suicide, I wasn't surprised. It was as if I already knew what was going to happen; all that guilt you had on your shoulders – it was as though it had already occurred. As if it were written somewhere.'

'Seneca: *Ducunt volentem fata, nolentem trahunt,*' he said darkly.

'You and your Latin. You see, that's why I left you. You think I left you for Francis? I left you because you were elsewhere. You were lost, haunted by memories, by your anger and your guilt. Being with you was like sharing you with ghosts, I never knew when you were with me and when—'

'Do we really need to talk about this now?' he said.

'If not now, when? Of course, I found out later what Francis wanted,' she continued. 'When I understood that it wasn't me, that it was *you* – that he wanted to get at you through me, I left him. He wanted to beat you at your own game, show you who was the strongest. I was just part of the stakes, I was a battlefield. Your bloody rivalry, your duel from a distance – with Marianne in the middle, like a trophy. Do you realise? Your best friend. Your alter ego, your brother. You were inseparable and all that time, there was only one thing he wanted: to take what you loved most in the world.'

His brain was on fire; he wanted to run away, not to hear another word.

'That's Francis all over,' she said, 'brilliant and funny, but deep down he's jealous and spiteful. He doesn't like himself. He doesn't like his face in the mirror. He likes only one thing: humiliating others. Your best friend. Do you know what he said to me once? That I deserved better than you . . . Did you know that he was jealous of your talent as a writer? Francis Van Acker has no true talent – apart from manipulating other people.'

He suppressed a desire to gag her with his hand.

'And then Mathieu came along. Bokha, as you called him . . . Oh, he wasn't as brilliant as you two. No. But he had his feet on the ground, and he was much cleverer than either of you suspected with your enormous egos. Above all, there was a strength about him . . . and kindness, too. Mathieu was all strength, patience and kindness, while you were fury and Francis was duplicity. I loved Mathieu. Like I loved both of you. Not with the same devouring passion. Not the same flame, but maybe in a deeper way – something that you and Francis could never understand. And now, today, there is Hugo. He's all I have left, Martin. Don't take him away from me.'

Servaz felt overwhelmed with fatigue. All the excitement of the night had disappeared. All the joy and lightness had evaporated, like champagne.

'Do you know Paul Lacaze?' he asked, to change the subject.

She hesitated for a moment.

'What has Paul got to do with any of this?'

He wondered what he ought to say. He couldn't tell her what he had found out.

'You know everyone in Marsac. What do you know about him?'

She examined him. She had understood it must have something to do with the investigation – and therefore, with Hugo.

'He's ambitious. Very ambitious. Intelligent. Provocative. He's got his political future all mapped out, on a national level. His wife has cancer.'

She looked closely at him again.

'You already know all that,' she concluded, still peering at him. 'Why are you interested in him?'

'I'm sorry. I can't say anything for the moment. What I'm interested in is not what everyone knows, it's what you know personally, that no one else knows.'

'What makes you think I would know things that no one else knows?'

'Because it might help me prove your son's innocence.'

Margot lay flat on her back, and could not sleep for worrying. She kept thinking about the mysterious conversation she had overheard in the maze. She tried to decrypt every word she'd heard. What did Virginie mean when she said that if necessary, they would help her father to understand? There had been a chilling threat in her words. Margot had clearly sensed the presence of danger. She thought she knew them, she thought they were simply the four most brilliant young people at the lycée: Hugo, David, Virginie and Sarah . . . But that night, she had stumbled upon something which would not leave her in peace. A shadow, a feeling. Vague but insistent. It was there, unspoken, but right at the heart of everything they said. And then there were those words of David's:

We have to call an urgent meeting of the Circle.

The Circle . . . what circle? The very word had an aura of mystery. She typed out a text to Elias:

They talked about some circle. What is it?

She wondered if he was already asleep, or if he would answer, and then her smartphone made its harp-like sound, and although she had been waiting for it, the sound made her jump.

Not the slightest idea. Important?

I think so.

She waited again for a reply.

In that case, we should start there.

How?

They said Circle meeting on the 17th. We won't let them out of our sight.

Okay. And meanwhile?

Keep watching. Careful, they've seen you.

Once again, she felt ill at ease on reading his final words. She remembered what Sarah had said: 'We have to be careful . . ..' She was in the middle of typing,

Okay, see you tomorrow

when her phone vibrated again with a final message:

Be really careful. I mean it. If one of them is the killer, it's bad news. Night.

Margot gazed for a long time at the words on the bright screen. Eventually she switched the phone off and put it on the night table. Then she did something she had never done before: she went to lock the door of their room.

24

The Stream

It was 7.30 in the morning and Zlatan Jovanovic was observing the other patrons at the Café Richelieu while finishing his cappuccino and croissant. Jovanovic would tell whoever wanted to listen that he could spot an adulterous husband, a bailiff, a flirtatious wife, a cop, a petty thief or a dealer, all in the twinkling of an eye. That customer in his fifties standing at the bar, for example, together with two younger colleagues wearing suits and ties: he had just received a text and was wearing a beatific smile. No message from work or from a long-time spouse could ever elicit that kind of smile on a bloke's face. And the wedding ring on his finger was the old-fashioned kind. Zlatan was willing to bet – from the way that he stood up straight and looked at his two companions with a superior, victorious air – that his mistress was much younger than him, and drop-dead gorgeous. Jovanovic took a sip of his coffee, wiped his upper lip and focused his attention on the bloke. He was typing a quick answer. *He's got it bad*, he thought. The double beep of a text echoed in the room less than a minute later. Hmm, it looked like their affair was going well . . . Then he caught a brief flash of annoyance in the man's eyes. Oh-ho! Had the young lady decided to move on to the next stage? Perhaps she was pressuring him to leave his wife. And the guy surely didn't want to . . . It was always the same old story: contrary to received opinion, seventy per cent of divorces were instigated by the wife, not the husband. Men were more cowardly. Jovanovic shrugged, put five euros on the table and got up. It was none of his business – but it was not altogether improbable that someday soon the guy's wife would show up at his office. Marsac was a small town.

He said goodbye to the barman, crossed the street and went into a building on the opposite side. There was one brass plaque by the front door, and it was his: Z. JOVANOVIC, PRIVATE DETECTIVES. SHADOWING/SURVEILLANCE/INVESTIGATIONS. AT YOUR DISPOSAL 24/7. REGISTERED WITH THE PREFECTURE. The plural of the word 'detective' was a dutiful exaggeration: Jovanovic was the only associate in the office. He had just the one secretary who came two days a week to tidy up his mess. The big sign on the door up on the third floor was more explicit: UNFAIR COMPETITION INQUIRIES, COLLECTION OF EVIDENCE, RESEARCH, VERIFICATION OF WORK STOPPAGES, VERIFICATION OF CVS, SOLVENCY INVESTIGATIONS, VERIFICATION OF DOCUMENTS, MISSING PERSONS SEARCHES, WORKPLACE THEFT, PHONE-TAPPING DETECTION, SECURITY AUDITS, MATRIMONIAL TRACKING AND SURVEILLANCE, SURVEILLANCE OF CHILDREN'S FRIENDS AND WHEREABOUTS. RATES CALCULATED BASED ON COMPLEXITY OF INVESTIGATION AND ON THE INVESTMENT REQD. BY OUR TEAMS. WE ARE BOUND BY PROFESSIONAL SECRECY (ARTICLE 226-13 OF THE NEW PENAL CODE), WE OPERATE IN FRANCE AND ABROAD WITH OUR NETWORK OF PARTNER AGENCIES, OUR REPORTS ARE ADMISSIBLE IN A COURT OF LAW, OUR DETECTIVES ARE REGISTERED WITH THE PREFECTURE. Half of this information was bogus, but Zlatan Jovanovic was not sure even a single visitor had ever gone to the trouble of reading the sign to the end. And a good number of his activities would certainly not have obtained the approval of the prefecture.

His appointment was already there. Zlatan caught his breath, and they shook hands. He slipped the key in the lock and gave the door a slight shove with his shoulder to open it. The tiny flat that served as his office smelled of stale tobacco and dust. Zlatan went straight through to the room at the back, a room that was as drab and grey as he was.

'Where is your team, Zlatan?' asked the voice behind him in a bantering tone. 'Do you keep them in the broom cupboard?'

Jovanovic didn't respond. To date, the detective had always known how to satisfy this client, with or without a team, and that was all that mattered. And anyway, he did have a partner – even if his partner never set foot in the office.

He lit an unfiltered cigarette and paid no attention to the person opposite him as he shuffled through a pile of papers until eventually he found what he was looking for: a little spiral notebook.

This tool would have caused his sole partner to smile, for the partner was a man who used neither pencil nor notebook and worked exclusively from home: a computer engineer whom Zlatan had recruited a year earlier. It was in this sector that the agency's sketchiest activities – from a legal standpoint – took place, but they were also the most lucrative: massive theft of electronic data, hacking into private mailboxes, computer piracy, phone tapping . . . It hadn't taken Zlatan long to figure out that companies had financial resources far superior to those of most individuals, and that he would have to subcontract these assignments to someone who had the skills he lacked. He puffed on his cigarette and listened attentively to the client's aims and objectives. This time, they would be doing more than merely flirting with breaking the law. When his client had finished, he let out a long whistle.

'I may have just the man you need,' he said finally, 'but I don't know if he'll go along with it. We will have to be . . . very convincing.'

'Money isn't a problem. But I want no traces in writing, anywhere.'

'That goes without saying. All the information you need will be loaded on to a USB stick, and there will be no copies. Your name will not be mentioned anywhere. No memos, no invoices, no notes, not a trace.'

'There is always a trace. Computers have an irritating tendency to leave traces.'

Jovanovic took out a handkerchief and wiped the sweat that was trickling down his neck. The heat was already stifling and he had no air-conditioning.

'The computer in this office is used only for ordinary paperwork and nothing else,' he said. 'It is as virginal as a nun's arse. All confidential tasks are dealt with elsewhere and no one but me knows where. And the person who assists me is ready to destroy everything the moment I give the signal.'

The client seemed satisfied with his answer.

Servaz was woken by a beam of sunlight. He opened his eyes and stretched, looking around him at the room illuminated by the new day. The chocolate-coloured walls, the light furniture and heavy pale grey curtains. Lamps and knickknacks everywhere. For a split second he was totally disoriented.

Marianne came in, wearing her blue satin pyjamas, a tray in her hands. Servaz yawned. He was ravenous as a tiger. He grabbed a piece of bread and dipped it in his bowl of coffee, then drank some orange juice. She watched him eat in silence, a little smile on her lips. When he had finished, he put the tray down on the bedside rug.

'Have you got a cigarette?' he said.

He had left his pack in his clothes. Marianne reached for hers, handed him one and lit it. The very next moment, she took his free hand in hers. Her fingers were warm and supple after sleep.

'Have you thought about what happened last night?'

'Have you?'

'No, but I'd like it to continue . . .'

He said nothing. He wasn't sure what he'd like.

'You're tense,' she said, with a hand on his chest. 'What's wrong? Is it because of me? Because of what I told you about you and Francis?'

'No.'

'Then what is it?'

He hesitated. Should he tell her? Why not. So he told her about the e-mail he'd received. As well as the image taken by the motorway camera. He merely said it was a man who'd escaped, a man who was trying to get in touch with him.

'There's something,' he said. 'I'm not exactly sure what it is . . . It makes me feel as if I'm being watched. It makes me feel as if someone is following everything I do, as if he knows wherever I go, even anticipates where I'm going to go, as if . . . I know it seems absurd . . . as if he could read my mind.'

'It does seem absurd, indeed.'

'You see, it's like when you play chess with someone who is much better than you are, and you know that no matter what you do, they already know your moves, as if they were inside your head.'

'Does it have anything to do with the investigation into Claire?'

He thought again about the CD they had found in her stereo.

'I don't know . . . the man escaped from a psychiatric hospital two winters ago.'

'It's that Swiss guy the newspapers were talking about, isn't it?'

'Mmm.'

'Do you think he *has* come back?'

'Maybe. I don't really know what to think. Or maybe it's me . . . You're right, I must be getting paranoid. And yet in spite of every-thing, I do sense something. A plan, a strategy somewhere, and it concerns me. It's as if I were his puppet. All he has to do is be increasingly provocative – an e-mail here, a little sign there, to get me to react in a certain way.'

'Is that why you asked me if I'd seen anyone lurking around the house the other evening?'

He nodded. He could see the gleam in Marianne's eyes. He knew what she was thinking: that his old demons were back.

'You should be careful, Martin.'

'Do you think I'm going mad?' he asked.

'Something strange happened, during the night.'

'Strange in what way?'

He could see her gathering her thoughts, a vertical line between her brows.

'It was after we made love for the second time. I couldn't get back to sleep. What time was it? Three o'clock in the morning? I got out of bed, I took my cigarettes and went to smoke one out on the balcony.'

He said nothing, waiting for her to continue.

'I saw a shadow near the lake. I can't be sure, but it seemed as if there were someone behind the trees in the garden. He went along the shore and disappeared into the woods. At the time, I thought it must be an animal. But now I think of it, it couldn't have been. There was someone there.'

He looked at her in silence. It was back, the chilling sensation that someone else was writing the pages of this story in his place, that he was a mere character and the author was in the shadows. Two separate stories: Claire Diemar's murder on the one hand, and Hirtmann's return on the other. Unless . . . He swung his legs out of the bed and stood up, grabbed his trousers and underwear from the chair, then went out onto the balcony, barefoot.

'Show me,' he said. 'The shadow, during the night, where did you see it?'

She followed him out and pointed to the foot of the slope, on the right, where the water met the lawn and the forest.

'There.'

He went back in, put on his shirt, and once he was on the ground floor he walked across the terrace on the lake side to go down the steps, then across the sloping garden. It was already hot. The sun had dried the vegetation and the lake sparkled like a metallic disc beneath its rays. A buzzing attracted his attention: a boat had just left its pontoon, and soon a water skier emerged from the water in its wake. It was a young boy, and judging from his intrepid zigzagging, he already had many hours of practice behind him. Claire Diemar's murderer had shown a similar dexterity, a similar experience in his field. Servaz told himself yet again that it had not been his first outing.

He looked all around him, but there was nothing. If someone had been watching, they hadn't left any trace.

Servaz went down to the water. He saw footprints, but they were old. He began walking along the shore. He reached the edge of the forest and went a few metres into the woods that spread down to the lake.

A dog barked in the distance. In Marsac bells were ringing. The boat went on buzzing across the lake.

A little stream ran through a bed of undergrowth and reeds. The morning light filtered through the foliage and sparkled on the water.

The tree trunk was lying across the path, near the stream. Servaz mused that all the youngsters in the neighbourhood must come here to sit and kiss and flirt, sheltered from view. And sure enough, there were two letters etched into the bark.

He bent closer and froze.

J H

He had sat down on another tree, a bit further along. The rapidly rising heat had left a film of sweat on his brow – or perhaps it was the discovery of the two letters. Insects were buzzing and for a moment he thought he was going to be sick. He shooed away the flies circling around him and dialled the number of the crime scene team to ask them to come and examine the place. As soon as he hung up, his telephone vibrated.

'Jesus Christ, what the fuck have you done? And why was your phone switched off?' roared a voice in his ear.

Castaing, the prosecutor from Auch.

'The battery was flat,' he lied. 'I didn't notice right away.'

'Didn't I tell you not to take any initiative without informing me first?'

Lacaze hadn't wasted his time, he thought.

'Didn't I say that, explicitly, Commandant?'

'I was going to inform the judge,' he lied, for the second time. 'I was about to do it, but you got there before me.'

'Bullshit!' replied the magistrate. 'Who do you think you are, Commandant – what do you take me for?'

'We found dozens of e-mails between Paul Lacaze and Claire Diemar,' he replied. 'E-mails proving that they were having an affair. Which Paul Lacaze himself acknowledged last night. They were clearly very much in love. I interviewed him as a witness.'

'And you showed up at his house, where his wife is dying of cancer, at eleven o'clock at night? I've just been told off by the Ministry of Justice. And believe me, I don't like that one bit.'

Servaz watched a water strider moving across the stream. With its long graceful legs, it skated over the surface; it didn't want to get its feet wet – just like the man on the other end of the line.

'Don't worry,' said Servaz. 'I'll take full responsibility.'

'Responsibility, my arse,' spat the prosecutor. 'If you mess up, it'll me on my head! The only thing that's keeping me from asking Sartet to take you off the case is that Lacaze himself asked me not to.' *He's afraid the story will get out,* thought Servaz. 'This is my last warning, Commandant. No further contact with Paul Lacaze without the judge's authorisation, do you hear me?'

'Loud and clear.'

He ended the call and wiped the sweat from his forehead.

Before he even realised what was happening, he leaned over and threw up his coffee and his breakfast.

Ziegler ran a finger between her neck and the stiff collar of her uniform shirt. It was incredibly hot and stuffy in her office, even though she had opened the barred window. Yet another thing that hadn't changed during her holidays: no one had repaired the air-conditioning. Nor was there any money to replace the old computers, or install an additional Internet connection, let alone broadband. As a result, it took at least five minutes to download a photograph of a suspect. As for her men, one was on sick leave and another was mowing the lawn. Such was the reality of a country gendarme's life.

The atmosphere was typical – when the boss was away, they would all take advantage of the fact to slack off: they were behind on most of the cases and everybody was sulking. One month without her had reminded them all that their life was infinitely easier when she wasn't there. Yet she knew that her men had good reason to complain: they were understaffed, had to work night shifts, weekends and holidays, and the number of hours was constantly on the rise. They had no family life, their salary didn't keep pace with the cost of living, their accommodation was run-down, as were the facilities and the vehicles – and up there, all the way at the top, were the politicians who pranced around and claimed that the fight against crime was their number-one priority. At the regional section she had got used to going it alone, but now she would have to find a way to create a team.

You'll just have to get down off your high horse, girl. You can be a real pain when you want to. Remember to take some croissants tomorrow morning.

The thought of it made her laugh. And maybe she should hold their cocks for them when they pissed, while she was at it. She frowned as she looked at the heap of files on her desk. Thefts from vehicles, traffic-related crime, burglaries, vandalism, destruction: no fewer than fifty-two acts of delinquency recorded in the vicinity and only five of them resolved. Brilliant. On the other hand, she was quite proud of her results where judicial crimes and offences were concerned – she had a clear-up rate of almost seventy per cent, a figure that was far superior to the national average. But the two cases that preoccupied her the most also had the biggest files. The first one was a rape case: the only information they had was the make and colour of the car, and a sticker on the rear windscreen which the victim had described in detail. She had known right from the start that this inquiry did not appeal to her men, and that they would be tempted to sit on it while waiting for new clues – in other words, a miracle – but Irène was determined to use her team, as long as they could be of service.

The second case was to do with a gang specialising in bank card theft, who'd been active in the region for several months. Ziegler had noticed that the same cash machine had been targeted three times in the space of fourteen months and that each time there was an interval of five months, give or take a few days. The cash machine in question seemed to offer a certain number of advantages in the thieves' eyes. At the top of the page she wrote:

Set a trap at the cashpoint. Check all movements in that period.

Through the half-open door, she heard one of her men come in at a brisk stride.

'Listen to this, guys!'

Everyone stopped what they were doing and Ziegler lent an ear, hoping that at last there was something new on one of the pending cases.

'Apparently Domenech is going to keep Anelka in the starting line-up against Mexico.'

'Shit, I don't believe it!' someone exclaimed.

'And Sidney Govou, too . . .'

A murmur of consternation arose from the other side of the door. Ziegler raised her eyes to the blades of the huge ceiling fan, which was stirring the hot air without making it any cooler. Her thoughts returned to the e-mail she had found in Martin's computer. She told herself that the files on her desk had waited an entire month for her return; they could wait a little bit longer. She got up.

Margot rolled a cigarette, wedging the filter between her lips and spreading the tobacco flakes across the paper while keeping an eye on the far side of the courtyard. It was filling with a crowd of students, and she watched the spot where the second-year students gathered. She had waited impatiently for the end of Van Acker's class. Ordinarily she enjoyed it, particularly when Van Acker was in a filthy mood, which was most of the time. Francis Van Acker was a sadistic despot, and he despised mediocrity. Along with cowardice, servility and yes-men. On a bad day, he absolutely had to find a scapegoat, and then the smell of blood would waft throughout the classroom. Margot took great delight in seeing how fear spread through the ranks of her fellow students. They had developed a real survival instinct, and the moment the literature professor came into the room, everyone could tell whether he was on the warpath that day. Margot and all her classmates were familiar with the way his blue eyes scanned them, and the grimace distorting the set of his thin mouth.

The bootlickers despised Van Acker. And they were afraid of him. At the beginning of the school year they had made the mistake of believing they could tame him with their bowing and scraping, and they had discovered that not only was Van Acker impervious to any form of flattery, he would make them pay a heavy price for their error in judgment. His favourite prey were those who made up for their limited abilities (limited on the scale of the Marsac elite) with an excess of zeal. Margot was not one of them. She wondered if Van Acker liked her because she was her father's daughter or whether it was because, on the rare occasions when he had put her to the test, she had answered right back. He liked it when others stood up to him.

'Servaz,' he had said that morning, while her thoughts were drifting back to what had happened during the night, 'aren't you interested in what I'm saying?'

'Yes . . . uh . . . of course . . .'

'Well then, what was I saying?'

'That a consensus exists regarding certain works; that if, over the centuries, a great many people have come together to agree that Homer, Cervantes, Shakespeare and Victor Hugo are superior artists, then that means that the phrase *to each his own* is a sophism . . . And that not everything is equal, that the rubbish sold as art is not equivalent to the great creations of the human mind, and that the basic principles of democracy do not apply to art, where there is a ruthless dictatorship of the excellent over the mediocre.'

'Did I say, "not everything is equal"?'

'No, sir.'

'Then don't put words in my mouth.'

Giggling in the class. The same students who ordinarily served as lightning rods for Van Acker's wrath had a field day when someone else was his victim. Margot discreetly raised her middle finger towards the courtiers seated at the bottom of the amphitheatre who had turned around to stare at her.

Now she filled her young lungs with smoke and studied the David–Sarah–Virginie threesome. They gazed back at her one after the other, in spite of the distance and the clusters of students between them, and she returned their stares, never taking her eyes off them for a moment. During the night, she had decided to adopt a radically different strategy. A bolder one. *Get the game moving.* Instead of being more discreet, she would make herself obvious, she would reinforce their suspicions, she would make them think she knew something. If one of them was the culprit, then maybe they would begin to feel vulnerable and lose their grip.

This strategy was not without risks.

But an innocent boy was in prison, and time was passing.

★

'Where was this photograph taken?' asked Stehlin.

'In Marsac. Near the lake . . . at the edge of the woods. Just next to Marianne Bokhanowsky's garden – she's Hugo's mother.'

'Is she the one who discovered the letters?'

'No, I did.'

The director's eyes grew bigger.

'What were you doing there? Were you looking for something?'

Servaz had expected this question. His father had taught him one day that truth was nearly always the best strategy; most of the time it was more embarrassing to others than to oneself.

'I spent the night there. I've known Hugo's mother for a long time.'

The director's gaze lingered on him. Espérandieu and Samira were also looking at him now.

'Fucking hell! She's our prime suspect's mother!'

Servaz said nothing.

'Who else knows about this?'

'That I was there last night? At the moment, no one.'

'And what if she decides to use it against you? What if she mentions it to her lawyer? If the judge finds out, he will take the entire department off the case and hand the investigation to the gendarmes!'

Servaz recalled the lawyer with glasses who had shown up that night asking to see Hugo – but he didn't say anything.

'Shit, Martin,' barked Stehlin. 'In the space of a single evening, you interrogate an MP without letting anyone know and after that, you . . . you spend the night with . . . with the prime suspect's mother! This could have serious consequences; it could invalidate the entire investigation, all the work the team has done!'

Stehlin could have used much cruder language, but Servaz understood that he was furious.

'Right,' said the director, visibly struggling to keep his composure. 'In the meantime, what does it change? We're still at the same point: we have no proof that Julian Hirtmann carved those letters. I find it very hard to believe that he spends his time running after you and leaving clues all over the place. All because of some bullshit music and because you had a chit-chat once upon a time. Particularly as it all started after Claire Diemar's murder.'

'Not after, at the same time,' Servaz corrected him. 'Which changes everything. It began with the CD in the stereo. Let's not forget that Claire has the same profile as Hirtmann's other victims.'

His words had the desired effect. They took the time to digest this information.

'And then there's another possibility,' he said. 'Maybe, in fact, Hirtmann never actually left the region. While Interpol and every police force in Europe have been watching trains, airports and borders, imagining that he's thousands of kilometres away, maybe he's been hiding out right nearby – and telling himself that the last place we would ever look is across the street.'

He looked up and saw in their eyes that he had made his point, and they were beginning to have their doubts. The atmosphere suddenly felt heavier; just talking about the serial killer, his murders and his violence, even indirectly, was enough to poison the air. Servaz decided to drive his point home.

'Whatever the case may be, too many things are pointing in the same direction for us to neglect the Hirtmann lead any longer. Even if it isn't him, it means that someone out there is imitating him and is connected with Claire Diemar's murder one way or the other – which throws Hugo's guilt into doubt. I want Samira and Vincent to focus full time on this lead. They have to get in touch with the unit in Paris which has been tracking Hirtmann and try and confirm whether our man is in this region or not.'

Stehlin nodded gravely.

'Fine. But there is something else,' he said.

Servaz looked at him.

'What about your security? Whether it's Hirtmann or not, that lunatic out there seems to be following you wherever you go. It seems he's never very far from you. And then there was that incident at the bank. Fuck, you nearly got thrown off the roof, Martin! I don't like it. Our guy has a fixation on you – and he's attacked you once already.'

'If he wanted to get at me, he could easily have done it last night,' Servaz objected.

'What do you mean?'

'The French windows in the bedroom were open. There aren't even three metres between the garden and the balcony, with a drainpipe and a Virginia creeper right next to it. He could easily have climbed up. And we – I mean, I was asleep.'

They were all looking at him. There was no longer any doubt that he had slept with the mistress of the house – with a person who was directly connected to the investigation in hand. An investigation that could be torn to shreds by any reasonably competent lawyer who cared to cite a conflict of interests. Stehlin collapsed in his chair, gazed at the ceiling and gave out a very long sigh.

'If we work on the assumption that it is Hirtmann,' said Servaz hastily, 'I don't think he is a threat to me personally. His victims are always the same type: young women with more or less the same physical characteristics. The only men he has ever killed, to our knowledge, were his wife's lover – so in that case it was a crime of passion – and a Dutch man who was in the wrong place at the wrong time. There's something else I want Vincent and Samira to do.'

His two assistants gave him a questioning look.

'I agree on one thing at least: it does seem that Hirtmann is fixated on me. But since his victims have always been young women, I want Vincent and Samira to ensure Margot's protection at the lycée in Marsac. If Hirtmann wants to get at me, he knows that's my weak spot.'

Stehlin's brow creased still further. He seemed very worried now. Then he looked over at Servaz's assistants. Samira nodded.

'No problem,' she said. 'Martin is right: if that arsehole has decided to go after him, and if he is as well informed as he seems to be, we can't risk leaving Margot without protection.'

'I agree,' said Espérandieu with conviction.

'Anything else?' asked Stehlin.

'Yes. If Hirtmann is still after me, there might be a way to catch him this time. Pujol could shadow me. From a distance, with a colleague. As discreetly as possible, with GPS or a chip. If Hirtmann really wants to keep an eye on me, he'll have to show himself, he'll have to take a risk, no matter how small. And we'll be there when he does.'

'An interesting idea. And what happens if he comes out of the woods?'

'Then we move.'

'Without back-up? Special forces?'

'Hirtmann isn't a terrorist or a gangster. He's not prepared for that type of confrontation. He won't put up any resistance.'

'It seems to me he has plenty of resources,' objected Stehlin.

'For the time being, we don't even know if this plan will work. We'll decide when the time comes.'

'Right, fine. But I want to be kept informed the minute anything happens, and you pass on everything you have, is that clear?'

'I haven't finished,' said Servaz.

'What else?'

'You have to call the magistrate; I need authorisation to collect evidence. From an inmate at the prison in Seysses.'

Stehlin nodded. He had understood. He turned around and reached for a newspaper, which he tossed in front of Servaz.

'It didn't work. No leak, this time.'

Servaz looked at Stehlin. Could he have been mistaken? Either the journalist hadn't found the information sufficiently important, or Pujol was not the leak.

The sky beyond the classroom windows was pale. Everything was still. A white heat hung like a transparent film over the landscape. Short, hard shadows underneath the oaks, lindens and poplars made them all seemed petrified. Only a jet's fluffy white vapour trail and a few birds provided some movement. And even the final-year students training on the rugby pitch seemed to be suffering, their game unfolding in slow motion, with no more enthusiasm or inspiration than that of the French national football team.

Summer had settled in and as Margot looked out of the window she wondered how long this whole business would last. She was listening to the history class with only half an ear, and the words slid over her like water on plastic. She thought back to the handwritten note she had found taped to her locker an hour earlier. On reading it she had blushed with shame and anger, then, from the gazes she met all around her, she realised that everyone already knew about it. The note said:

Hugo is innocent. Your father had better watch out. And you too. You're not welcome any more, filthy whore.

Her strategy was beginning to pay off . . .

25

Circles

On Tuesday afternoon at 13.05 Meredith Jacobsen was waiting in the arrivals hall at Orly-Ouest for the Air France flight from Toulouse-Blagnac. It was ten minutes late, but she knew why: the flight had been delayed to allow her boss, Paul Lacaze, to board. He had got his seat at the last minute on a plane that was already packed.

It was not his position as MP that had earned him such preferential treatment, but his membership of a very closed circle: the 2,000 Club. Unlike the usual frequent flyer programmes reserved for travellers who had clocked up tens of thousands of miles, membership of the 2,000 Club was granted only to a tightly restricted club of major economic movers and shakers, showbusiness personalities, and high-ranking civil servants and politicians. Originally the club had been limited to 2,000 members around the world, to delineate how exclusive and important it was, but it had gradually been enlarged and there were almost ten times the original number now. The 577 deputies of the National Assembly were not automatically granted access to the club, obviously; but Lacaze was a rising star, a media darling, and the airline pampered such high-profile personalities.

At last the doors opened, and Meredith waved to her boss as he came towards her. He seemed to be in a bad mood. She kissed him on both cheeks, grabbed his bag and they headed to a waiting taxi.

'We have to hurry,' she said. 'Devincourt is expecting you for lunch at the Cercle de l'Union interalliée.'

Lacaze grumbled to himself: 'the Whale' could have chosen somewhere more discreet. Officially, Devincourt was just one senator among others. He wasn't even a group president. But in reality, at the age of seventy-two, he was one of the big names in the party. He had been elected as an MP for the first time at the age of twenty-nine, in 1967, and he had served all the ministries of the realm one

231

after the other for over forty years; he had known six presidents, eighteen prime ministers, thousands of parliamentarians, and he had been in on more successes and failures than anyone. Lacaze saw him as a dinosaur, a man of the past, a has-been – but no one could afford to ignore the Whale.

Meredith tugged on her skirt as she settled into the back of the taxi and Lacaze thought, not for the first time, that she really did have nice legs. With an open file on her lap, Meredith went over his schedule for the day and he gazed out at the dreary fallow fields of Paris's southern suburbs while listening to her with one ear. By and large, he'd rather have the slums of Buenos Aires or São Paulo any day. He had visited them during one of the extravagant official voyages organised by the Assembly's friendship groups: those suburbs, at least, had some charm.

When he entered the grand dining room, Lacaze saw that the Whale had not waited to be seated. He was presiding triumphantly in the middle of the Salle à Manger, the Cercle de l'Union interalliée's restaurant on the first floor. The old senator preferred it to the terrace, which was always overcrowded in fine weather, or the cafeteria where the sporty thirtysomethings clustered whenever they visited the club's sports facilities. The Whale did not do sport and he weighed easily twenty-five stone. He had been a regular at the Cercle before those snotty-nosed kids were even born. Founded in 1917, when the United States officially entered the war, the Cercle de l'Union interalliée had originally been designed to welcome the officers of the Alliance, but it had long ago lost its original function. It had two restaurants, a bar, a garden, a library with 15,000 volumes, private drawing rooms, a billiards room, a swimming pool, a Turkish bath, and a sporting complex in the basement. The admission fee was roughly €4,000; the annual membership fee €1,400. Of course, money was not enough to obtain admission – otherwise every spotty computer genius, drug trafficker from the banlieue or newly wealthy secondhand-clothes merchant from the other side of the Atlantic would come and sprawl in its drawing rooms and trample the carpets in their trainers. One had to have a sponsor – and patience – and for some people the wait would last an entire lifetime.

Weaving his way between the tables, Lacaze observed that the senator had not noticed him yet. He could see the rolls of fat on his neck and the way his cushions of flesh stretched the fabric of his expensive suit.

'My young friend,' said Devincourt in his rasping voice when he saw the MP. 'Do have a seat. I didn't wait. My belly is more demanding than the most demanding of mistresses.'

'Hello, Senator.'

The maître d' arrived and Lacaze ordered a rack of lamb with bolet mushrooms.

'So, I hear tell that you stuck your nose in some pussy and she had the bad manners to snuff it? I hope she was worth it, at least.'

Lacaze shuddered. He took a deep breath. An acid mixture of fury and despair twisted his bowels. To hear the Whale speak like that about Claire made him want to smash the fat bastard's skull. But he had already broken down in front of that cop. He had to get a grip on himself.

'Well, at least she wasn't paid,' he retorted, clenching his jaw.

Everyone in Paris knew that the Whale resorted to the paid services of professionals. Girls from Eastern Europe whose pimps sent them to grand hotels that were not very particular. For a moment the senator stared at him, his gaze indecipherable – then he exploded with laughter, earning their table a few surprised looks.

'Shit, what a bloody fool! In love on top of everything!' Devincourt wiped his lips with the corner of his napkin and suddenly went serious. Coming from him, there was something obscene about the word *love*, and once again Paul Lacaze felt his stomach go into a knot. 'I was in love myself once,' said the Whale suddenly. 'A long time ago. I was a student. She was magnificent. She was studying at the Beaux-Arts. She was talented – oh, yes. I think those were the most beautiful days of my life. I had every intention of marrying her; I dreamt of having children, a big family, with her by my side. We would have had a sweet, long, peaceful life: we would have grown old together, watched our children grow up and have children them-selves. And we would have been proud of them, of our friends, of ourselves. A schoolgirl's daydreams – my head was full of them. Can you imagine? Me, Pierre Devincourt! And then I found her in bed with someone else. She hadn't even bothered to lock her door. Did your girlfriend have someone else?'

'No.'

His answer was firm and immediate. Devincourt gave him a cautious look, a brief spark of cunning beneath his heavy eyelids.

'People vote,' said the Whale suddenly. 'They may think they decide . . . but they have no power of decision. None whatsoever. Because all they do is re-elect the same caste, ad infinitum, from one term of office to the next. The same little group of people who decide everything for them. *Us.* And when I say "us", I'm including our political opponents. Two parties who've been sharing power for fifty years. Who pretend they don't agree on anything when in fact they do, on almost everything . . . For fifty years we have been the masters of this country and for fifty years we've been selling the good people this fraudulent notion of "change". Coalition should have started them thinking: how can two ruling parties with such radically opposing views work together? But it didn't: they have gone on swallowing the fraud whole, as if everything were fine and dandy. And we reap the benefits of their largesse.'

He lifted a lobster's claw to his mouth and sucked noisily.

'But lately, some people have wanted to divide the pie up rather too quickly. They forget they have to put on an act. You can piss on the people – but only if they believe it's rain.'

The Whale wiped his mouth again.

'You won't get to be head of the party if there are any scandals, Paul. Not any more. Those days are over. So do what you have to do to keep yourself out of that murder case – understood? I'll take care of the little commandant. We'll keep an eye on him. But I want to know: do you have an alibi for the night of the murder?'

Lacaze gave a start.

'Good Lord, what are you thinking? That I killed her?'

He saw the fat man's eyes flare with anger. The Whale leaned over the table and his bass voice rumbled like thunder between the glasses.

'Listen to me, you prat! Keep your wide-eyed innocent act for the courts, all right? I want to know what you were doing that night: were you screwing her, drinking with friends, snorting a line in the bog, was there someone with you, or no one – people who can testify, dammit! And stop putting on airs like you're so wholesome, you're pissing me off.'

Lacaze felt as if he'd been slapped. The blood drained from his face. He looked around to make sure no one had overheard.

'I was . . . I was with Suzanne. We were watching a DVD. Since her diagnosis, I've been trying to be at home as much as possible.'

The senator sat up straight.

'I'm very sorry about Suzanne. It's awful, what's happened to her. I am very fond of her.'

The Whale said this with brutal sincerity, then plunged his nose back into his plate. End of discussion. Lacaze felt a wave of guilt wash over him. He wondered how the man seated opposite would have reacted if he had known the truth.

26

Quarters

Sounds, to start with. Invasive, disturbing. They made a thick net of noise, unceasing, a relentless routine. Voices, doors, shouts, gates, locks, footsteps, key chains. Then came the smell. Not necessarily unpleasant, but typical. You would recognise it anywhere. All prisons have the same smell.

Here most of the voices were female. The women's wing of the prison of Seysses, near Toulouse.

When the warden unlocked the door, Servaz stiffened. He had left his gun and his warrant card at the entrance, signed in, and gone through the multiple security doors. He followed in the guard's footsteps, and he prepared himself mentally.

The woman motioned to him to go in. He took a breath and crossed the threshold. Prisoner number 1614 was sitting with her elbows on the table, her hands crossed in front of her. The neon light fell on her chestnut hair, which was no longer thick and long and silky, but short, dry and dull. But her gaze had not changed. Élisabeth Ferney had lost none of her arrogance, nor her authority. Servaz was willing to bet that she had carved out her niche here, just as she had when she had been head nurse at the Wargnier Institute. Everyone did her bidding there. And she was the one who had helped Julian Alois Hirtmann to escape. Servaz had attended her trial. Her lawyer had tried to insist that Hirtmann had manipulated her, tried to portray her as a victim – but his client's personality had worked against her. The members of the jury could see for themselves that the woman in the dock was anything but a victim.

'Hello, Commandant.'

Her voice was still just as firm. But there was a new weariness. Her intonation had a slight drawl to it now. Servaz wondered if Lisa Ferney was taking antidepressants. It was common practice here.

'Hello, Élisabeth.'

'Oh, first-name basis now, is it? Are we friends? News to me . . . Around here, it's usually Ferney. Or 1614. That slut who brought you here, she calls me the "head bitch". But that's just for show. In fact, she comes to see me at night and she's the one who gets down on her knees . . .'

Servaz looked at her closely, trying to tell how much was true and how much was false, but it was a waste of time. Élisabeth Ferney was unfathomable – apart from the little sparks of malice that danced in her brown eyes. Servaz had known a prison director who, when referring to his female inmates, would say 'that bitch' or 'those whores'. He insulted them systematically, harassed the youngest ones sexually, and went to the women's wing every night for blow jobs. He'd been dismissed, but there had been no criminal charges, as the prosecutor considered his dismissal sufficient punishment. Servaz knew that in the prison world, anything was possible.

'You know what I miss the most?' she continued, apparently satisfied with the reaction she saw on his face. 'The Internet. We all got hooked on that crap, it's crazy. I'm sure that being deprived of Facebook will cause the number of prison suicides to skyrocket.'

He pulled up a chair and sat down opposite her. He could hear sounds through the closed door. The echoes of voices, shouts, a cart being pushed – and then one particular noise: the clinking of metal on metal. Servaz knew what this meant. Exercise time. The guards used this time to go into the cells and make sure none of the bars had been sawn through by tapping on them with an iron bar. *That sound* . . . nothing could make the prisoners feel their solitude more than that permanent background noise.

'Seventy per cent of the inmates here are drug addicts, did you know that? Fewer than ten per cent of them get any sort of treatment. Last week there was a girl who hanged herself. It was her seventh attempt and she had told them she would try again. And yet they left her alone, with no surveillance. So you see, if I wanted to, I could escape. One way or another.'

He wondered what she was getting at. Had Élisabeth Ferney tried to commit suicide? He made a mental note to ask the medical staff.

'But you're not here just to see how I'm doing, are you?'

Servaz knew she would ask this question. He thought again of his father's advice. Sincerity . . . He wasn't sure this was the best strategy, but he didn't have any others in his arsenal.

'Julian wrote to me. An e-mail. I think he's here in Toulouse, or not far from here.'

Was there something in the former head nurse's gaze? Or was it just his imagination? She was staring at him, as impenetrable as ever.

'"Julian", "Élisabeth" . . . We're all chums now, are we? And what did it say, that e-mail?'

'That he was going to take action, that he was enjoying his freedom.'

'Do you believe him?'

'What do you think?'

The smile on her unpainted lips was like a scar.

'Show me the e-mail, and perhaps I'll tell you.'

'No.'

The smile vanished.

'You look tired, *Martin* . . . You look like someone who doesn't get a lot of sleep, or am I mistaken? It's because of him, isn't it?'

'You don't look too great either, *Lisa.*'

'You didn't answer my question. Is Hirtmann bugging you? Are you afraid he'll go after you? Do you have children?'

Beneath the table he dug his nails into his palms. Then he placed his hands flat on his thighs, uncrossed his ankles and tried to relax. There was something about Élisabeth Ferney that chilled him to the bone.

'And anyway, why you? If I'm not mistaken, you only met him once. I remember your visit to the Institute. With that little psychologist with a goatee and that female gendarme . . . such a pretty girl. What did you discuss for him to get so fixated on you? And you – you're fixated on him too, aren't you?'

He told himself he mustn't let her lead the conversation. Élisabeth Ferney belonged to the same race as Hirtmann: she was a narcissistic pervert, a manipulator who constantly tried to establish her hold over other people's minds. He was about to say something but she didn't give him the chance.

'So, you figure he might have been in touch with his former accomplice, is that it? Even if I did know something, why should I tell you? You, of all people?'

This question, too, he had foreseen. He confronted her gaze.

'I spoke to the magistrate. Access to daily papers, and you'll be enrolled in the micro-computing workshop. With Internet access once a week. I will personally make sure that the magistrate's decision is properly enforced by the administration of this . . . establishment. You have my word.'

'And what if I have nothing to tell you? What if Hirtmann hasn't contacted me? Does your offer still hold?'

She gave him a nasty smile. He didn't answer.

'And what guarantee do I have that you will keep your word?'

'None.'

She laughed. But it was a joyless laugh. He had hit the bull's eye. He could see it in her gaze.

'None,' he said again. 'No guarantee. Everything depends on whether I believe you or not. Everything depends on me, Élisabeth. But you don't have much choice, anyway, do you?'

She looked at him with a brief flash of anger and hatred. She must have said that sentence so often that, even coming from someone else's lips, she recognised it. The words of someone with the upper hand. Now the roles were reversed, and she was cruelly aware of it. She had been in his place when she ran the Wargnier Institute with Dr Xavier – threatening and cajoling her patients, making them see just what they had to win or to lose, telling them exactly what he had just told her: that everything depended on her.

'Unlike you, I have not had any news from Julian Hirtmann,' she replied, and he could sense a frustration and sadness in her voice that were not feigned. 'He hasn't tried to get back in touch. I've waited a long time for a sign. Something . . . You know as well as I do that there is nothing easier than to get a message to a prisoner. But it has never happened. I do, however, have some information that might interest you.'

He held her gaze, all his senses on the alert.

'Computer once a week and access to the daily papers, we agree on that?'

He nodded.

'Someone came here before you, someone who wanted to know exactly the same thing. And, oddly enough, she came by today.'

'Who was it?' he asked.

She flashed him a vicious smile. He got up.

239

'Anyway, all I have to do is ask the director,' he said.

'Fine. Sit down and I'll tell you. But don't forget your promise.'

He had someone else to see. In the juvenile wing. It was perfectly illegal, and he knew it. But Servaz had his contacts at the prison, and the director would not be informed about this meeting. That was why he had asked the magistrate for permission to question Lisa Ferney: to gain access to the prison.

Walking along the corridors, he thought about what she had just told him. Someone had been there before him. Someone he hadn't seen in a long time. Once again he saw himself in the avalanche.

The guard unlocked the door and Servaz gave a start. Good Lord! The hollow cheeks, the red-rimmed eyes, the desperate gaze. He knew Hugo had been placed in an individual cell, but suddenly he was frightened for him. If Marianne saw her son in this state, she would be terrified.

Servaz went back out and pulled the door behind him.

'I want him under special surveillance,' he said to the guard. 'Remove his belt, his shoelaces, everything. I'm afraid he might do something stupid. This kid will be getting out of here soon. It's only a question of time.'

He thought again about what Lisa Ferney had said: '*Last week there was a girl who hanged herself. It was her seventh attempt . . . And yet they left her alone, with no surveillance.*'

The guard simply smiled at him.

'Fuck, do I make myself clear?' said Servaz.

The guard gave him an indifferent look, then nodded. Servaz told himself he would have a word with the director before leaving, then he went into the cell.

'Hello, Hugo.'

No answer.

Just as he had done with Élisabeth Ferney, he pulled up a chair and sat down.

'Hugo,' he began, 'I'm really sorry about . . . this.' He made a gesture that took in the room and everything around it. 'I did everything I could to persuade the judge to let you go, but the accusations are too serious . . . at least, for the time being.'

Hugo stared at his hands. Servaz looked at the boy's nails: so bitten they were bleeding.

'There is some new evidence . . . there's a good chance you won't be here very much longer.'

'*Get me out of here!*'

His scream took Martin by surprise. Hugo's eyes were pleading, full of tears, his lips trembling.

'Get me out of here, please.'

Yes, he thought. *Don't worry. I'm going to get you out of here. But you have to be strong, kid.*

'Listen to me,' said Servaz. 'You have to trust me. I'm going to help you get out of here, but you have to help me, too. I have absolutely no right to be here: you've been indicted, and only the magistrates are allowed to talk to you, in the presence of your lawyer. I could be severely punished for this. But there is new evidence. So the judge will be obliged to reconsider his position. Do you understand?'

'What new evidence?'

'Do you know Paul Lacaze?'

Servaz saw his eyelids flicker. He hadn't been an investigator for fifteen years for nothing.

'You know him, don't you? Don't you?'

Hugo stared again at his gnawed fingers.

'Shit, Hugo!'

'Yes, I know him.'

Servaz waited in silence for him to continue.

'I know he was seeing Claire . . .'

'He was seeing her?'

'They had an affair . . . the top-secret kind. Lacaze is married, and he's deputy mayor of Marsac. But how did you find out?'

'We found his e-mails on Claire's computer.'

This time, Servaz detected no reaction. Apparently, Hugo was not surprised. So perhaps he was not the one who had emptied out the mailbox.

Servaz leaned across the table.

'Paul Lacaze had a top-secret affair with Claire Diemar. An affair no one was aware of, you said so yourself. So why do you know about it?'

'She told me.'

Servaz stared at him, stunned.

'What?'

'Claire told me everything.'

'Why would she do that?'

'Because we were lovers.'

Servaz continued to stare at him as he took in the news.

'I know what you're thinking. I'm seventeen years old and she was thirty-two. But we were in love . . . She met Paul Lacaze before me. She had decided to break up with him. He was really in love with her. And jealous. He had suspected for some time that she had someone else. She was afraid he'd blow a fuse, that he'd cause a scandal when he found out she was having an affair with one of her students – especially an under-age one. On the other hand, given his own situation, his hands were tied. He couldn't let it get out in the open.'

'How long had it been going on?' asked Servaz.

'For a few months. In the beginning, what I told you was true: we would talk about literature, she was interested in what I was writing, she really believed in my talent and she wanted to encourage me. She invited me over for coffee from time to time. She knew it would get all the gossips' tongues wagging, but she didn't care: Claire was like that – she was free, she was above all that. She didn't give a damn what other people thought. And then, gradually, we fell in love. It's strange, because she wasn't my type at all, to start with. But . . . I had never met anyone like her before.'

'Why didn't you tell the magistrate, or me?'

Hugo stared at him, his eyes round.

'Are you joking? Surely you know that would've made me look even more suspicious!'

He was right.

'Do you think Paul Lacaze knew about Claire and you? Think carefully. It's important.'

'I know what you're thinking,' said Hugo again, sadly. 'To be honest, I don't know. She promised me she would tell him everything. We'd had a long talk about it. I was fed up with the situation; I didn't want her to see him any more. But honestly, I don't think she ever told him. She kept putting it off, she always found some reason to postpone it . . . I think she was afraid of his reaction.'

Servaz thought about Claire Diemar's passionate e-mails, her declarations of eternal love to Thomas999. He thought about all the cigarette stubs in the woods, the shadowy figure leaving the pub

242

after Hugo, the kid's statement to the effect that he had passed out and woken up in Claire's living room. Maybe Paul Lacaze didn't need anyone to tell him anything, after all. Maybe he already knew.

Out in the prison car park, the heat struck him like an uppercut. The sun hung like a lamp in an egg-white sky and he felt as if he couldn't get enough air. He opened all the doors of the Cherokee to try and cool down the furnace inside the car. On his left were the walls and watchtowers of the other prison, known as Muret. It was a facility for long-term detainees, unlike the remand centre he had just left, and there was not a single woman among the 600 inmates.

There were 2,000 women imprisoned in France, spread among sixty-three of the 186 jails. Only six of them were reserved exclusively for female detainees.

He took out his mobile and dialled a number.

'Ziegler,' said the voice on the end of the line.

'I have to talk to you.'

'You're very suntanned.'

'I just got back from holiday.'

'Where did you go?'

He wasn't at all interested in her reply. But not to ask would have been discourteous.

'The Cyclades,' she answered, her tone indicating that she hadn't been taken in. 'Sunbathing, sightseeing, diving—'

'I should have called you earlier,' he interrupted. 'To find out how you were doing, but you know what it's like, I've been . . . hmm . . . busy.'

Her gaze wandered over the crowd on the pleasant terrace of the Basque Bar, in the shade of the trees on the place Saint-Pierre in Toulouse.

'You don't have to apologise, Martin. I could have called you, too. And what you did for me . . . that favourable report you wrote . . . They had me read it, you know,' she lied. 'I should have thanked you for it.'

'All I did was tell them what happened.'

'No. You told it from a certain point of view, in a way that exonerated me. It's always a question of point of view. You kept your promise.'

He shrugged, embarrassed. A waitress wove her way between the tables and set a coffee and a Perrier down before them.

'How's the new job going?'

It was her turn to shrug.

'Roadside tests, the odd fight between two drunks in a bar, burglaries, vandalism, or some guy caught selling dope outside the lycée . . . But now I can see how privileged I was at the crime investigation division. The station is run-down, the housing is unfit, absurd decisions are taken by superiors who are completely out of touch . . . Are you familiar with the syndrome of the "wriggling gendarme"?'

'The what?'

'The eggheads who oversee us have decided that the most urgent thing is to equip our offices with new chairs. The only problem is that the armrests are not set wide enough apart for gendarmes wearing a holster. As a result, all of us spend our time wriggling just to fit.'

The image made him smile. But not for long.

'You went to see Lisa Ferney yesterday,' he said. 'Why was that?'

'I . . . I read in the paper that Hirtmann had been in touch with you, that he wrote you an e-mail . . . I . . .' She was hesitating. 'Ever since what happened in Saint-Martin, I haven't stopped . . . thinking about him. Like I just told you, there's not much excitement at the gendarmerie. So, to pass the time, I've been compiling as much information as I can find on Hirtmann. It's become a sort of obsession . . . a sort of *hobby*. Like electric trains, stamp collections or butterflies, know what I mean? Except that the butterfly I dream of pinning to my board is a serial killer.'

She took a sip of water. Servaz observed her. She still had the little tattoo on her neck – a Chinese ideogram – and a discreet piercing in her left nostril. Not really your standard-issue look for a gendarme. He couldn't say he didn't like it. He appreciated Irène Ziegler. He had enjoyed working with her.

'You mean you collect everything that has been written or said about him?'

'Yes. Something like that. I try to see how much of the information overlaps, to see where it might lead. Up to now, I haven't had much success. It's as if he's disappeared from the surface of the planet. No one knows if he's alive or dead. So when I got back from holiday and I saw he'd been in touch with you, I immediately thought of Lisa Ferney. And went to see her.'

'It might be a hoax,' he said. 'Or a copycat.'

She saw him hesitate.

'But there's something else,' he added.

She didn't respond. She thought she knew what he was going to say, but she couldn't tell him what she had found on his computer.

'A biker who matches Hirtmann's description, speaking with an accent that could be Swiss, was seen at a service station on the A20 motorway. The images from the surveillance camera at a tollbooth a bit further south confirmed the shop manager's testimony. If it's him, he was headed for Toulouse at the time.'

'When was this?' she asked, even though she already knew the answer.

'Roughly two weeks ago.'

She looked around her, as if Hirtmann might be there, somewhere in the crowd, watching them. Most of the customers were students; the terrace, with its pink brick walls, Virginia creeper and stone fountain, was just like a little square in Provence. She recalled the exact contents of the e-mail. She would have liked to tell him what she thought – but again, she couldn't, not without confessing to him that she had hacked into his computer.

'This e-mail,' she said on the off chance. 'Have you got a copy of it?'

He reached into his jacket, pulled out a sheet of paper folded in four and handed it to her. She took the time to reread a text she already knew by heart.

'This must have you on edge.'

He nodded. 'What do you think?' he asked.

'Mmm.' She pretended to go on reading.

'Is it Hirtmann or not?'

She pretended to consider the matter.

'I think it sounds like him.'

'What makes you say that?'

'I told you, I've spent months studying his personality, his behaviour . . . I don't mean to boast, but I think I know him better than anyone. This message: it rings true, there's something there. It's as if I can hear his voice, the way it sounded when we were in his cell . . .'

'Yet a woman sent it, from an Internet café in Toulouse.'

'A victim or an accomplice,' she said. 'If he's found a woman

245

who's as perverted as he is, that's very worrying,' she added, looking at him.

He felt a chill, despite the heat.

'You say you're bored at your new post?' he said with a half-smile.

She looked right at him, clearly wondering what he meant by this.

'Let's just say that it's hardly the reason I joined the gendarmerie.'

He paused to think, then made up his mind.

'Samira and Vincent are gathering all the information they can about Hirtmann. Except that I've also asked them to keep an eye on my daughter. Margot is attending school at the lycée in Marsac. Like most of the students, she's a boarder, far away from me and her mother. So she's an ideal target.' He realised he had lowered his voice as he said this, as if he feared that saying things out loud might make them happen. 'Suppose I forward you all the information we get about Hirtmann? I'd really appreciate your input.'

He saw her face light up.

'A sort of consultant, is that it?'

'You said so yourself: you've become a specialist on Swiss serial killers,' he confirmed with a smile.

'You're not afraid you might get in trouble?'

'We don't have to go shouting it from the rooftops. Only Vincent and Samira will be in on it, and they're the ones who will pass on the information. I trust them. And I'm interested in your point of view. We worked well together, that winter.'

He saw that his compliment had touched her.

'Who told you I'd been to see Lisa Ferney in prison?' she asked.

'She did. I went to visit her roughly two hours after you did. Great minds—'

'And what did she tell you about Hirtmann?'

'That she's had no contact with him. You?'

'The same thing. You believe her?'

'She looks really depressed.'

'And frustrated.'

'Or she's an excellent actress.'

'Could be.'

'How would she behave if Hirtmann was in the neighbourhood and he'd got in touch with her?'

'She would probably act as if she'd had no news from him – and she would pretend to be depressed—'

'—and frustrated.'

'So you think that—'

'I don't think anything. But it might be a good idea to keep an eye on her.'

'I don't see how we can,' said Ziegler.

'Go and visit her regularly. She seems to be moping. Try and get closer to her. She might let something slip. Even if it's just to give you a little something in exchange for your visits, and to be sure that you'll come back and see her. But don't lose sight of the fact that she's a narcissist, like Hirtmann, and that she'll do whatever she can to exploit your weaknesses, to get round you, and she may only tell you what you want to hear.'

She agreed, looking preoccupied.

'I wasn't born yesterday. Do you really think that Margot is at risk?'

It was as if a bundle of worms were writhing in his belly.

'*Expressa nocent, non expressa non nocent,*' he answered.

Then he translated: '"Things expressed may be prejudicial; things not expressed are not."'

She sped through the countryside on her Suzuki GSR600, well over the speed limit, overtaking cars that seemed glued to the road. The sun shone on lush rolling green hills, and she felt full of energy and impatience. She was in on the action again.

Hirtmann in the area . . .

It should have frightened her but in fact the challenge excited her. Like a boxer training for the fight of his life who learns that his most formidable adversary, long withdrawn from competition, is on the circuit once again. Ready to put on his gloves.

'The results are in from the graphology test,' said Espérandieu.

Servaz was watching a woman crossing the street, backlit by the setting sun. It was a fine summer evening, but he was disappointed. When the phone had vibrated in his pocket, he had hoped it would be Marianne. He'd been waiting all day for her call.

'Claire Diemar didn't write that sentence in the notebook.'

Servaz took his eyes away from the woman. The baking urban landscape suddenly disappeared.

'Are we sure?'

247

'The graphologist was categorical. He said that there's not the shadow of a doubt, he would stake his reputation on it.'

Servaz focused his thoughts. Things were coming together. Someone had written a sentence in a notebook denouncing Hugo and had left it in plain sight in Claire Diemar's office. Hugo was the ideal scapegoat: a brilliant, good looking druggy. Above all, he was Claire's lover. He often went to her house. Servaz thought about what this implied. Not necessarily that whoever was trying to pin the blame on him knew about their affair. Maybe they simply knew about the young man's visits. Marianne, Francis and the English neighbour had all told him the same thing: news travelled fast in Marsac.

Then there was the other option, he thought, as he walked into the entrance to the car park. Paul Lacaze . . .

'One thing's for sure,' said Espérandieu. 'Whoever wrote it has an absolutely twisted mind.'

'If you wanted to get a sample of Paul Lacaze's handwriting without him knowing, where would you go?' said Servaz, remembering the warning he'd received from the Auch prosecutor that very morning.

'I don't know. The town hall? The National Assembly?'

'You can't think of anything more discreet?'

'Hang on a minute,' said his assistant. 'How could Paul Lacaze have dropped off that notebook at the lycée? Everybody knows him in Marsac. He certainly wouldn't have taken such a risk if he were getting ready to kill her.'

A point in his favour.

'Who else, then?'

'Someone who can move around freely at the lycée without being noticed. A student, a teacher, a staff member . . . there are plenty of people.'

Servaz thought again about the mysterious pile of cigarette butts in the forest. He slipped his ticket and his bank card into the machine, and punched in his code.

'This takes Hirtmann out of the picture again,' said Espérandieu.

Servaz pushed open the glass door into the car park, and walked along the vast echoing space between the rows of cars.

'How come?'

'Honestly, how do you think he could be so well informed about Marsac, and Hugo, and the lycée?'

'And the letters? The e-mail? The CD? What are they supposed to mean?'

Silence on the other end of the line.

'Maybe it's just someone trying to unnerve you, Martin—'

'For Christ's sake, the Mahler CD was in the stereo before the investigation was even assigned to us!'

Touché. This time his assistant had no answer. Suddenly Servaz heard the sound of footsteps behind him, ringing on the concrete.

'I don't know, it's weird,' said Espérandieu. 'Something's not right.'

Servaz could tell from his assistant's voice that he had come to the same conclusion he himself had: the whole business didn't make sense. It was as if they had all the keys, but not the right lock. He walked more slowly. He was level with the Cherokee. The footsteps behind him were coming closer. He pressed the remote and the vehicle made a double beep at the same time as the lights flashed to welcome him.

'In any case, watch out—' his assistant was beginning to say.

Servaz whirled round, a single quick fluid movement. He was there, only a few inches away . . . with his hand in the pocket of his leather jacket. Servaz saw his own reflection in his dark glasses. He recognised his smile. His pale skin and brown hair. Before Hirtmann had time to pull out his gun, he struck him with his free hand.

The punch sent a sharp pain into his knuckles, but he didn't give Hirtmann the time to recover. He grabbed him by his jacket and pushed him towards a car on the other side of the row, smashing his face against the rear window. Hirtmann swore. His sunglasses fell to the ground with a clatter. Servaz pressed himself against his back. His hand was already rummaging in the inside pocket of Hirtmann's jacket. His fingers found what they were looking for . . . or so he thought. Not a weapon.

A mobile phone.

He swung his opponent around. It wasn't Hirtmann. Now there was no doubt. Even cosmetic surgery couldn't have changed him to that degree. The man's nose was bleeding profusely. His gaze was wild, frightened.

'Take my money! Go ahead! But don't hurt me, please!'

Shit! Servaz picked his glasses up off the ground, put them back on his nose and patted the leather jacket.

'I'm sorry,' he said. 'I mistook you for someone else.'

'What? What?' croaked the man, relieved, indignant and stunned, while Servaz slipped his own telephone in his pocket and quickly walked away.

He turned the ignition and put the car in reverse, gears grating. Through the rear window he could see that the man had taken out his phone and was staring at his number plate. With his other hand he was trying to stop his nosebleed with the help of a thick pack of tissues.

Servaz would have liked to repair the damage, but it was too late. He had often thought that a time machine would have been the most wonderful invention for guys like him – guys who had a tendency to act before thinking. How many things might he have saved in his life with such a machine? His marriage, his career, Marianne . . . ? He put the car in first and drove off, tyres squealing on the slick surface of the car park.

Perhaps he was fantasising, he mused, as he took the exit ramp. Perhaps he had a tendency to complicate things. Perhaps Hirtmann had nothing to do with all this . . . Vincent was right: how could he? But perhaps he was the one who was right and they were all wrong, and he did have a reason to look behind him, to be on his guard, to fear the future.

A reason to be afraid.

27

The End of the Road

Drissa Kanté was awoken by the sound of a car horn in the street. Or perhaps it was in his nightmare.

In his dream, it was night time, in the middle of the sea, somewhere south of Lampedusa. In his dream, the sea was a succession of rolling hills, the sky a maelstrom of clouds and lightning. The rain assaulted them, blinded them, the women were screaming, the children were crying, the roar of the furious sea drowned out everything else.

Their motor had died not long after departure; the rotten hull of the old tub creaked with every blow of the sea. Drissa, his teeth chattering, turned his thoughts to the Libyan smugglers who had taken all their savings to sell them this raft, knowing full well they were probably sending them to their deaths; then he thought of all the vultures who had got rich at their expense at every stage of their 'journey' – and he cursed them.

When the lights of the Maltese trawler had appeared on the horizon, they thought their salvation had come. They had all stood up in the boat, at the risk of capsizing, and they had screamed and waved their arms. But the vessel did not stop. As the ship passed by they had seen the indifferent expressions on the faces of the Maltese fishermen; some were even laughing and waving to them.

That was when he woke up.

He looked around him, his mouth open, and his heart gradually stopped pounding as he recognised the room. He rubbed his eyes and repeated, like a mantra, *My name is Drissa Kanté, I was born in Ségou, Mali, I'm thirty-three years old and now I am living and working in France.*

It was a Spanish trawler, the *Rio Esera*, which came to their rescue. When the Spanish captain attempted to disembark his passengers on Malta, the authorities refused to let him. The trawler was stranded off the Maltese shore for over a week before at last his unwanted cargo was taken off his hands.

Once they were on land, Drissa was told to take bus number 113 and he would find a reception centre at the end of the line where he could sleep, wash and eat.

He boarded the bus and got out at the terminus. The Hal Far Camp: an old military airport transformed into a refugee camp. Sheet-iron containers with tiny windows, a tent village and a hangar with no planes. In the hangar alone there were over 400 people. He spent over a year living in one of the containers. Many of the migrants were sorry they had ever left home. And then, in 2009, there came a glimmer of hope: the French ambassador to Malta, Daniel Rondeau, agreed to take in refugees. That was how Drissa Kanté came to find himself in France.

Work was better paid than in Malta, where people like him had left the camp every morning to cluster at a roundabout near Marsa, where recruiters negotiated the price of a day's work from their cars. It had been the same thing here, in the beginning, until Drissa found a job at a cleaning firm. He was glad of it. He got up every morning at three o'clock to clean offices. It wasn't too hard. He had got used to the calming noise of the Hoover, the artificial smells of carpeting and leather armchairs, of bottles of cleaning products, and the routine simplicity of his task – all this despite the fact he had a degree in engineering. He was part of a small team – five women and two men – who went from one office block to the next. In the afternoon, he rested. In the evening he went out to meet people like himself in the town's cafés and he dreamt of another existence, the one he could see briefly as he walked past the shops and observed customers sitting in restaurant windows.

Something was bothering Drissa, though. Dreaming hadn't been enough. He had wanted to experience that life as well. And to do so, he had agreed to do something, and now he was sorry. It haunted him. Drissa Kanté was a fundamentally honest person. And he knew that if he were ever found out, he would lose his job. And perhaps a great deal more. He did not want to be sent back – not any more.

When he stepped out onto the pavement the streets of Toulouse were vibrating with that energy peculiar to summer evenings. It was 19.00 and the temperature was still close to thirty-five degrees. He was glad. He liked heat. Unlike most of the inhabitants of the city, he found it easier to breathe like this.

He sat down at the terrace of the café L'Escale, on the place Arnaud-Bernard, and greeted Hocine, the owner. He ordered a mint tea while waiting for his friends to arrive. At a neighbouring table a customer stood up, came over and stood right in front of him. Drissa looked up and saw a man in his forties, with greasy brown hair, a potbelly that stretched a shirt of questionable whiteness beneath a worn jacket, and an impenetrable face behind dark glasses.

'May I sit down?'

The Malian sighed.

'I'm waiting for friends.'

'It won't take me long, *Driss*.'

Drissa Kanté shrugged. Zlatan Jovanovic, glass of beer in his hand, flopped down onto the wobbly little chair. Drissa stirred the sugar in his steaming little glass with its gilded edge, as if it made no difference.

'I need you to do me a favour.'

Drissa said nothing.

'Did you hear me?'

He guessed that behind his dark glasses the man was looking at him.

'I don't want to do that sort of thing any more,' he said firmly, his eyes staring at the chequered tablecloth.

The booming laughter that greeted his declaration made him jump in his chair. Drissa looked anxiously at the other customers in the café, who were now all looking at them.

'He doesn't want to do that sort of thing any more!' said Zlatan loudly, leaning back. 'Did you hear that?'

'Be quiet!'

'Calm down, Driss. No one is interested in other people's business here; you ought to know that.'

'What do you want? I told you last time it was finished.'

'Yes, I know, but there is . . . something new. A new client, to be exact.'

'It's not my business. I don't want to know.'

'The client needs us, I'm afraid,' said the man, unperturbed, as if they were two partners discussing business. 'And this client pays well.'

'That's your problem – find another mug! I've moved on.'

Drissa felt his will growing stronger as he spoke. Maybe the man opposite him would finally understand that he couldn't count on

253

him any more. All he had to do was stand firm: the man would eventually give up.

'No one ever completely moves on, Driss. Not from the place you are in. No one can decide to stop just like that. Not with me. I'm the one who decides when it stops, understand?'

Drissa felt a tremor go through him.

'You can't force me to—'

'Oh yes I can. All the photocopies you made, all those papers you stole from dustbins, what would happen if they ended up in the hands of the police?'

'You'd go down with me, that's what would happen.'

'Really, you would do that, denounce me?' asked Zlatan in a tone of fake outrage as he lit a cigarette.

Drissa stared defiantly at the dark glasses, but the man's calm was unsettling. He could tell Zlatan was making fun of him, and that he wasn't afraid, while his own fear was increasing proportionately.

'Fine,' said the man after taking a puff on his cigarette. 'So, tell me, *who am I?*'

The Malian didn't answer, because he couldn't.

'What are you going to tell them, my friend? That a man with dark glasses you met in a café gave you 1,000 euros to put a microphone in a lamp? And you couldn't resist? And then he gave you 500 more to take pictures of some documents? And another 500 to collect the papers tossed in the dustbin every day? They're going to ask you what his name is: what are you going to say? Father Christmas? You're going to tell them that this man is in his forties, that he's tall and definitely overweight, that he has a slight accent? That you don't know his name or his address or even his telephone number: he's always the one who calls you from a withheld number? Is that what you're going to tell them? Believe me, you're the one who's in a mess, Driss, not me.'

'I'll tell them I'm prepared to reimburse the money if I have to.'

Once again, the man burst out laughing, and Drissa Kanté felt himself shrinking. He would have liked to vanish into the ground; he wished he had never met this man.

A big hand, damp and hot, came down on his own in a gesture of repulsive intimacy.

'Don't act more stupid than you are, Drissa Kanté. I know that you're not an imbecile.'

Hearing his name made him tremble from head to toe.

'So, let's go back over this. You have committed industrial espionage in a country where it's almost as serious a crime as killing someone, even though you arrived only recently, and you've only just found a stable job here and, who knows, maybe even a future. There's not a single element that can be authenticated other than that, amigo.'

Drissa glanced at the rings of sweat staining the underarms of the man's jacket.

'Plenty of people have seen you here,' he said. 'They can testify. You're not the product of my imagination.'

'Suppose they do – and then what? People round here don't like to talk to the police too much and anyway, it's obvious that someone paid you for the job. Big deal. It doesn't change anything for you. All these customers, what will they say? The same thing as you. The police will never be able to find me and you will rot in prison for a few years and then you'll be sent home. You travelled a long way, my brother; you crossed the desert, the sea, you crossed borders . . . Do you really want to be without papers again?'

Drissa felt all his strength draining away, his resolve taking on water like the cutter during the storm. Every one of the man's words felt like a hammer blow.

'Answer me: *is that what you want?*'

He shook his head, his eyes down.

'Fine. So I have some very good news for you. You have my word: this is the last time I'll ask you for anything. *The last time.* And there's 2,000 to back it up.'

Drissa looked up. The prospect of being set free, and of earning some money at the same time, had just reassured him a little. The man put his hand into his jacket pocket, then removed it and opened it. In his big fist the USB stick looked tiny.

'All you have to do is put this stick into a computer. It will take care of everything: it'll find the password and download the software it contains. It won't take more than three minutes. Then you take it back out, you switch off the computer and Bob's your uncle. All done. No one will ever notice the transaction. You give me back the stick, you get your two grand, and you'll never hear from me again. You have my word.'

'Where?' asked Drissa Kanté.

★

He felt as if he were driving through a wall of fire. The shade of every little cluster of trees was a blessing. Elvis Konstandin Elmaz had rolled down the window but the air was as hot as if he had opened the door to an oven. Luckily, it was getting late in the evening, and the patches of shade were quite frequent. He turned right in front of the sign at the crossroads:

KENNEL

LE CLOS DES GUERRIERS
GUARD AND DEFENCE DOGS

A bit further along he took an even narrower road, its surface potholed and cracked. A barn and a windmill stood out against the orange setting sun. It wasn't just the heat that was making him sweat. Shadows made him nervous. Elvis Elmaz was scared stiff. At the hospital he had managed to keep his cool in front of the cop and his weird sidekick, but he knew at once what had happened. Fuck! *It was starting again* . . . As he drove along, he began to feel as if his stomach were tying itself in an endless series of knots. Bloody hell! He didn't want to die. He wouldn't let it happen. Not like that slut teacher . . . He would show them! He pounded on the steering wheel, enraged, frightened. *Bunch of arseholes, go right ahead, I'm the one who'll get you!* He hadn't seen them coming the other night. Serbs, yeah right! Bullshit, more like! He'd made up the story about the woman and the Serbs for the sake of the police, and he'd asked one or two of his mates at the bar to back it up. That bar was full of blokes like him – on parole, or waiting for their trial. They'd almost got him, this time, but he'd stood up for himself and sent them packing. Too many potential witnesses. That's what had saved him. But for how long? He had one other solution: tell the cops everything. But then they'd reopen the case, and he'd have the families on his back. A trial, and a sentence to go with it. How long would they give him, with his background? He didn't want to go back into the rat-trap. No way.

Next to a rusty letterbox and the creamy cloud of a flowering bush, a second sign indicated he should leave the little road for an even bumpier track. The last hundred metres took him through a veritable tunnel of vegetation. It was getting ever darker and he was increasingly jittery. Another sign, a big one this time, informed him:

ROTTWEILERS, DOBERMANS, ALSATIANS, AMSTAFFS,
DOGOS ARGENTINOS, BORDEAUX MASTIFFS.

If the sign wasn't clear enough as it was, there was a rough drawing of a dog. Elvis had painted it himself. On his right, a terrifying commotion of barking and yapping greeted him in the silence. He smiled on hearing the chain-link clang as his beloved doggies hurled themselves furiously against the fence. The huge dogs seemed to excite each other to the point of barking until their throats bled – then they tired of it, and the noise abated.

No doubt they too felt the effects of the heat. Nothing was moving, not even the air, which was as inert as lead; the only sign of life came from the buzzing of flies and the clicking of the engine as it cooled down. He took a pack of cigarettes from his jeans pocket and stuck one between his lips. He inhaled the dogs' smell – wild and dangerous, deeply satisfying. Then he lit his cigarette and started walking towards the house. His torso was still wrapped in a dirty bandage covering a whole row of stitches, and in this heat it was incredibly itchy. Still, he was happy to have left hospital, and to be at home again with his precious hounds.

And his weapon.

A superposed Rizzini rifle, 20 calibre, for hunting big game.

Only a few more metres and he'd be in a safe place. He walked across the clearing, went up the steps to the veranda, and put the key in the lock. Living deep in the woods had been an advantage until today. An advantage for his little business, which required calm and discretion. But not today. Today he would rather have been in town, to lose himself in the crowd. The only thing was that he couldn't leave the mutts alone for too long. They must be famished after his stay in hospital. Tonight, however, he had neither the strength nor the courage to venture over to the cages. It was much too dark. He'd feed them tomorrow, as soon as he got up.

He went through the door, closed it behind him, and went to get his rifle and ammunition.

Go ahead, you'll see what you see. Don't go fucking with Elvis, he'll fuck you right back.

28

Lost Hearts

Margot couldn't stand the heat in the room any more. She splashed her face at the tap in the little sink. She reached for her towel and began to open the door to head to the showers, and then she heard them.

'What do you want?' Sarah was saying, two doors further down.

'You have to come. It's David.'

'Look, Virginie—'

'Move it!'

Margot peered through the doorframe. Virginie and Sarah were facing each other, one in the corridor, the other in the doorway to her room. Second-year students were entitled to private rooms. Sarah nodded and followed her friend towards the stairs.

Shit!

Margot wondered what she ought to do. You could hear the urgency and stress in Virginie's voice. She had mentioned David. Margot took a split second to decide, then put her bare feet into her Converse trainers and hurried out. The corridor was empty. She moved stealthily towards the stairway.

She could hear them going down.

She followed down the monumental staircase, her hand running along the balustrade. Through the big stained-glass window on the landing she could see the sun setting behind buildings huddled in the red dusk. When she emerged, the air seemed as solid as a pane of glass, but the evening was gradually bringing a soothing balm to the burning day.

Where were they?

She saw them at the last minute: two figures merging into the black mass of forest all the way at the end of the tennis courts.

She began running in that direction, as silently as possible, through

258

shadows and clouds of midges. But as soon as she reached the end of the path, the shadows grew darker and denser, melting into each other to create an ominous twilight – and she hesitated, no longer sure she wanted to continue.

Where had they gone? A cracking sound in the forest. Then Sarah's voice, from its depths: 'David!' Straight ahead of her there was a path. She could hardly see it in the murky undergrowth. She turned round to go back to the dormitory – no way was she going in there. Then curiosity, a need to know, got the upper hand and she spun round, back to the forest.

What the hell . . . ?

She made her way through the branches and thickets. Spiders' webs between the leaves brushed against her face; dozens of insects buzzed around her. She was treading cautiously but the girls ahead of her were making too much noise to notice her presence. The fading daylight left large patches of dusty light between the trees above her, but down by the ground it was darker and cooler.

'David, fuck, what the hell are you doing?'

Voices over there: they had found him. Margot's mouth went dry with fear; she stepped on a twig that snapped like a firecracker and for a moment she was afraid the noise might attract their attention, but they were far too preoccupied.

'My God, David, what have you done?'

Sarah's voice echoed in the forest, near panic. And panic was bloody contagious: Margot herself was on the verge of freaking out. She moved cautiously between the branches of the fir trees and found a clearing bathed in a twilight glow.

What the fuck was going on?

David was standing bare-chested on the far side of the clearing, his back against a grey tree trunk, his arms widespread. He was clinging to two thick branches that were almost perfectly horizontal, in a strange position that evoked a crucifixion. His head was down, his chin on his chest, as if he had lost consciousness. She could not see his face. Only his blond hair. And his beard. *A blond Christ.* Suddenly he lifted his head and she nearly leapt backwards when she saw his pale, mad gaze.

It was as if an electric current were flashing along her arms when she saw the red marks on David's chest. Very recent gashes. Then she saw the knife, in his right hand. The blade was red, too.

259

'Hey, girls.'

'Fuck, David, what's your problem?' said Virginie. 'What the fuck are you doing?'

Her voice echoed in the silence. David gave a little laugh as he looked down at his bloody chest.

'I really fucked up, didn't I? How do you do it? How do you manage to stay cool with everything that's going on?'

Was he on drugs? He looked completely out of it. He was trembling from head to toe, laughing and crying at the same time – or at least it looked like laughter, or a snigger . . . There were four gashes on his chest and the blood was still forming on each of them. It looked like smeared paint. Margot saw an enormous scar further down, directly across his abdomen, just above his navel.

'I can't take any more of this shit . . . it has to stop, we can't go on like this . . .'

Silence.

'Really, I'm serious, what's the point? What the fuck are we doing? How far will we go?'

'Get a hold of yourself.'

Virginie's voice. Yet again.

'And Hugo? Have you thought about Hugo?'

From her hiding place behind a bush, Margot saw David roll his head from side to side and look at the sky.

'What can I do about Hugo being in jail?'

'Fuck, he's your best friend, David! You know how much he cares for you; you know how much he cares for *us*. He needs us. He needs you. We have to get him out of there.'

'Oh yeah? And just how do we go about that? You see, that's the difference between him and me . . . If I were in his place, no one would give a damn. Hugo has always had people around him, he's always had his admirers . . . They're there for the taking . . . All he has to do is snap his fingers for Sarah to open her legs. Even you, Virginie; you'd never admit it, ever, but basically there's only one thing you dream of: that he'll give you one. Whereas I—'

'Shut up!'

Birds left the trees in a great rustling of wings, frightened by her shout.

'I can't take it any more . . . I can't take it any more.'

Now he was sobbing. Sarah rushed across the clearing to put her arms around him. Virginie seized the moment to take the knife from him. They sat David down in the grass at the foot of the tree. It was like watching a descent from the cross, thought Margot. Sarah was caressing his cheeks, his forehead; she kissed him delicately and tenderly.

'My baby,' she murmured, 'my poor baby . . .'

Margot wondered if they'd all gone stark raving mad. At the same time there was something about their madness – and David's pain – which made her heart bleed. Only Virginie seemed lucid.

'You have to deal with this,' she said firmly. 'You have to see a shrink, David, for Christ's sake! This can't go on!'

'Leave him alone,' said Sarah. 'Not now. Can't you see the state he's in?'

She stroked his blond hair, held him tight, maternally; shaking with sobs, he placed his head on her shoulder, even though she was a good ten centimetres shorter than him.

'You have to think about Hugo,' said Virginie again, lowering her voice. 'He needs us. Are you listening? Hugo would give his life for you! For every one of us! And you were behaving like . . . like . . . What the fuck, we have no right to abandon him. We have to get him out of there. And we can't do it without you.'

Frozen as if hypnotised by the scene, Margot could not move. A solitary bird let out a long, shrill cry that startled her, breaking the spell.

You have to get out of here. If they find you here, who knows what they might do? And the way they're behaving. Why do I think it's downright . . . unhealthy? It's as if something is binding them to each other. An indestructible bond. What would Elias make of it? And her father?

She wanted to get out of there – she was being eaten alive by insects on top of everything else – but she was too close. At the slightest movement, they would hear her. And that thought alone was enough to turn her stomach. She had no choice but to stay there, and she was finding it harder and harder to breathe, her palms damp on her thighs, her knees aching.

David nodded slowly. Virginie crouched down in front of him and lifted his chin.

'Get a grip, please. The Circle will be meeting soon. You're right – maybe it's time to put an end to it all. This business has gone on long enough. But we still have a job to finish.'

The Circle . . . This was the second time she had heard the word. Something oppressive, deeply sinister, was in the air. The buzzing of crickets and insects, nightfall: Margot could feel it in her nerves, her veins. She wished she could leave. Suddenly, they stood up.

'Let's go,' said Virginie, handing David the T-shirt he had tossed into the grass. 'Put this on. You'll come with us, right? No one must see you in that state.'

It was getting darker and darker in the clearing. David nodded silently. Margot saw him pull his T-shirt on over his thin torso and the four wounds, now more black than red in the fading light. She watched as Sarah and Virginie led him away from the clearing towards the path to the lycée and she withdrew deeper still into the shadow, her blood pounding in her temples. She waited for a long time among the bushes, until there was nothing left but the silence of the forest, a silence disturbed by various noises she could not identify.

She had the vague and paranoid impression that she was not alone. *That someone was there* . . . She trembled. The moon had risen above the trees. But the night was deceiving.

How long did she stay there without moving? She had no idea.

There was something *enchanted* – in the malevolent sense of the word – about the scene she had just witnessed. A strange atmosphere she could not define. What she had seen had upset her deeply. She sensed that they were beyond all salvation. She had a confused understanding that they had crossed a line, a boundary, and that they could no longer go back. Suddenly, she didn't feel like digging any more. She wanted to move on to something else. She would tell Elias to manage on his own.

She waited a little longer, then she began to move. And froze immediately.

A branch had just cracked, right nearby. As if someone had stepped on it. She stood stock still and listened carefully, but all she could hear was the pounding of her heart in her ears and the rustling of foliage overhead.

What was it? Like an animal on the alert, she swung her head from left to right. But the forest was getting darker and darker. Only the sky above was still a lighter grey. *What was it?*

She took another step towards the path, when she was brutally shoved forward and thrown to the ground. She felt an enormous weight come down on her back. She landed hard. She could smell marijuana on someone's breath, a warm exhalation against her chin, while a hand crushed her head into the earth and leaves.

'You were spying on us, bitch, weren't you?'

She wriggled, but David was crushing her. His cheek against hers. His coarse beard scratching her skin.

'You know I've always fancied you, Margot. I've always had a thing about your piercings and your tattoos, I've always wanted your tight arse. But of course you only had eyes for Hugo – like all of you sluts!'

'David, let me go!'

With horror she felt a warm, damp hand groping its way under her T-shirt, fingers reaching for one of her breasts.

'What are you doing, for Christ's sake? Stop it! Shit, stop it!'

'You know what we do to girls like you? Seriously, do you know what we do?'

His voice like a murmur in her ear. Suddenly his fingers twisted her nipple, and she cried out in pain. Another hand was already sliding into her shorts from behind. 'What's your problem? Doesn't the idea of a nice little quickie turn you on? Don't tell me you'd rather do it with that idiot?'

He was going to rape her. The prospect was so inconceivable, so unreal, that her brain would not allow it. Here, only a few dozen metres from the lycée . . . She was overwhelmed by a blinding terror. She struggled with all her might and he had to remove his hands to grab her wrists and pin her to the ground. He was strong. Too strong for her.

'*Granted, granted, I am a scoundrel, but she is a woman of a noble heart, full of sentiments, refined by education. And yet . . . oh, if only she felt for me!*'

His hand returned to its assault on her shorts, this time at the front, beneath her belly, while he was reciting. Inquisitive fingers in the space between her clothes and her skin. She gasped again. She felt David press up against her buttocks. He was hard.

'*But Katerina Ivanovna, though she is magnanimous, she is unjust . . .*'

'Tolstoy!' she guessed, to distract his attention, still wriggling vigorously.

'Ah-hah, nice try! Wrong! It's Dostoyevsky: *Crime and Punishment.* What a pity that idiot Van Acker isn't here. Especially as he's got a soft spot for you.'

263

A finger had found its way into her pants.

'Stop! Let me go! David, don't do this! *Don't do this!*'

'Shut up,' he murmured in her ear. 'Shut your mouth right now.'

Words uttered in a quiet voice. Quiet, but changed. Heavy with threat. He was no longer acting. He was elsewhere; he had become someone else.

He had slapped his other hand over her mouth to prevent her from screaming, and Margot tried to bite him. In vain. With absolute horror, she felt David's finger slide deeper into her pants. Incapable of reacting, her mind detached itself from her body. This was not her, either, it was someone else.

What was happening did not concern her.

He was going to take off her shorts, then he would rape her, there, on the ground . . .

It doesn't concern you . . .

Suddenly, David's hand withdrew from her pants and she heard him swear. There was a blow, then he gave a cry of pain, and before she could even get to her feet, she saw his face crushed on the ground next to hers.

'You're hurting me!'

'Shut up, fucking shitface!'

She recognised that voice. She rolled over and found herself looking at her father's assistant – the one with the strange face, but super-cool clothes – and she was putting handcuffs on David, her knee on his back.

'Are you all right?' asked Samira Cheung, looking at her.

She nodded, and wiped the earth and blades of grass from her knees.

'I wasn't going to do it,' moaned David, his cheek against the ground. 'I swear to you, fuck, I wasn't going to do it! It was just for fun!'

'What weren't you going to do?' Samira's voice was as sharp and threatening as a razor blade. '*Rape her*, right? You already did, you wanker. What you did is called rape, you stupid fuck.'

She saw David's shoulders shake with a sob.

'Leave him alone,' said Margot.

'What?'

'Leave him . . . he just wanted to frighten me. He didn't mean to rape me, it's true.'

'Oh, really? And how do you know that?'

'Let him go.'

'Margot . . .'

'I won't file a complaint, anyway. You can't make me.'

'Margot, it's because of this sort of—'

'Leave him alone! Let him go!'

She met David's gaze. There was a mixture of incomprehension and gratitude in his golden eyes.

'Whatever you say – but you can be sure I'll tell your father.'

She nodded, shameful, as the woman gave her a furious gaze. There was the clicking sound of the handcuffs being removed. Margot saw Samira pull David to his feet and stick her face not two inches from his, her eyes as black as tar.

'Are you scared? Because you should be. You were that close to messing up your entire life, and hers, and I'll have my eye on you from now on. Do me a favour: do something stupid. Just one thing. Anything. And I'll be there.'

David glanced at Margot.

'Thank you.'

In his eyes she saw an expression that was hard to decipher. Was it shame? Gratitude? Fear? Then he walked away. Samira turned to Margot, who was still sitting on the ground.

'You can find your own way home,' she said, coldly.

She left, taking the same path as David. Margot heard her go back up the lane past the tennis courts with a hurried step. She took several deep breaths, wondering why her father's assistant had turned up so miraculously. Was he having her watched? She waited for the silence to return, for the night to take possession of the forest. Only then did she roll over and stretch out on her back in the grass, her eyes to the sky, which was a deep grey, even darker through the black canopy. She rammed her earphones into her ears, asked Marilyn Manson to sing 'Sweet Dreams' – and then she began to sob.

Unaware that someone was watching her.

He heard the music and the sound of the motor to start with. *They were coming through the woods – and fast* . . . Elvis Elmaz switched off the telly, turned his head and looked over to the window. He could make out a glow in the forest. It was almost dark. *Headlights* . . . He leapt up off the sofa and towards the gun hanging on the wall. His heart began pounding. No one ever came to visit at this hour.

The dogs began growling, then barking, shaking their cages with their claws.

He made sure the gun was loaded, then went over to the window, when suddenly a shower of white light exploded in the room, blinding.

The car had its headlights on full beam. He had to turn his head away from the assault of the dazzling brightness. And then there was the music playing full blast, the bass causing the walls to vibrate.

Elvis hurried to the door, his gun pointed. He flung it open.

'Fuck, I know who you are, you bunch of faggots!' he screamed, bursting out onto the veranda. 'The first one who comes close, I'll blow his brains out.'

He felt the cold pressure of a rifle against his temple.

'This is Samira,' said the voice on the telephone.

Servaz turned down the stereo, and outside a siren was wailing. Once again he was disappointed. Once again, he had hoped it would be Marianne. *Why don't you call her?* he wondered. *Why wait for her?*

'What's up?'

'It's Margot . . . something happened this evening. Something not at all cool. But she's fine,' she hastened to reassure him.

He stiffened. Margot. Not at all cool. He waited for her to go on. Samira recounted the scene she had just witnessed: she'd been watching the back of the buildings, Vincent the front. She had seen two girls leave the building and walk towards the woods, then, just afterwards, Margot appeared, following in their footsteps; so she had trailed her, had found Margot watching the two girls and a boy named David in a clearing. She was too far away to hear what they were saying, but the young man called David seemed completely stoned. Then Samira saw the trio leave again while Margot was still hiding in the thicket. David reappeared several minutes later. Samira saw him make his way into the undergrowth then lost him again until he threw himself on Margot. Samira had rushed over, but she had been a good thirty metres away, the bloody forest was full of brambles, and she had stumbled on a root, and it had hurt like hell when she stood back up. It must have taken her roughly a minute and a half to intervene, *no more than that, boss, I swear.*

266

'At least this way he was caught in the act,' she said. 'And I'll say it again, boss: Margot is fine.'

'I don't get it! Caught in the act of doing what?' he shouted.

Samira told him.

'You're saying that David tried to rape my daughter?'

'Margot says he didn't. That it wasn't his intention. But he managed to . . . um . . . put his hand in . . . um . . . her pants . . .'

'I'm on my way.'

'Fuck, don't do that, don't do that, shit!'

He struggled. For appearances' sake. His wrists were tied behind his back and his legs were fastened to the chair legs with thick brown tape. His chest was tied to the chair back the same way. He even had some around his neck. Every time he struggled, the tape tugged at his skin and hair. He was sweating like a pig. 'Bunch of fucking bastards! Motherfuckers! Fuck the lot of you!'

The insults were helping him to resist. He knew they were going to kill him. And he knew it wouldn't be a pleasant death. He had only to think of what had happened to the teacher . . . He had never been very kind to women. He had beaten them, raped them, but what that teacher had been through was beyond comprehension – even for someone like him. A tremor went through him.

He inhaled the smell of the dogs and his own strong smell, then the more complex odours of the forest: they had tied him up outside on the veranda. Dust particles and insects danced in the harsh glow of the headlights burning into his eyes. Everything was coming to life around him with sharper intensity; everything was taking on a definitive value.

'I'm not afraid,' he said. 'Kill me, I don't care anyway.'

'Is that so?' said one of the figures, acting interested. 'Well, how nice for you!'

Like the others, his face was hidden in the shadow of the hood.

'You're going to be afraid, believe me,' said someone else, calmly.

Something about that voice made him tremble. It was so confident. And calm. And cold. He watched as they unwound a roll of cling film on the floor of the veranda. He felt dizzy. His heart was fluttering in his chest like a bird in a cage trying to find the way out.

'What the fuck are you doing?'

'Oh! All of a sudden you're interested?'

They got back up and began to wind the cling film around his torso and the back of the chair. He forced himself to smile.

'What is this?'

'This?' They laughed. 'This means: *yum yum time for doggies . . .*'

They disappeared from his sight. He could hear them in the house, opening and closing the fridge, then they came hurrying back. Suddenly gloved hands were sliding hunks of fresh, bloody meat between the cling film and his belly, and he trembled. When he had several steaks on his stomach, they went round the chair again, winding the film ever higher towards his throat then slipping new pieces of fresh meat – the cheap stuff that he used to feed the dogs – between the cling film, his chest and his neck.

'Fuck, what are you playing at?'

A sudden blow slashed his cheek. Warm blood began to spurt onto his chin.

'Ow! Fuck, you're sick!'

'Did you know that cling film is made up of fifty-six per cent salt and forty-four per cent petrol?'

They went on turning around him as if he were an explorer captured by natives, tied to a sacrificial pole. Again he felt the film against his throat then the chill of the pieces of meat. After that, they rubbed his face with the last hunks of steak. He shook his head violently from side to side, grimacing.

'Stop it! Stop it now! You bunch of—'

They went inside again. He heard them turn on the tap in the kitchen, washing their hands while they talked. He tried to move. As soon as they left, he would tip the chair over and try to set himself free. But would he have time? He blinked to banish the sweat that was dripping from his eyebrows and stinging his eyes. He had figured out what they were going to do and it filled him with terror. He wasn't afraid of dying, but not this sort of death. Fuck it, no.

He stared at the dazzling light from the headlamps. The night and the dark forest were all around. He could hear the insects buzzing in the woods; the dogs had stopped barking. Maybe they had already caught a whiff of the smell that meant food. His torturers passed him again, climbed into their car and slammed the doors.

'Wait! Come back! I have money! I'll give you money!' he screamed. 'Lots of money! I'll give you everything! Come back!'

He pleaded with them as he had never pleaded in his life before.

'Come back, come back, fuck!'

Then he began sobbing, while the car backed away into the night towards the cages.

There was no time to lose. They opened the cages in the darkness, one by one. The dogs knew them; they had come to feed them several times while their master was absent. 'It's me,' said one of them in a reassuring voice. 'You recognise me, don't you? I'll bet you're hungry. You haven't eaten a thing for twenty-four hours . . .' The dogs emerged from the cages one after the other and surrounded them, and they stood and let the huge beasts sniff them, dogs whose ancestors would not hesitate to attack a bear. The mastiffs rubbed against their legs, and walked around the car. Then they caught wind of that other smell wafting on the night air, and the visitors saw them raise their noses, their powerful necks turning in unison towards the house. They read the hunger and desire in their shining little eyes. The dogs licked their chops and all at once, as if responding to a signal, they began loping towards the house, barking. When the pack leapt onto the veranda, they heard Elvis's voice calling with authority, 'Titan, Lucifer, Tyson, good dogs, lie down! Lie down, I said!'

Then panic and pure terror overcame him: 'I said lie down! Tyson, no! NOOO!'

Despite themselves, they could not help but tremble when the screams tore into the silence and the dogs' growls of pleasure rose into the night as they devoured their master.

29

Breaking Bad

'I wasn't going to do it.'

He was sobbing, looking at them in turn.

'I wasn't going to do it, I swear. I – I just wanted to frighten her. I've never raped anyone! She was spying on us. It made me angry. I wanted to scare her, that's all! I wasn't feeling right today. I swear, fuck . . . I've never done anything like that in my life . . . You have to believe me!'

He put his head in his hands, his shoulders shaking with silent sobs.

'Were you on something, David?' asked Samira.

He nodded his head.

'What was it?'

'Meth.'

'Who gave it to you?'

He hesitated.

'I'm not a snitch,' he said, as if they were in a police drama.

'Listen to me, you little twat—' Servaz began, red in the face.

'Who was it?' said Samira. 'Don't forget you were caught in the middle of an attempted rape. You know what that means: expulsion from school, a trial, prison . . . not to mention what people will say. And your parents . . .'

He shook his head.

'I don't know his name. He's a student at the science faculty. His nickname is Heisenberg, like the character in—'

'*Breaking Bad,*' interrupted Samira, making a note to ask the narcs.

'And Hugo, does he take it too?' Servaz asked.

David nodded again, still looking at his hands.

'Had Hugo taken something that evening when you went to watch the match at the pub?'

This time, David raised his head and looked Samira straight in the eyes.

'No! He was clean.'

'Are you sure?'

'Yes.'

Samira and Servaz exchanged a look. It hadn't been Claire's handwriting in the notebook and clearly Hugo had been drugged. Tomorrow they would call the judge, but they weren't sure whether it would be enough to obtain Hugo's release.

Samira looked at Servaz. She was waiting for his decision. Servaz was staring at David, wondering if he should respect his daughter's wishes.

'Get the hell out of here,' he said finally. 'And spread the word: if you ever so much as touch a hair on my daughter's head, you and your little gang, your life will be hell.'

David stood up and walked out, his head lowered. Servaz stood up in turn.

'Take up your positions again,' he said to Samira. 'Get in touch with the narcs, and ask them if they know this Heisenberg.'

He left the room and went down the corridor. He knew the place like the back of his hand. There were memories connected to nearly every step. One of them surfaced. Him and Francis van Acker . . . they were twelve or thirteen years old. Francis was showing him a lizard warming itself in the sun on a wall. 'Look.' All of a sudden, Francis had sliced off the lizard's tail with a shovel or a rusty knife, he couldn't remember which. The tail had gone on twitching every which way, as if it had a life of its own, while the lizard ran off to hide. But while the young Martin remained fascinated by the tail, Francis had picked up a huge stone and crushed the reptile's head before it had a chance to disappear.

'Why did you do that?' Martin asked.

'Because it's a ruse: while the predator is fascinated by the tail, the lizard escapes.'

'Did you really need to kill it?'

'I'm a more intelligent predator than others,' Francis had said.

Servaz went through the second door on the left. A former class-room. Margot was waiting for him, biting her fingernails.

'Did you let him go?'

Servaz nodded.

'Now everyone is going to look at me as if I have the plague,' she said.

'It's not your fault.'

'I'm supposed to spend another year here, Dad. How am I going to make friends if I go around with the label "the girl you can't touch or go near because she's got police protection" stuck on my back?'

'Does the name Heisenberg mean anything to you?'

'The guy who created quantum mechanics or the character in *Breaking Bad*?'

He felt reassured. She had answered without the slightest hesitation. Clearly she had never heard of a dealer who went by the name.

'What is this *Breaking Bad* thing?'

'It's a TV series, about this chemistry teacher who finds out he's got terminal cancer and starts manufacturing and dealing drugs to ensure his family's future. Since when are you interested in TV series?'

'You overheard their conversation,' he said, changing the subject. 'What were they talking about?'

He saw her frown and think.

'I don't know . . . it was fairly disjointed, and rather strange. David said he was fed up with all of it, that he didn't want to go on.'

'Go on with what?'

'No idea. And then Virginie said they couldn't abandon Hugo, that Hugo loved all of them . . . Oh, and then she talked about something even weirder: the Circle. She said the Circle would meet soon.'

'The Circle?'

'Yes.'

She almost told him that the Circle was supposed to meet on the seventeenth of that month, but she held back. Why? *What's the matter with you?* Two of them knew about it: her and Elias. What was she thinking?

'Do you have any idea what it is?'

She shook her head.

'Go to bed,' he said, feeling weak with fatigue himself.

'How long are Vincent and Samira going to stay here?'

She was already putting her earphones in her ears. Servaz thought of something.

'As long as it takes,' he said. 'What are you listening to?'

'You won't know them, they're called Marilyn Manson.' She laughed: 'It's not at all your style.'

'Can you say that again?' he asked.

'What?'

'The name of the group.'

'Marilyn Manson. Why? What is it, Dad?'

Servaz felt as if an abyss had opened beneath his feet. *The music on the CD that someone left for him at the Internet café* . . . His mouth went dry and his fingers trembled as he opened his mobile phone to call Espérandieu and Samira.

Samira Cheung was once again hiding in the bushes behind the lycée, like some bloody commando. She was already regretting her choice of clothes: with her skinny jeans and her short tank top, the grass was itching her belly and she spent her time scratching.

She had a view over the back of the buildings, from the concrete cubes and the sports stand on the left to the entrance to the stables and the dormitory wing on the right, as well as the tennis courts, the lawn and the entrance to the maze. There was a light on in Margot's window, and it was open. She even thought she could see the red glow of a cigarette. *That's against the rules, young lady . . .* She had drunk a coffee and taken some Pro Plus, although the events of the evening had already given her enough adrenaline to keep her awake. She wouldn't have minded listening to some death metal to wake her up even more – Cannibal Corpse, for example. But she didn't want to be startled by someone coming up from behind out of the woods. To be honest, she hated the thought of the deep dense forest at her back.

As much as she could she avoided moving. She didn't want to attract attention. But from time to time she stretched and did a few flexes. Her walkie-talkie crackled and she heard Espérandieu's voice in the nocturnal silence.

'How are things at your end?'

'It's calm.'

'Martin's just left. He's completely losing it. He wanted to stay here. The gendarmes have posted a patrol on the road at the entrance to the lycée and Margot has orders to lock her door and not open it to anyone she doesn't know. She's gone to bed.'

'Not quite. I can see her: she's having a fag. But she's in her room.'

'I hope you're not listening to music.'

'All I can hear is some fucking owl. And what about you, is it calm there?'

'Deadly.'

'Do you really think he would have the guts to show up here?'

'Hirtmann? I don't know . . . I'd be surprised. But this business with the Marilyn Manson music is pretty creepy.'

'And what if he sees us?'

'Well, it will probably make him go back the way he came . . . I don't think he wants to get locked up again. If you want my opinion, he's miles away. And let's not forget that we're here to protect Margot, not follow him.'

Samira didn't say anything.

But that didn't mean she didn't have an opinion on the matter.

If the opportunity arose to get her hands on the Swiss killer, she would go right ahead and take it.

At the age of ten, Suzanne Lacaze had been convinced that the world was a marvellous playground and that everyone loved her. At twenty she had discovered that the world was a hurtful sharp-edged place where most people lie – when she'd seen her best friend steal the man she'd fallen madly in love with, tears in her eyes and spewing words like 'we're in love', 'we were made for each other', 'I'm so sorry, Suzie' from that pretty little mouth of hers, full of shit . . . Now, at the age of fortysomething, Suzanne knew, with unshakeable certainty, that the world belonged to the bastards, with God as the reigning champion bastard. For everyone else it was hell.

She stared at the ceiling and listened to her husband snoring next to her. He had come back an hour earlier, and although the cancer had weakened her sense of smell, she could still make out another woman's perfume. He hadn't even bothered to take a shower.

He had been so attentive, so patient with her lately. So . . . kind. Why hadn't he always been like this?

Don't go telling yourself stories, girl. He's not acting out of love, just to ease his conscience. He didn't even bother to shower: what further proof do you need?

She wanted to die in peace. Suddenly she understood that 'to die in peace' meant revenge. *Her* revenge. With blinding clarity, she realised that first thing tomorrow she would call that cop and tell him the truth.

Interlude 3

Confrontation

The needle. Before she lapsed into unconsciousness, she summoned her will.

Be strong. Now is the time.

She came to in the big old dining room. As she did every time. She was sitting in the high-backed armchair at the end of the long table, a wide leather strap around her waist, two more around her ankles.

Plates, candlesticks, glasses, wine, music. Mahler, of course. *That fucking stupid bastard Gustav Mahler . . .* She wondered whether she would be able to speak loudly enough after all these months walled up in silence.

She had no other weapons, only her voice.

'Cheers!' he said joyfully, raising his glass.

Usually, she reciprocated. She liked the taste of the wine, the liberating intoxication. And she liked her freshly ironed dress, the smell of soap on her skin, the delicious food – after all those days spent in her cellar eating the same colourless gruel. Her stomach and her brain shouted at her to throw herself on the wine and the steaming plate of food. She stared at the plastic glass. Tempting. She wanted it, wanted it so badly . . . almost as much as the drugs she thought she had weaned herself off, in those early days, down in her cellar, but had wanted so much she thought she would go mad.

She kept her hands flat on the table. She merely looked at him with an ironic little smile on her lips.

She saw him frown, puzzled.

'Aren't you drinking?' he said, still smiling. 'What's wrong? Aren't you thirsty?'

She was dying of thirst . . . Her throat was as dry as tinder.

'Go on, you know it's pointless,' he said in his most cajoling voice. 'Drink. You'll see: the wine is exceptional.'

She burst out laughing – her laughter loud, mocking, scornful – and this time, she saw a flicker of doubt in his eyes. Then he examined her the way a researcher does when he's observed an unexpected reaction in a guinea pig.

'Oh, I see,' he said. 'The idea is to provoke me.'

He laughed, but nicely. Without animosity.

'Your mother is sucking cocks in hell,' she said in a cold, hoarse voice.

He looked even more puzzled. He smoothed his dark little beard. His blond hair, cut short, shone in the candlelight. Then he managed to smile.

'That sort of language doesn't suit you,' he said indulgently.

She merely stared at him.

'*That sort of language doesn't suit you,*' she repeated, imitating his accent, his snobbish tones and his nasal twang.

There was a brief gleam of anger in his eyes, but his smile returned almost at once.

'Fucking scumbag, son of a whore, pathetic impotent twat . . .'

He didn't say anything.

'Your mother was a whore, wasn't she?'

He gave a joyful smile this time.

'You are absolutely right.'

His reaction threw her for a moment, but she pulled herself together. She gave a little snigger.

'Why are you laughing?'

'Your tiny cock: last time I wasn't completely asleep, and I saw it.'

She saw his gaze cloud over again at the far end of the table. She trembled; she knew what he was capable of.

'Stop it.'

'*Stop it.*'

A cloud of black ink passed one more time over his gaze then disappeared. He turned round and reached behind him to turn up the volume on the mini-stereo on the sideboard. The violins soared, the percussion rang out, the brass went wild. She began to imitate an orchestra conductor, with her arms in the air, her hands flailing. Smiling. She had neither knife nor fork – she had to eat with her hands. And the plate was made of paper. As she went on imitating a conductor, she grabbed the soup bowl and hurled it across the room before she began to sing, off key, above the music. The soup left a spot on the wall. *Her voice had returned* . . . She sang louder.

'THAT'S ENOUGH!'

He had stopped the music and was staring at her. Sternly. He wasn't smiling any more.

'You shouldn't play this game with me.'

This time the threat was explicit and for a fraction of a second she was overcome with icy fear. She could hear the anger in his voice. And like a well-trained dog, she was terrified by it. *Get a hold of yourself . . . you're on the right track . . .* For the first time, she had the upper hand – and with it came a brief feeling of triumph.

'Go eat your shit and die,' she said.

He pounded his fist on the table.

'Stop that! I despise such language!'

She giggled.

'You really are just an impotent little wanker, isn't that right, darling? You can't get it up. And you can't say "cock" or "cunt" or "balls" . . . I'll bet your mother played with your willy when you were little.'

She saw she was getting to him.

'You stupid bitch,' he growled. 'You stupid filthy whore. You're going to pay for that.'

He stood up. She felt a wave of fear, then panic when she saw what he had in his hand. *A fork* . . . She sank down into her chair. If she lost her nerve now, he would win.

When he was close enough, she spat at him. She missed his face, but managed to hit his shirt. He didn't wipe it off, but simply stared at her, his gaze empty.

Suddenly he grabbed her face and squeezed with all his might, his fingers crushing her jaw. He was hurting her. She struggled, tried to push him back with her hands, to scratch him, but he did not let go. An intense pain flashed through her. The fork was planted deep in her lips, biting into them like a rattlesnake. The blood spurted from her mouth, and she opened it to scream. The fork immediately struck a second time, landing in her gums. She thought she would go mad with pain. She sobbed, screamed, cried, and the fork struck again and again, on her cheeks, in her lips and her tongue.

Then the madness stopped the way it had started. All of a sudden.

Her heart felt as if it had trebled in size in her chest. Her mouth and face were burning, covered in blood. She was in agony. She tried to breathe normally. She could tell he was watching her, waiting for her reaction. Finally he went back to his chair, satisfied.

'*Queer, poof, little shit, worm . . .*'

She saw him stand stock still, his back to her now. She summoned all the strength she had left and tried to put the pain to one side.

'Ha, ha, ha,' she crowed. 'What a ridiculous little man! Mediocre . . . ordinary, insignificant, pitiful . . . isn't that right, Julian Hirtmann?'

He turned around. He was smiling again.

'You think I haven't figured out what you're up to? You think I don't know where you're trying to lead me? But you won't get away from me. We still have many long years to spend together, you and I.'

On hearing his words, she felt her courage wane. But she tried not to show it. She tossed her hair, then burst out laughing – a nasty laugh, a mocking gleam dancing in her eyes. Then she grabbed her dress and tore it, exposing her naked breasts.

'Do you really feel like spending your evenings with a vulgar, unpleasant girl like me? For years? I'm sure you could find someone more accommodating, couldn't you? A *new one* . . . Because as far as I'm concerned, it's all over, love. You'll never have me the way you used to . . . you can forget about it.'

With a violent gesture she sent the plastic wine glass flying, and pointed at his flies.

'Get it out. Show it to me. I'll bet it's all soft. You only get hard when I'm asleep, isn't that right? Don't you think that's a bit . . . *odd*? Do I frighten you? Prove that you're a man, go on, get it out; show me your little worm. You can't do it, can you? This is what our evenings will be like from now on, honey. You'd better get used to it.'

She could see how disappointed he was. She would have liked him to get it over with quickly. But she knew he wouldn't do her that favour. First he would make her pay. She prepared to suffer, she thought of all the harm she had done in her life, of the people she would have liked to say goodbye to . . . her son, her friends, the man she had loved so much and still betrayed . . . She sent her silent thoughts to all of them, words of love, while the tears streamed down her cheeks and he came closer, soundlessly.

She knew that this time it would work.

Wednesday

30

Revelations

It was 5.30 in the morning, and the sky was growing pale as Drissa
Kanté began to hoover office 2.84. No one aspires to do a job that
consists of cleaning carpets and dusting desks and computers, yet
to his great surprise, Drissa had eventually come to enjoy his job.

Even though there was no time to be wasted from one office
block to the next, even though he had to get up when everyone else
was still asleep, he liked the routine simplicity of his tasks. While
working he always found a way to escape, in his thoughts: back to
his country or into ideas inspired by his reading. This morning it
wasn't nostalgia that burdened him, but the fear of losing a job which
most of the inhabitants of his adopted country would have found
unworthy. He couldn't get the man's words out of his head: 'Do you
really want to be without papers again?' It was strange, he thought.
Of all the thousands of words you say, and the thousands you hear
every day, why does your memory have to pick a handful to haunt
you with, incessantly?

He took a duster and went to the office he'd been told to go to.
He stopped to listen. Even if he was early, there were cops on duty
at the other end of the corridor: he'd seen them on his way past.
When the fat man with the dark glasses had given him the address,
he knew his problems were not over.

His hand was trembling when he took the little USB stick out of
his uniform. There was only one computer in the office, he couldn't
go wrong. If he didn't do it now, he knew he'd never have the
courage. He glanced at the door.

Now . . .

The little USB stick fitted easily into the slot on the side. He hit
the 'on' switch and something inside the machine rumbled faintly.
He felt a rush of nervousness when the computer started up and

the USB stick flashed. He knew computers well. The fat man was right: the stick had been programmed to bypass the computer's start-up sequence. It was also designed to skip over the login and password stage, and to trick the antivirus – but Drissa knew it was relatively easy to find hackers on the Internet to do all that. The hardest thing was getting access to the actual computer – nothing could replace the human factor. *Hurry up* . . . He looked at his watch. The guy had told him that when the stick stopped flashing, it would be over. If someone came in now, they would immediately see that he had switched on the computer, which he was not supposed to do. *Faster, for Christ's sake!*

Suddenly he froze. The office door had just opened.

'What are you doing?'

Petrified, he stared at the person who had come through the door. He could not say a single word. It was Aïcha, a co-worker from the cleaning team, a nervy young woman who spent her time making fun of him. He saw her shining gaze pause on the computer screen, then return to him. Hard and inquisitive.

'Go away,' he said.

'What are you doing, Drissa?'

'Go away!'

She looked sternly at him, then closed the door. Never again! This was the last time. No matter the consequences, he would never agree to do anything illegal again. The USB stick stopped flashing. He took it out of the slot, slipped it into his pocket and switched off the computer.

He went over to the window and pulled up the blinds, then pressed the trigger of the blue spray. Beyond the window, the sky was turning pink, grey and pale orange above the rooftops, ever more luminous to the east. That evening, he would give the USB stick to the man and it would be over. But he had his own precautions to implement, too, to make sure the man never came after him again. This time, he wouldn't be so naïve.

'Commandant Servaz?'

He looked at his alarm clock. It must have rung and he hadn't heard it. He hadn't fallen asleep until four o'clock in the morning, and his sleep had been disturbed by nightmares he could not remember but which left him with an impression of unease as sticky as chewing gum.

'Uh-huh.'

'Commissioner Santos, from the GI.'

Servaz sat up straight. The National Police General Inspectorate. *The man in the car park*, he thought, sitting on the edge of the bed.

'We've received a complaint about you,' said Santos. 'A certain Florent Mattera, residing at 2A, boulevard d'Arcole, has accused you of assaulting him last night. He alleges that this happened in the car park at the Capitole. A man matching your description beat him, then apologised and drove away in a Cherokee, whose number plate he wrote down. And it was yours. Do you deny these facts, Commandant?'

Servaz thought for a split second.

'No.'

A sigh at the other end of the line.

'You'll have to come in for an interview.'

'When?'

'This morning.'

'Look . . . I'm in the middle of an extremely important investigation.'

'Aren't we all?' said the syrupy voice on the other end. 'Commandant, do you realise what you have been accused of? This is deadly serious. The era when cops could behave like gangsters is over, and I—'

'Okay, okay. I'm on my way.'

'Hi, Servaz.'

'Hi.'

'Morning, Martin.'

'Morning.'

'Morning, Servaz.'

'Hi.'

That morning, everyone seemed to want to show him their sympathy. It was as if he'd just been diagnosed with cancer. He got out of the lift and went down the corridor that led to the regional crime squad. It was 8.16 a.m. Taped to the brick walls were the same children's faces as always, watching him go past. Above and below the photographs were the words 'MISSING/DISPARUS', in English and French.

'Hi, Martin.'

'Hi.'

Ordinarily, he didn't even see them any more, those faces; he'd passed them so many times. But this morning, he saw them anew. All those missing children, never found. And the dates: 1991 . . . 1995 . . . *1986* . . . Sweet Christ. How had the parents survived?

'Good morning, Martin.'

'Hmm.'

Everyone seemed to know. It was the sort of information that gets passed on more quickly than an unpinned grenade. He hurried into his office. There was a note on his desk.

'The director wants to see you.'

Pujol's handwriting. Right. He didn't even hang up his jacket, but headed for the director's office. As he walked past the open doors, he could hear conversations come to a halt. He wanted only one thing: to avoid all those gazes. He went past the reception and the little waiting area with its leather sofas. He knocked on the door.

'Come in!'

On seeing him, the director stood up, his face a blank. Opposite him was a man who was considerably overweight, wearing a thickly knotted tie in spite of the heat, as well as the stubborn air of the civil servant who knows he's in the right. The man did not stand up, but he turned round to look at Servaz with his little yellow eyes.

'Morning, Santos,' said Servaz.

No answer.

'Martin, is it true, what Commissioner Santos has told me? Have you . . . confirmed the facts?'

He nodded. Stehlin shook his head. Commissioner Santos looked at Stehlin and raised his eyebrows, as if to say, 'Right, what happens now?'

'I—' began Servaz.

Stehlin held up his hand.

'I have spoken with Commissioner Santos. He has agreed to postpone your hearing until the investigation is over.'

Something must have happened . . . it was impossible otherwise. Santos would never have agreed to a deal if it weren't a matter of the utmost urgency. And Servaz was part of the equation. *Margot!* he thought, his stomach doing a triple flip.

'Something has come up,' said the director, confirming his hunch.

Servaz waited for what was to come.

'Do you remember Elvis Elmaz, the guy you interrogated at the hospital?'

Servaz nodded.

'Last night he was attacked. His life is hanging by a thread.'

'What happened?'

'Apparently someone tied him to a chair along with some meat and gave him to his dogs for dinner.'

Servaz looked at his boss, trying to grasp the meaning of his words, then to visualise the scene, but quickly changed his mind.

'He's in hospital,' continued Stehlin. 'Half his face has been torn off, his arms and torso have been chewed to the bone in several places, a number of organs are affected, and he has lost a great deal of blood. He's so gravely injured that they took him to the severe burns unit. It's not a pretty sight . . . and he's unlikely to recover. He went into a coma during the night. If he does make it, it will be thanks to his neighbour, who saw a car go by in the middle of the night and heard the dogs barking in a frenzy. But before he completely lost consciousness in the ambulance, something happened . . .'

They were getting there. *What was it?* thought Servaz impatiently. Stehlin reached for something on the desk and Servaz saw a transparent plastic evidence bag with a label.

'He managed to convey to one of the ambulance drivers that he wanted to write something. He had no lips and no tongue either, by then, so he couldn't speak. But . . .'

Stehlin picked up the evidence bag and handed it to Servaz.

'This is what he managed to write.'

Servaz took it. He looked at the pad in the bag. The wobbly, awkward, feverish handwriting:

Setvaz dug in past

Now he could understand why Santos had made the exceptional decision to agree to postpone his hearing. He felt both intense relief and a burning curiosity.

'Did you dig around in his past?' asked Stehlin.

Servaz shook his head. He felt dizzy.

'We dropped the Elvis lead as soon as his alibi turned out to be solid,' he replied.

'Then I think it must be a spelling mistake,' said Stehlin.

'It should be "Servaz dig in past", not "dug",' said Servaz. 'Whose past is he talking about? His own?'

'Probably.'

Servaz felt the wheels of his brain begin to turn.

'Maybe we dropped the lead too soon. Maybe we should have made sure that Claire Diemar and Elvis Elmaz didn't know each other.'

'Martin, you've only been on the case for four days. You did what you had to do.'

Servaz understood that this remark was aimed primarily at Santos.

'And there's something else,' added the director. 'Paris wants results. Above all, they want to clear Lacaze before everything gets leaked to the press and blows up in their face. So they asked us how far we'd got, and this morning they put pressure on the narcs. Your "Heisenberg" is one of their informers and they passed on his identity. For once they were only too eager to help out. Do you think he might have anything to do with the case?'

Servaz nodded. 'There can't be that many drug dealers in Marsac, can there? Who knows – maybe he's the one who provided the dope that drugged Hugo.'

Servaz was overheating by the time he left Stehlin's office, and it was only ten o'clock in the morning. He hesitated. He now had two new leads to explore. Where should he begin? To go digging in a past as full as Elvis Konstandin Elmaz's might make him lose time, but the Albanian's last words before he'd lapsed into a coma were flashing like a neon sign in Servaz's mind.

A man in his condition, who knew he might not make it out of hospital alive, had deployed his last ounce of strength to send that message. The message had to be of the utmost importance.

And the message was addressed to him, Servaz.

Elvis Elmaz knew who had killed Claire.

And it was the same person or persons who had fed him to his dogs.

He went through the fire door. A group had gathered in the corridor and Servaz realised that it must be something to do with the football. He tried to give them a wide berth, but he couldn't help overhearing some of their conversation.

'Martin, what do you think? Do you think France will beat Mexico tomorrow?'

Everyone on the squad knew how much he disliked sports – on television and in general. He caught a few people smiling sardonically.

'I hope not,' he said as he went past. 'That way we'll be able to talk about something else for a change.'

There was some half-hearted laughter.

Margot walked along the corridors, feeling everyone's gazes sticking to her like glue. She could tell they were murmuring, exchanging glances behind her back. Fortunately the school year was nearly over. In her ears, Marilyn Manson whispered, 'I want to disappear'. *Oh yes, mate, me too.*

She wondered just what they knew. How much was rumour, and how much was facts? Who had spilled the beans? Certainly not her father, or Vincent, or Samira. Was it David? Sarah? As she approached her locker she saw that a note had been taped to it. Here we go . . . She could just imagine how people's tongues would wag, spreading the rumour all through the school at the speed of sound: 'Did you see? Someone left another note on Margot's locker!' *Shit! You bunch of wankers!* There were times when bloody Armageddon seemed like the only solution.

She went straight up to her locker and saw that it wasn't a note, but a drawing. More precisely, a variation on the famous British army recruitment poster where an old general points and says YOUR COUNTRY NEEDS YOU. Uncle Sam's head had been replaced by a fairly blurry portrait of Julian Hirtmann.

Fucking morons! Didn't they have anything better to do?

She tore off the paper, crumpled it into a ball and threw it on the floor. Then she opened her locker. There was another note inside. She recognised the handwriting. *Elias, you little twat, how did you get into my locker?* The note said, 'I think I've found the Circle.'

Servaz hunted for an aspirin in his desk drawers, to no avail. He went into Samira and Vincent's office and opened Vincent's drawer. Paracetamol, ibuprofen, codeine, tramadol . . . Vincent and his chemicals.

When he returned to his office he saw that the message button on his desk phone was flashing. He looked at the number, but didn't recognise it. Servaz dialled, and a woman's voice answered: 'Suzanne Lacaze.'

He frowned. 'Good morning, Madame Lacaze. Have you been trying to get hold of me?'

A moment of silence.

'Yes.'

Her voice was even thinner than usual. A murmur stretched like elastic on the verge of snapping. Servaz was uncertain how to behave, but she left him no time to think.

'It's about my husband.'

There was tension in her voice. Extreme tension. The kind that accompanies a significant act. He felt his pulse beat faster.

'Yes, go on.'

'He lied to you the other night . . . about his alibi.'

Servaz swallowed. Another moment of silence.

'My husband wasn't at home the evening that woman was killed. And I don't know where he was. If I have to, I will say as much before the judge. And I hope you find the person who did it. Goodbye, Commandant.'

She had hung up. He let out a long breath. Fucking hell! He was going to have to make a few phone calls. He could just imagine the expression on the face of the prosecutor in Auch, and all of a sudden he felt that his day was actually improving.

31

Heisenberg

Servaz enjoyed the feeling that he was getting closer to his goal; the pieces were beginning to fall into place. There was a sound like a snare drum in his chest. The noise of victory. He sped down the motorway, his foot on the accelerator, the air so hot it trembled in mirages on the horizon.

He thought again about Santos and his summons. He knew that if he could solve this case quickly, the general inspectorate would have to take it into account. But what would happen if he sent the media darling Paul Lacaze to jail, the future head of the ruling party, the man who must not be touched? Wouldn't they be tempted to make him, Servaz, pay for it? They certainly would. And he had given them his head on a platter, back there in the car park. But for the moment, he didn't care. All that remained was the hunter's excitement when he sees the fox caught in the trap.

The fox had a nasty look about him. Lacaze gave Servaz one of those smiles that only he could give, but it changed into a grimace that didn't extend to his eyes. He listened to Servaz without moving, not expressing the slightest emotion in the face of his spouse's betrayal.

'You were at school in Marsac yourself, Commandant,' said the MP. 'Isn't that what you told me? Courses in the classics, is that right? Those were my favourite.' Lacaze was playing with a letter opener, feeling the tip with his forefinger. 'So I'm sure you're familiar with the notion of hubris.'

Servaz merely stared at Lacaze, unmoving. It was yet another alpha male confrontation, always the same things at stake. But this time Lacaze knew he had lost, and he was just trying to save face.

'Those who tried to rise too high exposed themselves to the

jealousy and anger of the gods. It would seem the gods have chosen my wife as their avenger . . . I must say, women are unpredictable.'

Servaz agreed with Lacaze on that point, but he did not show it.

'Has your wife told me the truth?' he asked, with a certain solemnity.

Once again they were sitting in the ultramodern house deep in the woods. Once Servaz had got through to him, they had come back here, at Lacaze's request. But this time there was no sign of Madame. The sun was coming in through the blinds in the picture windows, leaving stripes against the walls covered in photographs that glorified the master of the house.

'Yes.'

'Did you kill Claire Diemar?'

'I suppose I ought to remind you that you cannot accuse me unless I am in custody, which means a prior withdrawal of my immunity – and also that I must call my lawyer – but, to answer your question: no, Commandant, I did not kill her. I loved Claire – and she loved me.'

'That isn't what Hugo Bokhanowsky said. According to him, Claire was getting ready to leave you.'

'And why should that be?'

'Claire and Hugo were lovers.'

Lacaze looked at him in surprise.

'You can't be serious?'

'I am.'

Servaz saw Lacaze crease his forehead in doubt. 'The kid is nuts . . .Claire never mentioned him. And we were making plans for the future together.'

'However, you did tell me last time that she didn't want you to leave your wife.'

'Exactly. As long as she wasn't sure what *she* wanted. And also, as long as Suzanne was . . . in this state.'

'You mean, *alive*.'

A black shadow veiled the politician's gaze.

'Lacaze, had you been spying on Claire over the last few weeks? Did you have any doubts about her?'

'No.'

'Were you aware of her affair with Hugo Bokhanowsky?'

'No.'

'Were you with her on Friday evening?'

'No.'

Three firm responses.

'Where were you on Friday evening?'

Again the smile, and the empty gaze.

'That, I – I can't tell you.'

Lacaze said this with a smile full of irony, this time, as if he were aware of the comical side of the situation. Servaz let out a sigh.

'For Christ's sake, Lacaze! I'll have to call the judge and he will in all likelihood request a withdrawal of your immunity if you refuse to cooperate. You're in the process of destroying your own career.'

'You don't understand, Commandant: if I *do* tell you then my career will be destroyed. Either way, I'm trapped.'

Espérandieu was listening to what he considered one of the best rock albums of 2009, *West Ryder Pauper Lunatic Asylum*, by Kasabian, when someone knocked on the passenger window.

He turned down the sound before opening the door.

'There's someone we have to see,' said Servaz, climbing into the adjacent seat.

'What about Margot?'

'There's a gendarmerie van at the entrance.' Servaz pointed to the blue vehicle parked by the side of the road. 'Samira is keeping watch at the rear, and Margot is in class. I know Hirtmann. If he's going to act, he'll take no chances. Particularly not the chance of returning to jail.'

'So where are we going?'

'Just drive.'

They entered the town and Servaz gave Espérandieu directions. The meeting with Lacaze had dissolved all his enthusiasm. He couldn't understand why the MP was so obstinate in his refusal to say where he had been that night. Something wasn't right. He had sensed that Lacaze had good reasons to stand his ground. It wasn't the attitude of someone who has committed murder.

But perhaps Lacaze was simply very good at this game. He was a politician, after all, which meant an actor and a professional liar.

'Here we are,' said Servaz.

The university residence, on one of the hills overlooking the town, was a series of five identical buildings. They went through a small gate where a sign indicated PHILIPPE-ISIDORE PICOT DE LAPEYROUSE STUDENT RESIDENCE. They parked beneath the trees; the lawns were deserted. Unlike the lycée in Marsac, the semester at the faculty of science was over, and most of the students had left for the summer. The residence seemed abandoned. From the outside, the long four-storey building looked handsome enough with its rows of big windows, which ought to have made the rooms light and pleasant, but the moment they came in the entrance they understood that something was awry. There were banners hanging on the walls: 'WE PAY RENT, WE DEMAND THE MINIMUM', 'WE ARE FED UP WITH COCKROACHES', or even 'STUDENT WELFARE OFFICE = FILTH'. There was no lift. As they walked up the stairs, they soon realised that the banners were justified: the plastic strips on the ceiling were coming loose, the yellow paint on the walls was peeling, and on the door to the showers hung a sign that said OUT OF ORDER. Servaz even caught a glimpse of some insects scurrying along the floor. The narcs had told them room number 211. They stopped outside. There was music coming through the door, full blast. Espérandieu knocked and put on his most youthful tone of voice.

'Heisenberg, you there, mate?'

The music stopped. They waited at least thirty seconds, wondering whether 'Heisenberg' had escaped out of the window, when the door opened to reveal a thin girl wearing a tank top and shorts. Her hair was sticking up and its blonde colour was no more natural than her black roots. Her arms were so thin that her bones and veins were visible beneath her tanned skin. She was blinking in the half-light of the room, the blinds almost completely down, and her pale eyes studied them one after the other.

'Is Heisenberg around?' asked Vincent.

'Who're you guys?'

'Surprise!' exclaimed Vincent joyfully, waving his warrant card and pushing past her to enter the room.

The walls were almost entirely papered with photographs, posters and flyers. Espérandieu recognised Kurt Cobain, Bob Marley and Jimi Hendrix. The moment he stepped in the room, he identified the faint odour that lingered: THC, tetrahydrocannabinol; in its most common form: hashish.

'Is Heisenberg here?'

'What you want with him?'

'That's none of your business,' said Espérandieu. 'Are you his girlfriend?'

She gave them a look full of hatred.

'What the fuck is it to you?'

'Answer the question.'

'Get the fuck out.'

'We won't leave until we've seen him.'

'You're not the narcs,' she said.

'No, crime squad.'

'Call the narcs, you can't lay a finger on Heisenberg.'

'What would you know? Is he your boyfriend?'

She didn't answer, her big pale eyes darting from one to the other with an evil glow.

'Okay, well, I'm out of here,' she said.

She started to walk towards the door, and Espérandieu reached out and grabbed her wrist. Immediately, like a cat striking back, she spun round and dug her nails into his forearm.

'Ouch! Fuck, she scratched me!'

He grabbed her other wrist and tried to control her while she lashed out and struggled like a tiger.

'Let me go, you filthy cop! Get your dirty paws off me, fucking pig!'

'Calm down. Stop right now or we'll take you in.'

'I don't give a damn, you bastard! You have no right to treat a woman like this! Let me go!'

She wriggled, hissed and spat like a frenzied animal. Just as Servaz was about to come to Vincent's assistance, she banged her head violently against the wall.

'You hit me,' she screamed, a gash in her forehead. 'I'm bleeding! Help! Rape!'

Espérandieu tried to gag her with his hand to stop her screaming. She would rouse the entire building, even if it probably was three-quarters empty. She bit him. He shuddered as if he had received an electric shock, and was about to slap her when Servaz blocked his wrist.

'No.'

With the other hand, he locked the door. The girl calmed down a little, evaluating the situation, her sunken eyes shooting sparks of hatred when she realised she was trapped. Her forehead was bleeding. She rubbed her wrists, where there were red marks from Espérandieu's fingers.

'All we want is to speak to Heisenberg,' said Servaz calmly.

The girl sat down on the edge of the bed and looked up at them, dabbing at her bloody forehead with a corner of her tank top.

'What do you want to tell him?'

'We have questions for him.'

'I'm Heisenberg.'

Servaz and his assistant looked at each other. For a split second they wondered if she was bullshitting them again, then Servaz understood she was telling the truth. The narcs had deliberately not told them that Heisenberg was a woman, probably relishing the surprise and difficulties that lay in store for them.

'You can take me in, but I won't answer your questions. I have a deal with your colleagues. They even wrote it down somewhere.'

'We don't give a toss about your deal.'

'Oh, really? Well too bad, but it doesn't work like that, guys. I only talk to the narcs. You've got no right to grill me!'

'Well, let's just say the rules have changed. Call your contact if you like. Go ahead. Ask him. We want answers. You've got no more protection, you're stark naked. Either you talk to us, or you go to jail.'

Her pale green gaze watched them, trying to determine whether they were bluffing.

'Call your contact,' said Servaz again. 'Go ahead.'

She inclined her head, defeated.

'What do you want?'

'To ask you some questions.'

'What sort of questions?'

'Such as: is Paul Lacaze one of your clients?'

'What?'

'Paul La—'

'I know who Paul Lacaze is, sweetheart. Are you serious? You think a guy like him would risk getting his drugs from me? Shit, are you joking?'

'Who are your clients, students?'

'Not just them. Little middle-class people from Marsac, posh women you'd just love to slap in the face but who have tons of dosh, even labourers – these days, drugs are like golf: it's gone democratic.'

'You must have good marks in sociology,' said Espérandieu sarcastically.

She didn't even bother to look at him.

'How does it work?' asked Servaz. 'Where do you hide your supply?'

She explained. She made use of a 'childminder' – in police jargon, a person who agreed to look after the supply, generally an addict

294

who agreed to do it in exchange for the odd hit now and then. But Heisenberg's childminder was not an addict: she was an old lady of eighty-three who lived all alone in a private home; Heisenberg spent one afternoon there a week, keeping her company and chit-chatting.

'Do you keep a list of your clients?' asked Servaz.

She looked at him, her eyes round.

'What? No!'

'Do you know the lycée in Marsac?'

She gave him a wary look.

'Yeah?'

'Do you have any clients from there?'

She nodded, a gleam of defiance in her eyes.

'Uh-huh.'

'What? I didn't hear.'

'Not just students.'

Servaz felt a familiar tingle at the base of his spine.

'A teacher?'

She gave him a triumphant smile.

'Yup, a teacher. From Marsac. That elite lycée. That's shut you up, hasn't it?'

Servaz looked into her faded green eyes, wondering if she was bluffing.

'Their name?' he said.

'Sorry. You'll get bugger all from me. I don't inform on people.'

'Really? So how do the narcs go about it?'

'Not like that,' she said, stubbornly, as if he had offended her.

'The name Hugo Bokhanowsky, does that mean anything to you?'

She nodded.

'And David Jimbot?'

She nodded again.

'The name of the teacher,' he insisted.

'No can do, mate.'

'Listen, I'm getting fed up. You're wasting my time. The narcs have a file on you as thick as the phone book. And this time, the judge won't show any mercy. He's ready to send you down on a single phone call from us. You'll be behind bars for quite a—'

'Oh all right, for fuck's sake! Van Acker.'

'What?'

'Francis Van Acker. That's his name. He teaches I don't know what at the lycée in Marsac. A guy with a little beard who thinks he's the bee's knees.'

Servaz looked at her. Francis . . . of course. Why hadn't he thought of it earlier?

There are four of them in the car. They're driving fast. Too fast. At night. Windows down, on the road that winds its way through the woods. The rush of air makes their hair dance, and Marianne is leaning against him in the back seat, so her hair mingles with his and he inhales the straw-berry smell of her shampoo. On the radio Freddie Mercury is asking who wants to live forever and Sting whether the Russians love their children too. Francis is driving.

The fourth member of their party must have been Jimmy, or maybe it was Louis: Servaz doesn't remember. He and Francis are in the front seat, talking endlessly, mindless banter, laughing. They each have a beer in their hands; they look joyful, immortal and somewhat tipsy. Francis is driving too fast. As always, but it's his car. And suddenly in his free hand there is a joint, and he holds it out to Jimmy, who laughs stupidly before taking a drag. Servaz feels Marianne tense up next to him. She has the sparkly fingerless mittens that she wears all year round except in summer; her warm fingers emerge from the wool and mingle with his, their two hands joined like the links of a chain that no one can break. Martin revels in these moments, sitting in the semi-darkness in the back of the car, where they have become one person. The headlights cut through the tree trunks, the road speeds by, it smells like weed in the car, in spite of the night air blowing through the windows. On the radio, Peter Gabriel is singing 'Sledgehammer'. And suddenly, Martin feels Marianne's warm breath against his ear and her voice murmurs, 'If we die tonight, I want you to know that I've never been this happy.'

And he is thinking exactly the same thing, that their two hearts are beating in unison; he too is certain that he will never be as happy as he is at that moment, knowing the fulfilment of her love, and the friendship that fills the car, the carefree grace of their youth, until suddenly he sees Francis looking at them through the rearview mirror. The smoke from the joint is rising before his eyes in a thin spiral. Any trace of humour has vanished. It is a look of covetousness, of jealousy, of pure hatred. A moment later, Francis winks at him and smiles, and Servaz is certain he must have been dreaming.

*

Servaz parked in the centre of town. He had spent all afternoon thinking. He couldn't help remembering what Marianne had said about Francis the night before. About his lack of talent, and how he had always been jealous of Servaz's gifts. He pictured the literature professor they'd had back then, an elegant man who wore cravats beneath his striped shirt collars, and pocket handkerchiefs in his suits. He would spend a long while chatting with Servaz between or after classes and now he remembered how this used to make Francis sneer; he was perpetually denigrating the older man, and suspected him of seeking out Martin's company for reasons that were not purely intellectual.

Servaz had never suspected that Van Acker's sarcastic remarks might be due to jealousy: Francis was the centre of attention in Marsac, he had his little court of admirers –if anyone should have been jealous, it was Martin.

Marianne's words drummed incessantly in his mind: 'Your best friend. Your alter ego, your brother . . . There was only one thing he wanted: to take what you loved most in the world.' Even if he had subsequently hated Francis for having stolen the woman he loved, at the time he had believed that their friendship had something *sacred* about it. Hadn't Francis felt that way, too? He remembered his words in Marsac, only five days earlier: 'You were my big brother, you were my Seymour – and for me, in a way, that big brother committed suicide the day you joined the police force.' Was that a complete lie? Was Francis Van Acker the sort of person who sought revenge on those who were more talented or more handsome than he was? Did his sarcastic wit conceal a deep inferiority complex? Had he manipulated and seduced Marianne to make up for it – and because at the time she was easy prey? A possible answer was beginning to dawn in his mind. But it was simply too ridiculous, too absurd to be taken seriously.

Marianne. Why had she still not called? Was she waiting for him to call her? Was she afraid he might interpret a call as an attempt to manipulate the person who could get her son out of prison? Or was there something else? He was filled with anxiety. He wanted to see her again as soon as possible; he was already feeling that empty yearning he had had such difficulty getting rid of. He'd thought of dialling her number ten times since yesterday. And ten times he had decided not to. Why? And Elvis – what did he have to do with it all? He had narrowly escaped what looked like attempted murder, his life was hanging by a thread, and he had summoned his last remaining strength to tell Servaz to go digging in his past. Finally, there was Lacaze. Lacaze who refused to say where he had been on Friday evening. Lacaze who had a motive, and no alibi. Lacaze who at that very moment was in the judge's office, being heard as a target witness: the hearing had begun four hours earlier, but the MP was maintaining his suicidal silence. Elvis, Lacaze, Francis, Hirtmann: players doing a circle dance around him in a game of blind man's buff. He was the central player, the one whose eyes were blindfolded, hands outspread, and he had to grope his way towards the murderer.

Servaz climbed out of the Jeep, locked it, and set off. The little street away from the centre was lined with tall private houses surrounded by gardens. A great many cars were parked along the pavement. He spotted a parking space, but there was a lamppost nearby; it was not yet lit, although night was beginning to fall.

He went by without stopping, then back to the centre of town, where he found a shop about to close that sold DIY supplies and fishing gear. The old man gave him a puzzled look when he explained that he was looking for a fishing rod with or without a reel, but it had to be sturdy, and a certain length. Finally, he came out with a telescoping rod in fibreglass and carbon fibre which when fully opened could extend to four metres.

Servaz went back to the quiet little street, his fishing pole on his shoulder. He walked along the pavement, looking discreetly to the right and to the left, then he stopped beneath the lamppost and gave it two quick powerful blows with the end of the fishing rod. The second blow was enough to smash the bulb. It hadn't taken more than three seconds. He left again immediately, just as nonchalant.

Five minutes later he parked the Jeep in the space, praying that no one had noticed his little act of vandalism. A few dark facades now had light in their windows, and twilight was descending slowly over the street.

Francis Van Acker lived in a big T-shaped house that dated from the beginning of the previous century, one house down from the parking space. Servaz could discern its outline through the branches of a pine tree and the foliage of a weeping willow. As it was set on a little bank, rising out of a dark mass of bushes and hedges, it seemed to overshadow all the surrounding houses. There was light in the triple bay window on the first floor, on the right-hand side of the house.

He mused that the villa suited its owner: it had the same haughtiness, the same pride. Apart from the light on the right-hand side, the house was shrouded in darkness. Servaz took out his cigarettes. He wondered what he was expecting from this surveillance. He wasn't about to come back here every evening. He thought about Vincent and Samira, and a tremor went down his spine. He trusted his two assistants: Vincent would take his mission seriously because he knew Margot well. And Samira was one of his best agents. Except that the adversary they were dealing with was nothing like those who ordinarily graced the police station or the courtrooms with their presence.

He spent the next two hours observing the house and the rare traffic in the street: for the most part he just saw neighbours coming home late from work, or taking out the dog or the dustbins. And gradually the glow of televisions began flickering in living rooms, and lights came on in upstairs windows. He wondered where he had read this sentence: 'Wherever there is a television glowing there is someone staying up who does not read.' He would have liked to be at home listening to Mahler with the volume on low, a book open on his lap.

That night, Ziegler got home late. At the last minute she had had to deal with a drunken brawl in a bar in Auch: two men who didn't even have the strength to fight, they were so pissed, but capable enough to pull out a blade. They had felt so pathetically sorry for themselves by the time the law arrived that she wished there was a category of crime called 'first-degree stupidity' so she could lock them away. She removed her uniform and stepped into the shower. When she came back out, she saw she had three texts from Zuzka. She winced. She didn't feel up to calling her girlfriend after such a god-awful, irritating day. She had nothing to tell her. And besides, another task was waiting.

Thank you, Martin. I can tell it won't be long before I start having major problems with my girlfriend. Consultant – yeah, right!

She opened the windows to let in the evening air, though it was hardly any cooler outside. A quiet atmosphere reigned in the building. She put the television on low, popped a pizza in the microwave, then crossed the living room in her pyjamas and sat down at her Mac.

She blew on the pizza to cool down the burning cheese, took a swallow of gin and tonic, and started typing.

Espérandieu had sent her a photograph of the letters 'JH' which Martin had found carved into the tree trunk. She opened a second window, typed Marsac into Google maps, switched to satellite view and zoomed in on the north shore of the lake until she reached maximum enlargement. It was blurry, so she backtracked until three centimetres equalled fifty metres. She moved the cursor along the shore. Seen from above, some of the houses were veritable little castles: tennis courts, swimming pools and bathhouses, outbuildings, wooded parks, jetties on the lake for dinghies or motorboats, even greenhouses and children's playgrounds. There were only a dozen houses: the inhabited area of the lake was no longer than two kilometres. Marianne Bokhanowsky's house was the last one before the woods expanded into a forest that stretched for miles.

She moved the cursor until she found a road running through the forest, roughly 200 metres from the western edge of Marianne's garden. It was shaped like the letter J: the upper edge pointed north and the descending loop faced west. There was a parking area, with something that looked like two picnic tables, in the middle of the loop. She was willing to bet that Hirtmann had set off from there. Because the image was poorly defined and the foliage was dense she could not see whether there was a path. She decided to go and take a look the next day, if the usual troublemakers stayed calm despite the heat. The CSIs had explored the area around the stream: according to Espérandieu they hadn't found anything, but she doubted they had gone any further than that. She felt her excitement growing: there was a fresh lead. No need, now, to consult the information and files that others before her had pored over, data that had been sleeping in computers or gathering dust at the bottom of drawers for months: Martin had promised he would forward information to her as it came in. With the investigation in Marsac, he didn't have time to take care of it himself. And his two assistants were stuck with keeping watch over Margot.

This is your chance, my dear. It's up to you not to mess it up. You don't have a lot of time.

The cell in Paris hadn't sent anyone down there for the moment. One e-mail and two letters carved with a penknife into a tree trunk: that was a bit lightweight for them. But sooner or later Martin would stop having Margot watched, he'd wind up his investigation, and the police would take control again. If she could make a decisive breakthrough before that, Martin was not the type to claim others' findings as his own. Her superiors would be angry that they hadn't been kept informed, but no one would be able to take away the fact that she'd made headway in a case where other investigators, dozens of them, had been working themselves into the ground for months.

What makes you think you're going to do it? She spent the next two hours preparing her hack of the computer network at the prison where Lisa Ferney was interned. It took her a while, but in the end, she found herself with a made-to-measure variant of the famous Zeus software, the king of the Trojan horse programs (*The ancient world is never far away*, she mused). Zeus had already infected and besieged millions of computers the world over, including those of the Bank of America and NASA. The second manoeuvre consisted of finding a breach in the prison's computer network. But she had the e-mail address of the director himself. She had asked him for it before leaving. She incorporated the botnet into a PDF document, invisible to the Ministry of Justice's multiple firewalls and antivirus software, and then she moved on to phase three: social engineering, which consisted – here too, as in the famous scene from antiquity – in convincing the victim to activate the trap she had set. She sent the file to the director in an e-mail explaining that in the attachment there was some urgent information regarding an inmate. The only weakness in her method was having to use her own e-mail address. It was a calculated risk. If someone realised it was an attack, she could claim she too had been infected. When the director opened the document, Zeus would lodge itself in his hard drive system files without him realising a thing. He would open the file, see an error message, and he would either delete the e-mail or call her for an explanation. Too late. The program would already have made its nest.

Once it was installed, her personal version of Zeus would chart a map of the prison's computer system and she would receive it the moment the director went online. Ziegler could then read the map and target the files that interested her. She would place her order on the server, Zeus would read it, and at the next connection, Zeus would send her the files she had requested. And so on, until she had all the information she needed. Then she would send Zeus the order to self-destruct, and the software would vanish. There was no way anyone would ever know there had been an attack. No way to trace anything back to her.

When she had completed this task, she moved onto the next one. She felt a fleeting pang of guilt as she logged on to Martin's computer, but she consoled herself with the fact that she was acting on behalf of all of them, and that by getting her information directly from the source rather than waiting for him to pass it on she was saving time for everyone. Besides, it was his work computer. She supposed that if he had anything to hide, he would keep it for his computer at home. She went through his e-mail, then continued to the hard drive. Pouring the last drops of gin and tonic down her throat, she quickly scrolled through a number of files contained in C:\Windows, then frowned. *That software wasn't there last time . . .* Ziegler had an extraordinary memory for that sort of thing. Maybe it was nothing. She dug further and again raised an eyebrow: *another suspicious file*. She launched a scan of the hard drive and went to pour another gin and tonic. When she came back to her computer, she was puzzled by what she found. The Ministry of the Interior's security would not have let malicious software get through, and Martin wasn't the type to neglect security directives. If he had received a suspicious e-mail, or one coming from someone he didn't know, he would certainly not have opened it. So the only possibility was that the malware had been directly introduced by someone who was physically on-site.

She wondered how to proceed. She should warn Martin – but how could she do that without revealing how she had obtained the information? How would he react if he found out? She ran her fingers through her hair, pensively, her eyes riveted to the screen. First of all, she had to find out who had downloaded the software. She reached for a pad and pen and began to make a list of possibilities, but there weren't many:

colleague
detainee
outside visitor

In the last two cases, it was unlikely that Martin would have left them on their own long enough for them to be able to get anything done. She added one last possibility:

cleaning woman

32

In the Darkness

At around eleven o'clock at night, an old man took his dog out and gave Servaz a suspicious look, which he then transferred to the broken lamppost two metres from the car. Servaz hoped he wasn't going to call the gendarmes. Not taking his eyes from the house, he made two calls, one to Vincent and the other to Samira. The window on the first floor was still lit.

Shortly before midnight, his attention sharpened when a silhouette walked past the window. Then that light went out and another one came on behind a small stained-glass window where the two wings met, which must have been where the staircase was. Then a third window was lit on the ground floor. Servaz twisted his neck to watch the entrance. A few seconds later he saw the light in the vestibule come on, then the front door opened and Francis's head and shoulders appeared above the hedge. The last light went off inside the house. Van Acker was going out.

Servaz slid lower into his seat as he watched Van Acker come down the garden, open the gate, and emerge on the pavement twenty metres from his bumper. He saw his erstwhile friend head towards his car, a red Alfa Romeo Spider roadster parked a bit further along. With his hand on the ignition, he waited for Francis to start the car and drive to the end of the street before he turned the key and pulled out. He told himself that if Van Acker was on the defensive, it would be difficult to follow him without being noticed. But Van Acker hadn't seemed interested in what was going on in the street: he'd headed straight for the car without once looking around him.

Servaz came to the end of the street in time to see the car on his right, turning left 100 metres further on. He accelerated and turned at the same spot. Ahead of him, the roadster took the rue du 4 Septembre as far as the place Gambetta, and then headed southeast.

303

As he drove past the church, Servaz saw a student vomiting in the shadow of the presbytery; two schoolmates were waiting for him, laughing. The Spider sped past the lowered iron shutters of the little shopping streets, bouncing over the cobblestones, then round the fountain and onto the D939. He was leaving town. Servaz followed suit. The full moon shone on the dark wooded hillsides, and after a long straight line, the road went uphill and began to wind through the woods. Servaz kept a good distance, and he regularly lost the two rear lights before seeing them again as he came out of a bend. His GPS told him there would be no crossroads for four kilometres, so it would be useless to stay within sight, but Van Acker was driving fast and he must be careful not to allow too much distance between them.

It was obvious that Van Acker enjoyed testing the performance of his sports car, and he was driving well above the speed limit. Francis had never given a damn about the rules – except the ones that he himself established.

The road went up and downhill, winding like a snake. They were going so fast that the wheels of the Jeep tossed up dead leaves and gravel at every turn. Servaz got the impression that they must be audible from miles around. In the beam of the headlights he could see that the woods were getting thicker. From time to time he saw the full moon, but most of the time it was hidden by the vault of greenery. Twice, maybe three times, Servaz thought he saw headlights in his rearview mirror – but he was focused on what was happening in front of him, not behind.

When they reached the end of the valley, Servaz saw the Spider turn left 200 metres ahead of him and start down an even narrower road. He did likewise, and the little road began to climb, with hairpin bends. They went through a hamlet with three or four farms that clung to the top of the hill like a row of teeth in a crooked jaw. He forced himself to slow down to avoid being noticed. He reached a small junction and hesitated, until again he saw the rear lights off to his left, between the trees. The road began to climb again. Then it reached a plateau and followed a long open plantation of trees, with tall trunks regularly spaced like the pillars of a cathedral. There were hundreds of them.

Servaz was beginning to feel worried. Where was Van Acker going? His route had avoided the main roads, taking instead a series of small secondary roads with very little traffic – especially at this time of night. Servaz tried to think, but he was too focused on the car ahead of him.

At the next crossroads, right in the middle of a vast uninhabited plateau, he saw a sign: 'GORGES DE LA SOULE'. He searched for the Spider but couldn't see it. Shit! Servaz switched off the engine and got out. There was a special quality to the silence. There was not a breath of air and the night was astonishingly warm. He listened out. An engine noise . . . on his left. He strained to hear, and again he detected the change of gears and the faraway squeal of the tyres in a bend. He got back behind the wheel, took the Jeep in a large curve and headed for the gorges.

He reached them five minutes later, slowed down and parked the Cherokee at the side of the road. In daylight the gorges were a place of luxuriant vegetation, and the forest only opened to let in a few rays of sun and glimpses of the tall limestone cliffs. A wide, slow-moving stream ran through them. There were also several shallow caves by the side of the road, which people came to visit on Sundays when there was nothing else to do. At this late hour they seemed very different. In his youth Servaz had come here on more than one occasion, with Francis, Marianne and the others.

Something like a premonition told him that this might be where Van Acker was headed. There had always been a dark romantic side to Francis, and this place suited him well. It was a bit like the paintings of Caspar David Friedrich. If Francis had parked somewhere in the gorges and Servaz went that way too, his friend could not help but notice him. No one drove along this back road at this time of night. Francis would see him go by and realise that Martin was following him. And if Van Acker had simply driven on, Servaz would have lost him by now anyway – but he was willing to bet that he hadn't.

There was a track six feet from his rear bumper. He reversed down it very slowly until the vehicle was invisible from the road, in case Francis came back this way. He switched off the headlights, then the engine, and got out. Not a sound, other than the murmur of the stream that flowed on the other side of the road. He closed the car door gently. Listened. A nocturnal bird cried out somewhere. Nothing else. He tried to analyse the situation. He didn't have much choice; his only option was to go into the gorge. He knew that Van

Acker might be gone already, leaving him completely alone in the middle of nowhere, caught up in some wild-goose chase. He took his mobile from his pocket and switched it off. Then he began walking along the road, under the moonlit sky.

As he walked along the asphalt, he wondered what he actually knew about Van Acker nowadays – what had he been up to all these years? Their lives had gone in such different directions. Francis had always been a mystery. Can your best friend be the person you know the least? Two people who were so close and yet so different. We change. All of us. A part of ourselves stays the same: the kernel, the pure heart that comes from childhood, but all around, sediment builds up. Until it disfigures the child we used to be, until it makes the adult such a different person, so monstrous, that the child would not recognise the adult he has become – and no doubt he would be terrified at the idea of becoming that person.

Servaz went deeper and deeper into the gorge. Now the sound of the nearby stream concealed any other noise. He followed the long bends in the road, walking more and more quickly. He tried to see through the growth at the roadside, but to no avail. It was almost completely dark in there, deep in the forest. Still no sound . . . Where had Van Acker gone? Servaz went a few yards further and saw him at last, parked just beyond the next bend. A corner of the car and a headlight: the red Spider. Servaz froze; leaned forward slightly. Two more headlights appeared between the trees; there were two cars parked there. And two silhouettes in the Alfa Romeo. He hesitated about what to do next. Could he get any closer without being noticed? Or would it be better to wait for the second person to get out and return to their car? He figured he had one advantage over them. From inside the car, only what was in the beam of the headlights would be visible: the cliff dazzling in the harsh light.

If he crept through the woods, he would remain invisible. The question was whether he might make a noise as he went closer. But the two figures were deep in conversation, and the sound of the stream would cover him. He began to creep through the trees, but soon realised he could not go as fast as he had thought. The thickets were so dark and dense that it was impossible to make out the numerous obstacles in his way, and he was confronted with ever more impenetrable clusters of brushwood. Several times over he almost twisted his ankle in the dark because of the uneven terrain.

Low-hanging branches scratched his cheeks and forehead, and he snagged his shirt several times on the brambles. He had to stop frequently. He would observe the two forms in the car, then set off again. After what seemed like an endless amount of time he found himself confronted with an insurmountable obstacle: a brook flowed invisibly in the darkness; it must join the stream further down. Servaz only knew it was there because of a sudden incline beneath his feet, and the sound of water up close. He removed one shoe and sock, rolled up his trouser leg, and tried to put his foot in, but his leg went into the cold water up to his knee, and his foot hadn't even touched the bottom. The two figures were only a few metres away on the far side of the brook, but they had their backs to him. He moved along the brook until he could see the passenger more clearly. It was a woman. With long hair. He had no idea of the colour – any more than he could tell her age from where he stood.

Suddenly another solution occurred to him.

The road went all the way through the gorges, from one end to the other. There were two ways out, so either the woman had come from the other side, or she had been there well before them. Servaz was willing to bet on the first possibility. They didn't want to be seen together. They were taking a risk. He made his way back the way he had come, this time not worrying about any noise he might make. Time was of the essence. As soon as he reached the road, he began to run along the asphalt and gravel towards his car. He switched on the ignition and left the track, then headed down the road at thirty kilometres an hour. As soon as he was sure that the occupants of the Spider could no longer hear him, he put his foot on the accelerator. When he reached the previous junction, he saw a car parked beneath the trees, its lights switched off, but perfectly visible. He immediately recognised it. He pulled up alongside and lowered his window.

'What the fuck are you doing here?'

Pujol sat up.

'What do you think?' said Pujol, annoyed. 'Have you forgotten?'

Sweet Jesus! He had asked Pujol to tail him in case Hirtmann showed up. He had completely forgotten!

'I said, "at a distance"!'

'That's what we're doing. But you're driving all over the place.'

'Nice job with the fishing rod,' Pujol's teammate in the shadow said, sarcastically.

307

Servaz thought about Francis in the gorge: he might drive by at any moment.

'Go back to Toulouse! Get the hell out of here! I don't want you under my feet tonight.'

He could see the anger in Pujol's eyes, but he didn't have time for further explanations. He waited until their car had disappeared, then he set off again, turned left at the next junction, then left again. He went roughly two kilometres before he saw a new sign to 'GORGES DE LA SOULE' next to a ruined building: an abandoned farmhouse with a barn. He reversed the Jeep and parked against the wall, then switched off the engine and the headlights and began to wait.

After what seemed like forever, where he was beginning to wonder whether the woman had not gone the other way after all, the unknown car went by in front of him. He waited until she was out of sight and then started the car. For a few kilometres, he drove slowly, then accelerated when his GPS informed him that he was approaching the next junction.

He saw her turn left, and once again he took his foot off the accelerator to let her put some distance between them, then repeated the whole rigmarole as they drew near the following junction, just in time to see her carry on straight ahead. *The road to Marsac.* The one that went by the lycée before leading into town. He would have to get closer if he didn't want to lose her in the little streets. He was roughly 200 metres behind her, gradually closing the distance on the long straight stretch, when he saw her brake lights come on just before she veered into the oak-lined lane that led to the lycée. His mind was racing. If he turned into the long lane that led to the car park, there was no chance she wouldn't notice him. But from this distance, it was impossible for him to identify her.

He had a sudden thought. Vincent! He was parked somewhere, keeping watch over the entrance to the lycée. Servaz pulled into the verge. He already had his thumb on the call button.

'Martin! What's up?'

'There's a car coming into the car park,' he shouted. 'Do you see it? I have to know who the driver is!'

Silence.

'Wait . . . yes, I see it. Just a minute. She's getting out. A student . . . blonde. Judging by her age, she must be in the prep classes.'

'Go up to her – I absolutely have to know who it is!' he cried.

'Make something up, anything. Tell her the police have been watching the lycée ever since her teacher was murdered. Ask her if she's noticed anything. Tell her she shouldn't be walking around alone with what's going on. Exaggerate if you have to . . . And ask to see her ID card.'

He saw Espérandieu get out of the car; he didn't close the door but walked quickly over towards the other figure, who was now heading towards the entrance.

Servaz glanced at his dashboard.

The binoculars.

He leaned over and opened the glove box. They were in there, along with his torch, his notepad and his gun.

He grabbed the binoculars. Espérandieu was striding across the grass to catch up with the young woman. She still hadn't noticed him. Servaz trained the binoculars in their direction.

'Let her go,' he said suddenly, into his mobile.

'What?'

'Don't let her see you. It's pointless. I know who it is.'

He saw Espérandieu come to a halt and look in every direction before he noticed his superior at last. He ended the call, lowered the binoculars, and wondered feverishly about the significance of what he had just seen.

Sarah . . .

Margot made sure her door was locked and went back to her bed with its damp sheets. She looked for a moment at the empty second bed, and felt her heart contract. Her roommate had asked to be switched to another room after the news had gone round the lycée that Margot was the target of a threat.

She realised that, in spite of the lack of shared interests and their difficulty in communicating, she really missed Lucie. She'd taken all her belongings, and stripped the wall of all her family photographs. That side of the room looked sad and abandoned.

Sitting cross-legged on the bed, Margot began to reflect on the topic Van Acker had set them, but her mind was empty. Her homework was entitled: *Find seven good reasons never to write a novel and one (good) reason to write one.* Margot supposed that Van Acker wanted to open the eyes of all the aspiring writers in the class to the difficulties that lay ahead. Margot had already found the following reasons never to write a novel:

1. There are already too many novels. Every year a pile of new novels are published, not to mention the thousands that are written and will never be published.
2. Writing a novel requires a considerable amount of work for very little recognition.
3. Writing doesn't make anyone rich. At best the author can earn enough to go out to eat or pay for his holiday, but authors who can actually live from their work are an endangered species, like the snow leopard or the pygmy hippopotamus.

She dropped the last two comments; she could already picture Francis Van Acker dripping with sarcasm: 'Do you mean to imply that half the geniuses of our literature should have abstained from writing, Mademoiselle Servaz?' And besides . . . besides, she was drawing a blank. Her mind was focused on what was happening elsewhere, outside. Was *he* out there, somewhere in the woods, looking for her? Was Julian Hirtmann really hanging about or were they all just imagining things, like a bunch of lunatics? She thought back to the note that Elias had left in her locker that morning. 'I think I've found the Circle.' What the fuck did he mean by that? She had tried to speak to him, but Elias had stopped her, saying, 'Later.' *Shit, Elias, you piss me off.*

Her gaze fell upon the little black device on the bed. A walkie-talkie. Samira had given it to her and shown her how to use it, saying, 'Don't hesitate, you can call me any time.'

She liked Samira, with her alternative look and her wild clothes. Margot glanced again at the walkie-talkie. Finally, she reached for it.

'Samira?'

She let go of the button, the way they had told her to, so that Samira could answer.

'Yes, babe. I'm here. What's going on?'

'Uh . . . I . . . it's just . . .'

'You feel kind of alone in your room since your roommate left, is that it?'

Bull's eye.

'That wasn't too cool of her . . .' A crackling sound. 'It's getting really itchy over here. It's full of fucking horrible bugs. And besides, I'm kind of thirsty. I have two cold beers in a cooler. What do you say? We don't need to tell the headmaster or your father – after all, he told me to keep a close watch on you . . .'

A smile lit up Margot's face.

He felt too tired to go back to Toulouse. He wondered if he'd find a hotel room at this time of night, then he thought of another solution. He knew it wasn't a good idea, that she would have called him if she had wanted to see him – then he thought that she might be doing the same thing he was doing: waiting desperately for him to call. He was consumed with anxiety, doubt and the desire to see her. He reached for his mobile, saw the time in the corner of the screen, and put it back in his pocket. He didn't want to wake her up in the middle of the night. But maybe she wasn't asleep. Maybe she was waking up every night the way she had woken up two nights ago when he was in her bed. Maybe she was asking herself the same questions: why the hell didn't he call? Again he tasted her mouth on his lips, the perfume of her hair and her skin. There was a horrible emptiness in the pit of his stomach. He was craving her company.

'I'm going home,' he said to Espérandieu on the phone. 'Goodnight.'

He saw his assistant wave to him and trudge back towards his car. In an hour, another team would take over. He couldn't help but think about Margot, sound asleep. He wondered what Hirtmann was doing. Was he asleep? Was he lurking somewhere, stalking his prey? Had he found one, had he locked her up somewhere to play with her the way a cat plays with a mouse? He banished the thought. He had told Vincent to hide, but not too well; to remain noticeable to someone who was looking for signs of surveillance. He did not think that Hirtmann would take such a risk. Freedom was far too precious to him.

Servaz headed for the lake. He went by Le Zik, the café-concert restaurant on stilts. There were people inside, and strains of music reached him through the lowered window. He went along the east shore, closest to town, and then the north shore. He slowed down when he came to the gate of Marianne's house.

There were lights on on the ground floor.

His heart began to beat faster. He realised that he wanted her, desperately; wanted to kiss her and hold her. Wanted to hear her voice. Her laugh. To be with her.

Then his heart sank.

There was a car parked on the gravel under the fir trees. It was a red Alfa Romeo Spider. Servaz was aware of a wave of sadness swelling somewhere, the painful sting of betrayal. He faltered. Then he decided to give her the benefit of the doubt. He was angry at himself for thinking evil thoughts. He decided to wait for Francis to leave and then he would go over. There was surely an explanation. He drove a bit further along and parked in the shelter of the woods, at the edge of the property, then lit a cigarette and put Mahler in the CD player. At the end of the CD, he decided he would do without the music. He tasted bile; the poison of doubt was infecting him. He remembered the supply of condoms he had seen in the bathroom. He looked at the clock on the dashboard. Another hour went by. When the red Spider emerged from the garden, tyres squealing on the asphalt, Servaz felt a chill spread all through him.

The moon up there was a sad woman, the only one who would never betray him.

It was three o'clock in the morning.

Thursday

33

Charlène

He was twenty years old. Long brown hair, straight on top, curly at the ends and on his shoulders. He was holding a half-finished cigarette between his index and middle finger. He was staring straight at the camera lens with an intense, slightly cynical look, and the ghost of a smile – or pout – on his lips.

Marianne had taken the photograph. Even today, he wondered why he kept it. Two days after she took it, she left him.

Her voice, choked, as she told him. He had seen the tears in her eyes, as if he were the one who was leaving.

'Why?'

'I'm in love with someone else.'

The very worst reason.

He hadn't said anything. He had looked at her with the same gaze as in the photo (at least he supposed he had).

'Get the hell out.'

'Martin, I—'

'Get the hell out.'

She left without saying another word. Only later had he found out who it was. A double betrayal. For months he had hoped she would come back. And then he met Alexandra. He put the photo back where he had found it. This morning when he woke up, he had meant to tear it up and throw it away, then thought better of it. He was at the end of his tether. He had slept for only two hours, if that, and his sleep had been troubled, full of nightmares.

Hirtmann, Marsac, and now this . . . He felt as if he were an elastic band that someone was pulling on to see how far they could stretch him before he snapped. Not much further, he could tell. He went out onto the balcony. Nine o'clock in the morning. The sky was turning stormy again: a mass of black clouds was approaching from the west, even though the sun continued to shine. Waves of heat rose from the town, along with a chorus of car engines and horns. There was electricity in the air; the swifts were swirling, shrieking.

He got dressed and went out. His hair was uncombed, he hadn't shaved, his face bore the signs of his night-time expedition, and he hadn't washed in twenty-four hours, but he didn't give a damn. Walking through the streets did him good. He sat down at an outdoor café on the place Wilson and asked for an espresso and two lumps of sugar. An extra sugar to help with the bitterness . . .

He wondered who he could talk to, who he could turn to for advice. He realised there was only one person. He saw a lovely face, long ginger hair, a body and a smile to die for . . .

He drank his coffee and waited for opening time.

Then he took the rue Lapeyrouse, crossed the eternal construction site that was the rue d'Alsace-Lorraine, and turned down the rue de la Pomme. He knew the gallery opened at ten. It was 9.50. The door was already open, the gallery silent and deserted. He hesitated.

His soles squeaked on the light parquet floor. Jazz was playing quietly. His gaze did not linger on the modern canvases on the wall. He could hear footsteps upstairs, and a voice, so he went up the spiral metal staircase at the back.

She was there, on the phone, standing behind her desk near the big semi-circular plate-glass window.

She looked up and saw him. She said, 'I'll call you back.'

Charlène Espérandieu was wearing a white T-shirt that left one shoulder bare, and black harem trousers. Across her chest the word 'ART' was embroidered in brilliant sequins. Her red hair was ablaze in the morning light.

She was diabolically beautiful, and for a split second he told himself that this might be her, the one he was looking for, the woman who would console him and make him forget all the others. The one he could rely on. But of course not. She was his assistant's wife. And she no longer filled his mind the way she had two winters ago. She was on the periphery, in spite of her beauty – a pleasant thought, but without pain or passion.

'Martin? What brings you here?'

'I'd love a coffee,' he said.

She walked around her desk to kiss him on the cheek. She smelled of a light lemony perfume, like a breeze through a citrus orchard.

'My coffee machine isn't working. I need one too. Come on. You don't look too great.'

'I know, and I need a shower.'

They crossed the place du Capitole towards the cafés beneath the arcades. He was walking with one of the most beautiful women in Toulouse, he looked like a tramp, and he was thinking about someone else.

'Why do you never answer my messages?' she asked, once she had drunk some coffee.

'You know very well.'

'No, I don't. Why don't you tell me?'

He suddenly realised he'd been mistaken, that he couldn't talk to her about Marianne. He didn't have the right; he knew she would be hurt. Perhaps subconsciously that had been his goal: to hurt someone the way he had been hurt.

He wouldn't do it.

'I got an e-mail from Julian Hirtmann,' he said.

'I know. Vincent thought it was a hoax, that you were imagining things. Until you found the letters carved on a tree trunk . . . Now he doesn't know what to think.'

'So you know about the letters?'

'Yes.'

'And you know where—'

'Where you found them? Uh-huh. Vincent told me.'

'Did he also tell you in what circumstances?'

She nodded.

'Charlène, I—'

'Don't say anything, Martin. There's no point.'

'He must have told you that it was someone I've known for a long time.'

'No.'

'Someone that I—'

'Hush. You don't owe me any explanations.'

'Charlène, I want you to know—'

'Hush, I said.'

The waitress had come to collect the money but left again in a hurry.

'Really,' she added. 'It's not as if we were married, or even lovers, or anything.'

317

He remained silent.

'After all, who cares what I feel?'

'Charlène—'

'Was it only me, Martin? Didn't you ever feel anything? Did I dream it?'

He looked at her. She was so terribly beautiful in that moment. There was no more desirable woman in a hundred kilometres than Charlène Espérandieu. Married or not, she must be overwhelmed with propositions. So why him?

He had been lying to himself all these long months. Yes, he had felt something. Yes, he had thought about her often and imagined her in his bed – and in many other places besides. But there was Vincent. And their daughter Mégan. And Margot. And all the rest. *Not now.*

She too must have felt that it wasn't the right time, because she changed the subject.

'Do you think we're in danger? Or Mégan?' she asked.

'No. Hirtmann is obsessed with me. He's not going to go after every cop in Toulouse.'

'But if he couldn't get at you?' She seemed suddenly worried. 'If he's as well informed as you say he is, he must know that Vincent is your friend – have you thought of that?'

'Yes, of course. But we don't even know where he is. To be honest, I don't think there's the slightest danger. Vincent never met Julian Hirtmann. Hirtmann doesn't even know he exists. Be on the lookout, that's all. If you like, tell Mégan's school to make sure that no one is lurking about, not to leave her on her own.'

He had requested surveillance for Margot. Was he going to have to ask for the same thing for everyone who was close to him? Vincent, Alexandra?

Suddenly he thought of Pujol. Damn, he'd forgotten him again! Was Pujol still tailing him? What would he think if he saw Charlène and his boss deep in a very animated discussion at an outdoor café – without Espérandieu? Pujol couldn't stand Vincent. Servaz was sure he would be only too eager to dish the dirt.

'Shit,' he said.

'What's the matter?'

'I'd forgotten that I'm being tailed myself.'

'Who by?'

'Members of my team. People who aren't very fond of Vincent.'

'Do you mean the ones you gave a dressing-down to two years ago?'

'Mm-hm.'

'Do you think they saw us?'

'I have no idea. But I don't want to run the risk. You're going to stand up and we'll say goodbye and shake hands.'

She looked at him and frowned.

'This is ridiculous.'

'Charlène, please.'

'As you like. Take care, Martin. And take care of Margot . . .'

He saw her hesitate.

'And I want you to know that . . . I'm here, I will always be here for you. Any time.'

She pushed back her chair and stood up, then shook his hand very formally across the table. She didn't turn round, and he didn't watch as she walked away.

34

Pre-Match

He had an appointment at the general inspectorate at 10.30 a.m. When he went into the commissioner's office, Santos was talking to a woman in her fifties. Servaz thought she looked like an old-fashioned schoolmistress, with her glasses down at the end of her nose and her pursed lips.

'Sit down, Commandant,' said Santos. 'Allow me to introduce Dr Andrieu, our psychologist.'

Servaz glanced at the woman who went on standing, although there were two vacant chairs, then he focused his attention on Santos.

'She will be seeing you for treatment twice a week,' added Santos.

Servaz gave a start of disbelief.

'I beg your pardon?'

'You heard me.'

'What do you mean, "treatment"? Santos, you've got to be joking!'

'Are you depressed, Commandant?' asked the woman, straight off the bat, gazing eagerly at him over her glasses.

'Am I suspended, or what?' asked Servaz, leaning over the fat commissioner's desk.

Santos's little eyes studied him for a moment from between eyelids as puffy as a chameleon's.

'No. Not for the time being. But you need treatment.'

'I need what?'

'Counselling, if you prefer.'

'Counselling, my arse!'

'Commandant . . .' said Santos in warning.

'Are you prone to depression?' asked Dr Andrieu again. 'I would like you to answer this simple question, Commandant.'

Servaz did not even look at her.

'Where's the logic in this?' he asked the commissioner. 'Either I

320

need treatment and in that case you have to suspend me, or you acknowledge that I'm capable of working and this . . . *individual* has no business here. Full stop.'

'Commandant, it's not up to you to decide.'

'Commissioner, please,' he groaned. 'Have you seen her? Just the sight of her makes me feel suicidal.'

An involuntary smile flickered over Santos's fleshy lips.

'That is not how you will resolve your problems,' scolded the woman, piqued. 'Not by seeking refuge in denial or sarcasm.'

'Dr Andrieu is a specialist in—' Santos began, without conviction.

'Santos, you know what happened. How would you have reacted in my position?'

'Yes, that's why you have not been suspended. Because of the pressure you're under. And also because of the ongoing inquiry. And I am not in your position.'

'Commandant,' said the woman patiently, 'your attitude is counterproductive. May I give you a piece of advice? You ought to—'

'Commissioner,' protested Servaz, 'leave her in this office and I truly will go crazy. Give me five minutes. You and me, alone. After that, if you like, I will marry her. Five minutes.'

'Doctor,' said Santos.

'I cannot believe—' began the woman, curtly.

'Please, Doctor.'

When he went back out, he took the lift to the second floor and headed for his office.

'Stehlin wants to see you,' said one of the members of his squad.

Once again they had all gathered in the corridor to talk about football.

'Apparently it was pretty tense when he announced the selection,' someone said.

'Pff, if we don't win against Mexico, then we don't deserve to go on,' said someone else.

Couldn't they wait until they were in the bar to talk about stuff like this? thought Servaz. He walked up to his boss's office, knocked, and went in. The director was putting 'sensitive' packages – money or drugs – into the safe. Above it hung a bulletproof vest stamped 'Crime Squad'.

'I'm sure you didn't call me in here to talk about football,' he joked.

'Lacaze is going to be remanded in custody,' announced Stehlin as he closed the safe. 'Judge Sartet will request the withdrawal of his immunity. He has refused to say where he was on Friday evening.'

Servaz looked at him in disbelief.

'He's throwing his career down the drain,' said Stehlin.

Servaz shook his head. Something was bugging him.

'And yet,' he said. 'And yet I don't think it's him. I got the impression that what spooked him more than anything was to . . . to say where he had been. But not because he'd been at Claire Diemar's house that night.'

'What do you mean? I don't get it.'

'Well, it was as if revealing where he was that night might harm his career even more,' answered Servaz, puzzled. 'I know, I know, it doesn't make sense.'

Ziegler stared at the screen of her PC. Not the cutting-edge machine she had at home, but her far more sluggish desktop at the squad. She had stuck a few posters from her favourite films on the walls to cheer the place up a bit – *The Godfather Part II*, *The Deer Hunter*, *Apocalypse Now*, *A Clockwork Orange* – but it wasn't enough. She looked at the files on the shelves in front of her: 'Burglaries', 'Vagrants', 'Illegal trade in anabolic steroids' and gave a sigh.

It was a quiet morning. She had sent her men out and the gendarmerie was silent and empty, apart from the officer on duty at reception.

Once she had got her everyday chores out of the way, Irène went back to what she had discovered the night before. *Someone had downloaded malevolent software onto Martin's computer.* One of his colleagues? Why would they have done that? Someone in custody, when Martin was out of the office? No cop with any sense, let alone Servaz, would leave a detainee unmonitored in his own office. A member of the cleaning staff? *A possibility* . . . For the time being, Ziegler could see no others. If she was right, she needed to know which company had the contract with the Toulouse SRPJ. She could always call them, but she doubted they'd give the information to a gendarme without a warrant and a valid explanation. She could also ask Martin to find out for her. But she always came up against the same problem: how could she explain to him what she had discovered without admitting that she had hacked into his computer?

There might be another way round it.

She opened the online Yellow Pages, answered 'Cleaning Companies' to the question 'What, who?' and 'Greater Toulouse Area' to the question 'Where'?

Three hundred answers! She eliminated all the companies that also provided services such as housekeeping, gardening, pest control or thermal insulation, and concentrated on those that only cleaned offices and business locations. Now she had a list of about twenty names. This was far more reasonable.

She took her mobile and dialled the first number on the list.

'Clean Service,' answered a woman's voice.

'Good morning. I'm calling from human resources at the police station on the boulevard de l'Embouchure. We have . . . uh . . . a little problem.'

'What sort of problem?'

'Well, we haven't been too pleased with your company's *performance*, we find that the quality of the work has deteriorated of late, and we—'

'The police station, you say?'

'Yes.'

'Just a moment. I'll put you through to someone.'

Irène waited. Might she have landed on the right one on her first attempt? She waited for ages. Finally, a man's voice replied, sounding annoyed.

'There must be a mistake,' he said curtly. 'You did say the police station?'

'Yes, that's right.'

'I'm sorry, we don't clean the offices at the police station. I've been checking through our client records for a good ten minutes. There's nothing here about you. Where did you get your information?'

'Are you sure?'

'Of course I'm sure! And why are you calling us? Who are you, anyway?'

'Thank you very much,' she said, and hung up.

By the time she had made eighteen phone calls she was beginning to have doubts about her method. She dialled the nineteenth number and went through her little song and dance again. Once again, the person on the switchboard put her through to someone else. The same endless wait . . .

'You say you're not pleased with our work?' came a forceful-sounding man's voice down the line. 'Could you tell me a little bit more about that? What is it exactly that you're not pleased with?'

She sat up in her seat.

She hadn't prepared herself for the question so she improvised, feeling very guilty about the cleaners working in that building, who would now be upbraided for some completely fictional negligence.

'I'm making this call on behalf of some of my colleagues,' she concluded soothingly. 'But you know how it is: there are always some grumpy, dissatisfied people who need to criticise others in order to exist. I'm merely passing on their complaints. Personally, I've never had cause to complain about the state of my office.'

'I'll see what I can do,' said the man. 'I will emphasise the points you've made. Whatever the case may be, you were right to call us. We set great store by our customer satisfaction.'

The usual mercantile rhetoric – but which implied that the staff would be told off.

'Don't be too hard on your employees. It's no big deal.'

'No, no, I don't agree with you. We strive to offer excellent service, we want our clients to be fully satisfied, and our employees must be up to the task. That's the least anyone can expect.'

Particularly with the salaries you pay them, she thought.

'Thank you for your professional attitude. Goodbye.'

As soon as she had rung off, she went onto a website that showed companies' organisation charts, earnings and other key figures. She wrote down the name of the head of Clarion Cleaners on a Post-it. There was no telephone number, however. So she called the same switchboard, but this time from her landline at the gendarmerie, which would show her name and her employer.

'Clarion,' answered the same female voice as before.

'May I speak to Xavier Lambert?' she said, trying to change her own voice. 'Tell him it's for an inquiry for the gendarmerie, about one of his cleaners. It's urgent.'

Silence at the end of the line. Had the woman at the other end recognised her voice? Then a ringing tone.

'Xavier Lambert,' said a weary male voice.

'Good morning, Monsieur Lambert, this is Captain Ziegler of the gendarmerie, we are presently conducting a criminal inquiry that may concern a member of your cleaning team. I need a list of your staff.'

'A list of my staff? Who are you, did you say?'

'Captain Irène Ziegler.'

'Why do you need this list, Captain, if that's not indiscreet?'

'A crime has been committed in one of the offices cleaned by your company. The theft of sensitive documents. We found minute traces of industrial cleaner on the papers that were next to the stolen documents. But of course we shall keep this to ourselves.'

'Of course,' said the man, perfectly calm. 'Do you have a warrant?'

'No. But I can get one.'

'Then why don't you.'

Shit! He was about to hang up!

'Wait!'

'Yes, Captain?'

He seemed amused by her urgency. She felt herself getting angry.

'Look, Monsieur Lambert, I can get this warrant in the space of a few hours. The only problem is, we're working against the clock. The suspect may still have the documents in his possession, but for how much longer? We don't know when he will pass them on, nor to whom. We want to place him under surveillance. So you must understand that every minute counts. And you surely don't wish to be an accessory, even unintentionally, to a crime as serious as industrial espionage.'

'Yes, I understand. Of course. I'm a responsible citizen and if I can do anything to help you within a legal framework . . . But you in turn must understand that I cannot divulge personal information about my staff without a good reason.'

'I just gave you one.'

'Well then, let's just say that I will wait until this . . . excellent reason has been confirmed by the judge.'

The man's voice was full of arrogance. She felt the anger blaze through her now like wildfire. It was exactly what she needed.

'Naturally I cannot accuse you of obstructing the inquiry; you have the law on your side,' she declared coldly. 'But we gendarmes tend to carry a grudge, you know. So, if you persist in your attitude, I will be obliged to call in the Health and Safety Inspectors, the Departmental Office for Labour and Employment, and the Unreported Employment Committee. And they will ferret everywhere until they find something, believe me.'

'Captain, I suggest you change your tone, this is going too far,' said the man, clearly annoyed now. 'They will do no such thing. I will contact your superiors at once.'

He was bluffing. She could tell from his voice.

'Then if it's not today, it will be tomorrow,' she continued, adopting the same frosty tone. 'Because we won't let up, believe me. We will stick to your shoes like chewing gum. Because we gendarmes never forget a thing. I hope there is not the slightest irregularity in the management of your staff, Monsieur Lambert, I sincerely hope so, because if there is you can bid farewell to a number of your clients, starting with the police.'

Silence at the other end.

'I'll send you the list.'

'With all the information complete,' she insisted, then hung up.

Servaz was driving down the motorway. The air was still just as stifling and heavy, but a storm was clearly brewing. The wave of heat would soon give way to thunder and lightning. In the same way, he felt he was drawing close to a stormy conclusion, that they were closer than they realised. All the elements were there before their eyes. All they had to do now was bring them together and make them talk.

He called Espérandieu and asked him to go back to Toulouse to dig around in Elvis's past. At the lycée there were too many people about in the middle of the day, and Samira was not letting Margot out of her sight. Hirtmann would never strike under these conditions – assuming he did intend to strike, something Servaz was beginning to doubt. Once again, he wondered where Hirtmann might be. Any certainty he might have had regarding his whereabouts was beginning to falter. In his imagination Hirtmann was beginning to look more and more like a ghost, a myth. Servaz banished the thought. It made him nervous.

He parked outside the restaurant on the way into Marsac, forty minutes late.

'What the hell were you doing?'

Margot was wearing shorts, heavy shoes with steel toecaps, and a T-shirt of a pop group he hadn't heard of. Her hair was red, the gel in it making it stick straight up in the air. Without answering, he gave her a kiss and led her out to the little wooden bridge covered with flower boxes which spanned a stream where a few ducks were gliding along elegantly. The doors to the restaurant were open wide. It was pleasantly cool inside, and buzzing with discreet conversation. A few diners paused to look at Margot as she came in, and she ignored them disdainfully, while the maître d' led them to a little table.

'Do they serve mojitos here?' she asked once they were seated.

'Since when do you drink alcohol?'

'Since I turned thirteen.'

He looked at her, wondering whether she was joking. Apparently not. Servaz ordered a calf's head, Margot a burger. A television broadcast the images of players practising on the football pitch, the sound turned off.

'It's really giving me the creeps,' she began, without waiting. 'This whole business . . . this surveillance . . . do you really think he could . . .'

She didn't finish her sentence.

'You have nothing to worry about,' he hurried to reply. 'It's just a precaution. There's virtually no risk of him going after you, or even showing his face. I just want to be one hundred per cent sure that you're not in any danger.'

'Is it really necessary?'

'For the time being, yes.'

'And what if you don't catch him? Are you going to watch over me like this indefinitely?' she asked, playing with the fake ruby in her eyebrow.

Servaz felt his stomach contract. He didn't tell her that this question was nagging away at him too. Obviously a time would come for the surveillance to be withdrawn, when the prosecutor would decide it had gone on long enough. Then what? How would he ensure his daughter's safety? How would he sleep soundly?

'What you have to do,' he continued, not answering her question, 'is keep an eye out for anything that seems abnormal. If you see someone lurking around the lycée. Or if you receive strange text messages. Don't hesitate to go and see Vincent. You know him, and you get along well. You know he'll listen to you.'

She nodded, and thought about how she and Samira had been drinking, laughing and talking the night before.

'But again, you have no reason to panic. It's just a precaution,' he insisted.

It was like the dialogue from a movie, he thought. Like something he'd heard a thousand times. The dialogue from a very bad movie – one of those Z movies full of blood and guts. Once again he felt nervous. Or was it the approaching storm, putting his nerves on edge?

'Do you have what I asked you for?'

She put her hand into her khaki canvas satchel and brought out a bundle of dog-eared, handwritten papers.

'I don't understand why you asked me for this,' she said, pushing the papers across the table to him. 'You want to evaluate my work or what?'

He knew that black look. He'd had to confront it plenty of times in the past. He smiled.

'I won't read anything you've written. You have my word, okay? It's the notes in the margin that interest me. That's all. I'll explain,' he added, in answer to her frown.

Satisfied, he glanced at the pages marked with red ink, then folded them and put them in his jacket pocket.

It was 13.30 that Thursday, and the Whale was eating snails with garlic puree when the minister walked into one of the two private dining rooms (the smallest one) at Tante Marguerite, the restaurant on the rue de Bourgogne only a minute away from the National Assembly. The senator took the time to wipe his lips before turning his attention to the minister.

'Well?'

'Lacaze will be remanded in custody,' said the minister. 'The judge is going to ask for his immunity to be withdrawn.'

'That, I knew,' said Devincourt coldly. 'The question is, why wasn't that fucking arsehole of a prosecutor able to prevent this?'

'There was nothing he could do. Given the elements of the case, there was no way the examining magistrate could act any differently . . . I can't get over it: Suzanne told the police everything. That Paul had lied about his whereabouts. I wouldn't have thought she could do such a thing.'

The minister seemed crestfallen.

'Oh, really?' said the Whale. 'What did you expect? The woman has terminal cancer, she's been betrayed, scorned, humiliated. Personally, I think she ought to be congratulated. That little shit has only got what he deserves.'

The minister felt his temper flaring. The Whale had been having it off with prostitutes for over forty years and now he thought he could pass judgment?

'You're a fine one to talk.'

The senator raised his glass of white wine to his lips.

'Might you be referring to my . . . *appetite*?' said the fat man, unruffled. 'There's a great difference. And you know what it is? *Love* . . . I love Catherine every bit as much as I did on the first day I fell for her. I have the deepest admiration for my wife. The deepest devotion. The whores are for my health. And she knows that. Catherine and I have not shared a bed for over twenty years. How could that imbecile imagine that Suzanne would forgive him? A woman like her . . . so proud . . . a woman with character. A remarkable woman. Sleeping around is one thing. But to fall in love with that—'

The minister curtailed the discussion: 'What shall we do?'

'Where *was* Lacaze that night? Did he tell you, at least?'

'No. And he refused to tell the judge. It's insanity! He won't talk about it with anyone; he's gone mad.'

This time, the Whale looked up at the minister, clearly surprised.

'Do you think he killed her?'

'I don't know what to think any more. But he is looking more and more guilty. Dear Lord, the press will go wild.'

'Drop him,' said the Whale.

'What?'

'Back off. While you still have time. Give the media the union minimum: presumption of innocence, independence of the judiciary . . . the usual patter. But say he is accountable before the law like anyone else. Everyone will understand. A scapegoat: we always need one, I'm not telling you anything new. Lacaze will be burned at the stake by the press, they will tear him apart and gorge themselves on him until they've had their fill. The virtuous pundits will do their usual bit on television, and the crowd will bay with the wolves. And when they're done with him, it will be someone else's turn. Who knows? Tomorrow, it could be you. Or me. Sacrifice him. Now.'

'He had a brilliant future,' said the minister, looking at his plate.

'Rest in peace,' replied the Whale, stabbing another snail. 'Are you going to watch the match tonight? That's the only thing that might save us – if we win the World Cup. But we may as well dream of winning the next elections.'

At 15.15, Ziegler finally found what she was looking for. Or rather, she found two potential perpetrators. Most of the cleaners on Clarion's teams were women who had come fairly recently from Africa. The industrial cleaning sector had always been a source of employment for immigrant women, as the success of these companies rested upon an underqualified workforce who were unlikely to stand up for themselves.

There were only two men. Instinctively, Ziegler decided to start with them. First of all, because more men got in trouble with the law, even though the proportion of women was on the rise. And because all statistics showed that women were almost never involved in incidents regarding authority. Finally, men liked taking risks.

The first one was a family man, with three grown-up children. Fifty-eight years old, he had been working for the cleaning company for ten years. Before that he had worked for nearly thirty years in the automobile industry. She moved on to the next one. Much younger, he had arrived in France only recently. He lived on his own. No wife, no children. His entire family had stayed behind in Mali. A solitary man, lost and vulnerable in a foreign country. Trying to adapt and to blend into the crowd without attracting attention. Trying to make a few friends. Probably in a job that was unworthy of his qualifications. A man who was also probably deathly afraid of being sent home. She hesitated between the two, her gaze going from one information sheet to the other, until her finger stopped on the second one. It must be him; he was an ideal target.

His name was Drissa Kanté.

Espérandieu was listening to 'Use Somebody' by the Kings of Leon on his iPhone while gazing at the battlefield spread out before him. He sang along, then sent a silent curse in Martin's direction. He had come across the lads setting up a giant TV screen in the meeting room and filling the fridge with six-packs. He was sure that in an hour or so, all the offices would empty out, one after the other. He would have liked to join in the party, but he was stuck with tons of documents and faxes that he had divided into piles. There were dozens of them.

His research into the past of Elvis Konstandin Elmaz – who was still in hospital in a coma – had already taken him all morning and half the afternoon. He had already contacted the tax people and consulted the files of Social Security in order to try and reconstruct Elmaz's professional past. At the prefecture he had gone through the file with his insurance certificates and driving licences, had checked with the register office for any marital history and he had verified whether there were any offspring (not officially, in any case). He had also solicited the family benefits office and addressed a request to the Ministry of Defence to obtain any information regarding a possible military background.

The result was that Espérandieu now had an abundant but disparate pile of material in front of him. The worst possible scenario.

He sighed. There was something desperate and extremely unpleasant about having to reconstruct Elvis Konstandin Elmaz's life story. Elvis had an almost perfect profile of a repeat offender. Drug trafficking, grievous bodily harm, theft, sexual harassment, holding of hostages and, finally, rape. As Samira had said, it was a miracle he hadn't killed anyone yet. To which they now had to add the organisation of dogfights, if they were to believe what they had found on his property deep in the woods. During his spells of freedom, he had been the manager of a sex shop in Toulouse, rue Denfert-Rochereau; a bouncer at a private club on the rue Maynard a few hundred metres further along; a waiter in a café-restaurant on the rue Bayard a stone's throw from there, and he hung out in nearly every seedy place in the neighbourhood. Espérandieu found no other traces of known professional activity, but one detail did intrigue him: officially, Elvis's 'career' had started at the age of twenty-two, with a first conviction. Up until then he had been clever enough to fly under the radar, because Espérandieu had no doubts that with a CV like that he must have started much earlier. He looked down at the last document, opened it in desperation and skimmed wearily through the pages, hoping against hope that something in all these declarations would finally be worth his attention.

Well, this looks rather interesting, he thought, with a typical itching sensation as he read the last page.

He picked up the phone to call Martin. The name was there, on the page. Marsac. Before beginning his sinister 'career', Elvis Konstandin Elmaz had been a supervisor in a secondary school in Marsac.

35

The Rats

Servaz was driving through the hills. The warning signs of a storm were increasing: the countryside had changed to a grey metallic colour, the sky had darkened, and from time to time there were flashes of heat lightning. He stopped for a moment on a grassy verge deep in the forest to mentally prepare himself. Leaning against the car, he calmly smoked a cigarette. He watched as the flies and midges seemed to join in the general excitement. In the distance he could hear dogs yapping nervously. He swiped at a horsefly. And then he continued on his way. In five minutes he hadn't seen a single car go by.

Servaz's heart was pounding when he got out of the Cherokee at the end of the lane, at the edge of the clearing. Silence had reigned ever since the kennel had been emptied of its occupants. He tried not to think of their collective euthanasia. Under the stormy sky, the clearing seemed all the more sinister. He went up the creaky steps to the veranda, lifted the gendarmerie's tape, and unlocked the door with a skeleton key. Inside, he looked around as he pulled on a pair of gloves. The CSI team had searched every nook and cranny, but they hadn't been looking for anything in particular. Had they overlooked something? Servaz contemplated the pervasive chaos. The furniture, the floor, the kitchenette, the dirty dishes in the sink, the pizza and hamburger wrappings, the ashtrays full to overflowing and the empty beer bottles: everything had been left as it was, but now it was covered with multiple hues of powder. He wondered who would take charge of cleaning up all the mess.

He began exploring, slowly. The light that came in through the windows was a leaden grey. It was as if he were at the bottom of the ocean, and he switched on his torch.

It took him a good hour to get round the ground floor. The

bedroom was in the same repulsive mess as the living room: dirty underwear left on the unmade bed, empty video-game boxes. The same faint odour of cannabis and decay hung in the air. Everywhere, flies were buzzing noisily, overexcited by the approaching storm. He searched the bathroom in the same way, but didn't notice anything in particular, other than, on opening the medicine cabinet, what was an obvious addiction to all kinds of medication. The shower cubicle was green with mould; clearly, Elvis did not often flush the toilet, because a puddle of urine and toilet paper floated in the bottom of the bowl. Servaz went back down the narrow corridor that led to the living room–kitchen area. There was a trap door above his head. He went to fetch a chair, climbed up and reached for the handle.

The attic had a very low ceiling, and he had to bend over to move under the roof. It was vaguely lit by a skylight made of tiles and glass. Up here Elvis had shoved all the scrap from several years of his life: computers, printers, racks full of pilled clothing, boxes, folders, broken Hoovers, rolls of wallpaper, games consoles, VHS cassettes of porn films. On the dusty floorboards Servaz identified several tracks made by rats or mice. At the back of a wardrobe, behind some winter and après-ski clothing, Servaz found some metal boxes. He pulled them out onto the floor, sat down and lifted the lid on the first one. For a split second it was as if time had stood still. A child with his parents, playing on the beach with a bucket and spade . . . A little boy on his red plastic pedal car with a yellow steering wheel. A kid like any other. Not yet a bastard, not yet a monster. Servaz was sure this was Elvis. A few details hinted at the adult to come. But this child had the same sunny air, playful and innocent, as any other kid. Servaz told himself that lion cubs, too, looked like adorable cuddly toys.

He went on searching.

Pictures of Elvis as an adolescent, looking darker, more cunning. A furtive look at the camera lens. Was Servaz imagining something? There was a change. Something had happened. He no longer had the same person in front of him.

A woman, hugging Elvis. His wife? The one who had asked for a divorce? The one he had beaten and sent to hospital once she got that divorce? In the photo she looked happy, confident. She had her arms around her man, but while she was staring joyfully at the camera, he was looking elsewhere.

333

Other photos of people Servaz didn't know. He closed the box. Looked around. Followed the trail of rat turds distractedly.

The team of investigators had already searched the attic; he had read their report. They had looked for clues, any traces of the men who had attacked Elvis and fed him to the dogs. And what was he looking for? It wasn't Elvis's attackers who interested him for the moment, it was Elvis himself.

Dig in past, the Albanian had written.

He couldn't see anything here. Just an ordinary attic. He carried on, leaving no stone unturned, for a good hour, even opening the boxes of video games and porn cassettes, wondering whether he would have to look at them . . .

He felt like a rat.

Like the rats that had left that trail on the floor.

The trail . . .

There was one spot where it broke off, then continued a bit further along. As he stared at it, an alarm bell went off in his brain. He went over and knelt down. Peered closer. At this particular spot the floorboards were not as evenly joined as elsewhere, and the layer of dust was thinner. Servaz put his hands on the two uneven floorboards and wobbled them with his fingers. He looked for a way to get a grip on them . . . and found it. He pulled. The two floorboards came up. There was a hole underneath, a niche, and there was something in it. Servaz grabbed what was at the bottom of the hole and pulled it out of its hiding place.

A binder.

He opened the rigid cover and began turning the pages. *He was on to something.* He seated himself more comfortably on the dusty floor and looked at the photographs, one by one.

36

Diversion

You're being watched. We have to find a way to get you out without them seeing.

Margot reread the text and typed:

What for?

The answer came straight away.

Have you forgotten? It's tonight.

Tonight what? she wondered. Then she remembered. *The Circle* . . . The other night, in the clearing, they had talked about a meeting on the seventeenth. Elias was right: it was 17 June. Shit! She gave up texting and dialled his number directly.

'Hey,' he said, totally relaxed.

'Okay, then, I'm listening: have you got an idea?'

'Yes, I have.' He explained. Margot wasn't exactly enthusiastic. Particularly when she thought about that lunatic who might be wandering about out there. But Elias was right: something was going to happen that evening. It was tonight or never.

'Okay,' she said. 'I'll get ready.'

She ended the call and went to get the darkest hoodie she had as well as a pair of black trousers. She looked at herself in the mirror, took a deep breath and left the room. The corridor was so silent and dark that for a moment she was tempted to go back and tell him to forget it.

In these situations, there's only one solution, babe: don't think. No 'What if?'s, no 'Do I want to do it?' Just go.

She hurried to the stairway and went down the wide steps, her hand running along the stone banister. Beyond the big stained-glass window the day was leaden. She heard the distant rumbling of thunder. When she was downstairs, she called him.

'Okay, I'm ready.'

'Don't move. Wait for my signal. Not before . . .'

Hiding in the woods opposite Margot, Elias had Samira Cheung in his binoculars. The cop had her eye on the lycée, but most of the time she was looking directly at Margot's window. Margot had left the window open and the bedside lamp was on. The front door she normally used was just two floors down and Samira could not miss her.

Elias put two fingers in his mouth and let out a long, strident whistle. He saw Samira turn at once in his direction.

'Now!' he said. 'Hurry!'

Margot rushed through the door. She immediately felt the electricity in the air, like a presentiment. The leaves were rustling, the swifts were flying and circling in every direction, agitated by the approaching storm. She bent over the way Elias had told her to, and hugged the wall as she ran to the corner of the west wing. Then she dashed to the entrance to the maze.

'Good,' said Elias over the phone. 'She didn't see you.'

Margot wondered if that was really reassuring. Now she was out of doors, in the open – when Vincent and Samira thought she was safe inside.

A minute later, while she was making her way through the winding paths, Elias appeared before her like a mischievous ghost, and her heart leapt.

'Bloody fucking hell, Elias! Couldn't you say you were here?'

'Oh, yeah? And have your bodyguard jump on top of me? I don't feel like getting attacked by some girl who looks like a member of the Addams Family. You're not watching the football?'

'Fuck off.'

He paused for a moment. 'Maybe their famous meeting is just about the match, after all.'

'I'd be surprised,' she said, pushing him. 'Move!'

37

A Crack of Thunder

The roof beams shuddered with a crack of thunder. Still no rain. Servaz would have heard it splashing on the tiles. He looked up. The day was drawing to a close; it was getting darker and darker in the attic. But it was only six o'clock on a June evening.

He turned his attention back to the binder.

Prints. Taken with a good-quality digital camera. Carefully classified and protected with transparent sleeves. No names, just places, dates and times. The photographer did not have a great deal of imagination. Almost all the photographs had been taken in the woods, from the same angle, and represented the same scene each time, more or less: a mature man, trousers down, copulating in the grass in the middle of the thickets. Invariably, the prints that followed showed the man getting back to his feet. Invariably, the series ended with several close-ups of the individual's face.

He went on turning the pages. The monotony of the exercise almost made him smile. The positions did not betray an overabundant imagination, either. Urgency, if anything. A quickie in the woods. Click-click. Smile, you're on camera. Servaz concentrated on the partner, the bait. On most of the prints he could see only her legs, arms and a patch of hair. He thought there were freckles on her pale skin, but it was hard to say. He was willing to bet it was the same girl every time. She seemed very young, but that too was difficult to tell because of the angle of the shot. A minor?

Servaz was already halfway through the album and he had counted a dozen different individuals, a heap of possible suspects and motives, and a pile of alibis to check. But what was the connection to Claire Diemar? One thing was for sure: it wasn't enough that Elvis was a dealer, a rapist and a bastard who sent his dogs to kill or be killed

337

in sordid combats, he was also a blackmailer. When all was said and done, Elvis Konstandin Elmaz was a king-size scumbag.

Then Servaz got to the last photograph but one, and his head began to spin. This time he had it, the link he was looking for. This time too, he could see the face of the accomplice. *A kid . . .* Not a day over seventeen. He was willing to bet she was a pupil in Marsac.

When he got to the series' penultimate victim, he contemplated the close-up of the face. He felt as if someone were tapping him on the shoulder, saying, 'This time, we've got it.' But of course there was no one in the attic. Only him and the truth.

Ziegler tossed the cigarette butt onto the ground and was crushing it with the heel of her boot when the man came out of the building on the other side of the boulevard. She put on her helmet and straddled her Suzuki. Drissa Kanté began walking along the pavement and she waited for him to get ahead of her before easing her bike into the city traffic. He didn't go far. On boulevard Lascrosses, he turned off for the place Arnaud-Bernard. Ziegler drove slowly across the square, towards the entrance to the car park, while keeping an eye on her target, and she saw him sit down outside a bar known as l'Escale. She went down the ramp to the underground car park. She had no intention of leaving her motorcycle unattended around here. Three minutes later she was back out in the open air.

Drissa Kanté was chatting with another customer. Ziegler checked her watch, then headed for a café that was sufficiently far away from the first one.

'Look!'

Margot raised her head. An old Ford Fiesta had just come out of the lane from the lycée and onto the road, heading towards the town. *David's car.* It went right past them and they saw Sarah next to David at the wheel, Virginie in the back. Elias turned the ignition and pulled slowly out of the drive, the bonnet pushing aside the branches that had hidden them to some degree.

'Aren't you afraid they'll see us?'

He gave her an amused look.

'Well, that's the risk we take. I've never done this before. But I've seen Clint Eastwood do it plenty of times; that ought to help, no?'

She gave a smile and shrugged, but deep down she felt extremely nervous.

'I don't think they expect to be followed,' he continued reassuringly, as if he could sense it. 'And I'm sure they're too busy discussing their famous meeting.'

'The Circle,' she mused.

'The Circle,' he confirmed. 'For Christ's sake, it's like the name of one of those secret associations, like Freemasons or Rosicrucians or Skull and Bones! Do you have any idea what it might be?'

'In the note you left me you said you knew what it was.'

'I never said that; I wrote "I found it".'

'What do you mean?'

'I'll explain.' He ignored her furious glance. 'It's a good job I'm fed up with football,' he said before concentrating on his driving. 'Do you know the ball game the Romans played that was called *sphaeromachia*? Seneca talks about it in his letters to Lucilius.'

'It's a butterfly,' she said.

'What is?'

'*Sphaeromachia gaumeri*. Are you sure they're not on their guard? The other night in the maze they almost caught us – and they know they're being spied on.'

The look he gave her was half amused, then he shrugged and turned back to the road.

Servaz went down the steps of the veranda; the air was sultrier than ever. He walked across the clearing. The Cherokee was parked a bit further along. He was nearly there when something caught his eye: a white spot, in the vegetation to his left.

He walked over and held back the branches of the bushes. It was a pale piece of cardboard on the end of a plastic stick planted in the ground. Someone – one of the crime scene technicians – had written on it: '*Cigarette butts*'. Servaz frowned. The butts must have gone to the lab, like the ones he had found at Claire Diemar's place, at the entrance to the woods. The same person? Someone had been spying on Claire not long before her death. Had that person done the same thing here? *A witness? Or the murderer? Who was he? What was he doing here?* The number of butts found at Claire's place were proof of the time that person had spent there. They would have his DNA soon. But Servaz doubted that it was on file.

He went slowly back to the Jeep. In the distance thunder was still rumbling, but it seemed reluctant to come any nearer. Servaz thought of a wild animal, a tiger lurking on the outskirts of the village, or one that you hear deep in the jungle, at night – waiting for the moment to attack. He drove slowly to the end of the drive, turned left in the middle of the forest draped in shadow, and headed down the long straight stretch back to Marsac.

Ziegler recalled with apprehension that there was a match on that night. She wondered whether Drissa Kanté was going to spend his evening at l'Escale watching football, like, in all probability, eighty per cent of the inhabitants of Toulouse that night – or worse still, whether he might invite a few friends home to watch the match – but then she saw him stand up, shake hands, and leave on his own.

She had already paid for her drink. She waited one minute before getting up in turn to cross the square and collect her motorcycle from the car park, beneath the appreciative gazes of the consumers and dealers.

They had driven through Marsac and now they were heading south. The Pyrenees. The wall of mountains stretched into the distance, along the entire width of the horizon and beyond the hills – like a European Himalayas. They were driving along little regional roads, going through villages, bend after bend, and Elias tried to leave some distance between them without ever completely losing sight of his quarry. He had switched on the GPS in order to have an overview of the roads and junctions ahead of time, keying in an arbitrary destination that took into account, more or less, the direction in which they were heading. When it turned out that they were actually taking more of a southwesterly direction than a southern one, he reconfigured the GPS and keyed in 'Tarbes' as a temporary destination. He let them get further ahead when the device indicated there were no junctions for several kilometres, then accelerated to get sight of them again the moment they approached a turnoff.

Margot admired the dexterity he displayed both in driving and in his knowledge of how to tail someone. At the beginning of the year, with his hair hiding half his face and his air of always being elsewhere, she had taken him for a gentle dreamer. But Elias was full of surprises. He had never been very forthcoming about his family, about his brothers and sisters, but she was beginning to wonder what it was that had made him so resourceful.

Resourceful . . . Like the time he had taken a key out of his pocket and opened the door he was not supposed to open. Or the time he had left the note inside her locker.

'I don't know how you got my locker open, but don't ever do it again,' she said firmly.

'Roger that.'

But his purely diplomatic tone implied that he would try again at the first opportunity.

'You know you're a strange guy?'

'I suppose coming from you that's a compliment.'

'How did you get the key to that door, the other night?' she asked suddenly.

For a moment he took his eyes from the road.

'What's it to you?'

'How long have you and I known each other? Six months? Something like that? And the more I know you, the less I feel I know about you . . .'

He gave her a crooked smile, staring at the road and the evening light bursting from below the low ceiling of clouds.

'I could return the compliment.'

'What makes you tick? You act like a dreamer, like you're completely spacey, buried in your books and your daydreams, but in the end you're a real detective, some sort of fucking James Bond?'

This time he burst out laughing.

'Where did you learn this stuff, Elias?'

His smile faded.

'You really want to know?'

'Yep.'

'I was nine years old,' he said.

Aware that he had suddenly become very serious, she held her breath, waiting for what was next.

'I belonged to this group called "The Watchers". It was my big brother who created it. I was the youngest in the gang; the others were all big kids, the same age as him. Our thing was to learn to manage on our own in any circumstances – to survive. We thought we were some sort of fucking Robinson Crusoes, you see. We'd go out into the country and build cabins, and we wandered all over.

And during all that time, my big brother taught me loads of things, like how to use a compass, how to find out where I was, how to repair a moped, siphon off petrol, lay traps. He would say to me, "Elias, you have to learn how to get by all on your own, I won't always be here to help you." Sometimes we played football or rugby, or we went on treasure hunts, or scavenger hunts. On rainy days we would lock ourselves in a friend's garage. His parents didn't use it for their car, and there were all sorts of bits and pieces of old banged-up armchairs, greasy spare parts, broken odds and ends they were too lazy to throw out. They let us do whatever we wanted in there. So we'd spread all that stuff everywhere and pretend we were in a bomber flying over Europe during World War Two, or that we were at the bottom of the ocean in a submarine, that sort of thing. Of course my big brother was always the boss, he was the head pilot of the bomber, the captain of the submarine, the leader of the expedition into outer space: he loved giving orders, my brother.'

Suddenly she saw herself as she had been at the age of eleven, in the room at her father's where she slept every other weekend. She loved that room, because she could go to sleep later than at home, and because there was never any homework to do. It was late. Late, in any case, for an eleven-year-old girl. Her father had been reading her *20,000 Leagues Under the Sea* and when she closed her eyes, she was no longer in a tiny room of eight square metres but at the bottom of the ocean on board the *Nautilus*.

'What was he like, your brother?'

She saw him hesitate.

'He was just like . . . a big brother: protective, nice, a pain, really smart . . .'

'And what happened to him?'

'He died.'

'How?'

'The stupidest death on earth. A motorcycle accident, and an infection in hospital. He was twenty-two.'

'So it happened recently, then?'

'Yeah.'

'Right,' she said. 'End of discussion.'

'Drissa Kanté?'

He turned around. For a moment he stared, transfixed, at the apparition facing him in the middle of the hall, sheathed in black leather. He thought absurdly about a science fiction film. The opaque visor reflected his own gaping image. Then the apparition stuck a badge beneath his nose that transformed his spinal column into a refrigerator circuit.

'Yes, that's me,' he answered in a voice that sounded horribly guilty to his ears.

'Can I have a word?'

The apparition removed its helmet and he saw a lovely face framed with blonde hair. But the stern look she gave him was not reassuring.

'Here?'

'At your place, if you don't mind. Do you live alone? Which floor?'

He swallowed.

'Ninth.'

'Let's go,' said Ziegler firmly, pointing to the doors to the lift.

Inside the lift, which was as decrepit as the hallway, he looked straight ahead. Not saying a word, not looking at the woman next to him. The woman remained equally silent, but he could tell she wasn't taking her eyes off him. Every passing second made him more nervous. He knew it must have something to do with that recent job. He should have refused. He had known right from the start that it was a bad idea.

'What do you want with me?' he said, getting bolder, as they came out of the lift. 'I'm in a hurry. Friends are waiting for me, to watch the match.'

'You'll find out soon enough. You did something really stupid, Monsieur Kanté. Something unbelievably stupid. But maybe all is not lost. I've come to give you a chance to put things right. Your only chance.'

He reflected on what she had said as he unlocked the door to his flat.

A chance. The word resonated through his thoughts.

Where the hell were they going? For a moment Elias and Margot had thought they were heading west, but suddenly they changed course, heading due south towards the central Pyrenees, at the limit of the two regions of the Haute-Garonne and the Hautes-Pyrenées. They had left the plain and the hills and were now entering a valley several kilometres wide, surrounded by already high mountains, although the most impressive summits of the range were ahead of them, strung with villages like the beads of a rosary. Margot was beginning to wonder whether they wouldn't be spotted after all: they'd been following the Ford Fiesta for a good hundred kilometres or more.

But the stormy weather, darker and darker as the evening advanced, was on their side: in a rear-view mirror, any car headlights would look the same. Heavy clouds hung above the valley like anvils, and the light was turning greenish, both unusual and unsettling.

Margot found the landscape beautiful, immense, deep and hostile all at the same time. As for Elias, he was entirely absorbed by what was happening ahead of him. They went through a village of huddled houses, nestled in the confluence of two fast-moving streams, with two monumental bridges spanning them. She saw a few French flags hanging from the balconies, as well as a Portuguese flag. The steep peaks where they were headed, at the end of the valley, bit into the sky like a giant jaw. She was increasingly anxious to know just where they were going. If they ventured into the mountains, it would be hard to escape the vigilance of the Ford Fiesta's occupants. There couldn't be many cars driving up there in weather like this. The moment they hit the hairpin bends, David, Sarah and Virginie would see Elias's Saab below them.

'Fuck, where the hell are they going?' he said, echoing her thoughts.

'There are still a few cars on this road. But if they leave it for a smaller road, they're bound to notice us if we follow them.'

Elias gave her a reassuring wink.

'All the roads that lead into this valley, or almost all of them, are cul-de-sacs. If they take one, we'll let them get ahead and we'll wait for a while before following. That way, they won't get suspicious.'

How did he manage to keep his cool? *He's bluffing*, she thought. *He's as scared as I am, but he's playing the tough guy.* She was beginning to regret that she'd let herself be dragged into this. *I don't like the look of this, not one bit.*

Drissa Kanté's flat was tiny but very colourful. Ziegler was almost dazzled by the bursts of colour – red, yellow, orange, blue – everywhere on the walls. Fabrics, paintings, drawings, objects . . . a joyful chaos reigned and she had some difficulty finding her way to the sofa.

Drissa had clearly made an effort to revive something of his country in this tiny space. He sat down on a chair opposite her and didn't move. He looked at her, and she read the fear in his look. He told her in great detail about his meetings with 'the fat man with greasy hair'. She listened attentively and deduced that fat-ass was a detective. She wasn't surprised; in recent years such agencies had proliferated: in a world where the economy was looking more and more like a war, even well-established groups did not hesitate to avail themselves of their services. Lawyers representing small share-holders who were being hounded in their private life; members of Greenpeace who were victims of computer espionage; political personalities whose apartments had been 'visited': recourse to detec-tive agencies had become a common, widespread, established prac-tice.

Irène knew that in order to obtain sensitive information these agencies also resorted to the good offices of some of her colleagues who were not too scrupulous about supplementing their income: gendarmes, soldiers, former intelligence operatives. Drissa Kanté was simply one of their minions among hundreds of others. Truthfully, she couldn't care less about the missions the man from Mali had carried out on behalf of this detective. What interested her was the man himself.

'I'm sorry,' said Drissa. 'That's all I know about him.'

He handed her a drawing he had just done. He was a good artist – it was as good as any Photofit.

She looked up at him. Drissa Kanté was sweating profusely. His eyes were shining with fear and expectation, his pupils dilated.

'So you've got no surname, or first name, or pseudonym?'

'No.'

'And the USB stick, have you still got it?'

'No, I gave it back.'

'Okay. Try and remember some other details. Six foot three, twenty stone, greasy brown hair, dark glasses. What else?'

He hesitated.

'He sweats a lot. He always has sweat rings under his armpits.'

He looked at her, hoping for a sign of approval. She nodded her head to encourage him.

'He drinks beer.'

'What else?'

He took out a handkerchief to wipe the sweat from his face.

'An accent.'

She raised an eyebrow.

'What sort of accent?'

He hesitated.

'Sicilian or Italian . . .'

She fixed her gaze on him.

'Are you sure?'

He hesitated again.

'Yes. He talks a bit like Mario, the pizza guy.'

She couldn't help but smile. She wrote in her notebook: *Super Mario? Sicilian? Italian?*

'And that's it?'

'Mmm.'

Fear, once again, in his eyes.

'It won't be enough, will it?'

'We'll see.'

Espérandieu could hear them now, two doors down. They were chatting, laughing and predicting the results. He could even hear the commentator's voice announcing the line-up, shouting to make himself heard above the din of spectators in the stadium and the buzzing of the vuvuzelas. And the noise of beer bottles clinking together. For Christ's sake!

He closed the file. He'd finish the job tomorrow. It could wait a few hours, after all. He felt like a nice cold beer, and he wanted to hear the anthems. It was his favourite moment. He was about to get up when the phone on his desk rang.

'We have the results from the handwriting comparison,' said a voice.

He sat back down. *The notebook, on Claire's desk. And the notes in the margin of Margot's homework.* He figured at least he wasn't the only one working that evening.

Servaz parked in the quiet street. All the windows in the house were dark. Hot air came in through the lowered car window, bringing an aroma of flowers. He lit a cigarette and waited. Two and a half hours later, the red Spider drove past him in silence. A light began to flash at the top of a stone column, casting an orange glow onto the pavement, and the gate opened slowly. The Alfa Romeo disappeared inside.

Servaz waited for the lights to come on in the house before getting out of the car. He crossed the deserted street, taking his time, his shoes making almost no sound on the asphalt. There was a little door next to the gate on the other side of the pillar. He lowered the handle and the door opened silently. The only sound was the pounding of his blood in his chest when he walked up the flagstoned path that serpentined its way between the flowerbeds, the pine and the weeping willow. At this hour they were nothing more than masses of shadow blocking the light that came from the street lamp below the house. The enormous pine tree stood tall, like a totem, like the guardian of the place. Going up three concrete steps, Servaz reached a raised terrace surrounded by flowering bushes and again he could hear the distant sound of a television somewhere in a neighbouring house. Sports commentary and the clamour of an overexcited crowd. The match, he thought. He rang the bell. Heard the echo of the chime inside. Waited for a second. Then the door opened without him having heard any footsteps and he almost jumped out of his skin when Francis Van Acker's voice said, 'Martin?'

'Am I disturbing you?'

'No. Come in.'

Francis led the way into the house. He was wearing a satin dressing gown tied at the waist. Servaz wondered if he was naked underneath.

He looked all around him. The interior was nothing like the exterior; everything was modern. Minimalist. *Empty*. Grey walls almost devoid of any pictures, a light-coloured floor, chrome, steel and dark wood for the rare pieces of furniture. Rows of spotlights on the ceiling. Piles of books on the steps of the staircase. The picture windows on the veranda were open and the sounds of the neighbourhood came in – reassuring signs of normality, of ordinary lives, the echoes of children playing, dogs barking, and television. A summer evening. In contrast, the silence and emptiness that reigned inside the house seemed all the more heavy. They spoke the language of solitude. Of an existence turned entirely in on oneself. Servaz understood that no one had come here for a long time. Francis Van Acker must have realised how ill at ease Servaz felt because he switched on the television, with the volume off, and slotted a CD into the mini-stereo.

'Would you like something to drink?'

'A coffee. Strong and sweet. Thanks.'

'Have a seat.'

Servaz collapsed onto one of the sofas by the television. He recognised the piece that began to play a few seconds later: Nocturne No. 7 in C-sharp minor. There was a tension all through the music, where the bass notes predominated. Servaz felt a shiver go down his spine.

Francis came back with a tray, pushed aside the art books on the coffee table, and set the cups down before them. He nudged the sugar bowl delicately over to Martin. Servaz noticed that he had a scratch between his neck and shoulder. On the TV screen, a series of adverts silently elapsed, then he saw the players of the French team come back onto the pitch for the second half.

'To what do I owe the honour of your visit?'

His host had raised his voice above the music.

'Can't you turn that thing down a little?' Servaz blurted.

'That thing, as you call it, is Chopin. No, I like it like that. Well?'

'I need your opinion about something!' shouted Servaz.

Perched on the wide armrest, Van Acker crossed his legs. He lifted the cup to his lips. Servaz diverted his gaze from his bare feet, his calves as smooth as a cyclist's. Francis stared at him thoughtfully.

'About what?'

'The investigation.'

'How is it going?'

'It's going nowhere. Our prime suspect didn't do it.'

'It's going to be difficult to help you if you don't tell me more.'

'Let's say that I need your opinion on a more general, theoretical level, rather than a practical one.'

'Hmm. I'm listening.'

The image of the red Alfa Romeo Spider roaring out of Marianne's garden at three in the morning crossed Servaz's mind. He hastened to banish it. The notes of the piano rose and fell, hypnotically, in the room. He got a grip and forced himself to regain his lucidity. He breathed in.

'What is your take on a murderer who tries to make us believe that another murderer, a serial killer, is in the region, and who tries to pin the blame for his own crimes on this serial killer? He sends e-mails to the police. He disguises himself as a biker and deliberately speaks with an accent to a petrol station attendant. He puts a CD in his victim's stereo. He leaves little breadcrumbs wherever he goes, like Hansel and Gretel. He could also suggest there is a sort of . . . special relationship between the investigator and the murderer, even though there is a very precise motive behind his murders.'

'Like what?'

'The usual things: anger, revenge, or the necessity of silencing someone who's blackmailing you and threatening to ruin your reputation, your career and your life.'

'Why would he do that?'

'I told you: to lead us in the wrong direction. So that we believe someone else is guilty.'

He saw a spark in his friend's eyes. The ghost of a smile. The tempo of the music picked up; now the notes were resounding across the room, as the pianist articulated and hammered frenetically on the keys.

'Do you have anyone in particular in mind?'

'Perhaps.'

'And the suspect who is not the right one, that's Hugo?'

'It hardly matters. But what's interesting is that whoever tried to frame him knows Marsac very well – its local customs, what goes on behind the scenes. It's also someone with a literary mind.'

'Really?'

'He left a note on Claire's desk, in a brand-new notebook. A quote from Victor Hugo, talking about enemies . . . to make us believe that Claire herself wrote it. Only she didn't. It's not her handwriting – the graphologist is categorical.'

'Interesting. So, you think it might be a teacher, a staff member or a student, is that it?'

He looked Francis in the eyes.

'Exactly.'

Van Acker stood up. He went behind the counter and leaned over the sink to wash his cup, his back to Martin.

'I know you, Martin. I know what it means when you speak like this. You used to speak like this in the old days when you were close to the solution. You have another suspect, I'm sure of that. Out with it.'

'Yes, I do.'

Van Acker turned round to face him again and opened a drawer behind the counter. He seemed relaxed, calm.

349

'Teacher, staff member or student?'

'Teacher.'

The lower half of his body hidden by the counter, Francis went on absently staring at him. Servaz wondered what he was doing. He stood up and went over to a wall where, in the middle, a solitary painting hung. It was a large canvas, representing an imperial eagle perched on the back of a red armchair. The bird was fascinating, its feathers glinting golden, cloaking it in a mantle of pride. Its sharp beak and piercing gaze, focused on Servaz, expressed power and the absence of any doubt. It was a very fine canvas of striking realism.

'It's someone who believes he looks like this eagle,' he commented. 'Proud, powerful, sure of his superiority and his strength.'

Van Acker moved behind him. Servaz heard his steps coming around the counter. He felt the tension spreading through his back and shoulders.

'Have you mentioned this to anyone?'

'Not yet.'

He knew it was now or never. The painting was covered with a thick layer of varnish, and Servaz could see Francis's reflection moving in it above the eagle's shimmering feathers. Not towards him, but sideways. The music slowed and stopped.

'And why don't you follow your reasoning through to the end, Martin?'

'What were you doing with Sarah in the gorge? What were you talking about?'

'You followed me?'

'Answer my question, please.'

'Are you really so lacking in imagination? Reread your classics, for Christ's sake: *The Red and the Black*, *The Devil in the Flesh*, *Lolita* . . . the teacher and his student, the ultimate cliché.'

'Don't take me for a fool. You didn't even kiss.'

'Ah, you were that close? She came to tell me that it was over, that she was putting an end to it. That was the purpose of our little nocturnal rendezvous. What were you doing there, Martin?'

'Why is she leaving you?'

'That is none of your fucking business.'

'You get your drugs from a dealer nicknamed "Heisenberg",' said Servaz. 'Since when have you been taking drugs?'

The silence weighed on his shoulders. And seemed to drag on.

'That, too, is none of your fucking business.'

'Except that on the night of the murder, Hugo was drugged. Drugged and taken to the scene by someone who, in all likelihood, was at the Dubliners at the same time he was. And who poured something in his glass. There was a bit of a crowd, that night, wasn't there? It can't have been terribly complicated. I called Aodhágán. You were at the pub on the night of the match.'

'Like half the teachers and students in Marsac.'

'I also found a photograph at Elvis Elmaz's place – the guy who was fed to his dogs. You must have heard about it. A photograph where you're butt naked and with a girl who, by the looks of it, is under age. And I'll bet she's a student at the lycée, too. What would happen if word got out to the other teachers and the parents?'

He thought he heard Francis pick something up, saw his arm move in the reflection.

'Go on.'

'Claire knew, didn't she? That you were sleeping with your students. She had threatened to denounce you.'

'No. She didn't know a thing. At least, she never said anything to me.'

The reflection on the painting moved very slowly.

'You knew that Claire was having an affair with Hugo. You figured he would make an ideal culprit. Young, brilliant, jealous, quick-tempered – and stoned.'

'Like his mother,' said Francis behind him.

Servaz shuddered.

'What?'

'Don't tell me you haven't noticed anything? Martin, Martin . . . Clearly, you haven't changed. Still just as blind. Marianne has been hooked on certain substances since Bokha's death. She has a monkey on her back, too. And not a little one. More like a chimpanzee.'

Servaz saw Marianne again as she had been on the night they made love – her strange look, her erratic behaviour. He mustn't let himself get distracted – that was just what the man behind him wanted.

'I'm not sure I follow you,' said Francis, his voice echoing, although Servaz could not tell exactly where it was coming from. 'Did I try to insinuate that Hirtmann was the guilty one, or Hugo? Your . . . *theory* is not very clear.'

'Elvis was blackmailing you, wasn't he?'

'He was.'

A slight movement again behind his back.

'I paid him. After that, he left me alone.'

'You really expect me to believe that?'

'It's the truth.'

'Elvis isn't the type to let go of such a good source of cash when he's onto one.'

'Until the day he found his favourite fighting dog in its cage with its throat cut and the note, "Next time it will be you".'

Servaz gulped.

'You did that?'

'Did I say that? There are people who are very good at that sort of thing – even though their rates are somewhat . . . excessive. But I'm not the one who hired them. It was another of Elvis's victims. You know as well as I do that Marsac is full of important people – and money's no object. After that, Elvis gave up his blackmailing activities. Good God, Martin, the police: what a waste! You were so talented.'

Servaz saw the reflection reappear and take a step towards him in the varnish of the painting, then stop. Adrenaline was coursing through his veins, a mixture of panic and excitement.

'Do you remember that short story? The first one you ever had me read, called "The Egg". It was . . . it was absolutely marvellous.' A vibration, a genuine trembling in his voice. 'A jewel. There was everything in those pages, *everything*. It was like something written by an author already at the peak of his art, and you weren't even twenty! I kept those pages. But I've never had the courage to reread them. I remember how I wept when I read them, Martin. I swear: I wept in my bed, those sheets of paper trembling in my hand, and I screamed with jealousy, and I cursed God because it was *you*, a naïve, sentimental little fucker, that he had chosen. A bit like all that bullshit with Mozart and Salieri, know what I mean? And that way you had of always looking gently stunned: you had everything, you had talent and you had Marianne. God is a proper shit when he wants to be, don't you think? He knows how to hit where it hurts. So, yes, I wouldn't rest until I had taken Marianne from you, because I knew I could never have your talent. And I knew how to go about it with her. It was easy. You made it incredibly easy for someone to take her from you.'

Servaz felt as if the room were spinning. As if a fist were pressing against his chest to cause it to explode. He had to stay in control at all costs – this was not the moment to give way to emotion. That was exactly what Francis was waiting for.

'Martin . . . Martin,' said Francis behind him, and his smooth, sad, resigned tone made Servaz shudder.

In his pocket, his mobile vibrated. *Not now!* Behind him the reflection moved again. The vibration persisted . . . He plunged his hand into his jacket, took out the phone and answered, keeping an eye on the reflection.

'Servaz!'

'What's going on?' asked Vincent worriedly. He had heard the tension in his boss's voice.

'Nothing. Go ahead.'

'We've had the results from the graphological comparison.'

'And?'

'If those are his notes on Margot's homework, then it wasn't Francis Van Acker who wrote in Claire's notebook.'

Parked by the side of the road, Margot and Elias were peering at the narrow road down which Sarah, David and Virginie had disappeared. It veered off from the other side and immediately started to climb. A sign indicated, 'NÉOUVIELLE DAM, 7 KM'. Through the window Margot could hear the rush of a stream just nearby, in the shade below the road.

'What do we do?' she asked.

'We wait.'

'How long?'

He checked his watch.

'Five minutes.'

'Is that road a cul-de-sac?'

'No. It leads to another valley over a pass, 1,800 metres high. Before that, it goes past the Néouvielle dam and along the lake of the same name.'

'We might lose them.'

'It's a risk we take.'

'You thought it was me.'

The statement was voiced without emotion. Servaz looked at the bottle and Francis's hand. An amber liquid. Whisky. It was a fine glass decanter. Heavy . . . Did he intend to use it? In his other hand, Francis was holding a glass. He half filled it. His hand was trembling. Then his gaze enveloped Servaz, full of pain and scorn.

'Get out of here.'

Servaz did not move.

'Get the fuck out, I said. Why am I surprised? After all, you're just a cop.'

Exactly, he thought. *Exactly, I'm a cop.* He headed towards the door with a heavy step. As he placed his hand on the doorknob, he turned round. Francis Van Acker was not looking at him. He was drinking his whisky and staring at something on the wall he alone could see. And he looked so very lonely.

38

The Lake

A mirror. Reflecting clouds, the setting sun, jagged peaks. Margot thought she could hear something: a chime, a deep bell, glass breaking. The waves lapped against the steep shores in the half-light.

Elias switched off the engine and they got out.

Margot immediately felt dizziness drain all her strength: on the other side of the road, she had glimpsed the vertiginous drop that left them suspended between heaven and earth.

'It's called an arch dam,' said Elias, oblivious to her fear. 'This one is the biggest one in the Pyrenees. It's 110 metres high and the lake next to you holds 67,000,000 cubic metres of water.'

He lit a cigarette. She refrained from looking beyond him to the gaping void, and concentrated on the lake. On this side, its surface was less than four metres from the edge.

'The pressure is colossal,' said Elias, following her gaze. 'It's thrust back towards the shores by a flying-buttress effect; you know, like in cathedrals.'

A light wind ruffled the surface of the lake and caused the pine needles all around to dance. Unwooded areas gave way to a succession of grassy plateaus scattered with streams and rock piles. Then came the steep slopes of the mountain.

'Look. There.'

He handed her his binoculars. She followed the road, which rose to go around the lake, overlooking it by a dozen metres or so. Towards the middle of the reservoir there was a car park. Several cars were parked there, and even a minivan. Margot recognised the Ford Fiesta.

'What are they doing there?'

'There's only one way to find out,' he said, climbing behind the wheel.

'How can we get closer without them hearing us?'

He pointed to the end of the dam.

'We find a place to leave the car and do the rest on foot. Hopefully they won't have finished before we get there. But I'd be surprised. They haven't come all this way for nothing.'

'How will we get to them? Do you know this place?'

'No, but we have two good hours of daylight ahead of us.'

He turned the ignition and they drove to the end of the dam. There was a car park with a map at the entrance, sheltered beneath a little roof made of fir planking, but there was nowhere to hide the car. They left it there, and went over to the map. There were different trails available to hikers: three of them left from the second car park where the Ford Fiesta was parked, and a footpath joined the two car parks, following the shore and the road most of the way. Elias put his finger on the footpath and Margot nodded. At this time of day, in this weather, they probably wouldn't run into any tourists. Besides, apart from Elias's Saab, this first car park was deserted.

'Switch off your phone,' said Elias, taking his own out of his pocket.

The temperature was dropping rapidly. They began walking along the stony path. The evening air smelled of resin and the mountain flowers whose white forms dotted the twilight, and the slightly stagnant smell of the great reservoir.

The rocky dirt path climbed, looking down on the road, which in turn looked down on the lake. She supposed that at some point it would go back down to reach the second car park. The sky was turning a violet grey. The mountain was no more than a black mass, and what Elias had referred to as 'daylight' was less and less luminous. For all that they tried to step lightly, their shoes crushed the stones noisily enough to worry Margot. Because everywhere else there was silence.

They had gone what Margot guessed was roughly 500 metres when Elias stopped her with a raised hand and pointed to a spot slightly further along. Margot trained her gaze towards the steep shore 200 metres away.

It formed a sheer slope that dropped down from the road to the surface of the water, roughly ten metres below that. The top part of the slope, however, next to the road, was almost horizontal, and the slope only sheared off a few metres after that, forming a rocky escarpment prickled with bushes, thickets and pine trees. That was when she saw them. *The Circle* . . . She should have thought of it sooner. So simple. Too simple. The answer was there, before their eyes. She and Elias looked at each other and crouched down by the edge of the path, amidst the grass and the heather, while he handed her the binoculars.

They were holding hands, and their eyes were closed. Margot counted nine of them. One was sitting in a wheelchair. She saw another person standing, but in a strange twisted position, as if his legs were not quite on the same axis as his torso, as if he were one of those puzzle images made up of several different people, where each fragment is slightly out of joint. Then she noticed the shining poles on the ground at his feet: a pair of crutches.

They had made the circle on the flattest part of the terrain between the road and the steep slope. Those who were on the side nearest the lake had their heels almost above the abyss, the dark mass of water just behind their backs.

Margot looked at Elias in the encroaching darkness.

'You knew,' she said. 'You left me that note, "I think I've found the Circle." You knew about their existence . . .'

He answered without taking his eyes from the binoculars.

'I was bluffing. All I had was a map with this spot marked with a cross.'

'A map? And where did you find a map?'

'In David's room.'

'You got into David's room?!'

This time he didn't answer.

'So you knew all along where we were going.'

He gave her an amused little smile and she felt a surge of anger. Then he stood up.

'Come on. Let's go.'

'Where?'

'Let's try and get closer. To understand what's going on.'

Not a good idea, she thought. Not a good idea at all. But she had no choice. She followed him across the uneven terrain, while evening continued to descend.

David felt the tears streaming down his cheeks, his eyelids closed. The evening breeze dried them as the minutes passed. He was

357

holding hands with Virginie and Sarah. Alex had put his crutches at his feet, as had Sofiane. Maud was sitting in her folding wheelchair; they had had to push it along the road from the car park and then carry her for several metres, with her chair folded. They all held their arms out to their neighbours.

The Circle had formed again. As it did every year, on the same date: 17 June. A day that was carved in their flesh. Ten. That was their number. A round number. Like the circle. Ten survivors and seventeen victims. 17 June. God, chance, or fate had wanted it that way.

Their eyes closed, they let the memories invade, rise to the surface. They saw again that spring night when they had stopped being children and had become a family. They relived the enormous shock, the deafening sound of twisted metal, windows exploding in myriad shards of glass, seats torn from their fastenings, the roof and the sides crushed like a beer can in a giant's fist. They saw the night and the earth suddenly slipping, and they were rolling over each other, and the fragile pine trees were torn up, beheaded as they fell, the jagged rocks tearing the metal, their bodies projected every which way like weightless spacewalkers. They saw the beam of the headlights gone mad, illuminating the whirlwind with improbable flashing, gleams of panic, an absurd pattern. They heard their comrades screaming, and the adults, too. Then sirens, shouts, calls. Helicopter blades above them. The firemen, who came after twenty minutes. At that moment, the coach was still hanging ten metres above the surface of the lake, only a short way from where they stood now, momentarily held mid-slope by a few ridiculous shrubs and paltry tree trunks.

They saw again the moment when the last trees yielded in a sinister cracking and the coach slid with an agonising groan into the lake. And to the screams of those who were still trapped inside, it had foundered in the black water, illuminated by one of the headlamps, which continued to shine for hours at the bottom of the water.

The adults had wanted to evacuate them, but they had all refused. They were already together; they had stood their ground in unison, watching the rescue operation from a distance, the futile efforts, until the bodies of their little drowned comrades rose to the surface and began to float on the water, iridescent in the beam of that single headlight shining like a Cyclops's eye. One, then two, then three, then a good dozen little bodies rose like balloons until someone shouted, 'Get those children out of there, for fuck's sake!' It had happened on a June evening, an evening that should have symbolised freedom regained, the beginning of the holidays: the most exciting period of the year.

It was in the psychology unit at the hospital in Pau, where they had spent part of the summer recovering, that the Circle had been born. The idea came to them naturally, without any need for consultation. They had understood, instinctively, that they could never be separated. That the bonds with which fate had brought them together were much stronger than those of blood, friendship or love. It was death that united them. Death had spared them and marked them out for each other. That night they had understood that they could only ever count on themselves. They had had the proof. Adults were not to be trusted.

David felt the warmth of Virginie and Sarah's hands in his, and – through them – the warmth of the group. Then he remembered that there were not ten of them there that evening, but nine. Someone was missing. Hugo. His brother, his double. Hugo, who was rotting in prison despite all the signs he was innocent. It was up to him, David, to get Hugo out of there. And he knew how he would go about it. He was the first to break the Circle, then Sarah and Virginie in turn let go of the hands they were holding, and so on, like a chain reaction.

'Shit!' exclaimed Elias when he saw them move. 'They're going to see the Saab!'

He stood up, grabbed her hand and pulled her to her feet.

'Hurry!' he said in a loud whisper. 'It will take them a while to get the girl in the wheelchair back to the van.'

'Unless David, Virginie and Sarah leave first. They'll reach their car before us. And besides, we're too close. If we start running, they'll hear us!' muttered Margot.

'We're fucked,' said Elias glumly.

She could see his mind was racing.

'Do you think they'll recognise the car?' she asked.

'One car all alone in the car park at this hour? They don't need to recognise it. They're paranoid enough as it is.'

'Do they know your car or not?' she insisted.

'How the fuck should I know! There are dozens at school. And I'm just a first-year student, a nonentity as far as they're concerned . . .'

She saw them walk away along the edge of the road, speaking animatedly, their backs to them.

'No one's noticed us: come on, let's run. But no noise!'

She dashed off, zigzagging as silently as possible across the irregularities of the terrain.

'We won't make it!' he said, when he caught up with her on the path. 'They'll be just behind us on the way down and then they'll figure it all out!'

'Not necessarily. I have another idea,' she said, sprinting along the path.

He hurried after her. His legs were longer, but she was running flat out as if she had the devil on her heels. She scrambled down the slope to the Saab, opened the rear door, and motioned to him to climb in.

'Sit on the back seat! Hurry up!'

'What?'

'Do as I say!'

Already the sounds of cars starting rose above the silence of the lake and echoed back to them. *They're about to drive off, they'll pass right by us in a minute*, she thought.

'Come on!'

He did as he was told. Margot immediately lifted her hood over her head and sat astride him. She had left the door open facing the side of the road. She opened the zipper of her sweatshirt and her small white breasts appeared.

'Grab them!'

'Huh?'

'Go on! Feel me up!'

Giving him no time to react, Margot took Elias's hands and placed them on her breasts. Then she glued her mouth to his, darting her tongue between his lips. She heard the cars coming, they slowed down as they drew near, and she guessed that they were looking in that direction. She went on kissing him even as she felt the fear wash over her. Elias's fingers were pressing against her chest, more in response to a reflex than to any desire. She had put her arms around him and went on kissing him. She heard someone say, 'Fuckin' hell!',

360

there was laughter, then the cars accelerated. She turned her head cautiously. They were driving away. She looked down at Elias's fingers, still clinging to her breasts.

'You can take your hands off,' she said, sitting up.

She met his gaze, and there was something new in it, something she had never seen there before.

'I told you to let go.'

But he seemed to have decided not to do anything of the sort. He grabbed her by the neck and put his mouth on hers. She pushed him away violently and slapped him, harder than she meant to. Elias stared at her, his eyes wide. There was surprise, but also a dark fury in his gaze.

'I'm sorry,' she said, wriggling to extricate herself from the car.

39

Shots in the Night

Servaz went back to his car, dragging his feet. He felt overwhelmed. The lights from the street lamps filtered through the dark leaves of the trees lining the road. He leaned against the roof of the Cherokee and breathed deeply. He could still hear the echo of the same television. The commentary sounded lacklustre, and he knew that France must have lost.

He was gazing at a pile of ashes. Marianne, Francis, Marsac. It had not been enough for the past to re-emerge. It had only done so in order to disappear forever. Like a ship that rights itself and plunges up and down before sinking. Everything he had believed in, his best years, the memories of his youth, all that nostalgia: all illusions. He had built his life on lies. With a weight like a stone on his chest, he went to open the car door. Almost immediately his mobile beeped twice. A yellow envelope on the screen: a new message.

Espérandieu.

He opened it. For a fraction of a second he wondered what he was reading. He still had a hard time with text-speak.

Meet me Elvis house found sthg

He sat behind the wheel and called Espérandieu, but got an anonymous voice asking him to leave a message. Impatience and curiosity lifted the weight from his chest. What was Vincent doing in Elvis's house at this hour when he was supposed to be keeping an eye on Margot? Then Servaz remembered he had told him to dig into the Albanian's past.

He drove more quickly than usual as he left town. He reached the turnoff for the side road not long before midnight. The moon came out from behind the clouds and bathed the dark woods all around in its blue clarity. At the next crossroads, he took the rough track, every blade of grass lit by his headlamps. With his free hand, for the third time he pressed the 'call sender' option. In vain. What was his assistant doing? Why didn't he answer? Servaz was getting nervous.

He put down his phone and it began to vibrate.

'Vincent, you—'

'Dad, it's me.'

Margot . . .

'I have to talk to you, it's important. I think that—'

'Is something wrong? Did something happen?'

'No, no, nothing. It's just that – I really have to talk to you.'

'But you're all right? Where are you?'

'Yes, yes, I'm fine. I'm in my room.'

'Good. I'm sorry, sweetheart. I can't talk to you just now. I'll call you back as soon as I can.'

He hung up and put the telephone down next to him. Barrelling along the rough track, he went over the little wooden bridge, and the headlights lit up the tunnel of greenery leading to the clearing.

He didn't see any cars.

Shit! Halfway up the drive he switched off the ignition and got out. The sound of the slamming door seemed deafening. He remembered the winter evening when he had been attacked at an abandoned holiday camp and nearly been killed, his head wrapped in a plastic bag. There were times when he still went back there in his nightmares.

He opened the car door and hit the horn, but nothing happened, and the noise itself made him even more nervous. Servaz opened the glove compartment, took out his weapon and a torch. He slid a bullet into the gun. The moon had disappeared again behind the clouds, and he started walking through the darkness, swinging the beam of his torch into the bushes and the dark foliage. He shouted Vincent's name twice, but there was no answer. Finally he reached the clearing. The moon deigned to reappear for a moment, lighting up the wooden veranda and the house. The windows were dark. *Shit, Vincent, where are you?* If he had been there, Servaz would have seen his car, a sign, something.

All at once he was terrified at the idea of what he might find. The house projected an ominous shadow.

He climbed up the steps. *Was there someone in there?*

He realised that the hand holding his gun was trembling. He had never been a good shot; he had always been a cause of incredulous despair to his instructor.

Suddenly he no longer had any doubt. There was someone in there. The message was a trap, from someone who wasn't Espérandieu. From the person who had bound Claire Diemar in her bathtub and watched her die, who had rammed a torch down her throat, who had fed a man to his dogs. And that person had his assistant's mobile phone. He remembered the layout of the place. He had to go in there.

He went under the gendarmerie's tape, thrust the door open and immediately rolled onto the floor in the dark. A gunshot shattered the wood on the doorjamb. He had crashed into something as he dived, and cut his forehead. He fired twice in the direction of the shot and the deafening sound burst in his eardrums while the burning metal of one of the casings hit his leg. Despite the buzzing in his ears, he heard the gunman move backwards, knocking over a piece of furniture. There was a second shot, lighting up the room, but Servaz had already begun to crawl behind the bar in the open-plan kitchen. Then silence fell. The sharp odour of powder in his nostrils. He listened out for a noise, breathing. Nothing. His mind was racing. The sound the gun made hadn't been familiar; it wasn't a handgun – or a revolver or an automatic pistol.

A hunting rifle, he thought. Double-barrelled. And only two shots . . . The gunman had no more ammunition. He would have to open the rifle, eject the used cartridges and reload. Servaz would see him and kill him well before. The man was trapped.

'You're out of ammunition,' he shouted. 'I'll give you one chance: throw your rifle on the ground, stand up and put your hands in the air!'

With his free hand he groped behind him for the handle to the fridge door. That would give him enough light. He had lost his torch when he plunged to the floor.

'Go on! Throw down your gun and get up!'

No answer. Servaz felt something trickle into his eyes. He blinked, let go of the fridge for a second to wipe his eyes with the back of his sleeve. His forehead was streaming with blood.

'What are you waiting for? You've got no chance to get out. Your rifle is empty!'

Suddenly, a new sound. A door creaking. Shit, he was getting out the back! Servaz rushed in the direction of the noise and knocked over a metallic object that fell noisily to the floor. He reached the back door. The forest. Darkness. He couldn't see a thing. He heard a sharp click in the bushes to his right: a rifle being closed. His assailant had managed to reload. He crouched down. There was a first shot, then a second, and a sharp pain went through his arm and made him drop his gun. He reached out towards the ground, groping all around him to find it.

Fucking hell, where is the bloody thing?

His hands were scrabbling around desperately. He spun on his knees on the ground. He knew that he hadn't been shot, it was just a fragment from a ricochet. He heard the rifle being opened again a few metres away. When a bullet went through the bushes above him with a deadly whine, he set off in a random direction into the woods. A new bullet whistled past, slicing through the leaves. He heard the rifle being reloaded, then the gunman began to walk in his direction. Servaz could hear him pushing aside the bushes, unhurriedly. The gunman knew what had happened! That Servaz hadn't responded, that he'd been disarmed. Servaz ran, and stumbled on a root. Again he hit something. A tree trunk. His face was covered in blood now.

He got back up and began to run in a zigzag.

Two new shots, not as well aimed as the previous ones. He hesitated between continuing to run or hiding somewhere. *Run*, he decided. The further away he got, the greater the area his aggressor would have to search. The moonlight drifted through the foliage, making the landscape look unreal. It didn't help. He was trying to get through a new wall of undergrowth, but his shirt caught on some brambles. He struggled furiously, desperately, to get free, and tore it. Then, aware that its light colour made him an easy target, he unbuttoned it before rushing off again. His pale skin was not much better. What an imbecile he was – an imbecile who was about to die. A dishonourable death, a cop without his gun, defenceless, shot in the back by his own quarry. As he ran through the woods, increasingly out of breath, his throat on fire, he thought about Marianne, Hirtmann, Vincent and Margot . . . Who would protect her if he was no longer there?

He pushed aside a last bush and froze.

The gorge.

The sound of the river rose to him. He stepped back, gripped by vertigo. He felt nauseous. He was standing on the edge of the cliff. He could see the water shimmering among the trees, twenty metres below . . .

He recognised the dry little snap of a branch breaking.

He was dead.

He had the choice between jumping into the void and shattering against the rocks below him, or being shot in the back. Or turning to face his murderer . . . At least he would know the truth. *Small comfort.* He looked down. His knees trembled. He pictured himself falling, and again he felt sick. He turned back to the woods so he could no longer see the void; even bullets would be better than that.

He heard the gunman coming closer. In a moment he would see the face of his enemy.

He glanced over his shoulder again, towards the gorge, and saw that the cliff did not plunge straight to the bottom. Slightly off on his left, roughly four metres down, there was a little ledge suspended above the void to which a few bushes clung. It seemed to him that there was a black shadow under the rock face. Was it a recess? Servaz swallowed. Could this be his last chance? If he could get down there and slip under the rock? This would make things infinitely more difficult for the murderer: with a loaded rifle in one hand, would he follow him down the cliff, when he really needed both hands to hold on and avoid a deadly fall?

Impossible. He could never do it – even if his life was at stake. It was beyond him.

You'll die if you stay here. Vertigo won't kill you, but a bullet will!

There was a sound behind him in the woods. No more time to think. With his back to the gorge not to see the drop, he lay flat on his stomach, concentrating his gaze on the rock face a few centimetres from his nose, and began his downwards crawl, feeling with his toes for a foothold. Faster! He didn't have time to make sure of his footholds; he had no time for anything. In only a few seconds his pursuer would reach the edge of the cliff. He closed his eyes and went on. Urgency was pumping his blood, his legs were trembling violently. His left foot slipped. He felt himself go, carried by the weight of his own body. He screamed. A vain attempt to scratch at the rock face with his fingernails. He skidded down the rounded

rock face like a toboggan, his naked belly and chest scraping painfully over every jagged edge. He felt the bushes stabbing his back
and stopping his fall when he landed on the tiny platform. He saw
the void and rolled in the opposite direction, terrified. He crawled
and huddled beneath the rock face, in the recess, like an animal.

His hand groped for – and found – a big rock. He lay there, his
chest rising and falling in terror.

I'm waiting for you.

Go on, come down here, if you dare.

He was covered in blood, earth, scratches. He had returned to
his savage state. Fear and vertigo gave way now to anger, to a
murderous rage. If the bastard came this far, he would smash his
skull.

He couldn't hear a thing. The noise from the river echoed against
the walls of the gorge and drowned out any sound. His heart was
still beating wildly. The gunman might still be up there, his rifle
pointed calmly at the exact spot where he was hidden, waiting until
he dared put his head out of the hole. After a while, he relaxed.
There was nothing else to do but wait. He was safe as long as he
stayed there. His aggressor would not risk coming down. He checked
his watch, but it was broken. He stretched out – he could stay there
for hours. Then suddenly he thought of something.

His phone.

He took it from his pocket. He was about to call Samira for help
when he realised there was something not right. It took him a few
seconds to grasp the problem. Servaz sometimes felt as if he had just
climbed out of a time machine when it came to technology; he had
been one of the last people to buy a mobile phone, three years earlier,
and it was Margot who had helped him enter the names of his contacts.
He remembered very well that together they had entered *Vincent*.

Not *Espérandieu*.

He looked for his assistant's name in his contacts. Bingo! Two
different numbers. Someone had got hold of his mobile phone without
him knowing and had entered a new name before sending him a
text message. He tried to remember when he might have left his
phone unattended, but he couldn't think clearly.

He dialled Samira's number and asked her to send the gendarmes
urgently. He was going to ask her to come, too, when the word
'diversion' flashed in his mind. What if the gunman's aim was not

to kill him? None of the bullets had even grazed him, they had all gone wide. Either the gunman was a lousy shot, or . . .

'Be careful!' he said. 'And ask for back-up. Call Vincent and tell him to get here as quickly as possible. And tell the gendarmes that the guy is armed. Hurry up!'

'Fuck, what's going on, boss?'

'No time to explain. Be as quick as you can!'

Servaz realised how dreadful he must look when he saw the gendarmes' faces once they had got him back to the top of the cliff with the help of a rope and harness.

'We should have called an ambulance,' said Bécker.

'It's not as bad as it looks.'

They headed back through the forest to the house. The gunman had vanished but the captain leading the Marsac squad had made several calls. In less than an hour, Elvis's house and the surroundings would be swarming with the CSI team again, collecting the cartridges and any clues the gunman might have left behind.

Servaz headed to the bathroom while everyone was busy both inside and out. When he saw his reflection in the mirror, he had to concede Bécker's point. If he had seen himself coming, he would have crossed the street. His hair was full of dirt, he had black shadows beneath his eyes, and his dilated, shining pupils made him look completely stoned. His lower lip was split and swollen, and numerous black streaks were forming on his torso, neck and arms. Even his nose had a constellation of spots and scratches.

He really needed to clean himself up, but instead he took out his pack of cigarettes and calmly placed one between his lips. He went on examining himself in the mirror, holding the cigarette between his trembling fingers and inhaling deeply, until he burned himself.

Then, for no apparent reason, he burst out laughing.

They were gathered in one of the rooms at the gendarmerie in Marsac: Espérandieu, several gendarmes from the squad, Pujol, examining magistrate Sartet, who'd been roused from his sleep, and Servaz. Tired faces, men who'd been dragged out of bed and who now looked worriedly in Servaz's direction. They had also brought the doctor on call to the gendarmerie. He examined Servaz's injuries and cleaned them.

'When did you last have a tetanus shot?'

Servaz couldn't remember. Was it ten years ago? Fifteen? Twenty? He didn't like hospitals or doctors.

'Roll up your sleeves,' said the doctor, rummaging in his bag. 'I'm going to give you a shot of 250 units of immunoglobulins in one arm and one dose of the vaccine in the other, for now. And I want you to come to my office as soon as possible to take the test. I suppose you don't have time tonight?'

'You suppose right.'

'I think you should take better care of your health,' said the doctor as he jabbed him with the needle.

Servaz was holding a cup of coffee in his free hand.

'What do you mean?'

'How old are you?'

'Forty-one.'

'Well, it's time, I think, to take better care of yourself,' he said. 'If you don't want to have any nasty surprises.'

'I still don't understand.'

'You don't do much in the way of exercise, do you? Take my advice and think about it. Come and see me . . . when you have time.'

And he left, no doubt with the conviction that he would never see this particular patient again.

Servaz looked around the table. He summed up his conversation with Van Acker, along with the latest findings: the negative result of the graphological comparison, and the photos he'd found in Elvis's attic.

'Even if your friend didn't write in the notebook, that doesn't automatically prove his innocence,' Sartet pointed out. 'He knew the victims, and he had both the opportunity and the motive. Given that, to top it off, he was getting his drugs from that dealer, it seems we have enough to take him into custody. But I'd like to remind you that I requested the withdrawal of Paul Lacaze's parliamentary immunity. So, what do we do?'

'It would be a waste of time. I'm convinced it's not Van Acker.' Servaz hesitated. 'Nor do I believe that Paul Lacaze is guilty,' he added.

'Why is that?'

'For one thing because you already had your eye on him. What good would it do him to set a trap for me at this stage, when he refuses to say where he was the evening Claire Diemar was killed? It makes no sense. And he wasn't among Elvis's blackmail victims, he's not in his little catalogue of photos.'

'But he did lie about where he'd been and when.'

'Because if word got out about whatever he was doing that evening, his political career would be over.'

'Maybe he's gay,' suggested Pujol.

'Do you have any idea what the reason might be?' asked Sartet, ignoring Pujol's remark.

'Not the slightest.'

'One thing's for certain . . .' Sartet began.

They looked at him.

'If someone shoots at you, it's because you're on to the truth. And that person will stop at nothing.'

'We already knew that,' said Pujol.

'Moreover,' Sartet continued, turning conspicuously to address Servaz, 'Hugo Bokhanowsky's lawyer has reiterated his request for his release. As of tomorrow, the magistrate for custody is going to examine his request. In all likelihood he will meet the defence halfway. Given the present status of the case, I see no reason to keep the young man in detention.'

Servaz refrained from saying that he would have released him a while ago. His thoughts were elsewhere. All the theories he had put together were collapsing. Hirtmann, Lacaze, Van Acker. The magistrate and the murderer were both wrong: they were not getting closer to the truth. They were getting farther away. They hadn't been this clueless since the beginning of the investigation. Unless . . . Servaz looked at them thoughtfully. Unless he *had* come very close, without realising. How else could he explain the fact that he'd been shot at? In which case he would have to go over the different stages of the investigation one by one, painstakingly, to determine when he might have been on the verge of uncovering the murderer – and had frightened him into taking a risk like that.

'I still can't get over it,' said Sartet suddenly.

Servaz glanced at him questioningly.

'How we made such fools of ourselves.'

Servaz wondered what he was talking about.

'I have never seen a French team play so badly! And if it's true what happened in the changing room during half time, it's unbelievable.'

370

A murmur of general disapproval greeted his remark. That's right, thought Servaz, there had been a 'decisive' match earlier that evening. France-Mexico, if memory served. He couldn't believe his ears. It was two o'clock in the morning, he had nearly died – and they were talking about football!

'What happened in the changing room?' asked Espérandieu.

Maybe a bomb had exploded, blowing half the team to bits? wondered Servaz. Or one player had killed another? Or the despised manager had committed hara-kiri in front of them?

'They say Anelka insulted Domenech,' said Pujol, his tone one of deep shock.

Servaz was stunned. Every day, in police stations and in the street, cops were insulted. It simply proved that the French team was a true reflection of society.

'Anelka, wasn't he the player who was sent off last time?'

Pujol nodded.

'Why did they let him play again if he's so bad?' Servaz asked.

Everyone looked at him as if he had asked an excellent question. And as if the answer were almost as important as finding the murderer.

40

Surrounded

The refrains of 'Singin' in the Rain' penetrated her sleepy consciousness. Before she was wrenched from her dream, Ziegler had a fleeting vision of Malcolm McDowell wearing a derby hat, singing and dancing, and kicking her. Her mobile phone was ringing. She rolled over onto her stomach and reached with a groan towards the night table. An unfamiliar voice.

'Captain Ziegler?'

'Speaking. For God's sake, what time is—'

'I, uh, this is Monsieur Kanté. Listen, I . . . I'm sorry to wake you, but I have something important to tell you. It's really important, Captain. I couldn't sleep. I – I figured I had to tell you. But if I don't do it now, I won't have the courage later on . . .'

She switched on the lamp. The clock radio said 2.32. What had got into him? His voice was that of a man who was tense, but determined.

'Tell me what, Monsieur Kanté?'

'The truth.'

She sat up straight.

'What do you mean?'

'I lied to you, this evening. I – I was afraid. Afraid the man might find a way to take revenge, that if you arrest him I'll be judged, too – and deported. Is your deal still on?'

Her pulse began to race.

'I gave you my word,' she said finally, as he remained silent. 'No one will know a thing. But I'll have my eye on you, Kanté.'

She could tell he was weighing every word. But he had called her; he had already made his decision. She waited patiently, feeling her fingertips pulse as they squeezed the phone.

'They are not all like you,' he said. 'What if one of your colleagues spills the beans? I trust you, but not them.'

'Your name won't appear anywhere. I promise. And I'm the only one who knows it. You called me, Kanté. So out with it. Because there's no going back: I won't leave you alone now.'

'That man. He doesn't have a Sicilian accent.'

'I – I'm not sure I know what you mean.'

'I told you he had an accent, an Italian accent, don't you remember?'

'Yes. And?'

'I lied to you. He has an accent from Eastern Europe, a Slavic accent.'

She frowned.

'Are you sure?'

'Yes. Believe me, I've come across a lot of people during my . . . travels.'

'Thank you . . . but you're not calling me at this time of night just to tell me that, are you?'

'No, that's not all. I – I had him followed. He thinks he's so clever. But I'm smarter than him. Yesterday, when I gave him back the USB stick, I asked one of my girlfriends to follow him when he left the café. He was parked far away and he was being careful, but my girlfriend is careful, too. She knows how to make herself invisible. She saw him get into a car. And she wrote down the number plate.'

Ziegler sat bolt upright. She leaned over to grab a pen.

'Go ahead, Kanté, I'm listening.'

It was two o'clock in the morning by the time Margot got back to her room, exhausted and on edge. She wondered if she had just lived through the craziest night of her life. She wondered, too, if what they had seen up there by the lake was real. And if it was important. She was convinced it was. She couldn't explain why, but that spectacle had made a deeply disturbing impression on her, of something sinister, of impending catastrophe. And there had been David's threats, and his attempted rape, the note left on her locker . . .

Then there was what had happened with Elias in the car. His attitude all of a sudden. Until this evening, she would never have thought that Elias could be attracted to her – he hadn't even looked at her the night she had opened her door in her underwear. And until this evening, she had never felt drawn to him. She remembered, too, the anger in his eyes after she slapped him. She was sorry she had done it. It would have been enough to push him away, without humiliating him. The return trip had been long and tiresome; Elias had walled himself up in silence, and avoided looking at her.

She thought again of their kiss. A forced kiss, a strategic kiss – but a kiss all the same. A year earlier, she had had a lover her father's age, very experienced. Married with two children. He had broken off their affair suddenly and without explanation, and she suspected her father had had something to do with it. She had had three affairs since then. Altogether she had been with half a dozen men. With the exception of her first calamitous experience aged fourteen, Elias was certainly the least experienced of them all. She could tell from the way he had kissed her. So why did she want to repeat the experience as soon as possible?

She understood that the stress, excitement and fear they had shared had something to do with it. But that wasn't the only explanation. He might be clumsy, his behaviour was strange and unpredictable, but despite all that, she realised that she fancied him. Then her thoughts turned to something else.

She had to tell her father.

One way or another, what they had seen had something to do with what had happened to her teacher. She had to concentrate on that. She was tormented by an inexplicable feeling of urgency. Why didn't he return her call? Her thoughts were all over the place. Her father, Elias . . . She pictured Elias in his room, moping, and suddenly she felt she had to let him know that she was not indifferent about what had happened. She picked up her phone and keyed a message:

Are you there?

She waited a long time for the answer:

?

Meet me downstairs, in the hall

?

I have something to tell you

Don't feel like it

Please

What do you want?

I'll tell you there

Can't it wait?

No. It's important. I know I hurt you. I'm asking you as a friend

No answer.

Elias?

OK

She got up, hurried to the sink to splash some water on her face, and went out. He wasn't there when she got to the bottom of the steps and she was beginning to wonder if he was going to come when at last he appeared, his expression inscrutable.

'What do you want?' he said.

She wondered where to begin, tried to find something to say, and then suddenly she knew. She went up to him, very close, and kissed him. He did not respond. She felt him stiffen, cold as marble, but she continued until he melted, took her in his arms.

'Forgive me,' she murmured.

She was looking deep in his eyes when her phone buzzed in her pocket. She ignored it, but it went on buzzing. Elias pulled away before she did.

'Sorry,' she said.

She looked at the screen. Her father . . . *Shit!* She was sure that if she didn't answer, he would show up or send Samira.

'Dad?'

'Did I wake you up?'

'Uh . . . no.'

'Okay. I'm on my way.'

'Now?'

'You said you had something important to tell me. I'm sorry, sweetheart, but I couldn't get away before. Some . . . some stuff happened tonight.'

Don't I know it.

'I'll be there in five minutes,' he added.

He gave her no time to respond. He had hung up.

David had always thought of death as a friend. A close companion. It had been with him for so long. Unlike most people, not only was he not afraid of death, he saw it sometimes as a possible spouse. To marry death . . . it was a romantic notion, but he liked it. He knew that there was a name for what he suffered from. *Depression.* A word that was almost as frightening as *cancer.* And he owed it to his father and his older brother. To the black seed they had planted in his brain very early on by making him understand, day after day, year after year, that he was the failure in the family, the ugly duckling. Even the most inept psychologist could have read his childhood like a book. A distant, authoritarian father who reigned over tens of thousands of workers; a big brother, the heir, who had chosen his father's side very early in life; a little brother who had drowned accidentally in the family swimming pool when David was supposed to be looking after him; a self-obsessed mother, locked away in her little inner world. By the time he was seventeen, his mother had sent him to every therapist in the region – but his depression did not go away. There were times when he managed to keep it at bay, when it was nothing more than a vaguely threatening shadow on a sunny afternoon, where he could laugh, and mean it – but there were other times when the shadows overwhelmed him, like now, and he dreaded the day they would not release him from their embrace.

Yes, death was an option. The only one – he knew – that could rid him of the shadow.

Particularly if it could be used to get the only brother he had ever had out of prison. Hugo. Hugo had shown David that his father did not deserve admiration, that his blood brother was an idiot. Hugo had made him understand that there was no reason to envy them, that making money was a very ordinary talent. It wasn't enough, of course. But it had helped. When Hugo was around, David felt the melancholy loosen its grip. However, Hugo's time in prison had made him aware of a fact that up to now he had preferred to ignore: Hugo would not always be there. Sooner or later he would go away. And on that day, the depression would come back more avid, more famished, more cruel than it had ever been. On that day it would devour him whole, and spit out his empty soul like a little pile of bones. He could already sense its presence, hovering impatiently above him. He had not the slightest doubt: it was sure of victory. He would never be rid of it. It would have the last word. So why wait?

Stretched out on his unmade bed, his hands crossed behind his neck, he looked at the poster of Kurt Cobain pinned to the wall and thought about that cop, Margot's dad. Collateral damage, as the heroes in B movies say. The cop would be collateral damage. By setting himself up as the culprit and taking the cop down with him, he would prove Hugo's innocence once and for all. The idea seemed more and more attractive. Now he just had to pull it off.

41

Doppelgänger

He moved around in the bushes, did some stretching exercises, then he unscrewed the thermos of coffee, and like Samira a few hundred metres away, put a tablet of Modafinil on his tongue and swallowed it down with a sip of Arabica. He had added a splash of Red Bull. The taste was peculiar but this way, in spite of the late hour, he was wide awake.

And he could hold out for quite a few hours.

There was an interesting view from the hill. The buildings of the lycée might be several hundred metres away, but with his night-vision binoculars he could see everything that was happening. He had recognised the commandant. The other people were unknown to him. He had spotted the young female cop hiding in the bushes behind the lycée, and her colleague sitting in the car. The one in the car wasn't even trying to hide. Hirtmann knew immediately that Martin had put him there to dissuade him, Hirtmann, from going closer. And he liked the idea. He liked to know that Martin was constantly thinking about him.

Martin . . . Martin . . .

He had grown attached to the policeman. Since the day of his first visit to the Wargnier Institute, when he had made his clever remarks about Mahler. Hirtmann had not forgotten that moment. While waiting for his visitors he had occupied himself as best he could, his mind absorbed by the first movement of the Fourth Symphony. Then Dr Xavier brought them in. That was the first time he saw Martin. He had not failed to notice the way Martin had started when he recognised the music. Then to his great surprise, Martin had said his name, 'Mahler'. Hirtmann couldn't get over it. And he had felt a surge of joy when he understood, with a wave of emotion he had difficulty concealing, that the man sitting before him was his *doppelgänger*, his kindred spirit – a double who had chosen the path of light instead of darkness. To live is to choose, after all. A single meeting had shown Hirtmann that Martin resembled him much more than he thought. He would have liked to convince him of their affinity, but it was a good thing that Martin thought about him as often as he did. He had sensed that this was a man who, like him, despised the vulgarity of the present generation, the poverty of their taste and their interests, their sheep-like behaviour and their incurable philistinism. Oh yes, they understood each other. Even if Martin might have trouble admitting it.

Since that day, Hirtmann simply could not stop thinking about Martin. About Alexandra, his ex-wife, and Margot, his daughter. He had made enquiries. And little by little, it was as if Martin's family had become his own. He had slipped into his life without him knowing, and he was never far away. It was better than watching a reality TV show. Hirtmann couldn't get enough of it.

He re-focused his attention on the lycée. They were all climbing back into their cars. He had parked his own car 500 metres away, in the forest. If anyone went near it, an alarm would go off and Hirtmann would be notified.

He trained his binoculars on the facade of the dormitories. The lights were all off except in Margot's room. Then he saw Martin in the room, and she was speaking to him animatedly. The unexpected sight of this little domestic scene filled him with happiness, an emotion that caught him off guard. Something which bore a curious, distant resemblance to love. In his hiding place in the woods he could not help but smile at the thought.

42

The Lake 2

He parked at the side of the road, at the edge of the property, and waited for the right time. The day was breaking, with a patience he did not have. He smoked one cigarette after the other and when he held out his hand he saw it was trembling like a leaf in a stream. The image reminded him of the sentence they had all learned in philosophy class.

No man ever steps in the same river twice.

Never, he thought, had he known a more appropriate phrase. He wondered if back then he had loved a girl who did not exist. He looked at the house beyond the trees, and his pain returned. He opened the car door, tossed his cigarette to the ground, and got out.

He walked along the fence to the gate, then up the drive. His shoes crunched noisily on the gravel in the dawn silence. Anyway, she wasn't sleeping, he could tell when he saw the front door was open. Six o'clock in the morning, not a soul around, and the door was wide open. *For him.* She must have wanted to see him arrive. He wondered if she had got up early or simply hadn't slept. He was willing to bet on the second option. How long had she been awake? To the east the sun was breaking through, beneath the grey ceiling of cloud, and it created long shadows that extended throughout the garden. He went up the steps, unhurriedly.

'I'm in here, Martin.'

The voice came from the terrace. He went through the rooms, one by one. Her form against the light; she had her back to him. He emerged into the open air. The lake was motionless, reflecting the sky and the curtain of trees on the far shore with the precision of a mirror. An impressive calm. Even the grass on the slope seemed greener in this pure light.

'Did you find the answers you were looking for?'

Her tone was distant, almost indifferent.

'Not yet. But I'm getting close.'

She turned slowly and stared at him. Her face was pale and exhausted. Her eyes were red, her cheeks hollow, her hair dry. He tried to read a message in her eyes but there was nothing. And yet the sorrow was there; this woman was not the Marianne he had loved, not even the Marianne to whom he had recently made love.

'They're going to release Hugo,' he said.

A gleam of hope.

'When?'

'The magistrate for custody and release will give his ruling this morning. He'll be out by this time tomorrow.'

She nodded. He understood that she did not want to get carried away, that she was waiting to hold her son in her arms.

'I spoke to Francis,' he said. 'Last night.'

'I know.'

'Why didn't you say anything?'

She looked right at him. A deep, green, shifting look, like the forest opposite. Her expression was impassive, but not her voice.

'What? That I'm an addict? You really think I was going to tell you all that just because we fucked?'

The expression wounded him. As did her tone.

'What did Francis tell you, exactly?'

'That you began taking drugs after Bokha's death.'

'Not true.'

He shot her a questioning glance.

'It would seem that Francis was afraid to tell you the whole truth. Maybe he was afraid of your reaction. Francis is not a very brave person.'

'What truth?'

'I started messing with drugs aged fifteen,' she said. 'At a party.'

He gave a start. Fifteen . . . They already knew each other then, though they weren't together.

'I've always thought it was a miracle you never realised,' she added. 'I was constantly afraid you would find out, that someone would tell you . . .'

'I suppose I was too young and naïve.'

'Oh yes, definitely. But there's something else: you were in love. How would you have reacted?'

'And you, were you in love?' he asked, not answering her question.

She gave him a black look and for a moment, he thought he could see the old Marianne.

'I forbid you to even doubt it.'

He inclined his head, sadly.

'The drugs,' he suddenly realised. 'Francis was already supplying you back then. How – how could I have been so blind? Not to notice . . . all that time we were together . . .'

She went up to him, her face so close he could see every one of the little wrinkles that had appeared around her eyes and mouth over time, every part of the complex design of her irises.

'So is that what you think? That I left you just because of the dope? Is that your opinion of me?'

He saw the black flame in her eyes. The anger. The spite. The pride . . . and suddenly he was ashamed of himself.

'You stupid idiot! I told you the truth, the other night: Francis was there for me, while you were lost, distant, elsewhere. Haunted by your guilt, your memories, your past. Being with you meant living with the ghosts of your parents, with your nightmares. I just couldn't do it any more, Martin. There were so many shadows in you, and so little light, in the end. It was more than I could handle. I tried, oh yes, God knows I tried. And Francis was there for me when I really needed it. He helped me to let go of you.'

'And he supplied you with dope.'

'Yes.'

'He manipulated you, Marianne. You said so yourself: that's his only real talent. Manipulating people. He used you. Against me.'

She raised her chin. A hardness disfigured her features.

'I know. When I realised, I wanted to hurt him in turn, and I knew his weakness: his pride. So I left him. I dumped him and I made it clear to him that he had never mattered to me, that he was nothing.'

There was something infinitely weary and broken in her voice, a guilt that went far back into the past.

'And then Mathieu came into my life. He's the one who helped me out of it. He didn't know anything about all that. Bokha managed to do what neither one of you could: he saved me.'

'How could I have saved you from something I didn't even know about?' he pleaded.

She ignored him.

'And how long has it been since you . . .'

'Relapsed? Since Mathieu's death. We're in a town where there are almost as many students as there are inhabitants. It wasn't very difficult to find a dealer.'

'Do you know Heisenberg?'

She nodded.

'Margot told me about something,' he said, changing the subject because he couldn't stand talking about it any more. 'A scene she witnessed last night, in the mountains. Up by the Néouvielle lake.'

He saw the expression on Marianne's face change. He told her what Margot had described to him.

He could see the surprise increasing in her gaze as he spoke.

'Yesterday was 17 June,' she answered when he had finished. '17 June, 2004,' she added.

He waited for her to continue.

'A coach accident. It was in all the headlines, in all the regional papers. You should remember.'

Yes, he vaguely remembered something. A news item swept away in the flood of other news items. Disasters, massacres, wars, accidents, murders . . . a coach accident. Neither the first nor the last. There had been a great number of victims, including children.

'Seventeen children were killed. And two adults: a teacher and a firefighter,' she said. 'The driver lost control of the coach, went off the road, and into the lake. But before that, the coach was stuck for two hours halfway down the slope, and a number of children were rescued.'

He looked at her.

'How come you remember this so well?'

'Hugo was in the coach.'

'Do you know David, Sarah and Virginie?' he asked.

She nodded.

'They're Hugo's best friends. They're at prep school with him. Brilliant young people. They were in the coach that night, too.'

Servaz looked at her closely.

'You mean, like Hugo, they survived the accident?'

'Yes. They were all traumatised, as you can imagine. I remember when we went to pick up the children. It was awful. They had watched their schoolmates die.'

'They got treatment for it, didn't they?'

'Yes. Physical and psychological. Some of them were severely injured. Some of them were disabled for life.'

She broke off and paused to think. 'They were already close before the accident. But I get the impression that this brought them even closer. They're thick as thieves, now.'

She hesitated.

'If you'd like to know more, just look it up in the local newspaper. They had a field day with the story.'

He stared at her. He felt sad and empty. She intercepted his gaze.

'I warned you, Martin: all the people I care about come to a bad end.'

He hesitated to ask her something he had been dying to ask since he had entered the house. He dreaded the answer. But his need to know was overpowering.

'What was Francis doing here the other night?'

He saw her give a start.

'Have you been spying on me?'

'No, I was spying on him – because he was the one I suspected.'

'He'd just been dumped by his girlfriend, a student from Marsac – that Sarah you mentioned. It's not the first time that . . . that he slept with one of his students. Or that he's come to cry on my shoulder. It's strange, don't you think: when Francis needs to confide in someone, he comes to me. He's a very lonely person. Like you, Martin. Do you think it's because of me?' she asked suddenly. She made an odd gesture with her hand. 'I've often wondered: what do I do to you? What do I do to the men in my life, Martin, that other women don't? Why do I destroy them?'

She was shaken by a sob, but he could see no tears in her eyes.

'You didn't destroy Bokha,' he said.

She looked at him.

'He was happy with you, you told me so.'

She nodded, her eyes closed, a bitter line distorting her mouth.

'Do you think I can? Actually make a man happy? And stop? *Once and for all?*'

They looked at each other. It was one of those moments where the scales could tip either way. She could forgive him – everything he had said, thought, believed; or she could reject him and banish him from her life forever. And what did he want?

384

'Hold me,' she said, 'tightly. I need it. Now.'

He did as she asked. He would have done it even if she hadn't asked him. He looked over her shoulder at the lake, the morning light. Now it was her turn to squeeze Servaz, and he felt submerged by her embrace, by the warmth that flooded him.

'You've always been there, Martin. In my mind. Even when I was with Bokha, you were there. You've never left me. Do you remember "UDDUP"?'

Yes. He remembered. 'Until death do us part.' They always said goodbye with these five letters. Her voice and her breath in his ear, her mouth so close. He wondered if it was true, if he could trust her. He decided he could. He was fed up with suspicion, a profession that rubbed off on every aspect of his life. This time it was simple and clear. How long had it been since he had loved in this way? He felt that it was the same for her: it had been a near thing, for both of them – and he understood that they wanted to travel at least some of the way together. To believe in a future.

On the lake, a heron gave a long lonely cry. Servaz turned his head just in time to see it take off into the stormy sky with a great beating of its wings.

Friday

43

The Lake 3

He dreamt he was dying. He was lying on the ground, in the sun, his head turned to the sky, and thousands of black birds were flying high overhead, while his blood drained from him. Then a shadow appeared and lowered its head to look at him. In spite of the grotesque wig and the huge glasses, he did not have the slightest doubt as to its identity. He woke up with a start, his head still full of the birds' cries. He heard a sound from downstairs, and he could smell coffee.

What time was it? He pounced on his telephone. Four missed calls. The same number. He had slept for more than an hour. He dialled the number.

'For Christ's sake, what the fuck are you doing?' said Espérandieu.

'I'm on my way,' he answered. 'We're going straight to *La République de Marsac*. It's a local newspaper. Find their number and call them. Tell them we need everything they have on the coach accident at the Néouvielle lake on 17 June 2004.'

'What's this business about a lake? Have you got something new?'

'I'll explain.'

He rang off. Marianne came into the bedroom with a tray. He drank the orange juice and black coffee straight down, and gobbled a buttered slice of bread.

'Will you come back?' she asked suddenly.

He looked at her as he wiped his lips.

'You already know,' he said.

'Yes. I think I do.'

She was smiling. Her eyes were, too. Her eyes so deep and so green.

'Hugo will soon be free, and you'll be here . . . all the misunderstandings between us will be over. I haven't felt this good for a long time. I mean, this . . . *happy*.'

She had hesitated to say the word – as if to say it might cause the happiness to vanish.

'Is that true?'

'I've never been this close to it, at least,' she corrected.

He took a shower. For the first time since the beginning of the investigation, he felt a renewal of energy and a desire to rush ahead, to move mountains. He wondered whether this business about the accident was important, and instinctively he knew it was.

When he was ready to go, he took Marianne in his arms and she leaned against him. In spite of everything, he couldn't help but wonder if she had taken something since last night. As if reading his thoughts, she threw her head back, with her arms around his waist; she was almost as tall as him.

'Martin . . .'

'Yes?'

'Will you help me?'

He looked at her.

'Will you help me get rid of the monkey?'

'Yes. I'll help you,' he said.

Bokha had managed to. Why shouldn't he? It was love she needed. The only thing that could fill the void . . . He remembered her words a few hours earlier: 'You've always been there . . . You've never left me.'

'Do you promise me?'

'Yes. Yes, I promise you.'

La République de Marsac had not yet digitalised all its archives. Only the last two years were on CD. All the rest – including the year 2004 – had been preserved in boxes of microfiches stacked in a wooden cupboard at the end of a corridor.

'Oh, boy,' said Espérandieu, contemplating the work ahead.

'2004, here it is,' said Servaz, pointing to a pile of three plastic boxes. 'There's not that much. Where can we find a reader?' he asked the secretary.

The secretary led them into a windowless room in the basement. An anaemic neon light flickered and the microfiche reader appeared: a big cumbersome machine, which, judging from the layer of dust on it, was not used often. Servaz rolled up his sleeves and approached the monster.

They opened the boxes of microfiches and looked for the one for 18 June 2004, the day after the accident. Bingo. The moment they slotted it in the viewer, the title of the article leapt out at them:

FATAL COACH ACCIDENT IN THE PYRENEES

Seventeen children and two adults lost their lives in a coach accident at Lake Néouvielle last night at approximately 23.15. According to initial reports, the vehicle is said to have gone off the road in a bend then fallen on its side, where it lay trapped on the slope between the road and the lake for several minutes. The rescue workers, who arrived on the scene very quickly, managed to save ten children and three adults before the vehicle continued its slide and sank into the lake before their eyes, leaving them helpless. The cause of the accident is not known. The victims were all students from a secondary school in Marsac. They were on their end-of-year class trip.

They went over the following pages. More articles, black-and-white pictures of the disaster. They could see the long outline of the coach lying halfway down the slope before it slid into the lake. Human forms stood out against the harsh glow of headlights. Firefighters walked by. Then another photograph . . . the lake. Lit up, from deep below . . . Servaz shuddered. He looked at Espérandieu. His assistant seemed paralysed.

Servaz removed the microfiche from the reader and reached for another one in the box. The articles published the next day and the following days added more details:

The funerals of the 17 children and two adults who died in a tragic coach accident two days ago at the Néouvielle lake will be held tomorrow. The 17 victims, who were aged between 11 and 13, were all pupils at the same secondary school in Marsac. Of the two adult victims, one was a firefighter trying to help the children trapped in the vehicle, the other was a teacher from the school. Ten other children survived thanks to the efforts of this teacher and the firefighters. The adults who were rescued include the coach driver, a school supervisor and another teacher. For the time being the investigators have ruled out excessive speed, and the analysis carried out on the driver showed he had no alcohol in his blood.

The articles that followed described the funerals and evoked the parents' sorrow, tugging at the readers' heartstrings. There were more photographs, taken with a telephoto lens, of the families gathered around the coffins and then at the cemetery.

Emotion and a time for contemplation yesterday in Marsac for the funerals of the 19 victims of the coach accident, held in the presence of the ministers for transport and national education.

Many rescue workers are traumatised after the terrible night they experienced at the Néouvielle lake. According to one of the workers, 'The worst thing was hearing the children's screams.'

Then, once the emotion had passed, the tone of the articles began to change. No need to be an expert to understand that the journalists had smelled blood.

Two articles questioned the role of the driver.

FATAL ACCIDENT AT LAKE NÉOUVIELLE:
DRIVER QUESTIONED

And then:

FATAL COACH ACCIDENT: WAS THE DRIVER
RESPONSIBLE?

According to the prosecutor in Tarbes, there are two theories regarding the coach accident that cost the lives of 17 children and two adults on the night of 17 June at Lake Néouvielle: the poor condition of the vehicle, or human error. According to the testimony of several children, the coach driver, Joachim Campos, 31, lost control of the vehicle during a moment of inattention while he was deep in conversation with one of the teachers, just at the moment when the narrow, winding lakeside road required constant vigilance. However, the prosecutor has refuted this report, explaining that there are several leads, 'including human error', but that statements would first have to be verified.

'Why did you do it, Suzanne?'

Paul Lacaze was stuffing his belongings into an open suitcase on his bed. She was watching him from the doorway. He turned to face her and the look she gave him, her eyes sunken with illness, made him sway as if she had punched him. As if all the energy she had left was concentrated in that tiny burst of pure hatred.

'You bastard,' she hissed.

'Suzanne . . .'

'Shut up!'

He gazed sorrowfully at her, with her hollow cheeks, grey skin and synthetic wig. Her teeth were protruding, skull-like, beneath her bloodless lips.

'I was going to leave her,' he said. 'I was going to end our relationship. I had already told her—'

'Liar.'

'You don't have to believe me, but it's the truth.'

'So why won't you tell me where you were on Friday night?'

He guessed that she wanted to believe in it for just a little bit longer . . . He would have liked to convince her that he loved her, that what they had had together was something he had never shared with anyone else. So that she could take that certainty with her, at least. He would have liked to remind her of the good times, all those years when they had been the perfect couple.

'I can't tell you,' he answered regretfully. 'Not any more. You've already betrayed me once. I can no longer trust you. How could I?'

He saw her sway in turn, the gleam flickering deep in her eyes. For a split second he was tempted to take her in his arms, then the temptation passed. Like two boxers in a ring, they were each giving as good as they got. He wondered how they had reached this point.

'Oh my God!' exclaimed Espérandieu.

Servaz's eyesight was not as good as his assistant's, and he wasn't as quick at reading the tiny, somewhat blurry characters on the microfiche, but on hearing the excitement in Vincent's voice his heart began to race. He rubbed his eyes, leaned closer to the luminous screen and read:

The cause of the accident has not yet been determined, but the theory of human error would seem to have been confirmed. The testimonies of the surviving children all seem to point in the same direction: Joachim Campos, the coach driver, 31, was in the midst of a deep discussion with one of their teachers, Claire Diemar, at the time of the incident, and he took his eyes off the road on several occasions to speak to her. Claire Diemar, along with the coach driver and a 21-year-old supervisor named Elvis Konstandin Elmaz, is one of the three adults who survived the tragedy. A fourth adult, also accompanying the children, was killed while trying to save them.

'What a business, huh?' said a voice behind them.

Servaz turned and saw a man in his fifties standing in the doorway – a mass of dishevelled hair, a four-day beard, his glasses stuck in his hair – gazing at them with a smile. Even if they hadn't been in the basement of a newspaper office, Servaz could have stuck a fluorescent Post-it marked 'journalist' on the man's forehead.

'Were you the one who reported on the accident?'

'I was.' The man stepped closer. 'And believe me, it's the only time in my professional life I would have preferred to give someone else the scoop.'

'What do you mean?'

'By the time I got there, the coach was already at the bottom of the lake. I've seen quite a few things in my life, but that . . . The firefighters from the valley were there. There was even a helicopter on site. Those poor guys were devastated. They had done everything they could to get as many children out as possible before the coach went into the lake, but they didn't manage to save all of them, and one of their own men was stuck on the bottom too. Two other firefighters were in the coach when it crashed into the lake, but they managed to swim to the surface. They dived down again, even though their bastard of a captain forbade it, and they managed to save one more, but the others were already dead. And for the entire duration of the operation, or as near as dammit, that fucking headlight went on shining. In spite of the absolute battering the coach had taken, can you imagine? It was like . . . I don't know, a luminous eye. That's it: the eye of some fucking animal, like the Loch Ness Monster, know what I mean? With those children in its belly, at the bottom of the lake. You could make out the shape of the coach. I even thought I could see . . . Ah, shit!'

He was choking up as he spoke.

Servaz thought of Claire in her bath, with the torch rammed down her throat, the strangely twisted position her murderer had left her in. He found it very difficult to conceal his emotions. The journalist came closer, and shifted his heavy-framed glasses onto his nose as he leaned over to read what was on the screen.

'But the worst of it was when some of the kids' bodies began to float to the surface,' he continued. 'The windows were broken and the coach was lying on its side. Over half the children were stuck down below but the others, after a few hours, eventually got free of whatever had been holding them there, and they did what all victims of drowning do when they don't have 200 pounds of concrete attached to their feet. They floated to the surface, like fucking balloons, like puppets.'

Like dolls in a swimming pool, thought Servaz. Almighty God!

The man seemed to extricate himself from his memories and suddenly looked like a dog who has sniffed a bone.

'Tell me, why does this old business interest the cops all of a sudden?'

Servaz saw the journalist's gaze go back and forth between Vincent and him. 'Holy shit! Claire Diemar! The teacher who was murdered . . . she was in the coach, too!'

Shit, indeed she was, thought Servaz. He could see the wheels begin to spin wildly in the reporter's mind.

'Bloody hell! She drowned in her bath! You think it was one of the kids who did it? Or a parent? But why six years later?'

'Time to go,' said Servaz.

'What?'

'Get out.'

The journalist bristled. 'I warn you, there will be an article in *La République* first thing tomorrow. Are you sure you have nothing to say?'

'Out!'

'We're in for it now,' said Espérandieu, once he had gone.

'Let's go on looking.'

The following articles reported that the driver was released due to lack of proof. As time went by, the articles became less and less frequent, today's news effacing yesterday's. From time to time, when something new came to light, a short article mentioned the tragedy, increasingly briefly. As it did in this piece:

SAD IRONY OF FATE: FIRE CHIEF FROM COACH TRAGEDY

DROWNS IN THE GARONNE

'Looks like the Grim Reaper has been keeping his accounts up to date,' remarked Espérandieu philosophically.

But Servaz felt all his alarm bells go off when he skimmed through the article:

Last night one of the participants in the Néouvielle tragedy lost his life in circumstances strangely reminiscent of the death he helped others to escape last year. It would seem – although the investigation has only just begun – that, for reasons that are as yet unclear, the former fire chief came to blows with a group of homeless people who were loitering on the Pont-Neuf in Toulouse. A witness who saw the scene from a distance declared that things rapidly became heated, then 'it all happened so quickly'. After a brutal beating, the fire chief was thrown from the bridge. His body was recovered after the witness alerted the police, but it was too late. A search is under way for the culprits.

'Shit!' exclaimed Servaz, leaping up out of his chair. 'Call the division! I want everyone on it. Find a list of all the people who had anything to do with the tragedy even remotely and go through every single record! Tell them it's urgent. Tell them we've got the press on our tail.'

Once she had logged into her office computer, it took Irène Ziegler less than three minutes to find the owner of the vehicle with the number plate Drissa Kanté had given her. And hardly more than two minutes to find his profession.

'*Zlatan Jovanovic, Private Detectives. Shadowing/Surveillance/ Investigations. At your disposal 24/7. Registered with the prefecture.*'

With an address in Marsac . . .

Irène flung herself back in her seat and stared at the computer screen. *Marsac* . . . What if her initial theory had been wrong? What if it wasn't Hirtmann who had been paying someone to spy on Martin? A detective in Marsac. Martin's investigation was focused on the town. She checked her watch. She had an appointment at the courts in Auch for a domestic violence case, then she was expected at the office of her unit commander. Two wasted hours at least. Probably more. After that she would hurry to Marsac to find this Zlatan individual.

She didn't have a warrant, but she'd think of something.

She got up and put her cap on, and wiped a few specks of dandruff off her uniform shirt. A poster on the wall featured a pair of gendarmes posing for the great glory of the gendarmerie. They looked like Barbie and Ken. Ziegler inspected her uniform with a sigh.

'That was fast,' said Pujol on the other end of the line. 'The coach driver, Joachim Campos, is in the missing persons database.'

Servaz felt a rush of adrenaline.

'Why?'

'Suspicious disappearance. 19 June 2008.'

His heartbeat accelerated. The fire chief had been tossed in the water in June 2005, one year after the tragedy. The coach driver had disappeared in 2008. Claire Diemar had drowned in her bath in June 2010. How many more victims – one per year? Always in the month of June? There was one detail that didn't square with the others: Elvis. His death didn't follow the pattern. He had been the victim of what had to be called attempted murder only a few days after Claire.

Had the perpetrator decided to speed things up? Why? Was it because of the police investigation? Maybe he had been frightened. Maybe he had realised that Elvis, one way or another, could lead the police to him.

'Ring the hospital,' said Servaz. 'Ask them if there is any chance Elvis will come out of his coma, so we can question him.'

'No chance,' Pujol said. 'The hospital phoned a few minutes ago. He just died from his injuries.'

Servaz swore. Rotten luck. And yet they were close, he was sure of it.

'Regarding the incident on the bridge, and the fire chief the homeless people tossed in the Garonne: find me the name of the witness,' he said to Pujol.

He put down the phone and turned to Espérandieu, who was behind the wheel.

'Back to Toulouse. I want a thorough investigation into that Campos guy's file.'

'I can't take it any more.'

Sarah looked at David. He seemed about to choke, his voice fragile and trembling. She wondered if he was already high or if something else was going on. She knew the extent of his depression. She often thought that while the accident may have been the trigger that had enabled the black angel camped out in David's psyche to spread his wings, it had already been there. Hiding somewhere. She knew about the little brother who drowned in the swimming pool, the one they had entrusted to him though he wasn't even nine years old. She also knew what his bastard father and brother had done to him. She and Hugo talked about it often. Hugo said that David was like a headless duck. Hugo was very fond of David. But David liked Hugo even more. There was a bond between them that was greater than just fraternal. A bond she could not explain. A bond that was even stronger and deeper than the one that united all of them.

Sarah had been one of the first children out of the coach, through the window, when the vehicle was still lying on the slope, held in place by a few trees. It was the young teacher who had died who helped her out; she still remembered how embarrassed he had been, his muttered apologies as he put his hands on Sarah's bottom to shove her out, before he turned round to try and save one of her little schoolmates stuck beneath a seat. Oddly enough, she could remember the young professor's round face perfectly, and his glasses that were just as round (they all made fun of him in class because he had no authority; he was a laughing stock, and Hugo excelled at impersonating him), but she couldn't remember his name. And yet she owed him her life, as did David, as did several members of the Circle. He had ended up at the bottom of the lake with the other victims. On the other hand, she had never forgotten the name of the pretty new teacher who all the pupils adored. That pretty bitch of a teacher had got out first, crawling on all fours, screaming hysterically and leaving the children to their fate. Deaf to their calls for help. Claire Diemar. Not one of them had ever forgotten her. Imagine their astonishment when there she was at the prep school in Marsac. They remembered how distraught she had seemed when she read the roll call and recognised their names.

All these years, too, Sarah had not forgotten the supervisor with the funny name: Elvis Elmaz. Elvis, who would encourage them to smoke on the sly even though they were only twelve; Elvis, who lent them his Walkman and let them listen to rock music; Elvis who told the boys how to get it on with girls, and who felt her up on the quiet because at the age of twelve she looked sixteen. They admired him and feared him at the same time. They would have liked to be like him. Until the night they discovered that their demi-god was a coward.

Nor had they forgotten the fire chief. He wouldn't allow his men to go in the coach, on the grounds that it could tip into the lake at any moment – but almost all of them had disobeyed his instructions and one of them had lost his life. It was thanks to those disobedient firefighters that there were ten of them in the Circle, and not just two or three. And then there was the driver: not only had he lost control of his vehicle because he was paying more attention to Claire Diemar than he was to the road, but he had also been one of the first to escape. The only person he had helped had been that filthy bitch. No doubt because she was pretty, and because they had flirted on and off, discreetly, during the trip.

'What was the name of that teacher?' asked Sarah, before placing her lips on the bong and breathing in.

David gave her a glassy look. He seemed completely stoned.

'The one with the glasses?' said Virginie. 'The one who saved us? The Frog.'

'That was his nickname. Doesn't anyone remember his first name?'

'Maxime,' said David in a thick voice, taking the bong when Sarah handed it to him. 'His name was Maxime Dubreuil.'

Yes. Now she remembered. Maxime, who pretended not to hear the farts, whistles and laughter behind his back. Maxime, who was constantly pushing his glasses up his nose when he spoke. Maxime Dubreuil. *A hero.* His body had been fished out the next day along with the others, when the crane lifted the coach out of the water. Sarah remembered how his mother had wept at the funeral, a fragile little woman with a mane of white hair like a cloud of candyfloss.

Would Maxime have approved of what they had done? Surely not. Why did she get the feeling, more and more often, that they had lost their way? Why did she have the impression they were becoming worse than those who had abandoned them?

'We have to do something about that cop,' said David.

He spoke in a lifeless, apathetic voice. Virginie looked at him, but for once she didn't say anything. They were in the abandoned chapel in the middle of the woods, roughly two hundred metres from the lycée, where they were in the habit of meeting to drink, plot and smoke.

'It's up to me to take care of it,' he added after a moment.

He passed the pipe on: the water was now a greenish colour.

'What are you going to do?'

'You'll see.'

The case of Joachim Campos's disappearance had begun, as usual, with a telephone call. From his girlfriend, who was waiting for him at the La Pergola restaurant on the evening of 19 June 2008, and who was surprised he was so late, then panicked when he didn't show up. The report explained that she had tried to reach him on his mobile twenty-three times that evening, but each time she got his voicemail.

The next morning, she called in sick and went to his workplace. Joachim was no longer a coach driver. Even though there had been no charges against him, he had been sacked for another professional error six months after the accident. He was now a warehouse man. A job that did not offer nearly as many opportunities to flirt with pretty strangers. At his workplace, they told the girlfriend that Joachim had not come in that morning. By mid-afternoon she decided to contact the gendarmerie, who made it clear to her that there was not much that could be done.

But Joachim Campos's girlfriend, as witnessed by the fifty-three new calls she made to the former driver's mobile, was the stubborn type. She harassed the gendarmerie and the police, and finally got what she wanted when a witness came forward, asserting he had seen someone who matched Joachim's description in an old grey

Mercedes on the night of his disappearance – only a few kilometres from the restaurant where they had been due to meet. An interesting detail, according to the same witness, was that there were two men with him in the car.

The case was reclassified as a suspicious disappearance. For obscure procedural reasons, it was taken over by the police in Toulouse – who had worked the union minimum, and as always in these matters, the prosecutor had wasted no time closing the case for lack of evidence.

Servaz took the sheets from Campos's file one by one. He handed half of them to Espérandieu. It was 14.28.

At 15.12, Servaz began to go through the list of calls made to and from Joachim Campos's mobile phone.

One number cropped up a great many times, on the evening of the disappearance and the following days, and Servaz knew without even checking that this would be the stubborn girlfriend. Other people had tried to reach him in the days that followed: his sister, his parents, and a number that turned out (once Servaz had delved into the investigation report) to belong to a young married woman who had been having an affair with Joachim for several months.

At 15.28 Servaz turned to the location of the last calls made and received by Joachim Campos. These might enable them to retrace his steps.

'A map,' he said. 'I need a map of the central Pyrenees.'

Espérandieu fiddled on his keyboard and opened Google Maps.

'Here's your map.'

Servaz looked at the screen.

'Can't you make it a bit bigger?'

Espérandieu moved the vertical cursor down and the territory covered by the map grew larger while the distances between the villages shrank.

'A little bit further south and east,' said Servaz.

His assistant complied.

'There,' said Servaz, putting his finger on the spot.

Espérandieu looked at the spot indicated. *La Pergola*.

'Yes. And so what?'

'There's the restaurant, and there's the last transmitter that recorded Joachim Campos's mobile. It's thirty kilometres from the restaurant, but in the opposite direction from his house. A witness claims to have seen someone resembling Joachim in his Mercedes near the restaurant roughly half an hour before the transmitter recorded him passing by, in the company of two men. Assuming the witness was right, this means that Campos wasn't heading home.'

'So what? God knows where he was going. Maybe to his other woman.'

'No, it's not in that direction either. What's interesting is that no more transmitters were activated after that one, in spite of the calls his desperate girlfriend made.'

'As though his telephone had been destroyed or switched off and abandoned somewhere,' suggested Espérandieu.

'Exactly. And that's not everything. Make it bigger.'

Espérandieu moved the cursor further down and the territory expanded further. Servaz ran his finger from the restaurant to the transmitter then extended its trajectory.

'Bloody hell,' said Vincent as he watched his boss's finger move closer and closer to a place whose name they had read at least a hundred times in the last few hours: Lake Néouvielle.

Ziegler was outside the courts, sitting astride her Suzuki, when 'Singin' in the Rain' chimed in her pocket. She unzipped her leather jacket and looked at the screen of her iPhone: Martin.

'You did some diving when you were in Greece, didn't you?' he asked. 'With or without air tanks?'

'With,' she answered, her curiosity instantly aroused.

'And are you good at it?'

She gave a short little laugh.

'Ha ha! I'm a federal instructor, first degree, and a Two Star Instructor with the World Underwater Federation.'

She heard him let out a long whistle.

'That sounds pretty cool. I suppose it means yes?'

'Martin, why do you want to know?'

He told her.

'And have you ever done any diving?'

'With a mask and snorkel, yes, once or twice.'

'I'm serious. What about with an air tank?'

'Uh . . . yes, a few times, but it was a long time ago.'

This was a lie. He had only dived once in his life with a tank, at

Club Med . . . in a swimming pool . . . along with Alexandra and an instructor.

'When was that?'

'Hmm . . . fifteen years or so ago, I think. Maybe a bit longer.'

'It's a very bad idea.'

'It's the only one I have. And we can't afford to wait for permission from the prosecutor's office to have a team of divers at our disposal. The press will be all over the case in the next few hours. It's a very small lake, after all . . . and there are no sharks,' he joked, lamely.

'It's a fucking bad idea.'

'Do you have all the gear we'd need? Do you have a diving suit for me?'

'Yeah, I should be able to find one.'

'Great. How soon shall I come and pick you up?'

'I have an appointment with the company commander. Give me two hours.'

She would deal with Zlatan Jovanovic later. She was dying to know what Martin had found.

Air tanks, diving, a lake . . .

With treasure at the bottom, she thought.

44

The Dive

It was already late afternoon when they started along the dirt track. They bounced along the road as far as a chain stretched between two squat poles. A rusty sign swung from the middle:

NO BATHING

The lake and the dam appeared before them. Servaz looked at the far shore, 200 metres away; the road overlooked the lake in a sharp bend. It was there that the coach had left the road to careen down the slope. It was impossible to get to the lake from there: the shore below the road was a steep cliff to which only a few old trees still clung; their roots, laid bare by successive landslides, reached into the water; a raft of dead wood and debris floated on the surface between the branches. All around, the slope was not as sheer, but still too steep.

So there was only one way to get there: the track they were on.

Servaz opened his door, and immediately the heat of the day cloaked his shoulders like a piece of clothing forgotten in the sun. Irène had already walked around the Cherokee to open the boot. She was hurriedly removing her clothes and Servaz could see that she was very suntanned. She pulled her black rubber suit over her pink thong and bra and he set about changing too.

'We'd better hurry,' she said, looking at the clouds.

Thunder was rumbling and swirling in the distance. From time to time, there came the flash of a lightning bolt. But still no rain. She took the second set of gear from the boot and helped him pull on the diving suit. He tried to recall the explanations she had given several times over in the car, and he was beginning to regret his plan.

'It looks as if the storm is about to break,' she said. 'I'm not sure this is a good idea.'

'I don't have any others,' he said.

'We could wait until tomorrow. A team of divers can comb the lake. If there's anything to find, they'll find it.'

'Tomorrow *La République de Marsac* is going to publish an article stating that the police are trying to establish a link between the accident and Claire Diemar's murder, and all the media will get hold of the story. If there is something down there, I don't want the press to see it.'

'Why don't you tell me what we're looking for?'

'A grey Mercedes. And maybe someone inside.'

'Is that all?!'

For a split second he almost backed down. But a remnant of pride prevented him from giving up. Irène saw it in his eyes, and shook her head. But she didn't say anything. She repeated her explanations about breathing, placed the tank on his back and arranged it. Then she adjusted the straps and set the hoses of the mask and the breathing tube on his shoulders and torso.

'This is the stab,' she said, pointing to the stabilising jacket. 'You inflate and deflate it with these valves, here, like I showed you. Always inflate it on the surface. It will allow you to stay above water. The stab is attached to the tank by this strap. The tank is connected to the regulator. You insert it in your mouth like this. Bite down lightly on the rubber if you're afraid you'll lose it.'

He tried to breathe. He thought he could sense resistance in the hose, but it was probably due to stress. Irène checked his belt and his flippers; she fastened the dive computer – a fat watch – around his wrist.

'This is the depth, and this is the temperature. And here you have the time elapsed. In any case, I won't take my eyes off you and we stay a maximum of forty-five minutes in the water, got it?'

He nodded. Tried to move. Took two steps forward, raising his knees to avoid stumbling on the flippers, then stopped. He felt clumsy, unbalanced. The weight of the air tank made him feel as if he was going to fall on his back at any moment.

Ziegler closed the boot and the noise caused a cluster of birds to scatter on the other side of the lake. A warm wind stirred the leaves, and the thunder still hovered, but otherwise silence reigned.

'Okay, let's go back over this. With the fading daylight, it's going to get dark down there very quickly: always put your torch in front

405

of your hand so that I understand what you want to say. If everything is fine, you make the sign "okay".' She joined her thumb and forefinger to shape a circle. 'Given the fact that you're a beginner, you're going to use up your reserve much faster than me, so don't forget to check it regularly. You have enough air for a good hour. Finally, if you have a problem, or if we get separated, wave your torch in all directions and don't move. I will come and find you. Is that clear?'

It was clear that he had less and less inclination to go through with it. But he nodded his head, his teeth clamped a bit too tightly on the nozzle of the regulator, his jaws clenched.

'One more thing: breathe in, but don't forget to breathe out at regular intervals. Underwater, lungs that are filled with air for too long will want to make you rise to the surface. If that happens, remember to exhale slowly. Since the air gradually expands in your lungs as you go back up, it could be dangerous.'

Great.

'This is completely idiotic,' she added. 'Are you sure you want to go through with it?'

Once again he nodded.

She shrugged, turned round and stepped slowly into the water, backwards, her face turned to the shore. He imitated her and immediately felt the chill of the water through his suit. It wasn't unpleasant, because he had been so hot, but he wasn't sure it would be as pleasant after he'd been down there for an hour. *A mountain lake,* he thought. It was a long way from the Seychelles.

When the water was up to their chests, Irène spat into her mask, spread her saliva over the Plexiglas surface, and rinsed it just before adjusting it on her nose. Servaz copied her. Then he immersed his mask in the water and inspected the floor of the lake. The silt they had disturbed was filling the water with thousands of particles, preventing him from seeing anything. He hoped they would see more clearly at the bottom.

'One last thing: when I let go of your hand, stay level with me. Don't go any more than three metres away. I want to be able to keep an eye on you. And don't forget to equalise the pressure in your eardrums by pinching your nose and breathing out. It will calm the buzzing in your ears. This lake is deep and you'll feel the effects of the pressure after only two or three metres.'

He made the 'okay' sign and she gave a faint smile. She seemed even more stressed out than he was.

'Put your regulator in your mouth,' she ordered.

She took his hand and they lay back against the water, kicking their flippers. When they were well away from the shore, she motioned to him to deflate his jacket and they started to descend in a cloud of bubbles.

It took him a few seconds to get used to the regulator, and he noticed he had to make a real effort to breathe underwater. Memories of his experience in the swimming pool came back, although it had been almost twenty years earlier, and he remembered that even then he hadn't really liked it very much.

They were already in what seemed like endless darkness in spite of the double beam from their torches. Irène squeezed his hand and guided him. They went down. The air whistled when he breathed in and bubbles sparkled all around him when he breathed out. Then silt danced in the beam of their torches and they could see the bottom of the lake – irregular, sloping and covered with a great prairie of algae, which undulated like a head of hair in the current, five metres below. At the same time, he could feel the pain growing ever more acute in his eardrums; a buzzing that was louder and louder. He made a face, and let go of Ziegler to put his hand on his ear. Irène immediately grabbed him by the jacket and obliged him to go back up. She looked at him through her mask and imitated the gesture of equalising. He did as she told him, pinched his nose and breathed out. He felt something like a big air bubble leave his ear. The pain vanished. There was only a slight buzzing. Bearable, he concluded. Again he made the 'okay' sign and they started down once more, stopping twice to equalise the pressure.

At the bottom, thick fronds of algae brushed against their bellies. They swam in the probable direction of the sheer drop from the edge of the road. Irène was still clutching his hand, yet he felt all alone in the world. Alone with his thoughts.

Light.

He felt as if he were weightless.

Silence.

He could hear nothing around him except the gurgling sound. And the echo of his breathing, which was getting easier.

He glanced at his dive computer.

Fifteen metres.

After a while, Ziegler let go of his hand and looked at him. He motioned to her that everything was okay, and she moved away from him, continuing to swim in the same direction. Servaz looked all around. There wasn't much to see. They were alone at the bottom of a lake where no one would think to look for them, and he felt extremely vulnerable and exposed. His stress was growing by the minute, now that she was no longer holding his hand. *Calm down, you're only a few metres from the surface, all you have to do is inflate your jacket to get back up there.*

Except that Ziegler had told him about observing gradual stages. Even at this depth. And the importance of not panicking. *Shit.* He looked towards the surface and saw a vague light. Far away. More grey than blue. Maybe the storm had broken. The thought made him more anxious than ever. *Calm down. Breathe out.* He concentrated on what was in front of him and inspected the silty bottom with the beam of his torch. Turning his head, he saw Ziegler only three metres away, continuing to explore by sweeping her torch from side to side, light and easy, undulating like a mermaid. She was paying no attention to him. He could scream all he liked, she'd never hear him. *If you have a problem, or if we get separated, wave your torch in all directions and don't move. I will come and find you.*

The lake bottom was more irregular now: there were rocks, and tree trunks, an entire landscape as irregular as it was on the surface, and looking more and more like an outdoor tip. Servaz lit up a big tree trunk with his torch, gained a little altitude to get past the obstacle then dived again towards the prairie of algae. Then the ground seemed to rise quite abruptly. He glanced at Ziegler. They were even further apart now and he felt his panic return. He was alone with himself, thousands of cubic metres of hostile water pressing against the thin Plexiglas of his mask.

A school of little fish swam past his nose, catching silvery glints of light.

There was something a bit further along, in the middle of the algae and the silt. Probably some household appliance that had been tipped in from the shore: the slope indicated they were getting closer. He kicked his flippers to propel himself closer to the object. Now he could see the pale reflection of glass among the algae. He forced himself to breathe out slowly, in spite of his impatience and curiosity. Two more kicks of the flippers and he saw it. Joachim Campos's grey Mercedes. Almost intact in spite of the corrosion gnawing away at it. Half of the number plate had vanished, but there was still an X, a Y, a double zero, and the number for the region, 65, clearly identifiable.

There was something inside.

At the wheel.

The windscreen was covered with a thin green translucent film, but he could see through it.

Pale.

Motionless.

Staring straight ahead.

The coach driver.

He could tell his pulse was pounding too hard, he was breathing too quickly. He twisted his way round the vehicle, and approached the door on the driver's side.

He reached out to squeeze the handle, expecting it to be blocked, but against all expectation the door opened with a creak muffled by water. But there wasn't enough room to open it all the way.

Servaz leaned inside through the opening and lit up the shape at the wheel.

Still in place, held by what remained of the seatbelt. The beam from his torch revealed details Servaz would have preferred to ignore: prolonged immersion in the water had transformed the body's fat into adipocere, or 'corpse wax', a substance that was like soap to the touch, and Joachim resembled a perfectly preserved wax figure. It was the process of adipocere transformation that had halted decomposition and preserved the body all this time. His scalp had been destroyed, and it was a bald, waxy head that Servaz saw before him, emerging from what remained of his shirt collar. The epidermis of his hands had also become detached, and looked like two leather gloves. His eyes had vanished, leaving two black sockets. Servaz observed that the car had protected the corpse from predators to some extent. He was breathing more and more quickly. He had often looked at corpses, but not deep under the surface of a lake, imprisoned in a diving suit. The water was getting colder and colder. He shivered. The encroaching darkness, the bubble of light, and now this body . . .

Then Servaz saw the hole near the corpse's temple. The bullet had gone through his cheek near the left ear. Servaz looked more closely. He had been shot at point-blank range.

The corpse suddenly moved. He was overwhelmed by panic. And again, the tatters of the shirt on the corpse's torso stirred, and Servaz recoiled violently. His head banged the metal frame of the car. He let out a cloud of panicked bubbles. With the shock, he dropped his torch, and it drifted slowly to the floor of the car, between the dead man's legs, capturing the corpse, the dashboard, and the roof of the car in its luminous eddy.

At the same time a tiny fish emerged from what was left of the shirt and swam away. Servaz's ears were buzzing. He didn't have enough air. He realised he'd forgotten to look at his dive computer. He reached inside, grabbed the torch from between the pedals and the dead man's shoes, and waved it every which way to call for help.

Where was Ziegler?

He didn't have the courage to wait. With a few desperate kicks of his flippers, he rushed towards the surface. After only a few metres he found himself caught in a tangle of white, tentacular roots.

Something was clutching his leg. He struggled furiously to get free, when another piece of wood struck his mask violently. Dazed by the shock, he tried to go left, then right, but once again he banged into the hard, rigid roots. They were everywhere. He was a prisoner, only a few metres from the surface. He felt he was losing control, he couldn't think straight any more. He couldn't face the idea of going back out the way he had come or going back down. He had to find a way up at all costs.

Now!

Suddenly the nozzle of his regulator was torn from his mouth. He groped, terrified, found it, pulled on it, but the regulator was stuck among the branches and the roots! He pressed his mouth to the nozzle and breathed in the oxygen, greedily. There was something wrong. The regulator was still connected to his air tank. How could it be stuck among the roots? He carried it to his mouth, breathed in again, tried desperately to free it by shaking it. There was nothing for it. Panic was blinding him. He could hear the fizzing of bubbles all around him, a symptom of his distress.

He did not want to stay another minute in the water, trapped like this. He undid the straps of his air tank and struggled to get free from his harness. He breathed one last time, as much as he could, from the regulator.

Then he grabbed the roots, shook them, but in the water he lacked strength. He kicked with his flippers, pulled, arched his body. Pushed on his legs. There was a muted cracking sound. He forced his way up, blindly, slipped through, swam up some more, bumped against the roots, shook them, climbed, struggled, bumped, got free, swam up, and up, and up . . .

The rain came from the west. Like an army bent on conquering a territory. After the vanguard announced its arrival with salvos of lightning and violent gusts of wind, it unfurled on the woods and the roads. Not just an ordinary rain: a deluge. It swept the roofs and streets of Marsac, caused the gutters to overflow, and whipped the old stone facades before continuing its way across the countryside. It drowned the hills, caused them to vanish under a heavy liquid shroud, and it was spiking the surface of the lake when Servaz's head burst through the raft of dead wood and debris that floated among the roots near the shore.

His mask was stuck to his face like a suction cup. He had to pull very hard to yank it off and he felt as if his cheeks were going to come off with it. He opened his mouth wide to swallow the fresh air in great avid lungfuls. He let the rain ripple over his tongue. He turned his head and looked around and the panic returned. What time was it? How long had they been down there, since it was already dark? He heard Ziegler break the surface next to him. She took him by the shoulders.

'What happened? *What happened?*'

He didn't answer. He was shaking his head back and forth, his eyes wide open, his mask on his forehead. He heard the crash of nearby thunder. The sound of the storm pounding on the surface of the lake.

'My God!' he roared. 'Can you see me?'

She was still holding his shoulders. She looked around them, trying to determine how to get to the shore. She turned back to him. He was looking everywhere but, oddly, without looking anywhere in particular, and without looking at her.

'Can you see me?' he said again, even louder.

'What? What?'

'I can't see a thing! I've gone blind!'

★

411

He observed them, as silent and invisible as a shadow. A shadow among shadows. They could not imagine that he was so close.

He had followed them to the abandoned, ruined chapel where they were clearly in the habit of meeting. He had hidden in the tall shrubs and, through the window whose glass had disappeared long ago, listened to them holding forth while they smoked. He had to admit that they were considerably more interesting than most of their peers, all those semi-literate young primates. He had a better idea now of why Martin had become who he was. This place turned out quite promising adults. What if there were a school of crime that trained its students in a similar fashion – he could have taught classes there, he mused, and a smile spread across his face.

Crouching in the bushes in the rain, he watched them leave the chapel and take the path towards the lycée. And then he went into the deserted little building. Christ and any signs of worship had vanished long before. The place was littered with beer cans, empty Coca-Cola bottles, snack wrappers and magazines, the vulgar symbols of that other religion, the dominant cult of mass consumerism.

Hirtmann was not religious, but he had to admit that certain faiths, Christianity and Islam in particular, had bypassed all the others where torture and savagery were concerned. He could picture himself quite easily, preaching with the same eloquence that he had applied in the courts. Now he was preparing himself to be both judge and executioner. In his own way he was going to revive the good old joke of the biter being bit.

Originally he had believed that the usurper, the one who had dared to pretend to be him, must be one of these young people. But as he listened to them, and nosed about here and there, he realised his mistake. And the irony of the situation appeared to him in all its cruelty. *Poor Martin* . . . he had already suffered so much. For what might have been the first time in his life, Hirtmann felt a surge of compassion and comradeship. It almost brought tears to his eyes. It would have been a real surprise to Martin to know that he could have this effect on him. *Martin, my friend, my brother* . . . he thought. He was going to mete out a harsh punishment to the guilty party. The crime was double, since there had been two victims. She would pay for her crime of lese majesty on the one hand, and her betrayal on the other. A punishment that would remain branded upon her body and her mind forever.

45

Hospital

'Retinal haemorrhage,' said the doctor. 'Boyles's law, where the variation in pressure is accompanied by variation in the volume of the gas
space: like all gases, the air contained in your mask was subject to
changes in pressure. Given the effect of the pressure, the air was
compressed when you went down, and expanded when you came back
up. You are the victim of what is known as barotrauma: a trauma due
to extremely abrupt changes in atmospheric pressure. I don't know
what happened down there, but a total loss of vision is extremely rare.
Even a momentary one. But rest assured, you will not remain blind.'

Great, thought Servaz. *Couldn't you have said that sooner, stupid bastard?*

The doctor's voice, which was deep and steady as it pontificated,
horrified him. In all likelihood, if he'd been able to see the rest of
him, he would have felt the same.

'The haemorrhage may take a certain time to evolve,' continued
the voice, learnedly. 'The macula has been affected, the central zone
of vision. There is no specific treatment. We can only act on the
cause. And obviously in this case, the cause is already behind you;
therefore all we can do is wait for things to go back to normal. We
may need to resort to a surgical ablation to recover your eyesight
completely. We will see. In the meantime we will keep you under
observation. And you will keep this bandage over your eyes. Whatever
you do, don't try and take it off.'

Servaz nodded, wincing. There wasn't much he could do; he
couldn't see a thing.

'One might say you don't do things by halves,' said the doctor,
ironically.

He wished he could have come up with a scathing reply, but
oddly enough, these words reassured him. Perhaps because of the
doctor's positive tone.

'Right, I'll come by later. Get some rest.'

'He's right,' said Ziegler next to him, when the doctor's footsteps had faded away. 'You really don't do things by halves.'

He could tell from her voice that she was smiling. And concluded that she too had some reassuring news.

'Tell me what he told you.'

'The same thing he's told you. It could take several hours or several days. And if they need to, they will operate. But you will get your sight back, Martin.'

'Fantastic.'

'It was a mistake, that dive.'

'I know.'

'I'm going to have to explain it to my superiors.'

He made a face. She was going to get into trouble again, he knew it. And again because of him.

'I'm sorry. I'll take all the blame. I'm going to ask Sartet and the prosecutor if we can pre-date the request. Otherwise I'll say that I lied to you, and claimed I already had approval.'

'Hmm. Well, they're not going to sack me over it. And they can hardly do any more to me than what they've already done. Besides, there's the corpse: that justifies everything, don't you think?'

'What's going on with the car and the body?'

'This time, they're sparing no expense: they're taking everything out of the lake. The body will be sent for autopsy tonight. Everyone is on a war footing.'

He could hear the persistent noise of the storm, and ordinary hospital sounds: nurses' voices, footsteps in the corridors, trolleys being pushed along.

'Am I all alone in here?'

'Yes. Do you want me to station someone outside your door?'

'What for?'

'Have you forgotten that someone shot at you last night? You can't see a thing, you're even more vulnerable. And it's a hospital. Anyone can just walk right in.'

He sighed. 'No one besides the police knows I'm here,' he replied.

She squeezed his hand. Then he heard her push back her chair.

'In the meantime, you have to sleep. Do you want a sedative? The nurse can give you one.'

'Only the liquid variety. And then only if it's been aged at least twelve years.'

'I'm afraid that won't be reimbursed by Social Security. Get some rest. I have something to see to at my end.'

He straightened up a little. He could hear the tension in her voice.

'It sounds important.'

'It is. I'll fill you in tomorrow morning. There are several things I have to tell you.'

He could sense her awkwardness.

'What sort of things?'

'Tomorrow.'

Ziegler paused under the hospital's glass canopy and looked out at the downpour. The lightning formed an electric arc in the darkening sky. A second later, the thunder made the air vibrate.

She put on her helmet and ran to her motorbike. The summer storm had transformed the road into a rushing stream. She went down to the centre of Marsac, gliding like a shadow through the deserted streets, riding very slowly over the flooded cobblestones. It was almost eight o'clock in the evening and she wondered if she would find him at home or at his office. The business address was nearest. When she looked up at the yellow facade of the shoddy building in the centre of town, she saw that there were lights on the top floor. Her hunter's instinct was immediately aroused. It had been a long time since she had gone hunting, really hunting: the kind that gave her a sensation that even sex or motorbikes couldn't match. She parked on the pavement, removed her helmet, smoothed her streaming blonde hair and headed to the door. There was no intercom or lock and all she had to do was climb the creaking stairway up to the top floor. She rang the bell and waited.

'Yep?' said a voice on the intercom after twenty seconds or so.

'Mr Jovanovic?'

'Uh-huh.'

'My name is Irène Ziegler and I'd like to make use of your services.'

'We're closed. Come back Monday.'

'I'd like someone to tail my husband. I know you're not cheap, but I'm prepared to pay whatever it takes. Please give me fifteen minutes.'

For a few seconds, there was silence, broken by the crackling of the intercom, then the lock clicked open and she pushed against the door. She was in a tiny apartment which smelled of stale tobacco. There was a light at the end of the corridor so she went towards it. Zlatan Jovanovic was locking some documents in a safe. An old-fashioned model, not much better than a cupboard. It would take a real professional only one minute to force it open. She understood that the safe was only there to impress the clients. He must do this with every new arrival: the trick of putting the documents in the safe. Important things would be elsewhere, probably encrypted on a computer. He closed the heavy door and turned the cylinder lock. Then he collapsed into his office swivel chair.

'Go ahead.'

'That's a good one, the trick with the safe. I'm impressed.'

'I beg your pardon?'

'It's sort of old-fashioned, that model, isn't it? I know at least twenty people who could open it blindfolded with one hand tied behind their back.'

The man's eyes narrowed.

'You're not here about a fickle husband.'

'How observant.'

'And who are you?'

'Does the name Drissa Kanté mean anything to you?'

'Never heard of him.'

He was lying. The tiniest retraction of his pupils. In spite of his poker face, the name was like a slap.

'Listen, Zlatan – you don't mind if I call you Zlatan? – I don't have much time to waste, so if we could dispense with the preliminaries . . .'

She took a USB stick out of her pocket and slid it across the desk to him.

'Does this look like the memory stick you gave Kanté?'

He didn't even look at it. He was staring at her.

'Let me repeat the question: who are you?' he said.

'The person who's going to have you sent down if you don't answer me.'

'My activity here is legal, I'm registered with the prefecture.'

'And installing spyware on police computers, that's fine with them, I suppose?'

Again, the blow struck home. But only for a tiny fraction of a second. He must be a very good poker player.

'I don't know what you're talking about.'

'Five years in jail: that's what you've got coming to you. I'm going to request an identity parade. We'll see whether Kanté identifies you. Besides, we have a witness: a friend of his followed you and wrote down your number plate. Not to mention the owner of the café, who saw you with him several times. Seems rather a lot, don't you think? You know what's going to happen? The examining magistrate will request a remand in custody, and the magistrate for custody and release will decide your case. It will take him only ten seconds and a quick glance at your file. Believe me, it won't be a moral dilemma. You will be locked up for sure.'

He wiggled on his chair, and gave her a black look. Despite his disdainful manner she saw a familiar gleam: fear.

'You seem nervous all of a sudden.'

'What do you want?'

'The name of your client. The one who asked you to spy on Commandant Servaz.'

'If I tell you, my business will be fucked.'

'You think you'll be able to conduct your business from inside? Your client is a murderer. Do you want to be charged as an accessory to murder?'

'And what do I get in exchange?'

She took a deep breath. She had no trump card: no orders, no warrant. If this got out, she would be dismissed for sure.

'I just want a name. That's all. If I get it, I leave and we wipe the slate clean. No one will know a thing.'

He opened a drawer in his desk and she recoiled slightly. His big paw rummaged inside. She watched him, ready to jump. His hand came back out with a cardboard folder, which he set down in front of her. She noticed that he bit his fingernails.

'In here.'

Standing in the rain, Lacaze gazed at the entrance to the new courts of law. It was already several minutes past eight, and he wondered if the man he was looking for would still be in his office.

The new law courts had opened a few months earlier. The architects had preserved the original maze of old buildings and courtyards around the rue des Fleurs, but they had extended the listed building with very modern additions, an artificial eloquence of glass, brick,

concrete and steel. Lacaze thought the concept reflected, unintentionally, the state of justice in this country: an ultramodern facade and
entrance hall masking the dilapidation and lack of funds behind it.

An attempt at modernisation that was doomed to fail.

He had to empty his pockets onto a little table before going
through the metal detector. After that, he walked across a lobby
dominated by a lofty glass ceiling, and turned left, passing the doors
that led to the courtrooms. Just beyond them a woman was standing.
He needed a badge to go further and he didn't have one.

'Thank you for waiting for me,' he said.

'Are you sure he'll still be there?' asked the woman, scanning her
badge and pushing open the bulletproof door.

'I was told he worked late.'

'Naturally you won't tell him I'm the one who let you in.'

'Don't worry.'

Servaz heard the door to his room open and for a moment, he was
truly apprehensive.

'Good God,' came Cathy d'Humières' powerful voice. 'How do
you manage it, constantly getting yourself in these situations?'

'It's not as bad as it looks,' he smiled, relieved.

'I know. I've just seen the doctors. If you could see yourself,
Martin. You look like that Italian actor in that film from the sixties
. . . *Oedipus Rex* . . .'

His smile turned to a grin and he felt his cheeks pulling on the
large bandage wrapped around his temples and forehead.

'Coffee, boss?' said another voice, and he recognised his assistant.

He held out his hand and Espérandieu pressed a warm coffee
into it.

'I thought visits weren't allowed after eight p.m.,' he said. 'What
time is it?'

'8.17,' said Vincent. 'Special dispensation.'

'I won't stay long,' said the prosecutor. 'You have to get some
rest. Are you sure the coffee is a good idea? I gather they just gave
you a sedative.'

'Uh-huh.'

He had wanted to refuse, but the nurse left him no choice. He didn't
need to see her to understand that she wasn't joking. The coffee was
remarkably bad, but his throat was dry; he would have drunk anything.

'Martin, I'm here as a friend. This investigation is under the exclusive jurisdiction of the county court in Auch, but between you and me, Lieutenant Espérandieu explained what's going on. If I've got it right, you think the same murderer killed all those people over the last few years because of the coach accident. And that would be the motive?'

He nodded. *They were so close* . . . That was where they had to look: the Circle, the accident, the death of the fire chief and of the coach driver . . . It was right there. But deep down, he still had doubts. It had come to him while they were on their way to the lake and getting ready to dive. There was something wrong. A piece of the puzzle that didn't fit with any of the others. Except that he couldn't put his finger on it, and his headache didn't help matters.

'I'm sorry,' he said, to avoid answering. 'I've got a horrible headache.'

'Of course,' said Cathy d'Humières apologetically. 'We'll talk about all this when you feel better. In the meantime, we've had no sign of Hirtmann,' she said, changing the subject. 'There ought to be an agent outside your door.'

He shuddered. Apparently, everyone wanted him guarded.

'It's pointless. No one knows I'm here, other than the emergency team, and a few gendarmes.'

'Yes. Well. Hirtmann has popped up more than once, after all. I don't like it, Martin. I don't like it one bit.'

'I have a buzzer next to my bed, if need be.'

'I'll stay for a while,' interrupted Espérandieu. 'Just in case.'

'Fine. If you're up and about tomorrow, we'll go over everything in detail. We'll give you a white cane if we have to,' she said, opening the door to his room.

He made an evasive little gesture with his hand.

'Goodnight, Martin.'

'You're not actually going to spend the night here, are you?' he asked Vincent when the door had closed.

He heard the scraping of a chair being moved.

'Would you rather have a nurse? In any case, in your state, you wouldn't even know what she looked like.'

Ziegler closed the folder. Zlatan Jovanovich was staring at her from the other side of the desk. There was a gleam in his eyes that hadn't been there earlier. He had had plenty of time to think while she was reading. Did he really believe she would leave and draw a line under everything he had done? Maybe he was thinking that she hadn't shown him any official documents. Suddenly she was on her guard.

'I'll be taking this with me,' she said, pointing to the folder.

He merely stared at her. She stood up. He did likewise. She looked at his hands hanging down next to his body. Drissa Kanté was right: he must weigh at least twenty stone. He walked slowly around the desk. She stayed still, waiting for him to go ahead of her, ready to dodge if he jumped her. He did nothing of the sort, however. He merely walked down the dark corridor. As she followed him, staring at his wide back, she put one hand in the pocket of her jacket where she kept her weapon, when all of a sudden he disappeared through an open door on the right. She didn't have time to react. She could see the darkness beyond the door. She grabbed her gun, removed the safety catch, and chambered a round.

'Jovanovic! Don't be stupid! Show yourself!'

She had her gun ready now. She stared at the dark doorway, less than a metre away. She froze. She didn't want to go any further. She didn't want twenty stone worth of flesh to burst out of the shadow, his fists coming down on her like sledgehammers.

'Come out of there right now, for fuck's sake! I won't hesitate to shoot, Zlatan!'

Nothing. Jesus Christ! *Think!* He was probably just around the corner, waiting in ambush, with a club or even a gun. She held her weapon in both hands, as she'd been taught. She took the top hand from her grip and moved it slowly towards the pocket containing her iPhone.

Suddenly she heard a click from the other side of the room: the light went out and the apartment was plunged into darkness. A glow of lightning briefly illuminated the corridor, followed by a boom of thunder outside, and then everything returned to darkness. The only source of light were the street lamps and the neon of a café downstairs. The rain was streaming down the windows, drawing shadows that slid across the floor like black snakes. She could feel her nervousness growing. From the start, she had known she was dealing with someone experienced. She had no idea what this guy had done before becoming a private detective, but she was sure he knew all the tricks of the trade. She thought of what Zuzka would say in such circumstances: 'Not looking good.'

Judge Sartet was about to lock the door to his office when the footsteps in the corridor caught his attention.

'How did you get in here?'

'Have you forgotten I'm an MP?' replied the visitor.

'These law courts are a complete sieve. I don't think we had an appointment. And my day is over. To the best of my knowledge your immunity has been withdrawn, Monsieur Lacaze,' he added. 'So don't worry, I will listen to you when the time comes: I haven't finished with you.'

'This won't take long.'

The judge had difficulty hiding his exasperation. All the same, these politicians. They thought they were above the law, they went on about how they were serving the country or the state but in fact they were only serving themselves.

'What do you want?' he asked, not even trying to be polite. 'I don't have time for games.'

'I want to confess.'

Thunder and lightning rattled the windows. The phone vibrated at the same time and he gave a violent start. Servaz stuck out his hand, groping to find his mobile on the night table, but Espérandieu was quicker.

'No, I'm his assistant. Yes, he's right here. Yes, I'll pass you over.'

Vincent put the phone in his hand and went out into the corridor.

'Hello?'

'Martin? Where are you?'

Marianne's voice.

'In hospital.'

'In hospital?' She seemed genuinely frightened. 'What happened?'

He told her.

'Oh, my God! Do you want me to come and see you?'

'No more visits as of eight o'clock,' he replied. 'Tomorrow, if you like. Are you alone?' he added.

'Yes, why?'

'Lock your door and close your shutters. And don't let anyone in, all right?'

'Martin, you're frightening me.'

I'm afraid, too, he almost answered. *I'm scared shitless. Get out of there. Don't stay alone in that empty house. Go and sleep somewhere else until we find that fucking maniac . . .*

'You have no reason to be afraid,' he said. 'But still, do as I said.'

'I heard from the prosecutor's office,' she told him. 'Hugo gets out tomorrow. He was weeping when I spoke to him. I hope this experience won't have . . .'

She didn't finish her sentence. He could sense her relief, her joy and her fear, all at the same time.

'What do you say to a celebration, the three of us?'

'Marianne, don't you think that . . . that it's a bit premature? After all, I'm also the cop who locked him up.'

'Maybe you're right.' He could hear her disappointment. 'Later, then.'

He hesitated.

'This dinner . . . does that mean that . . . ?'

'The past is the past, Martin. But "future" is a fine word too, don't you think? Do you remember that language we invented? Just the two of us?'

Of course he remembered. He gulped. Felt his eyes misting over. It was probably the effect of the medication, all this emotion . . .

'Yes . . . yes . . . of course,' he answered, his throat tight. 'How could I have—'

'*Guldendreams*, Martin,' said the voice on the other end of the line. 'Look after yourself, please. I . . . We'll talk soon.'

Five minutes later his mobile vibrated again. Again, Espérandieu answered before passing him the phone.

'Commandant Servaz?'

He immediately recognised the young voice. Even though the tone was totally different from the last time he had heard it.

'My mother just called. They've told me I'll be released first thing tomorrow morning, and they've dropped all the charges against me.'

Servaz could hear the usual prison sounds behind the voice, even at this time of the evening.

'I wanted to thank you.'

He felt himself blushing. He had just done his job. But Hugo seemed very moved.

422

'Uh . . . You did a great job,' he said. 'I know how much I owe you.'

'The investigation isn't over,' Servaz hastened to point out.

'Yes, I know, you have another lead, I've heard . . . the coach accident?'

'You were there, too, Hugo. I'd like us to talk about it. As soon as you have the strength, of course. I know it's not easy, that it's not a pleasant memory. But I need you to tell me everything that happened that night.'

'Of course. I understand. Do you think the murderer might be one of the survivors?'

'Or the parent of one of the victims,' said Servaz. 'We found out . . .' He hesitated. 'We found out that the coach driver was also murdered. Just like Claire and Elvis Elmaz, and probably the fire chief. It can't be a coincidence. We're very close.'

'Gosh,' murmured Hugo. 'I might even know him . . .'

'Yes, you might.'

'I don't want to disturb you any longer. You should rest. Just remember I'll be eternally grateful for what you did. Goodnight, Martin.'

Servaz put the phone down on the night table. He felt strangely moved.

'If I understand correctly,' said the judge, stunned, his fingers linked beneath his chin, 'you were in Paris, in the company of the likely future presidential candidate for the opposition on the evening Claire Diemar was killed.'

The magistrate was no longer in the slightest hurry to go home.

Paul Lacaze nodded. 'That's right. That night I was on the motorway. My chauffeur can confirm it.'

'And, naturally, there are other people besides him who could confirm it, if need be? This member of the opposition, for example? Or someone in his immediate entourage?'

'If it becomes absolutely necessary. But I hope it won't.'

'Why didn't you say anything?'

Lacaze gave a sad smile. The building had emptied and the corridors were silent. They looked like two conspirators. Which, ultimately, is what they were.

'You do realise that if this gets out, my political career will be over. And you know as well as I do that there is no secrecy in this country, that everything always ends up in the papers. So you see that it was extremely difficult for me to talk about it here or at the police station.'

Sartet clenched his jaw. He didn't like it when someone questioned the integrity of representatives of the law.

'But by running the risk of being indicted, you also put your career in jeopardy.'

'I didn't have time. I had to react, and choose between the two evils. Obviously, I couldn't know that my meeting would be on the same night as . . . as what happened. And that's why you have to find the culprit as quickly as possible, your Honour. Because that way I'll be cleared, and those who suggested I might be guilty will be discredited, and I'll be able to resume my place as the politician of integrity whom others sought to destroy.'

'But why have you told me all this now?'

'Because it's my understanding that you have another lead . . . this business with the accident . . .'

The judge frowned. Lacaze was clearly well informed.

'And?'

'That means it might not be necessary to keep a record of this informal meeting we've had. And I don't see any clerks about,' said Lacaze.

Sartet in turn gave a vague smile. 'Hence the late hour of your visit . . .'

'I trust you implicitly, your Honour,' insisted Lacaze. 'But only you. I don't trust the people around you nearly as much.'

Sartet smiled at this rather vulgar flattery but it did have an effect. He was equally flattered to find himself – a minor examining magistrate – in the middle of what might be termed an Affair of State.

'Your relationship with Diemar has begun to filter into the press,' he pointed out. 'That could also be harmful to your career. Particularly given your wife's condition.'

Lacaze's brow creased, but he banished the argument with one hand.

'It'll be far less harmful, however, than murder or collusion with the opposition,' he replied. 'And the press will get its hands on the letter I wrote to Claire not long before her death. It says that I had decided to break off our relationship to devote myself entirely to my wife. I should point out that I really did write this letter. It's perfectly genuine. I just hadn't planned to make it public.'

Sartet shot him a look of disgust mingled with admiration.

'Just tell me one thing. The reason for this high-risk meeting with the opposition – was it to imitate Chirac's move in 1981? You come to an understanding with the probable opposition candidate for the presidency, and you ensure that a great many votes from your party will go to him in the second round. That way, five years later, you stand against him.'

'It's no longer 1981,' corrected Lacaze. 'The people in my party won't vote for the opposition unless – perhaps – his economic policies are reasonable and he has already proved himself elsewhere. And if they disapprove of the policies of our current president. I'm afraid he has no chance to be re-elected.'

'This assumes, all the same, that the person you met last Friday will definitely be selected as the candidate,' said the magistrate, who seemed to be enjoying himself more and more. 'Two years from now . . .'

Lacaze smiled back at him.

'That's a risk I can take.'

There was a knock at the door. Servaz turned his head in that direction. He could hear Vincent moving on his chair.

'Oh, excuse me,' said a young man's voice. 'I came to see if he was asleep.'

'No problem,' said Espérandieu.

The door closed again. Espérandieu went back across the room and the chair creaked when he sat down. There was less noise now in the corridors.

'Who was that?'

'A nurse, or an intern . . .'

'Go home,' he said.

'No, it's fine, I can stay.'

'Who's looking after Margot?'

'Samira and Pujol. And two gendarmes.'

'Go and join them. You'll be more useful there.'

'Are you sure?'

'If Hirtmann wants to get at me, it's Margot he'll attack.' His voice quivered. 'He doesn't even know I'm here. Besides, he would rather attack a woman. I'm worried, Vincent. Worried about Margot. I'll feel easier if you're there with Samira.'

'And the person who fired at you, have you thought about them?'

'Same thing. They don't know I'm here. And shooting someone at night in the middle of the woods is not the same as doing it in a hospital.'

He could tell his assistant was thinking.

'All right. You can count on me. I won't let Margot out of my sight.'

Espérandieu took Servaz's hand and put his mobile phone in it.

'Just in case,' he said.

'Okay. Get going. Tell me when you get there. And thanks.'

He heard the door close and the silence fall. Beyond the window echoes of thunder reverberated throughout the sky. They seemed to be calling to each other, surrounding the hospital.

The shrill blast of a car horn sounded in the street. Ziegler sensed movement behind her. She understood that he'd gone around to get her from behind, and waited until there was some noise to move. She turned round. Too late. The punch hit her temple with a violence that made her fall to her knees, stunned. Her ears were ringing. She had scarcely had time to turn her head to cushion the blow.

Then she felt a kick in the ribs, her lungs emptied and she rolled on the floor. There came another kick in the stomach, but she had curled into herself, her hands around her head, her knees up, and her elbows close to protect herself, so he only partially reached his target. Then came another shower of furious blows.

'Filthy bitch! You really thought you could fuck me over like that? What do you take me for, stupid cow?'

He went on insulting her, spluttering, as he hit her. The pain was atrocious. He bent down, grabbed her by the hair and banged her face against the floor. Her vision was invaded by a cloud of black dots, and for a moment she thought she would pass out. He grabbed her by the ankles, turned her over, even though she was lashing out, and fell with all his weight on to her, crushing her to the floor, one knee in the hollow of her back. He twisted her arms behind her and she felt him putting thin plastic handcuffs on her wrists, which he tightened until they were biting painfully into her flesh.

'Fuck! Do you understand what I'm going to have to do now? Do you understand, you stupid bitch?'

426

His voice was enraged and whiny at the same time. He could have killed her right then. But he was still hesitating: killing a cop was one hell of a step to take, a decision that required some reflection. Perhaps she was still in with just a tiny chance . . .

'Don't be stupid, Zlatan!' she cried. 'Kanté knows all about it, and so do my superiors. If you kill me, you'll be sent down for life!'

'Shut it!'

He gave her another kick, not as hard this time, but it was somewhere he'd already struck and she winced with pain.

'You're really taking me for a fool, aren't you? You didn't even get out your badge. And you're not on assignment. I'll take care of Kanté. Who else knows about this?'

He kicked her again. She clenched her teeth.

'You don't want to talk? No problem: I've dealt with tougher ones than you.'

He spat on the floor. Then he leaned down, searched her pockets, took her iPhone and her gun, and went back to his office, leaving her handcuffed and frantic in the middle of the corridor.

Servaz wasn't asleep. He simply couldn't fall asleep. Too many questions. Caffeine was galloping through his veins, along with the sedative the nurse had given him – and he didn't know which one out of the arabica, the adrenaline and the bromazepam would be first over the finish line.

All he could hear was the storm outside and from time to time footsteps outside the door to his room. He had tried to imagine what the room was like, but he couldn't. He felt completely helpless.

He stared at the void in front of him and let his thoughts come.

The discovery of the corpse in the Mercedes was the proof that his assumption was right: the murders were connected to the coach accident. The fire chief's fight with the homeless men had, in all likelihood, been staged. The men had never been found. The murderer or murderers had been very clever: it would be difficult or even impossible for an investigator to find a connection between a fight that went wrong in Toulouse and a disappearance 100 kilometres away, three years later. Not to mention the fact that other cases might come to light, concerning other people involved in that tragic night.

But there was still something wrong.

The nagging feeling he'd had earlier was back. There was some-thing that wasn't clear. *If these were murders and not accidents, the driver's and fire chief's deaths were carefully disguised. But not Claire Diemar's . . .*

The painkiller they had forced him to take was beginning to work. His head was spinning. It seemed in the end that Sister Morphine stood the best chance of winning. He cursed the doctors, nurses and all the medical staff. He wanted to stay lucid. All these doubts were blossoming in him, like a poisonous flower. Claire Diemar had been killed in a way that connected her, beyond the shadow of a doubt, to the coach accident. *The torch in her throat, the lit bath, even the dolls in the swimming pool . . .* But this was the first time that the murderer had wanted to make the link. Claire's death very clearly evoked the accident. And it testified to the murderer's rage at the moment he committed the crime. His lack of control.

Suddenly everything fell into place. Why had it taken him all this time to see what had been right in front of him from the start? He recalled how he'd felt at the very beginning of the investigation, when he found the cigarette butts in Claire's garden. How he'd had the unpleasant impression that he was watching a magician's trick: *someone wanted to make him look the wrong way.* He had sensed the presence of a hidden shadow moving behind the drama, unbeknownst to all. Except that now, he knew. He felt a wave of nausea. He hoped he was wrong, prayed that he was. He was still staring out at his room without seeing it. The thunder in his ears was incessant. In the same manner, the thought came back to him. Why hadn't he seen it sooner? No one was better positioned than he was to under-stand. He had to warn Vincent. Immediately. And the magistrate.

He groped for his mobile. His fingers curled around it, his thumb found the big on-switch in the middle.

Then the smaller keys below. Except that he couldn't open his contacts, let alone read them. He tried to dial a number, and lifted the phone to his ear, but an implacable voice told him it was invalid. He tried again. Same result. *The buzzer.* He groped next to his bed looking for it, found it, and pressed it. And waited. Nothing. He pressed it again. Then shouted, 'Is anyone there?' No answer. Fuck, where were they all? He threw back the sheet and sat up at the edge of the bed. A strange sensation came over him. *There was something else.* Another thought was lurking at the edge of his consciousness, trying to catch his attention. It was something to do with what had happened since he had been in this room. He was having trouble clarifying his thoughts. The sedative was beginning to work; he felt heavier and heavier, groggy. But urgency was driving him on. He had to stay awake no matter what. He had been on the verge of a very important thought. Something . . . *vital*.

46

A Draw

He had made only one mistake, but it was enough.

Ziegler thought of the way he had briefly touched her breasts. Because of the pain in her torso, her breathing was shallow. She was lying on her back in the middle of the corridor, handcuffed. Twisting like a worm on the ground, wincing, clenching her teeth, she managed to grab the hem of her T-shirt and pull on it violently. Good God, this cheap shit was tougher than it looked. No matter how hard she tugged, the material refused to tear. God dammit! She put her neck on the dusty floor to catch her breath, and forced herself to think. Then she turned her head to the skirting board. *A nail* . . . Clearly the hammer had missed it, because it was sticking out one or two centimetres. She edged sideways to get closer to the wall. It was a flat-headed nail, fairly big. It was a crazy idea, but it wouldn't hurt to try. She slid so that the nail was level with her belly button, then she tried to roll over in that direction. She was amazed to discover how difficult it was when you were handcuffed with your arms behind your back. On her third attempt, however, she managed it and found herself with her cheek and shoulder crushed against the wall just above the skirting board, the rest of her body jammed between the floor and the base of the wall, and the nail just below her T-shirt. *You're almost there* . . . She wedged her hips as close as she could against the skirting board, then began wiggling slowly downwards. That, too, was bloody difficult. But she was relieved to see that she had caught her T-shirt on the nail. And once the nail had lifted the T-shirt far enough, she took a deep breath. *One, two, three* . . . She pulled away from the wall as violently as possible. The sound of her T-shirt ripping made her almost exultant.

She closed her eyes, paused for a second and listened out. She could hear him rummaging in a desk drawer, then loading a cartridge into his gun. A wave of fear went right through her. Then she realised that he was making a phone call.

A brief respite.

Goaded by urgency, it was almost as if she didn't feel her pain. She hurried to grasp the back of her jeans between her handcuffed hands, and wriggled until her hips, buttocks and almost all her thighs were out of her trousers, then she struggled like a devil, edging along the floor to make her trousers slide along her legs until she could push them off with her feet. Her entire body was screaming with pain but she managed. *That bastard doesn't know who he's dealing with.* Wearing only her leather jacket opened onto her torn T-shirt, her bra and her pink thong, she waited for him to come back, her legs spread suggestively. *It's now or never*, she thought. *The big scene between Little Red Riding Hood and the Big Bad Wolf.*

'Fuck, what have you done?'

She raised her head. Saw his oily gaze take in her breasts, belly, knickers . . . And she knew she had chosen the right strategy. That he belonged to that category of men. Maybe it wouldn't work, but there was a tiny chance. Zlatan's gaze stopped at the top of her thighs. He seemed puzzled. He knew this wasn't the right time, of course – but he found it hard to turn his eyes away. She lay sprawled at his feet, and she was in his power.

'Untie me,' she said. 'Please . . . don't do it . . .'

She spread her thighs, she wriggled and arched her back, as if she were trying to get free. He was staring at her: a hard, black gaze. Shining. *Primitive.* A predator. Once again she could read the dilemma in his eyes. He was torn between the urgency of getting rid of her, and what he saw before him: a very beautiful woman, practically naked, at his mercy. And the allure of the flesh was almost irresistible for a depraved man like him. He'd never have such an opportunity ever again, that's what he was thinking. She could tell that arousal was blurring his reasoning.

He put his hand on his belt and unfastened the buckle. She took a deep breath.

'Stop . . . no . . . don't do that,' she said.

She knew that it would have the opposite effect on this man. He reached for his flies, slowly, without taking his eyes off her. He took a last step forward. It was just as he was struggling with a stubborn button, his gun still in his other hand, that Ziegler's legs closed abruptly around his ankles like a pincer – and she snapped them violently towards her, her own ankles crossed in a deadly vice.

She saw the flash of surprise in his eyes as he lost his balance. He paddled the air with his hands. Fell with all his weight. His head banged hard against the skirting board. But it was the gun that Ziegler did not take her eyes off as it fell. It went off, with a deafening sound. A shrill whistle pierced her ear, and a warm gust of air caressed her cheek as the bullet went right by her to land in the wall behind with a sharp thud. There was a cloud of smoke and a bitter smell of cordite. She was already crawling, wriggling, wiggling, pushing desperately with her feet along the floor, and she grabbed the pistol just in time. She rolled over onto her side, her shoulder crushed against the floor, looking straight at Zlatan's feet and, beyond, at his face, with the gun in her bound hands, pointed at him.

'Don't move, you bastard! If you make the slightest move, I'll empty it into your belly, you bloody fucking shitface!'

He gave a nasty laugh. His eyes were two pools of darkness, staring at the black hole of the barrel, his eyebrows creased.

'And what are you going to do, now?' he said mockingly. 'Kill me? I doubt it. Are we going to stay here for long? Have you seen the position you're in? In two minutes, your arm will be completely numb.'

He was looking at her with the tranquil assurance of the predator who has all the time in the world. He was right. The blood was already hardly circulating in the shoulder jammed beneath her, and the hand holding the gun was shaking uncontrollably. Soon she would be trembling too hard to aim correctly and he would have recovered sufficiently to hurl himself on top of her.

'You're right,' she agreed with a smile.

He gave her a surprised look. Immediately afterwards, she fired, and he screamed with pain when his knee exploded.

'Fuck, you're crazy!' he screamed, writhing in pain. 'You could have . . . you could have killed me, fuck!'

'Exactly,' she said. 'In this position, I fired blind. I could have got you anywhere . . . in the belly, the chest, the head . . . Who knows where the next bullet will go?'

She saw him turn pale. Paying no more attention to him, she pulled both handcuffed arms back at an angle of forty-five degrees, the gun forty centimetres from the floor, and she kept her finger on the trigger, shooting blindly into the little room behind her, towards the window she had seen on her way past. Behind her back she heard the glass shattering. She thought she could hear shouts from the street below.

'Now the cavalry should be on its way,' she replied, satisfied.

A new thought came to him, obvious, spontaneous, terrifying: if his hunch was right, he was in danger, too. Right then. Because contrary to what he had assumed, the murderer knew where to find him. He was more vulnerable than ever.

He was probably already on his way, thought Servaz, with another wave of nausea.

Sitting on the edge of his bed, he could feel the terror race through him. He didn't have a minute to lose; he had to get out of there. Quickly. Hide somewhere. He reached again for the buzzer and pressed it. Nothing.

Stupid idiots!

Instinctively he looked all around him, although he couldn't see a thing, and he got up, his hands held in front of him. He groped his way along the wall, felt its coarse surface beneath his fingers, pipes going every which way, and finally he found a chair by the head of the bed with a plastic bag on it. He felt inside. His clothes. He hurried to put them on, then grabbed his mobile from the night table and headed towards the place where the door ought to be.

He opened it. The corridor seemed strangely silent. He wondered where all the staff had got to. Then a word lit up in his brain: *football*. There must be other matches to watch, even without the French team. Unless they'd all been called to another floor. It was getting late, and the daytime staff had gone home. He felt fear invading him. He turned his head from left to right. He suddenly felt very exposed and vulnerable.

With all his senses on the alert, he held his arms out in front of him until his hands reached the opposite wall. He chose to go left at random. He was bound to find someone sooner or later. He almost stumbled over a cart that was against the wall, then went round it and resumed his progress. Pipes, papers pinned to a cork board, a box with a key and a chain – maybe the fire alarm. For a split second he thought of turning the key. Then he reached a corner, and went around it. Stood up straight.

'Is anyone there? Please, help me!'

No one. He felt a tightness in his chest, and a cold sweat rolled down his back. He continued to grope his way along the wall. Suddenly he froze. His fingers had just touched a metal surface that protruded from the wall, and there was a button . . . *a lift!* His hands trembling, he hurriedly pressed it and heard a ping in response. He could hear the rumbling of the lift beginning to move. The doors opened a few seconds later with a whoosh. He stepped inside when a voice behind him called out:

'Hey! Where are you going?'

He heard the man come in and the doors of the lift closed behind them.

'Which floor?' asked the voice next to him.

'Ground floor,' he replied. 'Are you a staff member?'

'Yes. Who are you? How did you get here in that state, anyway?'

The man's tone was suspicious. Servaz hesitated, choosing his words.

'Listen. I don't have time to explain. But you have to do me a favour: call the police.'

'What?'

'I have to get out of here. Immediately. Take me to the gendarmerie.'

He could tell that the man was examining him closely.

'Why don't you start by telling me who you are?'

'It's complicated. I – I'm . . .'

The doors opened. A recording of a woman's sugary voice called out through the loudspeaker, 'Ground floor/reception/cafeteria/newsagent's'. He took a step outside, heard voices a bit further away, and sensed from the slight echo they produced that they were in a vast space, probably the hospital entrance hall. He started walking.

'Hey, wait, take it easy!' called the man behind him. 'Not so fast!'

He froze.

'I told you: I can't stay here.'

'Oh really? Why not?'

'I don't have time. Listen, I'm a policeman and—'

'So what? What does that change? You're in a hospital, you're our responsibility and have you seen the state you're in? I can't let you out like this! You can't even—'

'Which is why I'm asking you to help me.'

'To do what?'

'Get me out of here! Take me to the gendarmerie. I told you . . . For Christ's sake, there's not a minute to lose!'

There was a silence. The man must have thought he was crazy. On edge, Servaz listened out, trying in vain to identify the voices and sounds around them, to locate any possible threat. But the man's presence at his side reassured him.

'In that state, wearing those clothes? You're completely nuts! Have you seen the weather? It's pissing it down. Tell me why you're so eager to go to the gendarmerie. Maybe we can call from here. Why don't we get the staff from your floor so we can talk it over quietly with them?'

'You won't believe me if I tell you.'

'Try me.'

'I think someone is trying to kill me, and I'm afraid he'll come here.'

As he was speaking he realised that his words would cast doubt on his sanity. But he was no longer in a state to think calmly. The sedative was taking effect; he felt exhausted, disoriented by his blindness, and increasingly woozy. Again, silence.

'I see,' said the man, sceptically. 'Seriously, do you expect me to swallow such a crazy story?'

Suddenly Servaz recognised the voice. It was the young man who had come into the room earlier on, when Espérandieu was there.

'You came into my room,' he said.

'I did.'

'There was another man with me, do you remember?'

'Yes.'

'He was a policeman. Like me. What do you think he was doing there?'

He could tell the young man was thinking. He took the opportunity to put his hand into his pocket.

'Here. Take this. It's my mobile. His name is in my contacts: Vincent. He's a police lieutenant. Call him. Right away. Tell him what I just told you. And then give me the phone. Quick! It's an emergency!'

People went past them, chatting. Outside, an ambulance siren wailed then stopped. The man took the phone from his hands.

'Your pin code?'

Servaz gave it to him. He waited, all his senses on alert. Voices and footsteps all around, and no way of knowing who they belonged to. He was struggling against the fog spreading through his skull.

'What's his last name?'

'Huh?'

'Your lieutenant! What's his name?'

'Espérandieu.'

'And you?'

'Servaz.'

'I'd like to speak to Lieutenant Espérandieu,' said the young man into the phone. 'On behalf of . . .'

He listened to him explaining the situation awkwardly to Vincent. The tension in his voice grew noticeably.

'Okay, I'll bring him to you,' he said finally, grabbing Servaz by the arm. 'Let's go. This is crazy!' Servaz could hear the panic in his voice now.

'I told you I wanted to speak to him.'

'Later! We have to get out of here, quickly. If you're in danger, then so am I! I don't suppose you have a weapon?'

Good question. Where had his gun got to? He remembered he had left it in the glove box, before the dive.

'No,' he said. 'And anyway, you wouldn't know how to use it.'

They went through the hospital doors and were immediately absorbed into the ferocity of the storm. The air smelled and tasted like ozone, and there was an ear-splitting crack. The young man took Servaz by the arm and they hurried across the car park. Servaz was immediately drenched. The rain dribbled down his neck and soaked his hair. The puddles seeped up through the soles of his shoes. He began to shiver. Another thunderclap.

He heard the young man open a car door.

'Get in!'

He collapsed onto the passenger seat and let out a nervous laugh when he realised that, driven by reflex, he was looking for the buckle of the seatbelt.

'Why are you laughing?' asked the young man, slamming the door and turning the key in the ignition.

He didn't answer. The man put the windscreen wipers on and they took off like a shot. He felt the car swerve as they took a tight turn out of the car park and he was thrown against the door. He told himself it was just as well he couldn't see anything.

'I think we've lost him,' he joked feebly. 'Do we really need to go so fast?'

'Don't you like speed?'

'Not really.'

They took the roundabout at the same diabolical speed and Servaz's head bashed into the window.

'Shit, slow down!'

'Put your belt on,' ordered the driver, simply.

He could hear the rush of water against the undercarriage of the car, the spray it threw up. Echoes of thunder everywhere. He felt both relieved and worried. A thunderclap, louder than all the others, made him jump.

'Incredible weather, isn't it?'

Servaz thought the comment was rather strange, given the situation. There was something about the young man's voice, a tone . . . Now he knew what it was. Right from the very start, when the young man had opened the door to his room, something had rung a bell. Not that it was a familiar voice. But he thought he had heard it at least once before.

'Have you been working in his hospital for long?'

'No.'

'What exactly do you do there?'

'Huh? I'm a nursing auxiliary.'

'Shouldn't we have informed your superiors?'

'Make your mind up! You and your assistant both told me to hurry up, to get the hell out of there and now—'

'Yes, but still,' he said. 'To go off like that into the blue with a patient without telling anyone . . . Don't you have a pager or something?'

Silence. Servaz felt his nausea return. Instinctively, his hand gripped the handle above the door.

'We'll call the hospital as soon as we get there,' said the young man.

'Yes, you're right. So what exactly does your job consist of?'

'Listen. I don't think this is the right time to—'

'How did you know that Lieutenant Espérandieu is my assistant?'

The sound of the engine, the beating of the windscreen wipers and the drumming of the rain on the roof of the car were the only answer.

'Where are we going, David?' he asked.

47

Exit

The night of 18 June was one of the most turbulent of the year. There were gusts of wind of 160 kilometres an hour, trees were uprooted, cellars were flooded, and an impressive number of lightning strikes were observed in the countryside around Marsac. The firefighters were constantly in demand. The night of 18 June was also one of the longest in Servaz's life. While David and he drove through the torrential downpour, it occurred to him, sitting slumped in his seat with the sweat stinging his eyes beneath the bandage, that the weather was exactly the same as the night they had discovered Claire's body in her bath.

'A nice show you put on,' he said in a voice that he tried in vain to keep steady. 'I almost fell for it.'

'You did fall for it,' his neighbour corrected him.

'Where are we going?'

'Don't you want to hear my confession, Commandant?'

'I'm listening.'

They went round another roundabout, tilting dangerously. The furious blast of a car horn followed in their wake.

'I killed Claire Diemar, and Elvis, and Joachim Campos, and several other people,' said David, raising his voice to be heard over the din. 'They got what they deserved. That's what I say. And you, Commandant, what do you say?'

'Why, David?'

In response, the young man seized Servaz's left hand and slipped it under his T-shirt in a gesture of surprising intimacy. The policeman shuddered when his fingertips felt something like a wide pucker of skin all the way across his belly.

'What is that?'

'An Asian speciality. Hari-kiri. When I was fourteen. But I didn't have the courage to go through with it. And besides, with a blunt knife, it's not as easy.' He sniggered. 'Not everyone can be Mishima,' he concluded bitterly.

For an instant Servaz was sorry he had no particular skill in dealing with this type of behaviour; sorry he was a cop and not a psychiatrist.

'You know Camus' question, don't you, Commandant?'

'"There is but one truly serious philosophical problem and that is suicide. Judging whether life is or is not worth living amounts to answering the fundamental question of philosophy,"' said Servaz mechanically. 'I'm not sure I follow you. Is that your idea, David: we're going to kill ourselves?'

All Servaz got for an answer was silence. He swallowed. He had to find a way to stop this madness. But what? He couldn't see a thing, he was imprisoned in a metal shell hurtling at breakneck speed through the rain. He had no control over the situation.

'And why not? It would be both my farewell and my confession,' said David in an icy voice. 'A confession signed in blood and metal.'

Servaz managed to roll down the window. He felt sick. He breathed in the damp air, greedily, filling his lungs. He wondered what would happen if he jumped from the moving car.

'I don't think it's a good idea to get out just now,' said David. 'There are trees and electricity pylons everywhere. There's a good chance they'd find your head on one side and your body on the other. I don't think Margot would appreciate it.'

Servaz rolled the window back up.

'You didn't answer my question: why?'

'Do you know anyone who is truly innocent, Commandant? I challenge you to name even one.'

'Stop the chat. Why *you*, David? You're not the only survivor of that accident. Why not Virginie, or Hugo, or Sarah? Or is it to avenge the others – the one who goes round on crutches, for example? Or that other one in a wheelchair? The . . . *Circle*, is that it?'

'You're an astonishing man, Commandant. I didn't think your investigation would get this far. But they're innocent. I'm the only guilty one. All they did was fantasise.'

'Did you and Hugo talk about it? About what you were going to do? Did you confide in him? You swapped ideas, didn't you? He knew about everything.'

'Don't involve Hugo in this! You've already persecuted him enough. Hugo has nothing to do with this!'

'Hugo called, he told you what I had just told him, that I was nearly there, that I had found out about the coach accident, and that I was going to go after the Circle.'

'What are you talking about?'

'According to a witness, there were two people in Joachim Campos's car,' said Servaz. His fingers were gripping the door handle. He was ready to jump out if the car slowed down even the slightest bit.

'And several people tossed Bertrand Christiaens into the Garonne,' he added.

'Christiaens' death has nothing to do with the rest,' said David. 'But you have to admit it's crazy, the irony of what happened to him . . .'

'You're lying.'

'What?'

'You were in on the murder of Bertrand Christiaens. And you were in Joachim Campos's Mercedes before he died – but I'll bet you weren't the one who shot him. You were there when Elvis died, smoking one cigarette after the other in the bushes while they fed him to his dogs. But you didn't kill Claire Diemar . . . because I know who did.'

'What are you talking about?'

'How did Hugo get you into this state? How does he manage to manipulate people, huh? How did he convince you to write that sentence in Claire's notebook?'

There was wheezing silence next to him. Then David said, very calmly, 'You're wrong. It's not Hugo who got me into this *state*, as you call it. It's my father, my brother, my fucking family . . . All those people who are so sure of themselves, and who never doubt; all those ambitious fucks who saw me as a pathetic failure. Hugo did everything he could to help me. Hugo saved me. He made me understand that there was a place even for someone like me, that other people were no better than I was. He's my brother, you understand? My big brother. My true brother. The one I should have had. I would do anything for him.'

Servaz suspected that this time David was desperately sincere. And his sincerity was terrifying. Hugo had a deadly hold over him: deadly for both of them.

'Yes, it's my handwriting in the notebook. And it's my DNA on the cigarette butts. So everyone will believe I'm guilty. And the fact I took you with me to my death will confirm it. I won't let you go after the others.'

Servaz's fingers felt for the ends of his bandage, and tugged. The skin came first, then bits of sticking plaster pulled away. He opened his eyes.

A light . . . through the fog of his tears and the rain flooding the windscreen . . . He could see!

It was still blurry, but he could see. It took him some time to get used to it. The headlights of the cars coming in the opposite direction were blinding. The purplish, flickering eye of a traffic light appeared, through the back and forth of the windscreen wipers and the downpour. He clung to his seat when David hurtled through the red light.

'Fucking hell,' he screamed.

The young man turned briefly in his direction.

'What the fuck are you doing? You took off your—'

'David, you don't need to do this. I'll testify in your favour! I will say you were acting under the influence. You'll get treatment, and they'll release you. You'll be free. Cured!'

A booming laugh came in response.

'Listen to me, dammit! You can get treatment! David, I know you're innocent, that Hugo manipulated you. Do you want to die with this burden on your conscience? To become a monster in everyone's eyes?'

A No Entry sign: the motorway exit. Servaz felt his blood drain into his belly and legs, his entire body pressed instinctively back against his seat. They were about to go the wrong way onto the motorway!

'Fuck, what are you doing? Stop!'

Irène looked out at the waltz of squad cars from the gaping doors of the ambulance. The flashing alarm signals swept intermittently through the interior of the vehicle, then over the puddles and the face of the paramedic next to her. He was checking the lines that connected her to a number of different devices.

'How do you feel?'

'I'm okay.'

She dialled Martin's number again, to no avail; she got his voicemail every time. She wondered anxiously if he had fallen asleep. She absolutely had to tell him what she had read in Jovanovic's file.

Marianne . . .

It wasn't difficult to work out her motive. The only possible motive. She had spied on Martin to protect Hugo, to find out where the investigation stood. Because she would have done anything for her son. But by resorting to someone like Zlatan Jovanovic, she had gone outside the law. Ziegler may have won, but her victory left her with a bitter aftertaste when she thought of Martin, how he would react when he found out the truth. Even if he didn't show it, Martin was fragile. He was a man who'd been wounded since childhood. How would he take this new setback? Suddenly she realised the paramedic was looking outside, his eyes open wide and his smile broader still.

'Yes?' he said to the person who was standing by the ambulance.

Ziegler turned her head and saw Zuzka looking at her. Her long black hair rippled down to a very short cream-coloured leather jacket, and underneath she was wearing layers of necklaces and charms, a tank top that showed her belly button, and a pair of print shorts that were even more minimalist. Her lipstick was as bright as a neon light. For a split second, Ziegler forgot everything else.

'Can I go?' she said.

The paramedic looked from one to the other; he seemed to be wondering whom he would rather spend the night with.

'Uh . . . you have to see the ENT specialist, then get your back and ribs checked out . . .'

'Later.'

She jumped down from the stretcher and the ambulance, took Zuzka in her arms and kissed her. Her girlfriend's tongue had the bittersweet taste of Campari, rye and vermouth. *A Manhattan,* concluded Ziegler. Zuzka had come straight from the strip club, the minute Irène had called her.

Servaz thrust himself against the door when they went around the bend at breakneck speed, and prayed they would overturn before they reached the motorway. But he saw the asphalt rush up to them and headlights in the distance coming closer. He swallowed. The car left the exit and hurtled down the centre lane the wrong way.

'David, please, think! You still have time to stop. Don't do this, for Christ's sake! Watch out!'

A furious wailing of car horns in front of them. Headlights flashing frenetically. He closed his eyes. When he opened them again, the two cars that had passed them were continuing on their way, warning lights flashing in a panic in the night. Sweat was streaming like water down his face. Stinging his eyes. He wiped it with the back of his sleeve.

'David! Answer me, for Christ's sake! You're going to fucking kill us!'

David was staring at the road and Servaz could not read anything in his eyes other than their certain death. His hands were clinging so tight to the steering wheel that the knuckles were white. Servaz realised he was miles away. He stared at the motorway in front of them, hammered with rain, and he waited for the next vehicle to appear, all his senses focused on the coming collision, certain and inevitable.

He sunk deeper into his seat when he saw the headlights in the distance. More luminous flashes as the oncoming cars understood they were going the wrong way. Headlights higher up in the dark . . . more powerful. Blurred in the rain. A deafening roar pierced the night. A lorry! Even though he was half blinded by the headlights, Servaz could see the driver trying to swerve, heavily, into the other lane, saw the massive form move with exasperating slowness from one lane to the other, saw the gigantic spray of water thrown up by the mammoth's whirling tyres. He curled in on himself, waiting for the terrible crash, waiting for the moment when David would jerk the steering wheel over and propel them into the steel juggernaut.

But nothing happened. The monster's horn blasted his ears as it went close by; he turned his head and through the fog of water saw the driver's gawping eyes as he looked down on them, terrified, from his cabin. Servaz took a deep breath. Suddenly he understood that everything that had happened since he had set foot in Marsac had been destined to lead him here, to this motorway; that this flooded road was like a symbol of his own story, his attempt to go the wrong way back into his past. He thought about his father, Francis, Alexandra, Margot and Charlène. His mother, Marianne . . . destiny, chance. Like particles hurtling towards each other, crashing, smashing up – being born and disappearing.

It was written.

Or was it?

Suddenly he thrust his hand into David's pocket, where the young man had put Servaz's mobile. He yanked it out.

'What are you doing? Leave that!'

The car zigzagged perilously from one lane to the other. Servaz looked away, no longer paying attention to what was happening in front of them. He lifted the phone to his lips while David's hand grabbed his wrist and tried to tear it away from him.

'Vincent, it's me!' he began screaming, before he had finished dialling. 'Can you hear me? Vincent, it's Hugo! Hugo is the guilty one! Do you hear me? *Hugo!* The words in the notebook, that was just a trick. He's going to try and pin the blame on David. Do you understand what I'm saying?' Vincent's voice came through on the other end: 'Hello? Hello? Is that you, Martin?'

They were driving in all three lanes at once, even swerving onto the hard shoulder.

'Get hold of the judge! Hugo mustn't be released! I don't have time to tell you more!'

He hung up. This time, he had David's full attention.

'What did you do? What did you just do?'

'That's it, Hugo won't be getting out. Pull over onto the verge. There's no point! You have my word: they'll take care of you! Who will go and see Hugo in prison if you're not there to do it?'

Once again headlights were bearing down on them, slightly to their left. Four lights in a row. Ultra-powerful. High above the road. Another lorry. David had seen it, too. In a fluid movement that seemed almost choreographed, he slowly left the middle lane to slip gently into the one where the articulated vehicle was approaching.

'No, no, no! Don't do that! Don't do that!'

New flashes of headlights. The roar of the horn. The metallic creaking of the juggernaut as it moved, trying to find a way out. This time there wouldn't be one. The truck wouldn't have time to swerve. The two vehicles were rushing towards each other. So this was where the road ended. It was written. The end of the story. A titanic crash and then nothing. The void.

On their left Servaz saw the exit to a rest area, coming down the hill towards them.

'If you kill us, you'll kill two innocent people! There's no way out for Hugo! It's all over for him! Who will go and see him in prison if you're not there? Turn left! Turn leeeeft!'

He saw four round, blinding eyes bearing down on them; four daggers of light reflected on the surface of the road. He closed his eyes. Held his arms out in front of him and put his hands on the dashboard in an absurd reflex.

Waited for the terrible crash.

Felt they were swerving, suddenly, to the left. He opened his eyes.

They had left the motorway! They were heading up the exit at top speed, the wrong way.

Servaz saw the gigantic lorry go by beneath them on their right. Saved! Then he gave a start when he saw a car leaving the rest area above them. David yanked the wheel, and they went up onto the grass, bouncing roughly as they swerved past the car on its way down. They tore several branches from one of the low hedges and landed in an almost deserted car park. Servaz could see the neon lights of a café and service station at the far end. David rammed his foot on the brake. The car swerved sideways, the tyres squealed.

It came to a stop.

Servaz unfastened his belt, opened the door and rushed outside to vomit.

He knew that from now on death would always have a face. That of a huge lorry, with its four headlights in a row. He knew it the way he knew he would never forget that image. And that every time he got into a car with someone else behind the wheel he would be terrified.

He inhaled great lungfuls of the damp night air. His chest was rising and falling, his legs were trembling. His ears were buzzing as if a beehive had been opened and the bees let loose all around him. He walked slowly round the car and found David sitting on the ground, leaning against the rear wheel. His fingers were digging into his blond hair; he was trembling and sobbing, staring at the ground. Servaz knelt down in front of him and placed his hands on the boy's shoulders.

'I'll keep my promise,' he said. 'We'll help you. Just tell me one thing: did you put the Mahler CD in Claire Diemar's stereo?'

The boy gave him a puzzled look, clearly failing to understand, so he shook his head, as if to say, 'It doesn't matter', then he squeezed

445

David's shoulder and stood up. He took out his phone and walked away, aware of what a sight he must be, in his hospital gown, soaking in the pouring rain, his fingers covered with scratches, his face still bearing the traces of the bandage he had torn off.

'Christ almighty, what was that phone call? And why didn't you answer?'

It was Vincent. He seemed in a panic. Servaz realised that his phone must have rung several times, though he hadn't heard a thing in the midst of the maelstrom. But it was good to hear his assistant's voice.

'I'll explain. In the meantime, get the judge out of bed. You have to cancel Hugo's release. And we need authorisation to interrogate him in prison this evening. Call Sartet.'

'But you know he'll never agree. It's illegal. Hugo was indicted.'

'Unless he's interrogated about another case,' said Servaz.

'What?'

He explained what he had in mind.

'Do as I say. I'll join you as soon as I can.'

'But you can't see a thing!'

'Oh yes I can. And believe me, there are times when it's better not to see anything.'

There was a puzzled silence at the other end.

'You're not in hospital?'

'No. I'm at a motorway service station.'

'What? What on—'

'Forget it. Hurry up. I'll explain later.'

A door slammed behind him. Servaz turned round.

'Hang on a minute,' he said to his assistant.

He thought he could see a smile on David's face as he sat behind the steering wheel. Their gazes met through the windscreen. Servaz felt something like an electric shock. He broke into a run as the Ford Fiesta started slowly backing up. As if in a dream, while he was running towards it, he saw the car make a gracious arabesque on the asphalt surface of the car park, turn towards the exit then take off.

Servaz told himself David wouldn't get far. Then, in a fraction of a second, he understood.

He ran as fast as his legs could carry him, propelled by despair, fear, anger and the knowledge he would never forgive himself for having been so stupid. He ran uselessly in its wake as the car pulled away, already out of reach as it sped through the opening between the hedges and down the slope, then entered the motorway again.

And stopped in the middle of the lanes.

From where he stood Servaz could hear David switch off the engine. And heard almost immediately the hysterical blaring of a horn on his left. He turned his head just in time to see an articulated lorry in the wide bend at the bottom of the hill. He saw the juggernaut brake too late and too suddenly, swerving across the three lanes, losing control of his trailer which hurtled with all the rest of its cargo onto the tiny Ford, engulfing it in an explosion of crushed metal, pulverised plastic and flesh.

He saw all the rest as if through a fog, much later: the ambulances, the police cars, the flashing lights slicing through the darkness; he hardly heard the wailing of sirens, the messages crackling over the radios, the orders, the hissing of the extinguishers and the shrill buzzing of electric saws; he hardly paid any attention to the news vehicles that came to join the melee, the TV cameras, the popping of camera flashes, or even the face of the young reporter who stuck a microphone under his nose and whom he shoved away, roughly. He dreamt of them more than he actually saw them or heard them. He dragged himself to the café and a strange thought occurred to him when he saw people were rushing about like bees disoriented by smoke. He told himself that these people were out of their minds and didn't even know it. That only madmen could want to live in a world like this and carry it with them, day after day, to its ruin. Then he ordered a coffee.

Interlude 4

In the tomb

In her mind there was a cry, nothing more.

A moan.

Which rose and devoured her thoughts.

A cry of despair, screaming with rage, pain, solitude. Everything which, for months on end, had deprived her of her humanity.

She was pleading, too.

Please, oh please, have mercy, please . . . let me out of here, I beg you. In her mind, she was shouting and begging and weeping. But only in her mind: in fact not a sound came from her throat. She was gagged, the strap tightly knotted at the back of her neck. Her hands were behind her back, stuck together from palm to fingertips with superglue. It was a very uncomfortable position. It made her lean forward all the time, including when she slept. She had tried to tear the skin of her hands, but it was impossible.

She changed position in the darkness to relieve the tension of her muscles; she was sitting on the dirt floor leaning against the stone wall. Sometimes she lay down. Or went over to her shabby mattress. She spent most of her time drowsing, curled up in a foetal position. Sometimes she got up and took a few steps. Not much more. She didn't feel like struggling any more. He only fed her once every other day now; he gave her just enough to keep her from dying of starvation. He no longer washed her. She had lost so much weight. She had a constant bad taste in her mouth, and there was a horrible pain gnawing away at the left side of her jaw and tongue: an abscess. Her dirty hair caused her scalp to itch. She felt weaker and weaker.

He had stopped taking her upstairs to the dining room. No more meals, no more music, no more rape in her sleep. That was the only relief. She wondered why he kept her alive.

Because she had a replacement, now. He had introduced them

once. She was so weak she could hardly stand and he had had to support her while she climbed the stairs up to the ground floor. 'God, you stink,' he had said, wrinkling his nose. She saw the young woman sitting at the dinner table, in the chair that used to be hers. Her torso bound to the back of the chair, the way she had been bound. She recognised that look: it had been hers several months or several years earlier. At first she didn't say anything, she no longer had the strength. She merely wobbled her head. But she read the horror in the eyes of the woman wearing her dress; she smelled her freshly washed hair, her perfumed body. Finally she managed to croak, 'That's my dress.' He took her back down to the cellar. That was the last time she saw her, but from time to time she heard music up there and knew what was going on. She wondered where in the house he kept the other woman locked up.

She had struggled to retain her sanity for a long time, she had tried to cling to reality. Now she was letting go. The madness that lurked at the edge of her consciousness, like a predator certain of its prey, had begun to devour her lucidity, to feast on it. The only way to escape that madness was to think of what her life had been – the life of a different woman, who bore her name but no longer resembled her. A beautiful life, eventful, tragic – but never boring.

Her throat tightened with remorse when she thought of Hugo. She had been so proud of him. She knew all about his drug use, but who was she to throw the first stone? Her handsome son, so brilliant. Her greatest success. Where was he now? In prison, or out? The anxiety crushed her chest when she thought about him. And then sorrow threatened to break her when she imagined Mathieu, Hugo and herself together again, reunited, sailing across the lake on a fine morning, surrounded by friends during a barbecue on a spring afternoon. She could hear their laughter, their exclamations, again she saw her five-year-old son lifted up to the sun in his father's arms, an expression of absolute happiness on his chubby face. Or father and son sitting at the head of the bed, Hugo with his thumb in his mouth, attentive, terribly serious, then gradually falling asleep while his father read to him. Mathieu had died in a car crash, and he had left them behind – her and Hugo – at the beginning of their life together. Sometimes she was very angry with him for that.

And she could see the house by the lake, the terrace where she liked to have breakfast when the weather was fine, a book in her hand, the smooth and placid mirror of the lake reflecting the trees on the opposite shore, the haven of peace she never tired of.

And then she thought about Martin. She often thought about him. Martin: her greatest love, her greatest failure. She remembered the classes when their gazes would meet twenty times an hour, their impatience to be together. Her anger, when he remained uninterested in the music she loved. She had nicknamed him her 'Old Man', or her 'Dear Old Man', although he was only one year older than her. By God she loved him.

She loved him, she admired him – and she had betrayed him. Now she crouched down in the darkness of her tomb, her mind empty, her body trembling. Suddenly a rush of despair took away all these fine sunny images, and the darkness, the cold, swooped down on her. The madness was back, and she felt it closing its sharp claws around her mind. In those moments, she clung with all her strength to a vision, the only one that still saved her.

She closed her eyes and began to run. All alone, along a beach left bare by the tide. A luminous dawn caused the waves and the damp sand to glitter, and the breeze stirred her hair. She was running, running, running, ever further. For hours, with her eyes closed. The cries of the seagulls, the regular sound of the sea, a few sails on the horizon and the dawn light. She could not stop running. On this endless beach. She knew she would never see the daylight again.

48

Finale

Searchlights lit up the outer wall of the prison. The car park was deserted. Servaz parked as close as possible to the entrance. His anger had not left him. A rage which replaced weariness and fatigue.

The director was waiting for them. He had received several calls during the night: from the prosecutor's office, the crime squad. He didn't understand why this case was such a big deal; he didn't know that an MP from the ruling party – the hope of his party – had nearly been arrested, and had now been cleared, and that first thing tomorrow the party would hasten to inform the press that he had been exonerated once and for all, and would vehemently denounce 'all the absolutely regrettable leaks', and would show up in every news programme to protest that 'in our country we have something known as presumption of innocence and in this case it was trampled on by members of the opposition'. In Paris they had felt the wind changing: one mustn't appear to have dropped Paul Lacaze too quickly, now he'd turned out to be innocent. Time to close ranks.

As for the prison director, he was still extremely uncertain of the police commandant with his bloodshot eyes and dilated pupils and the young lieutenant in his silvery jacket, looking like an adolescent. The commandant had bruises and scratches all over his hands and face, and a bandage in his wild hair – as if he'd had his skull stitched back together. The director was about to close the door behind them when Servaz raised his voice:

'We're waiting for someone.'

'The prosecutor's office only mentioned two people.'

'Two, three – what difference does it make?'

'Listen, it is already well after midnight. Am I going to have to hang around here until you've finished? Because I would like to—'

'Here she is.'

There was the sound of a motor and a gendarme's car appeared. The door opened on the passenger side and a woman got out, a big bandage shaped like a cross over her nose and cheeks. She also had her left arm in a sling. Ziegler hunched down in the driving rain, and hurried to cover the last few metres to the entrance. She had been grilled for a good hour by a deputy public prosecutor from the prosecutor's office in Auch as well as several officers from the gendarmerie crime investigation division, but she had still managed to get hold of Martin. In a few words she explained what had just happened, once again omitting to mention that she had hacked into his computer.

'How did you find all this out?' he said, puzzled.

He hadn't seemed surprised to learn that Marianne had been spying on him. On the other hand, Irène noticed how immensely sad he was.

'She's with us,' said Servaz now to the prison director.

Good God, thought the director, when he saw the dishevelled blonde approach. *What sort of circus is this?* But he had orders. From high up. 'Do everything they ask, is that clear?' the director of penitentiary administration had said on the phone. He shrugged, signalled to the guards to pay no attention when the three visitors set off the metal detector alarm, and he preceded them into the bowels of the prison, their steps resounding down the corridors. They went through three security doors and finally the director took out a key ring, and opened the door to the visiting room.

'Go ahead. He's waiting for you.'

He walked away quickly. He didn't want to know what was going to happen in there.

'Good evening, Hugo,' said Servaz as he walked in.

The young man seated at the Formica table raised his head and looked at him, his hands crossed.

Then his gaze shifted to Espérandieu and Ziegler as they came in behind Servaz, and Servaz saw a momentary little gleam of surprise in his blue eyes when he saw the gendarme's face.

'What's going on? The director got me out of bed and now here you are . . .'

Servaz made an effort to contain his anger. He sat down and waited for Vincent and Irène to do likewise. All three were on the opposite side of the table facing Hugo. From a strictly legal point of view, they no longer had the right to interview the kid regarding Claire's death, since he had been indicted. But Servaz had obtained an authorisation from Sartet to talk to him about the investigation into Elvis's murder – a separate case.

'David is dead,' he said quietly.

He saw the young man wince with pain.

'How?'

'He committed suicide. He went the wrong way up the motorway, and his car collided with an articulated lorry. He died on the spot.'

Servaz gave Hugo a piercing look. He could see the kid's sorrow was sincere as he struggled not to cry, his lips twisted as if he had swallowed a box of nails.

'Did you know he was suicidal?'

Hugo raised his chin. He stared at Servaz, his eyes shining, and nodded.

'Yes.'

'For a long time?'

The young man shrugged as if to say, 'What the fuck does it matter, now?'

'For as long as I've known David he's been depressive,' he said, his voice flat and mechanical. 'Even when we were kids, he was always . . . strange. He would have these sort of black moods . . . and that sad smile. When he was twelve years old he was already smiling like that.'

Servaz saw him take a sort of deep breath, as if he were preparing to hold his head under water.

'Sometimes he had unpredictable reactions – he could go from joy to despair in a second. When he was like that, his mates avoided him – but not me. His mother sent him to shrinks for years, until finally he told her to fuck off. It was all the fault of his dirty bastard of a father.' Hugo's words were flowing like lava. 'And that wanker of a brother. They're the ones who screwed him up. I remember one time when David was fourteen he brought a girl home, a nice girl. His brother got such a kick out of humiliating him in front of her that she never wanted to go to their place ever again or even speak to him. His father wouldn't allow him to read or even have books in his room: he said that reading made you effeminate. His father would brag about how he got where he was without reading a single book in his entire life, even at school.'

'Had he ever made other suicide attempts?'

'Yes, several. Once he even tried to stab himself in the stomach with a knife. Like samurais, you know what I mean? That was just after the episode with the girl.'

Servaz remembered the scar beneath his fingers. His throat tightened and he swallowed. Hugo looked at them in turn.

'Is this why you came to wake me up in the middle of the night? Why all three of you came? To tell me that David was dead?'

'Not exactly.'

'They're letting me out tomorrow morning, right?'

Servaz could hear the concern in his voice. He didn't answer.

'Fuck, David, my brother . . .' moaned Hugo suddenly. 'What a shit life you had, my friend . . .'

'He did it for you,' said Servaz softly but clearly.

'What?'

'I was with him in the car. David confessed to the murders of Claire Diemar and Elvis Elmaz. And of Bertrand Christiaens and Joachim Campos.'

'Who?'

Good acting, thought Servaz. *You didn't fall into the trap.*

'Those two names don't mean anything to you?'

Hugo shook his head.

'Should they?'

'Those are the names of the fire chief who came to your rescue at Néouvielle lake, and the coach driver.'

'Oh, right. Now that you mention it—'

'And Claire Diemar was in the coach that night, too, wasn't she?'

Hugo gave Servaz a strange look. A clap of thunder boomed beyond the window.

'That's right. She was. You think there's a connection between the accident and her death. You say that David confessed to Claire's murder? Before he killed himself?'

Hugo seemed to be sincerely stunned. The kid was an incredibly good actor.

'If he committed suicide by crashing into a truck, and you were in the car, how come you're here right now?'

He was staring suspiciously at Servaz. It was all Servaz could do not to lunge at him across the table.

'Enough now,' said Ziegler calmly.

Hugo swung his gaze around to her.

'Well done about the notebook idea. It was risky, but clever. First it accused you. Then it made you innocent.'

No answer.

'I suppose that if the policemen in charge of the investigation hadn't dug further in their search, if they hadn't shown, shall we say, sufficient curiosity and professional conscience, you yourself might have asked for a handwriting examination.'

For a fraction of a second, it was there. The spark. The sign they were waiting for. But it vanished at once.

'I don't know what the fuck you're talking about! It's not my handwriting in that notebook.'

'Of course not,' said Servaz. 'Since it's David's.'

'So, is it true? He's the one who killed her?'

'You fucking filthy little bastard,' said Ziegler. 'Are you the one who asked him to write those words in the notebook, Hugo? Or did he do it on his own initiative?'

'What? What are you talking about!'

Another flash. Closer. Deep in the prison, someone shouted. A long, painful cry, which ended as soon as it had begun. A guard's footsteps in the corridor. Then silence, once again. But it was never silent for long in prison.

'Claire slept around quite a bit, didn't she?' said Servaz.

'Were you jealous?' asked Ziegler.

'How many did you kill, you and your little friends?' asked Espérandieu.

'The fire chief, that was you,' said Servaz. 'Sarah, Virginie, David and you: four people threw him in the water.'

'And in Joachim Campos's car, a witness saw two men with him. Was it you and David?' suggested Ziegler.

'Were there two of you there, that night, to kill Claire Diemar?' continued Vincent. 'The camera filmed two people leaving the pub. Was it you and David then as well? Or did David merely stand guard?'

'What I don't understand is why you stayed there,' added Servaz. 'Why take the risk? Why not do what you'd done with the others? Why didn't you disguise her death as an accident or a disappearance? Why did you sit next to her swimming pool? Why?'

Hugo's gaze flickered to each of them in turn in the neon light. Servaz saw doubt, anger and fear in his face. Servaz's phone gave a double beep in his pocket. A message. *Not now* . . . He did not take his eyes off Hugo.

'You have to stop this!' said Hugo finally. 'Call the director, I want to speak to him! I have nothing to say to you. Get out of here!'

'Did you kill her all by yourself, Hugo? Or were there several of you? Did David take part?'

Silence.

'No, I was alone.'

Hugo looked up at them, his eyes thin shining slits. They said nothing. Servaz felt his heart pounding. He knew the others felt the same.

'I went there to warn her of the danger she was in. I'd been doing lines at the pub, and I'd drunk too much. I knew the others were about to put their plan into action. It was June. And I knew it was her turn, this time. We had talked about it, amongst ourselves.'

He made a little gesture with his hand, just like his mother.

'I knew she'd been a coward, that night, six years ago. That she left us to our fate, me and the others. But I also knew that she'd been haunted by it ever since. She had told me so. She thought about it all the time, she was obsessed by it. The fact that she'd behaved so badly. "I was afraid, I panicked that night. I was a coward. You should hate me, Hugo." She said it all the time. "Why are you so kind, so nice to me?" Or else, "Stop loving me, I don't deserve it, I don't deserve all this love, I'm not a good person." And the tears would stream down her cheeks. And then there were other times when she was the happiest, funniest, most surprising, most marvellous person I've ever met. She could turn every moment into a miracle. I loved her, do you understand?' He paused for a moment, and his voice changed, as if there were two actors sharing a role. 'I was drunk and completely stoned that night when I left the pub. I went to see her while everyone else was watching the match. I told her about the Circle. In the beginning, she could hardly believe it, she thought I was making it up, that I was drunk; and then when I told her in detail about the death of the driver, she suddenly realised I was telling the truth.'

Servaz looked at Hugo's eyes. The gleam deep inside. Like embers poked and kindled beneath the ash, like a fire burning for a long time.

'And then I saw her change. It was as if someone else had taken her place. She wasn't the Claire I knew . . . the Claire I knew encouraged me to write and swore to me she had never seen such a talented student. She sent me twenty texts a day to tell me she loved me and that nothing would ever keep us apart, that we would grow old together and still be as much in love as we had been on the first day. And she would quote authors and poets who spoke about love, and she'd make up songs about us, or she'd find a name for every part of my body as if it were the map of a country that belonged to her. And she wasn't afraid to say, "I love you" again and again, a hundred times a day . . . Suddenly that Claire ceased to exist. She was . . . *gone*. And the one who replaced her looked at me as if I were a monster, an enemy. She was afraid of me.'

Hugo's words hung suspended. Every one of them seemed to find an echo in Servaz's heavy heart.

'She wanted to call the police. I did everything I could to dissuade her; I couldn't stand the idea that my brothers and sisters might go to prison. Or the thought that they'd have to pay all over again, what with everything they had already been through. I didn't know what to do. I told her I would convince them to stop, that it was all over, there would be no more victims, but she didn't have the right to do that to them after what she had already done. She didn't want to listen, it was as if she'd gone mad, she was deaf to all my arguments. We started to quarrel; I pleaded with her. And then suddenly she came out with it: she told me she didn't love me any more anyway, it was all over between us, she loved someone else. She'd been meaning to tell me, soon. She spoke to me about this guy, the MP: she said she was madly in love with him, she was sure of him. I wanted to protect her and all she could think of was to send us to prison and get rid of me! I couldn't let her do that. I was furious, I was drunk with anger. I told myself: what kind of woman can swear to a man on everything she holds dearest that she will love him until the end of time, then the next day she loves someone else? What kind of woman can be so wonderful and then suddenly as ugly as can be? What kind of woman can play with people like that? And I thought: the kind who leaves children to die because she's a coward. She was young and beautiful and carefree, and only thought about herself. All the remorse eating away at her, her guilt, it was all show. As was her love. A lie. She lied to herself the way she lied to others. That night I understood that

457

Claire Diemar was nothing but selfishness and pretence. That she would always be poison for anyone who crossed paths with her.'

'So you hit her,' said Servaz. 'You found a rope and tied her up before you put her in the bath. And you turned on the tap.'

'I wanted her to understand before she died what the children had been through because of her. For once in her life she would know all the harm she had done.'

'Well, she got the picture, that's for sure,' said Servaz. 'And then you threw the dolls into the swimming pool and sat there by the water. Why the dolls? Was it because they symbolised your drowned schoolmates floating to the surface?'

'Whenever I went to her place, that collection of dolls gave me the creeps.'

'And then?'

Hugo raised his head and looked at them.

'What then?'

'You were in a state of shock, paralysed by what you'd done, still under the effect of alcohol and drugs: who came that night to take Claire's laptop and empty her mailbox and make it look as if someone else was trying to cover their tracks? Who put Mahler on the stereo, who was there?'

'David.'

Servaz slammed his fist on the table so hard that he made the others in the room jump. He stood up and leaned over the table.

'You're lying! David just committed suicide trying to save you – you, his brother, his best friend, and you're already defiling his memory? That night, David left the pub after you did, he was on the bank's video surveillance cameras on the other side of the square. He even attacked me so that he could steal the recordings! But the CD, that wasn't him. When I asked him about it, right before he died, he just stared at me: he didn't know what I was talking about!'

Hugo remained silent. He seemed shaken.

'All right,' he said finally in a dead voice, a voice filled with self-disgust. 'David just came out of the pub that night. He wanted to stop me from telling Claire everything. I sent him packing and he went back inside. He only stole the recordings to make sure no one could find out about the Circle, and because it reinforced the theory that someone else was guilty.'

A chill went through Servaz's veins.

'And the cigarette butts they found at Claire's place, in the woods?' he said. 'Before he died he told me that it was his DNA on them.'

'He disapproved of my affair with Claire. He despised her. Or maybe he was jealous, I don't know. But what I do know is that he was there, sometimes, spying on us from the woods and smoking one cigarette after the other. David could be like that.'

'Who was it, then?' insisted Servaz, even if he was more and more afraid to hear the answer. 'Who came to clear up after you? Who put the CD in that fucking stereo?'

Another beep in his pocket. He took out his mobile. There were two messages. At this time of night? What could be so urgent? He opened the inbox. The number was not one he recognised. He opened the first message. And fear rushed through him again.

'Margot!' he shouted, leaping up from his chair.

The SMS was signed, 'J H'.

And it said:

Take care of your loved one.

He hunted feverishly for Samira's number, then pressed the call button.

'Boss?' said Samira, surprised.

'Go and find Margot! Run! Hurry!'

He could hear her trotting across the grass, then running on the gravel. He heard her race up the steps to the dormitory, pound on the door and say: 'It's Samira!' He heard the door open and a familiar voice answer, a sleepy voice, a voice that felt like balm on a wound. Then Samira's voice on the phone again, breathless.

'She's fine, boss. She was asleep.'

He took a deep breath, looked at the others who were staring wide-eyed at him.

'Please, do me a favour. Stay with her tonight, take the other bed. You understand?'

'Copy,' said Samira. 'I'll sleep in her room.'

'Lock the door.'

He closed his mobile, puzzled and relieved at the same time. He looked again at the text message.

'What's going on?' asked Ziegler, who was on her feet now, too.

Servaz showed her the message.

'Oh, shit,' she said.

'What?' said Servaz. 'What is it?'

'He's going to go after Marianne.'

'What's this about my mother?' said Hugo suddenly from the other side of the table.

They looked at him.

'She's the one who put on the CD, isn't she?' said Servaz in a flat voice.

'Tell me what the fuck is going on!'

Servaz showed him the screen of his mobile and saw Hugo go pale.

'Fuck, *this time it's really him!*' shouted Marianne's son. 'He's going to punish her for taking his place. Yes, she's the one who put on the CD, before she rang you. I called her for help, that night. I told her it was too late, because they had seen me from across the street. She knew the gendarmes would show up any minute. So she had this idea. She remembered your investigation, all those articles she'd read in the paper at the time: Hirtmann, the Institute, your shared love of Mahler. So she came as quickly as she could, and she put the CD in the stereo and left again right away. She was crying. She told me over the phone to try and empty Claire's mailbox. I didn't see the point, I was in a daze, but I did it and then I wiped the keyboard. If the gendarmes had found her there, she would simply have told them the truth: that I had called her for help. But they took a while to get there. They didn't know they were going to find a corpse . . . and they'd probably all been watching the football. That's what saved us. They showed up right after she left. Then she called you. She figured that if they gave the investigation to you, and you found the CD, she might be in with a chance to make you doubt my guilt. And then she sent you that e-mail from a cybercafé.'

Everything that had happened that week, everything Servaz had been through was coming to the surface. The manager of the Internet café had told him it was a woman who came in. Hugo and Margot had hung out together. Hugo must have told his mother what Margot's favourite music was. And who else would have had the chance to fiddle with his mobile, enter a fake contact, while he was asleep? Who had been careful to avoid aiming straight at him with the rifle? Who had calmly carved the letters on the tree trunk during the night? He thought back to what he had said to Espérandieu over

460

the phone in the car park: 'The Mahler CD was in the stereo before the investigation was even assigned to us.' And for good reason.

'What are you waiting for?' screamed Hugo, shoving back his chair, which fell noisily to the floor. 'Don't you get it? Don't you see what's happening? He's going to kill her!'

There was a crack of thunder, then lightning; there were lights, flashing and glowing and swirling. The rain was pouring down the windscreen, messages crackled on radios, there were sirens and speed, and the road rushing by as if it were a fast-running river; the night spreading all around. Various sounds in his head, fear, his muddled conscience. The terrifying certainty that they would get there too late.

Driving through Marsac in a fog . . . The lake . . . With Ziegler and Espérandieu, driving along the east shore, then the north shore, Vincent at the wheel. The vehicles from the gendarmerie were already there. Half a dozen of them. They went in through the wide open gates. In the house all the lights were on, both downstairs and up. Light was streaming from every window, illuminating the garden. There were gendarmes everywhere; Servaz had called them from the prison, almost an hour earlier. He leapt out of the car and hurried towards the entrance, running up the steps. The front door, too, was wide open.

'Marianne!' he called.

He rushed into the deserted rooms.

He came upon Bécker, the captain who had been at Claire's house at the very beginning, speaking earnestly with other officers he didn't know.

'Well?'

'She's nowhere to be found,' answered Bécker.

He went through the curtains dancing in the wind, and out onto the terrace, facing the lake brimming with rain in the darkness.

Where had she gone? He called her name. Again and again. He met the gendarmes' puzzled gazes. She would show up any second now, and ask them what was going on, and he would hold her in his arms and kiss her, and would absolve her for her betrayal and her sins. They would watch as the police cars drove away, and then they would open a bottle of wine. Then she would ask him to forgive her – it was her own son, after all – and they would make love.

461

No, it wouldn't happen like that; he had to tell her that Hugo would be staying in prison. And it was his fault. He knew this would keep them apart, forever, that after this there would be no going back. He felt the despair descend upon him. But at least she would be alive. *Alive* . . . He went down onto the soaking lawn, his shoes sinking into the spongy grass, and he approached the gendarmes who were searching through the shrubbery. He turned round: the glow from the revolving lights, on the far side of the house, seemed to rebound from the belly of the clouds, enhancing the black form of the big house with its bright windows. But beyond the pools of light on the grass, there was only darkness.

'She's not here,' said one of the gendarmes.

'Are you sure?'

'We've searched everywhere.'

He pointed to the end of the garden near the woods, where he had found the carved letters. Even though he knew, now, that it was not Hirtmann who had carved them.

'Go and have a look over there. There's a spring, and a long fallen log. Check the entire area.'

He went back inside. Where had she got to? Had Hirtmann taken her with him? The thought of it made him feel sick.

'Martin . . .' said Ziegler tentatively.

'Was everything like this when you arrived?' he asked Bécker.

'Yes. The doors and windows were open. All the lights were on. Ah . . . and there was some music.'

'Music?'

He froze. Bécker pressed the button on the stereo and the music filled the room. Full blast. *Mahler.* Brass and strings raging throughout the house, booming in every room thanks to the speaker system, punctuated by the shrill chiming of the triangles, the deeper voice of the cellos, the entire orchestra hurtling towards the ultimate catastrophe.

Servaz gasped. He recognised the piece: the Finale from the Sixth Symphony, the music of defeat – his defeat, a piece that Adorno himself had referred to as, 'All is bad that ends badly.'

He slid down the wall to the floor. His entire body was trembling. The gendarmes looked at him, failing to understand. They stopped the music, and then they heard him sobbing. They were embarrassed: a cop was not supposed to cry, at least not in front of his colleagues, not when he was on duty. A moment later they heard him scream with laughter, and they told themselves that he'd gone mad. It wouldn't be the first time. They weren't robots; they had to deal with all the shit in the world; they were living sewers, they collected shit and took it as far away as possible from the rest of the population. But really it was never all that far. The shit always came back in the end.

And then they realised he had a piece of paper in his hand. They looked at each other, dying to move closer so they could read it, but they didn't dare.

On the paper it said:

She betrayed your trust and your love, Martin. She deserved to be punished.

Epilogue

Summer 2010. Spain.

It was hot. He went slowly down the cobbled streets bordered with lanterns and flowered balconies towards the Plaza Mayor, and he saw dozens of happy people in the warm Spanish night. It was strange, he thought, how a simple football match can make millions of people happy for a few hours.

As he swayed through the crowd that was dancing, singing, shouting their joy to his face, he could hear the hysterical chatter of the television presenters from the balconies above him.

The Plaza Mayor was lined on all four sides by arcades, its facades decorated with eighteenth-century frescoes. Its bright colours made it look so much like an Italian piazza that several pasta brands had used it in their commercials. The thought of it made him smile, a ghostly smile, due to the fact that he'd been drunk since five o'clock in the afternoon and now it was past midnight.

He collapsed into the only empty chair on the terrace.

'You've been drinking,' said Pedro, putting down his beer and staring at him, laughing.

'Mmm . . . What will you have?'

Pedro pointed to his empty glass.

'Same again.'

He saw his friend was about to talk to him about the French team. He liked to tease Servaz about it.

'Well, did they get rid of the manager?' asked Pedro.

'Not yet,' said Servaz.

'And that player who insulted him, and the ones who went on strike during training, will they be punished?'

Servaz gave him an almost delighted smile: there could be only one country where multimillionaire players were capable of going out on strike during the World Cup: his own. Suddenly he was thirsty.

464

He stood up unsteadily and went into the big café to order *una caña* and a *carajillo de cognac*. He watched the barman as he poured the powdered sugar into the bottom of a tiny glass, added two coffee grains, lemon zest, a shot of brandy, then brought the potion almost to the boil with the coffee maker's steam spout before setting it on fire with his lighter and pouring black coffee into it. Servaz narrowed his eyes with an air of absolute seriousness which betrayed the extent of his drunkenness.

When he went back out, with his scorching glass on a little plate, Pedro was still there, going back over the match for the tenth time with the people at the next table. Servaz went over to his chair but missed it when he tried to sit on it. The coffee and brandy splashed over his shirt and as he lay on the ground he burst out laughing, oblivious to the looks from the other tables.

'That's enough,' said Pedro. 'Time to go home.'

He grabbed the policeman under his arms and dragged him into the adjacent street. He was smaller than Servaz, but stronger. Servaz leaned on his shoulder. He looked above the roofs at the starry night, a night like a poem by García Lorca. He had decided to take every holiday day, every hour he was entitled to, and no one at the Criminal Division had found any reason to object, in the circumstances.

Not long after he'd put in for his holiday, Sarah Lillenfeld and Virginie Croze had been indicted and imprisoned, other members of the Circle had been remanded in custody, and the investigation was continuing – but without him, now. He had packed his suitcase and gone to see Ziegler, who'd been granted ten days' medical leave after the attack, and who would have to appear once again before the gendarmerie's disciplinary board. He wondered what the sanction would be this time. He knew that Irène was close to handing in her resignation, and the thought of it made him sad. She had told him, too, that she had hacked into the computer system at the prison where Lisa Ferney was locked up, and that Lisa was her bait: she had a strange conviction that Hirtmann would get in touch with her someday. Then he had gone on his way and found refuge in this little village on the other side of the Pyrenees, in the province of Huesca in the Alto Aragon, four hours' drive from Toulouse. In the middle of nowhere, the region was breathtakingly beautiful. No one would come looking for him here. No one knew him. Here he was *el Francès*. Except to Pedro and a few others, whom he'd known for only two weeks, but whom he presumptuously considered his friends.

Now Pedro stopped every three yards, with Servaz leaning on him, to celebrate Spain's victory with everyone he met – which seemed like the entire town. Servaz had got a phone call from the director a few days earlier, too: they had discovered the origins of the leak in the press. There had simply been no leak. At least not from inside the force. They went back to grill the manager of the Internet café – Servaz recalled Patrick, the manager with cold stubborn eyes behind his glasses – and Patrick admitted that he had called the papers as soon as they had left. By the sound of it the reporter himself had deduced Servaz's identity from the manager's description. When Patrick had told him that the cops had received an e-mail sent from his Internet café, that they were looking for a tall man who spoke with a slight accent and that they had seemed in a bit of a panic, the reporter immediately recalled the most sensational criminal affair in recent years.

'You're a lucky man,' said Servaz in a thick voice as they made their way arm in arm.

'Why?'

'To live here.'

Pedro shrugged. They went through the door of the *hostal*, along the corridor until they reached the inner patio. White walls and galleries of varnished wood ran around each floor, decorated with green pot plants and antique furniture. There was a sweet smell of clean laundry and jasmine. They climbed the stairs to the third floor, and Pedro pushed open the door of the room, which was never locked.

'One day you'll tell me what happened to you,' he said, putting him down on the bed. 'I'd be interested to know. You don't destroy yourself like this without a reason.'

'You are a . . . philosopher, *amigo*.'

'Yes. I'm a philosopher. I probably haven't read as many books as you,' added Pedro, glancing at the Latin authors lined up on the dresser as he pulled off Servaz's shoes. 'But I've read a few. And I know how to read people's hearts. You only know how to read words.'

There wasn't much in the little room apart from the books: a suitcase, some clothing, a Walkman of the kind no one, except Servaz, used any more, and CDs – Mahler's symphonies. That was the

466

advantage of music over books, he always said to himself. Music took up less room.

'I love you, *hombre.*'

'You are drunk. Goodnight,' said Pedro.

And he switched off the light.

Servaz was roused at seven in the morning by the din of a pneumatic drill, car horns blaring, and workers calling to each other, and once again he wondered how this country got by on so little sleep. As inert and empty as a puppet that's lost its strings, he lay for a long time staring at the ceiling. He could tell his mouth was furry, his breath was heavy. He had a terrible headache. He got up and dragged himself to the bathroom. Without hurrying. Nobody was expecting him anywhere. There was no more urgency in his life.

He let the lukewarm water flow over his neck and shoulders. He brushed his teeth and put on his last clean shirt. He filled a glass from the tap and dropped an aspirin into it.

Ten minutes later he was heading up the main street, passing underneath an arch to turn into a narrow shady street that led up through the arid hillside. All around him the village was waking up. He inhaled the smells of coffee, and of flowers enlivened by the morning. He could hear children shouting. Radios celebrating the victory – they couldn't get enough of it. All this energy that he felt around him, all this *life*. He thought about the economic crisis, all those reporters talking airily of people and things they knew nothing about, repeating numbers and statistics until they were blue in the face. And all the bankers, economists, speculators, corrupt financiers and blind politicians – they should come here, to understand. People here were alive. They wanted to work. To exist. To live. Not just survive.

Unlike me, he thought.

He climbed up the hill. Above the rooftops, a plane left a white trail in the pale blue sky. He reached the cathedral built against the cliff amidst the pine trees. He followed the long gallery of colonnades, went up a few steps and found himself in the cool shady cloister. He walked around the green basin of water and continued climbing up the path that wound its way up to the top of the cliff. This was where you had the best view. A huge Christ, eight metres high, spread his arms, extending his futile blessing to the entire region.

467

It was a magnificent panorama. But what brought him here every morning was not the view: it was the cliff. And the void. The call of the void. It was a temptation. A possible liberation. He had been toying with the idea for a while, but one thing kept him from going through with it: Margot. He knew as well as anyone what it meant to lose a father in this way. He thought a great deal about David, too. Once you opened the door to it, suicide was like a tenant you couldn't evict. He had given it a great deal of thought and had reached the conclusion that if he made his decision, he would make it happen here. This would be the best way. A fall of thirty metres – no way to bungle it. No sordid death in a hotel room. He would take flight. Into sunlight and blueness.

He'd been toying with the idea for several days – perhaps weeks. It was just an idea. He had no intention of going through with it. At least not for now. But the idea in itself was comforting. He knew that he was depressed and that there were ways to treat depression – but he didn't feel like it. He had seen too many dead people, had buried too many of them, had been betrayed too often. He was weary. All he wanted was to rest and to forget, but it all kept coming back, again and again. He was tired of seeing Marianne's face in his memory, and his parents', and others' as well. He was convinced that she was dead and, like Hirtmann's other victims, she would never be found. She had wanted to save her son, but she had also betrayed Servaz. He wanted to believe, in spite of everything, that there had been something sincere about their reunion, that she had not slept with him merely out of self-interest. But every time he thought about what she must have gone through before dying, staring at the thought head-on was as unbearable as staring at the sun.

He could see Pedro leaving his workshop, a tiny figure in overalls all the way down below. Pedro raised his head to look up at the sky, in his direction, but he didn't see him. He was watching the children as they headed off to go swimming in the river.

'They told me I'd find you here.'

The voice made him jump. He turned round. Ordinarily, he would have been happy to see her. But that morning, he didn't know whether he was happy – or ashamed. She had changed. She had removed her piercings and her hair was once again its natural colour. She looked several years older.

'How did you find me?'

'It looks like it wasn't just your love of books you gave me but also your investigator's genes, Dad.'

She had obviously prepared her words in advance, and it made him smile. She was suntanned, wearing a tank top and a pair of denim shorts.

'I remembered that you and Mum and I came here when I was a kid, and that you liked this place a lot. But it's not the first place I've been to. I've been looking for you for over a week.'

She took two steps and leaned out – and immediately recoiled.

'Wow! What a view – but it's so high up!'

She did not see him blush with shame, his stomach churning.

They spoke. In the days and nights that followed, they spoke. Drank. Spoke. Smoked, laughed, spoke – and even danced. He got to know his daughter. Elias was there, too, a silent beanpole of a boy with hair that covered half his face. Servaz realised that he liked him. Sometimes he kept them company; sometimes he left them on their own. They had wonderful days where they were together in a way they had never been, and other days when they argued. Like the night she found him dead drunk after she had spent the evening with Elias. He began to drink less. Then not at all. They seemed to have all the time in the world. School did not start for weeks and he wondered if she had planned to work during the summer holidays. Eventually he asked her when they would be leaving.

'Whenever you're ready,' she answered. 'You're coming with us.'

He introduced them to Pedro and others, and they made a happy little team. Elias began to talk – at least, a little bit. They went to bed late, but he realised that when he got up in the morning he had more energy. And he no longer stayed on his bed staring at the ceiling. Margot and Elias had a room on the floor below his, and it looked out onto the patio like his, and on mornings when he was making a slow start she would come up and knock on his door. They went on long walks or drives through the region, and they discovered vistas which left them speechless, whole villages of stone and slate straight out of a Western. They bathed in streams of ice-cold water. They went cycling and canoeing. They chatted with the locals and with tourists, they went to parties to which they were given last-minute invitations. She took photos and for once he didn't mind having his picture taken. To his great surprise he discovered that he could smile. When they came back from their outings, they were always famished.

The days went by, halcyon days, simple, perfect. Nothing was planned, nothing really mattered. Nothing was at stake. And then one morning, shortly before dawn, he woke up, very calm, took a shower and packed his suitcase. That night he had dreamt about her. Marianne was alive. Somewhere. And she needed him. If Hirtmann had already killed her, he would have found a way to let him know. Servaz left his room. Everyone was still asleep on the other floors, but daylight had already reached the patio. He went down, his suitcase in his hand, took a deep breath to fill himself one last time with the perfume of jasmine and laundry, of wax polish and departure. He had loved this place. Then he knocked on the door.

'I'm ready,' he said, when it opened.

Acknowledgments

As a rule, I have taken great liberties with geography. Some people might locate Marsac in one place, other people will think it is elsewhere – and they will all be both right and wrong. Of course there is no 'Oxford or Cambridge of the Southwest'. My Southwest is a country almost as imaginary as Tolkien's marvellous Middle Earth.

I also took some liberties with the everyday reality of police work when I felt constrained, as if I were wearing a pair of shoes that were too small, and even greater liberties with the complicated justice system. Nevertheless I must extend my thanks to a number of people for their precious advice, their guided tours and their assistance, which prevented me from making glaring mistakes. In order of appearance, Sylvie Feucher, general secretary of the union of senior police commissioners and officials, Paul Mérault, Christophe Guillaumot, José Mariet and Yves Le Hir from the Toulouse police force. As always, any errors (intentional or not) that remain are mine. Thanks too to Stéphane Hauser for his musical advice; he will forgive me for not always following it. Finally, I must extend my thanks to my editors at XO who, once again, have performed the miracle of changing water to wine, and to the incredible editorial team at XO and Pocket; to my wife, who, as ever, makes my life easier; and to Greg, my first reader, friend, confidant, coach and sparring partner combined. Finally, I would like to dedicate this book to someone who had the poor taste to depart ten days before the publication of my previous novel: my mother, Marie Sopena Minier. The fact that she didn't have the time to read it was not easy to accept.